D1557543

VILLAINS RULE

by

M. K. Gibson

Copyright © 2017 by Michael K. Gibson

Published by

Amber Cove Publishing

PO Box 9605

Chesapeake, VA 23321

Cover design by Raffaele Marinetti

Visit his online gallery at www.raffaelemarinetti.it

Cover lettering by M.K. Gibson

Book design by Jim Bernheimer

Visit the author's website at www.mkgibson.com

First Publication: February 2017

Printed by Kindle Direct Publishing

ISBN-13: 978-1544135496

ISBN-10: 1544135491

Dedication and Acknowledgements

How about that? My publisher actually gave me another shot to write a book for him!

HA! Sucker!

This particular piece of fiction is, despite the mocking nature, my love letter to the fantasy genre and table-top gaming. Tolkien, Dragonlance, Forgotten Realms, Joel Rosenberg, D&D, Whitewolf and so many more from my childhood cemented my eternal geek. But for this work, I wanted to do an action-comedy about the devices which make the stories work, and that is the villains.

…While also Taking the Piss out of my beloved genre.

Thank you to my lovely wife who, despite a complete lack of caring towards geek culture, endures my ideas, supports me, and edits my drivel.

Thank you to Jim Bernheimer and Amber Cove Publishing for once again, giving my codified fever dreams a home.

Thank you to my mother, Bonnie H., who always encouraged my writing.

Massive shout out to Erik J., whose back and forth email conversations with me were the original genesis for this stupid, stupid book.

Thank you to my friends who support and mock me. Love ya bastards.

And lastly, thank you to the fans I've made who've given me support to keep on writing. It isn't time to quit my day job, but my evenings are filled with making new worlds for people who wish to visit them. Love you!

M. K. Gibson

Table of Contents

Villains Rule

The Third Rule of Villainy

Heroes are arrogant, predictable, and really, really dumb.

Prologue

(Look, I know prologues can be boring. But they are there for a reason. So just read it. And if it helps, imagine it being read in a fancy accent.)

The warrior rode home.

What was left of the Elder River village still smoldered. Almost a year to the day, smoke rose from the magically immolated land the warrior called home.

Home.

The warrior had been gone so long, the word "home" had nearly lost meaning. Through the trials he endured and the dangers he faced, the warrior had stayed focused.

When his village and his family were slaughtered and burned by the half-fire giant General Anders, the war leader for the hordes of the Baron Grimskull, he was lost. He was destroyed inside. But the warrior had been taken in by his mentor, Zachariah Greywalker. It was in the home of the elves of the Whispering Woods where the warrior was taught to fight, taught to use his mind, and taught to live again. It was there where the warrior fell in love with the elf maiden Lady Alianna.

The warrior promised his mentor and his beloved he would find the Baron Grimskull's weakness and bring peace to the land. And to the horizon, he set off.

Death the warrior courted, and death he delivered upon the enemies who barred his way. The Nameless Sea could not claim him. The Waste of Sand and Tears could not contain him. The bleak rock of the Grey Spire Mountains could not deter him.

And finally, deep beneath the Peak of Inverness, the Bray Beast of D'hoom Dungeon fell to him. It was there in D'hoom Dungeon the warrior found the source of Grimskull's power: Amulet of the Ember Soul. Armed with the amulet, the warrior could strip the baron of his power. With this, he could bring an end to Grimskull's tyranny. With this he could usher in a new age of peace.

The remnants of the Elder River village were in view. The sun set on the horizon. Blue and purple wove a tapestry of twilight across the valley sky. The warrior wanted nothing more than to return to the woods and to his lady love. But first, he had a promise to keep. A promise to himself.

The warrior rode through the remnants of the village gates, charred from the attack. He slipped off his horse and closed his eyes and breathed in deeply the scent of his home. He felt right, true, and just.

"Mother, Father, my friends . . . your deaths will be avenged. I wish I had been stronger then. I wish I could have saved you. But with this amulet, I will destroy Grimskull. And I will rebuild here. Your sacrifice will be the foundation of a stronger tomorrow. On this, I swear!"

The warrior had left this place a fearful boy. Now, the boy was a man, and the man would defeat any enemy that stood before him.

"By the gods above and below, I dare any to stand between me and my sacred vow," the warrior growled.

From the shadows behind the warrior stepped a rather large man dressed in all black tactical gear with night-vision goggles. The man in black cracked the warrior over the head with a rubberized metal baton, dropping him into the dirt.

Nudging the warrior on the ground with the steel toe of his combat boot, the man in black judged the warrior unconscious. The man in black took the pouch holding the Amulet of the Ember Soul from the warrior's belt. Opening the bag to inspect that the Amulet of the Ember Soul was intact, the man in black nodded with satisfaction.

The man in black leaped up on the warrior's horse and steered the horse away, leaving the village. With a backwards glance at the fallen warrior, the man in black muttered in dismissive, eye-rolling disgust:

"Heroes are so fucking stupid."

Prologue pt. 2 - Electric Boogaloo

In a pocket dimension, between the real world and the fantasy realms, and slightly to the right of the world where your left socks go missing, existed the executive office of The Blackwell Corporation, Evil Consulting Agency. The ultra-modern building sat atop a lone barren mountain, seemingly floating in a void.

The waiting area inside the lobby of Blackwell Inc. contrasted the building's exterior. The retro 1970s décor was lit by harsh flickering fluorescent lighting. The rectangular off-white ceiling tiles were intermittently stained the color of weak tea. The area resembled the airport lounge of days gone by, complete with rows of piss-yellow, hard plastic chairs attached to scratched chrome frames with nary an armrest to be found.

Muzak versions of fantasy realms madrigals droned painfully from the tinny, crackling speakers. The waiting room walls were floor-to-ceiling glass windows that looked off into the nothingness of the pocket dimension. The view gave the lobby a perpetual nighttime look and radiated cold.

But mostly, the lobby stank. It stank of many things: stale cigarette butts in full ashtrays, burnt coffee in the antique percolator, and the stale popcorn of a 1980s K-Mart.

The waiting room also stank from the presence of the eternal rotting corpse of the Dread Zombie Lich Lord Morakesh and his nine mummy high priests.

Just ask Sophia.

Sophia Rose DeVrille, Blackwell Corporation's one and only receptionist, sat in her chair behind a fuck-all awesomely ornate cherry and mahogany desk. She typed away at her keyboard while sitting in her ridiculously expensive chair. Sophia felt that her lower lumbar was not only being supported, it was practically being made love to.

Sophia wasn't really typing any kind of letter or email. She was just choosing to ignore the increasingly impatient Lord Morakesh, despite the stink. The Dread Lord's nine high priests sat in the lobby reading out-of-date magazines like *Better Homes & Gardens*, various parenting magazines, and *Highlights*. Lord Morakesh stood in front of Sophia's desk with his arms crossed, tapping his undead foot impatiently. Little necrotic bits of the Dread Lord were falling into piles despite his bandages and ceremonial armor.

It was quite disgusting.

Lord Morakesh continued standing in angry silence while the clock on the wall ticked.

Tick.

Tick.

Tick.

Tick.

"Excuse me, but I have an appointment!" Lord Morakesh belted out in exasperation.

"No. You don't," Sophia mumbled without looking up, continuing her fake typing.

"Well, no. But do you know who I am?"

"Yes."

"Yes? And?"

"And I do not care, sir."

"I am the Dread Lord Morakesh!"

"And that," Sophia gestured absently, "is the Infamous Alpha Werewolf, Grey Fang, of the Dessemark Bloodpack."

Grey Fang inclined his head slightly in a sign of acknowledgment, shifted his *Boy's Life* magazine, crossed his legs, and began to lick-clean his crotch. Thoroughly.

"Over there," Sophia continued, "is The Torment. Non-Corporeal Manifestation of Abstract Evil. Master of the Never Realm's Sphere of Pain and Suffering."

The Torment floated above his chair in a seething cloud of smoke, fire, and pain. There was the faintest outline of a man within the billowing despair. While not having an apparent face or mouth, The Torment seemed to greatly enjoy the Blackwell complimentary cookies and juice box. Drunk, of course, with a crazy straw.

"And over there is—" Sophia began again in the same bored tone, but The Dread Lord Morakesh cut her off.

"Fine, fine. I get the point. When will he be free to see me then?"

Sophia took a deep breath and sighed, preparing the canned statement: "The Blackwell Corporation, Evil Consulting Agency, greatly appreciates all its current and future clients. We endeavor to expand our evil family. Know that you are a valued client, and your needs are our needs."

Morakesh stood there baffled, then blinked and shifted in his bandages.

"What does that mean?"

"It means sit the fuck down and Mr. Blackwell will see you when he sees you. This dimension's passage of time does not reflect your own. You will not be missed from your realm. Please enjoy our refreshments."

It was obvious from her "that's final" tone that the conversation was over. The Dread Lord Morakesh sat down next to his high priests and began idly flipping through an *Entertainment Weekly* from 2001, featuring *Lord of the Rings*. The Dread Lord Morakesh found this "Sauron" chap to be quite intriguing.

The room was silent, save for the errant magazine shuffling noises and the constant sloppy crotch-licking coming from Grey Fang.

"Do you mind?" Morakesh croaked, revolted.

Grey Fang paused his public pubic bath for a moment and looked up at Morakesh.

"Jealous?" the great lycanthrope asked and promptly returned to his cock-and-balls.

"A little," Morakesh sighed with dusty air as he read his magazine. Being an undead Lich with vast power was great and all. But, thanks to being technically dead, he really missed having a working penis.

The Fourth Rule of Villainy

Villains are frequently as dumb, or dumber, than the heroes.

Chapter One

Where I Introduce Myself

Let me begin simply and to the point: My name is Jackson Blackwell.

I am forty-one years old, yet I look thirty. I am well built for my five-foot, ten-inch frame and I like to dress sharply. My background is a mix of Anglo and Middle Eastern. But my description is not what you are here for.

Some call me Shadow Jack, due to my nefarious activities. But there are some circles where I am known by my professional name: The Shadow Master.

I am a villain.

Let me be more clear. I am *the* villain. You see, I make other villains better and I profit from that. Consider me . . . a villain adviser, if you will. I exploit them—other villains, that is—for my own gain. Please, do not confuse this for a redeemable quality. I do for them, the weaker villains, what they cannot do for themselves. I help them try to defeat the hero. And I have wealth and power beyond measure because of it.

You see, true villainy doesn't stem from a desire to do wicked things. Deviants who kill, rape, and torture are pure sociopaths.

Garbage.

Beneath me.

Just like those pompous, pretentious fools who cling to the Oxford comma.

I ensure that I destroy them whenever I encounter them.

Please note: I am above those things. Killing, for example, has to happen from time to time. But my kills come with purpose, not from wanton, base desire. I derive no pleasure in them.

True villainy comes from another desire. And I have that desire—to be the top power. To know I am better than everyone else I encounter. To take what I want, when I want, and how I want. Again, I see your juvenile sensibilities confusing this with ruling.

Any idiot can rule. In fact, most who do rule are idiots. I am the power to the side of them. The one guiding them, the one whispering in their ears. Until they no longer serve my cause. When that happens, I simply remove them and allow another pliable idiot to "rule."

Seems simple, doesn't it?

Why do I do it? Because I like it. I like being a villain. I am not a nice man. I have never been, nor will I ever be, a "nice man."

Nor am I a pathetic anti-hero. Gods, I hate anti-heroes.

I have not the rough and gruff exterior of a sometimes killer with a compassionate heart. The kind of dirty *you people* tolerate. And do you want to know why you tolerate them?

Because you are evil.

Deep down, in the dark place of your heart, you wish you were as free as I. A villain. You wish you could cut loose and do what your dreary, boring, piss-ant lives won't allow.

So you root for your anti-heroes. Because that is as close to my villainous freedom as you can come. Your beloved smugglers, berserkers, and vigilantes kill bad guys like me. And then you cheer.

Evil is punished. Anti-hero gets the girl and you relish in the villain's demise.

Do you want to know another secret about you? Hmm?

Good people do not take joy in the fall of others. Good people do not take joy in the death of anyone. Even villains. Those that do? They are villains in waiting. That is you. But you are too cowardly to admit it.

It is OK, simple ones. The world needs villains.

You may disagree, which is understandable. Weaker minds often refuse to accept truth when it is presented to them. So, lie to yourself all you like. Heroes do not use fear and pain to succeed.

That is my domain. A villain's domain.

It is the villain who sets the stage. It is the villain who causes the drama we love to watch in TV and movies. In the books we read. Without the villain, the hero is nothing. He or she has no motive. No ambition. Nothing.

I am Jackson Blackwell. I am a villain. And villains rule.

"Um, whom are you speaking to?" a voice said out loud, bringing me from my thoughts.

Across my desk sat Baron Martin Viktor Grimskull, the warlock, warlord, and ruler of the Great Eastern Empire. He sat in a garish ensemble of purple-stained leather and black plate armor. Atop his head and across his face, the Baron wore a helmet made from the bleached skull of a demonic animal.

I hated him. But his gold was excellent, pure, and seemingly never-ending.

"My apologies, Baron. Sometimes when my mind wanders, I forget that since I own this dimension, I am technically a god here. Ergo, my thoughts are sometimes broadcasted."

The intercom on my desk buzzed to life. "Sir. You were doing it again," Sophia scolded me.

I tapped the comm with growing irritation. "Thank you, Sophia. I am aware."

"Your waiting room is growing as well, sir."

"Who now?" I asked.

"Morakesh. A lich from—" Sophia said, but I cut her off.

"I know who he is. Annoying as hell and pushy. Well, he's undead, so he isn't going anywhere. Let him wait."

"The others, sir?"

"*They* had appointments. I will see to them in turn."

"Yes sir," Sophia acknowledged as she clicked off.

"Now, where were we?"

"You summoned me here," Grimskull stated. "I do not enjoy being summoned. By anyone."

"Baron, have you ever heard the legend of Darth Vader?"

"What is a 'Darth Vader'?"

"I'm glad you asked. The story of Darth Vader is an ancient legend from my world. A parable, if you will. You see, Darth Vader was a Dark Lord of the Sith. A master of arcane magics, who wore all black armor with a flowing black cloak and wielded a sword made of pure crimson energy. He was the right hand and enforcer of an emperor. Where he went, people trembled in fear. And all you heard was his fearsome breathing as he approached."

"He sounds amazingly dreadful," the baron said, trying to sound bored. But from the way he leaned slightly towards me, his body language betrayed his words.

"Would you like me to continue?" I asked as I lit up a black cigarette with silver tips from a small box on my desk. A gift from an old friend whom I helped hunt the most dangerous game. The cigarette gave off the scent of incense as I smoked it.

"If you must," the baron said, wafting the smoke from his face. "So, this Vader chap, I assume he becomes the realm's greatest warlord?"

"You would think so. Alas, it turned out the fearsome Vader was in fact a hero all along."

"Disgusting!" the baron exclaimed.

"Indeed," I agreed. "It turned out this villain was nothing more than a whiny, self-absorbed, arrogant child who only turned to a darker path to save the woman he loved."

"For love? Weakness!" Grimskull decreed, and I nodded along. "And did he save her?" Grimskull asked.

"That's best part: No!" I laughed and Grimskull laughed with me.

"Get this—he accidentally . . . oh my . . . he accidentally killed her!" I chuckled thinking about it. "During his transformation from being a guy named 'Ani' into Darth Vader, his tenuous grasp of his magical abilities reached across the realm and killed her while she was in childbirth."

"Ha! That is incredible!"

"I know, I know," I sniffed. "But after he killed her, he screamed 'Nooo!' when he found out. And what I always found odd was he never even bothered to ask about his children, who in fact survived. Twins. A boy and a girl."

Baron Grimskull gave as quizzical a look as possible through his skull mask. "Why are you telling me this?"

I sobered my face and deliberately rested my elbows on my desk so I could lean in and stare into Grimskull's beady yellow eyes. "Because this story of Darth Vader has a point. You see, not following up on the existence of his children proved to be his downfall. The boy became a follower of the same mystical arts as he did. And eventually, the son confronted Darth Vader before the emperor and destroyed the dark master. Vader turned back to being a hero and died in his son's arms. Redeemed."

"What does this have to do with me?" Grimskull asked.

"Because, Baron," I said as I gestured with my left hand to a shadowy corner of my large and ornate office while snubbing out my cigarette with my right, "you to failed to follow up on your lineage's actions."

A very large black man, one of my elite soldiers, stepped from the shadows and presented himself to my left. The soldier was decked in head-to-toe black tactical gear from our world. He wore his balaclava pulled down and his night vision goggles covering his forehead. Grimskull leaned away, obviously intimidated.

The man in black handed me a leather pouch, saluted, and returned to his post in the shadows.

"Thank you, Courtney," I said to the soldier. Courtney had been a soldier, bodybuilder, bouncer, and mixed martial arts amateur back in our world. Here, he was a highly trained operative in my employ. Plus, with a name like Courtney, he had a lot of aggression to work out.

I reached into the pouch and produced the gaudy and heavy Amulet of the Ember Soul. "Look familiar, Baron?"

Chapter Two

Where I Discuss Fantastical Beasts and How to Feed Them

How did you come by that?!" Grimskull demanded as he jumped to his feet.

"Sit down, Baron," I said flatly.

"That is mine and I demand you return it to me this instant or else you will feel my—"

"SHUT UP," I said, raising my voice and cutting the baron off. My voice echoed from the walls as I used my influence over this realm to amplify my will.

"Sit, Baron," I ordered. Instead of complying, Baron Grimskull began to manifest a ball of fire in his right hand.

Well, he tried. This was my realm, after all.

When the warlock's magic refused to answer his call, he looked to me, confused. I in turn produced a Colt 1911 .45. A gift from a yellow-eyed demon for helping to torment a pair of monster-hunting brothers. I calmly aimed the weapon and fired one round into the baron's breastplate.

Grimskull roared, more in shock than in pain, as the round knocked him over his chair onto the ground. The baron's breastplate was made of a dragon-skin weave and was very resistant to damage. With this being my realm, I could have willed the bullet to pass through his body. But I decided it was best to get his attention for now.

Bloodshed could always come later.

"Baron, I assume you are willing to listen to me now?" I asked after Grimskull ceased his wailing. The baron rose to his feet and I gestured with the barrel of the 1911 to sit back down.

"In case you have not realized, this place responds to my wishes, not yours. Your magic is useless here, while I, on the other hand, could commit every act of savagery I wished upon you and there would be nothing you could do to stop it."

"What?" Grimskull asked loudly. Obviously his ears were not reacting well from the tinnitus. The ringing from the weapon's discharge would pass.

Sighing, I shortened my previous statement to "Sit the fuck down and listen." That, the good baron comprehended.

"This amulet of yours is the result of our deal with a Never Realm demon. You give up a portion of your soul for power. But if anything happens to this amulet, what happens?"

"The denizens of the Never Realm come and claim the remainder of my soul and my mortal body," Grimskull recited like a scolded child.

"Exactly. I worked very hard to negotiate that deal with the demon Y'ollgorath for you. So, please explain to me why the fuck this was left unguarded in a hole in the ground."

"It was not left unguarded in a hole in the ground, as you so basely state it! The Amulet of the Ember Soul was guarded by the Bray Beast deep within D'hoom Dungeon."

God, that sounded so cliché and badly written. The fantasy realms were positively the worst when it came to their naming conventions.

"Baron, the Bray Beast? Really?"

"Have you ever seen the Beast?" Grimskull asked. "It is a behemoth! With heavy natural plate armor, giant tusks, a deadly barbed tail, and acidic saliva. Oooh . . . the Beast is truly a monster to behold!"

"Mm-hmm," I muttered. "And . . . what do you feed the Beast?" I asked.

"Excuse me?"

"Feed . . . it," I said, my intonation suggesting that the good baron was an idiot.

"I don't understand the question. The Bray Beast feeds off the flesh of those foolish enough to dare venture into the D'hoom Dungeon."

"Uh huh. And where exactly is the D'hoom Dungeon?"

"High atop the Peak of Inverness lies the ancient path of Kara'Thum. The stone stairwell leads deep within the mountain, and there you will find D'hoom Dungeon."

"Right," I said, seeing if Grimskull was picking up what I was laying down.

He was not.

"So, let me get this straight, Baron. You have several tons of flesh-hungry monster in this dungeon."

"Yeah."

"And the only way to reach said dungeon is by climbing up one of the tallest peaks in the entire realm?"

"Exactly."

"So, the only way the Beast eats is when a foolish adventurer climbs said mountain peak, braving the incredibly harsh terrain, descends almost the entire way back down the mountain along a winding stairwell, and stumbles into the Bray Beast? I have the facts correct?"

"Yes! Devilish, if I say so myself."

"Then how did you expect the Beast to put up a fight against a worthy opponent if the damn thing is starving and emaciated from the lack of freaking food?"

Grimskull looked at me like I'd just spoken gibberish to him. "I don't think you understand. Let me explain again. High atop the Peak of Inverness lies the ancient path of Kara'Thum—"

"No no no," I cut him off. "I get the concept. I do. What you and all your ilk fail to realize is that when you place a monster, be it a Bray Beast or a dragon or whatever, to guard the treasure, sooner or later a smart hero is going to get the treasure. He or she is going to pack to survive the elements, have enough food for the trip, have perhaps a magical instrument or two to bypass traps, and face a mostly-starved monster who has survived, barely, off two to three humans a year. Did you honestly think that plan was going to work?"

" . . . Yes?"

I sighed. I had to remind myself for the thousandth time, I am rich because they are dumb.

"I'm not a fool, Mr. Blackwell. The Amulet of the Ember Soul can only be destroyed by the blood of an innocent, a measure I demanded when the deal was brokered. But you also forget, I placed a spell on the amulet so that only one of my royal bloodline may remove it from its resting place. Since I have no offspring, the amulet should have remained there!" Grimskull exclaimed.

"Ahh, yes. That was the crux of this and my story of Darth Vader. Baron, do you have children?"

"No."

"Well, I have this amulet here, which was taken by Courtney from an adventuring hero. So . . . thoughts?"

"Impossible. I have no wives, thus no royal children."

I wanted to hang my head. "No wives. But any mistresses?"

"Concubines? Oh, hundreds. My favorite one was a little thing from Elder River village. Twenty-one years after she left me, I had the whole village burned to the ground."

"Why did you wait twenty-one years?"

"It took me a while to get around to it?"

Shaking my head, I continued the conversation to the next logical conclusion that Grimskull was missing. "So, what do you think the chances are that she was pregnant when she left?"

"Oh. I see what you are getting at. You truly think I am stupid, don't you?" Grimskull asked, crossing his arms.

"The thought did cross my mind," I said, nodding.

"Well, 'Shadow Master,'" Grimskull said, using my title as an insult, "I'll repeat myself. I have no *royal* children. Sure, I have bastards out there. Who doesn't? But my spell kept anyone but a royal child from taking the amulet. No royal wives, therefore, no royal children."

"Baron, do you know why they call me The Shadow Master?"

"A nickname you gave yourself?" Baron Grimskull sniffed as he crossed his arms and looked away.

Petulant child.

But he was still a client. "No, Baron. It's because working in mysterious and dark places is what I do. I find out things that others do not know. And I use that information for my benefit. For example, did you know that the Elder River village is built upon the ruins of an ancient civilization?"

"No?"

"Indeed. And that civilization was once called The Eld. Or, the First Men of the Elder Race. They were the people who crossed over from the Land Beyond into your realm of Caledon. They settled in the rich and fertile basin of the Elder River. They were the ones who dominated the existing population and taught them mathematics, science, and technology. A new age of prosperity rose. Well, until the powers that be turned on them, fearful of their science over magic."

"You are referring to The Rift. The war of magic and science between man and elf that shaped the land. That was over a thousand of years ago," Grimskull said.

I nodded. "Exactly. People believe The Eld were all killed off. After all, magic won. But what if several members of the The Eld High Tower were secreted away. What if members of their royal lineage survived? And hundreds and hundreds of years later, some of their descendants returned to their ancestral home to begin again. This time, in a simple life. Keeping their love of science hidden over the generations, lest they ever be discovered and destroyed again."

"So . . . my concubine Greta?"

"A descended royal princess of The Eld."

"Oh. Shit."

"Exactly, Baron. So, here's the new plan. You keep the Amulet of the Ember Soul in your castle. You keep it on you at all times. If someone comes for it, they will need to infiltrate your keep and confront you directly. If you leave your keep, you will take a regiment of armed guards with you, everywhere. You will now create a new squad of soldiers whose sole purpose is protecting you and that amulet. These soldier will be well paid and given benefits above all others. You will ensure that being one of your elite guard is something all within your domain should seek to become."

"Well . . . *paid?*"

"Yes, well paid. As with the rest of your staff."

"I have indentured servants," Grimskull sniffed, "not *staff.*"

"Not anymore," I said, shaking my head and pointing at the baron. "Now, you have a paid workforce. You will do everything in your power to make your staff love you and never betray you."

"Is all this . . . necessary?"

"How many times have you had an assassination attempt against you? A direct attack? Someone poisoning your food?"

"Hmm." The baron considered the question. "It does seem to happen a lot."

Of course it does. Fantasy worlds are nothing if not predictable. "Yes, Baron, they do. Because your people hate you and wish to see you dead. That is why we are going to change your image."

"But I am Baron Viktor Grimskull! All serve me! All bend their knee to my will! Those who oppose me die!"

"Which is why everyone is trying to kill you. You will still be Baron Grimskull, ruler of the Eastern Empire. But with a few modifications."

"Modifications?"

"Yes."

"Such as?"

"Other than a staff of well paid and fairly treated employed servants? Well, off the top of my head, you will also need an armed and trained standing army made up of loyal soldiers."

"What about my recruitment drives?"

"Are you referring to the purging of the villages wherein you abscond with formidable fighting men and child soldiers?" I asked.

"Naturally."

"Gone," I stated flatly.

"What?!"

"Next come your taxes and tariffs."

"What are those?"

"What you should be doing to the people of the Eastern Empire. Instead of taking what you want, you will impose a fair tax to generate revenue."

"Your words confuse and anger me," Grimskull said, narrowing his eyes.

Ignoring him, I continued. "You will use a portion of the revenue you receive to put back in to the empire's infrastructure for road maintenance, houses for healing the sick, and schools for educating the masses."

"OK, that is enough of that!" the baron declared, standing and pointing his finger at me. "You claim to be the master villain? The darkest of us all? Yet you advise benevolence, education, and . . . fair taxation? This audience is ended. I demand to be returned to my realm, immediately!"

Chapter Three

Where I Discuss Politics, Ex-Wives, and Have a Visit from my Sister

I said nothing at first. I watched the baron calmly with my elbows on my desk and my hands steepled under my chin. The baron held his pose, pointing at me, waiting for a reaction. When I gave him none, I saw his arm begin to tremble from holding the "intimidating" pose.

I leaned back slowly and then lit another black cigarette with a silver tip and waited. This was a mental pissing contest. A game of chicken, if you will. And I did not get to where I was by flinching first.

"I mean it!" Grimskull said, breaking the silence. "I demand to be returned."

"Fine. You may go." I waved in dismissal.

Calmly I placed my cigarette in the glass ashtray's cradle and began shuffling a few papers on my desk. Grimskull turned to leave.

"It's a shame. You may have been even greater than Countess Skullgrim," I said.

The baron stopped. "What did you say?"

One of the many sub-rules of villainy: Everyone has a rival. Discover it and exploit it.

In this case, Baron Viktor Grimskull had a longstanding hate-hate relationship with Countess Elsbeth Skullgrim, Empress of the Western Empire. But what did you expect from ex-wives?

"The Countess Skullgrim. The Power of the West, as I hear she is called these days. You could have been even more infamous than she. But you know what is best for your dwindling empire. Good day, Baron."

The baron stood there thinking. It did not take a psychic, even though I had several in my employ, to know what he was thinking. Was I bluffing? Was I using a trick to get him to come back? Baron Grimskull was at a crossroads. If he came back to the table, he may be perceived as weak. If he left, then he would be foolish.

Decisions, decisions.

Grimskull, his back straight, walked back to my desk and sat down, trying to make it appear that it was his decision.

"What do you know of Countess Skullgrim?"

"Everything," I said, picking my cigarette back up. "I was the one who organized her empire to rival yours."

If looks could kill, I would have been nothing but pink mist along my office walls.

"You . . . what?!"

"Don't look so shocked, Baron. When you divorced your wife all those years ago, she fled your lands with nothing but the clothes on her back and a title that was worth nothing without people to follow her. So, I found her, cultivated her, set her up as the Countess Skullgrim and put her on the throne she is on. But now, I have chosen to assist you these last few months."

"Why?"

"Simple. She no longer needs me. And I no longer have her income. So that brings me to you. What you see as weakness in my plan to brighten the shit-hole you call an empire is, in fact, brilliance. Yet you choose not to see it."

"Enlighten me," the baron said, watching me with wary eyes.

"Let me ask you, Baron. Is it better to be feared or loved?"

"Feared, of course."

"A foolish answer," I said, not caring about the baron's ire. I held up a hand, stalling his building tirade. "The answer is loved. A man who serves you out of fear will do so, as your empire does now, until the day comes when they can let you die or rise up against you. That is why there are so many attacks against your life. But . . ." I trailed off.

"But what?" Grimskull asked. Obviously this line of reasoning never occurred to him. Just like the idea hadn't occurred to Countess Skullgrim when I'd pitched it to her.

"But a land that loves its ruler will die for him, or her, willingly. They will throw their bodies on the machines of war in the hopes that their blood slows, or stops, the threat against their beloved ruler. And while they love you, you will take what you want from them as they sit fat, happy, and content. Give them games. Give them fair wages and reasonable taxes and they will sing your name. The poor are dangerous, for they have nothing to live for. Those with more, a middle class if you will, are easily fooled provided you give them something else to hold their attention. And while you give them things like literacy, alcohol, public games, sex, and the illusion of free commerce, they will do nothing more than claim you are the greatest ruler of them all, defending you while you rob them blind. All you have to do is reap the benefit of a blind populace who are too occupied with their own boring lives. *That*, my Baron Grimskull, is villainy. Let others die for you and pay you while they do."

After finishing my little speech, I stood up and poured two tumblers full of a nice spiced wine from a favorite dimension of mine. I offered Grimskull one of the heavy glass tumblers and held my drink out.

"What do you say, Baron?"

"How do you know this will work?" he asked. A fair question.

I winked at him. "Because I've done it before. The Western Empire, all of Countess Skullgrim's lands, are thought of as the cradle of civilization in your world. Why is that?"

"Because she bewitched her people with her magic."

"No magic at all, Baron. False democracy. Let the people believe they have a say in how the country is ruled and they will flock to your lands. Trust me, where I come from, it is an everyday occurrence."

The baron looked at me for a moment or two, and then we clinked glasses. "So be it. We shall try it your way."

I noted that the baron did not drink his wine first. I smiled and sipped at mine, keeping my eyes on him. When the Baron was satisfied I was not trying to poison him, he drank the contents of his tumbler as well.

"It is settled then. Courtney will escort you back to the rift-gate to where your world's escort is waiting. As far as they are concerned, you have been gone mere seconds. I will start the arrangements."

"No," the baron said.

"No?"

"If you want to change my lands and take my gold for it, you will oversee this yourself. I want you close if things go wrong. In your world, you are the god. In mine—well, you will be my guest."

The baron was not truly stupid. I knew this. I shrugged. "Why not? It has been a while since I've done any field work. I will be in your lands within the week. Do we have a deal, Baron?"

"We have a deal."

The baron turned and left my office, with Courtney on his heels. I sat back down at my desk and began preparing my ledger, outlining the plan and the supplies I would need.

"Sir, you have a visitor," Sophia's voice said over the intercom.

I pressed the intercom. "I am a little busy right now, Sophia."

"Sir . . . it's your sister."

Shit.

Of all the dark and twisted things in all the realms across the known and unknown universe, my sister was by far the most sinister and hateful thing ever created.

"And she brought your nephew," Sophia amended.

I stand corrected.

Chapter Four

Where I Entertain Bad People, Worse Ideas, and Give My Nephew a Job

"Julie!" My sister, Paige, called out in her obnoxiously high-pitched warble as she burst into my office. "Oh Julie, you never come to visit anymore! Figures I would have to come . . . here to see my baby brother."

I hated when she called me that.

"Mr. Blackwell, I'm so sorry, she just barged in past me despite my telling her you were occupied," Sophia said as she chased after my sister. The chase wouldn't be too long; it appeared that Paige was once again off her latest fad diet. I could smell the fast food grease and the diet Coke before she wrapped me up in her massive arms for a hug.

"Julie?" Grimskull asked.

Damn it. I thought he had left already through the office portal.

"Oh hello!" Paige said, turning to the baron, releasing me. My suit now reeked of curly fries. "Aren't you terribly frightening?"

Paige pushed past Courtney, who made a move to block her path, but I waved him off. Courtney did not possess empathy for human life. The suffering of others was simply a part of his job. As much as I would have loved to see him perform acts of violence on my sister, I had promised our parents that I would look after her—a promise she abused as often as possible. If she were here, there was no doubt she was out of money already.

"A pleasure to meet you, m'lady," the baron said as he took my sister's garishly lacquered, corpulent hoof of a hand and kissed it. "I am Baron Viktor Grimskull, Lord of the Eastern Empire. Who may you be? And, if I may I ask, why did you call Mr. Blackwell 'Julie'?"

Paige blushed. "I am Paige Blackwell, Julian's big sister. And I've been calling him Julie since we were kids. Isn't that right, Julie?"

"I call myself Jackson now, Paige. As you are well aware," I said, attempting to maintain my composure.

"Jackson? Really? Your middle name? You know that was just Mom's maiden name."

"I am aware. I am also aware that Julian was not the most popular of names while growing up. Hence, Jackson. Now Paige, I assume you want something. Please allow the baron and I to conclude our business, as he was just leaving. I will see to you momentarily."

I raised an eyebrow and willed the gate to Grimskull's realm to open wider. My realm responded to my will and the gate emitted a powerful, pulsating light, a reflection of my growing temper.

"Nonsense, Julie," Paige said as she waved her hand, and the gate shut down immediately.

"You have dominance over this place as well?" Grimskull asked.

"Of course!" Paige exclaimed. "He may be a god here, but as his sister, that technically makes me a goddess!"

"Indeed you are, m'lady."

"Oh, aren't you a charmer." Paige blushed. If Grimskull weren't careful he would find himself in the trailer park, one hundred pounds overweight and dead from a heart attack like her last two husbands.

"Paige, the baron needs to return to his realm. Now."

"Lighten up, Julie. You haven't even said hello to your nephew!"

Nephew. Damn it. I'd momentarily forgotten.

I turned my attention from the baron and my sister flirting to the wasteful lump of flesh reclined on my office's leather sofa with his feet on the armrests. His expensive headphones were on, which meant he was lost to a sea of wretched music as he stared intently at his new smartphone.

I steeled myself.

"Hello Randy," I said as I scanned the room for missing items that my felonious nephew might have crammed into his oversized jeans. Beneath the mop of unkempt, greasy hair and hoodie, the 23-year-old man-child ignored me.

Seriously—Randy. Who names their child Randy anymore?

"Hello Randy," I repeated, my voice growing in power.

Randy showed a moment of cognitive capability as he looked briefly up at me, then back to his smartphone. "'Sup dude."

'Sup...dude? The paltry words of the hack Shakespeare should be stricken from the annals of history, for my nephew Randy redefined eloquence in only two syllables.

"Welcome, Randy. I trust nothing of mine has found its way into your possession . . . again."

"What's your wifi password, dude?" Randy asked, not looking up.

Looking at Randy, I could hardly believe he was of my blood. At 17 I had already made my first million in fenced gold and illegal magical items sales. Randy, on the other hand, dropped out of community college, lived with his mother, ate half-frozen microwave meals, and masturbated to bland internet porn. He steadily grew greasier, as he lived off the privileges my enterprising initiative provided to my equally parasitic sister.

I imagined storming across the space between us, grabbing his smartphone, and stuffing the rectangular brain-wasting device up my nephew's rectum.

Instead, I altered the subtle reality around the phone and gave him full access to the internet. Tunneling a data plan into my dimension was not very difficult. Besides, if the worthless shit was engrossed in vapidity, then he was too occupied to rob me.

"Really?" I heard Paige say, giggling.

"Indeed," Grimskull said.

Leaving Randy to his withering brain cells, I returned to my sister and the baron. I focused my will tighter and reopened the portal from my realm. I inclined my chin to Courtney, who had been keeping his ever-present eye on the two of them. Courtney nodded and stepped towards the baron.

"Baron, if you would please follow me. Now," Courtney insisted.

Grimskull, who cut an imposing figure, looked up at Courtney and shrunk back slightly. "Yes, Shadow Master, I suppose it is time. Lady goddess Paige, I do hope you will consider my offer. My empire is quite lovely."

"Oh Viktor, you couldn't handle all this," Paige said as she slapped the cheap Lycra that barely contained her well-traversed . . . womanhood. "But I'll keep it in mind."

The baron bowed to my sister and departed with Courtney through the portal.

"Oh, he is wicked. I like him," Paige said.

"Of course you do. You are always drawn to evil men. And idiots." *And apparently the allure of the all-you-can-eat Old Country Buffet*, I thought to myself. "Now, may I ask, why are you here?"

"Oh Julie, you know, I've been thinking."

I somehow doubted that.

"All you do is work, and somehow, you still look younger than me."

"Because in this realm, time does not pass the same. It obeys my wishes. So, here, I do not age. Now, what is your point exactly?"

"You are not married and you have no children," Paige said.

"That is by design. Family is weakness. Caring for something other than myself leads to love and love leads to trust. Trust leads to betrayal. It is the inevitable nature of all things."

"But I'm your family."

"I stand by what I said." I lit another cigarette and tried to enjoy something while I was subjected to this familial hell. Paige stood there, slack-jawed, confused, and crestfallen. In other words, in one of her five natural states. The others were sleeping, eating, rutting, and watching reality television on a couch.

"OK, I am going to ignore that and get to why I'm here."

"Please, don't hurry on my account. It isn't like I have a business to run," I said as I ashed my cigarette.

"Your business is why I'm here. I think you should consider teaching Randy the family business. An heir."

I stared blankly at Paige, deciding if my promise to Mother and Father had a statute of limitations. The 1911 *was* still on the desk.

"You cannot be serious," I said.

"Why not? He's your nephew. He's your blood."

"Please, don't remind me that I am related that walking advertisement for proper condom use."

"Dude . . . I'm sitting right here. I can hear you."

"I wasn't whispering."

"Julian Jackson Blackwell!" Paige announced in her loudest authoritative tone. She used her will over this dimension to flicker the lights for effect. "Do not talk about my child that way!"

Have you ever noticed when an asshole is presented the truth, they get offended? And they replace the word "kid" with the word "child" when they feign indignity? I've found the same applies for "house" and "home" when you aptly describe someone's garbage pile thusly.

"Paige, what do you want? More money? I will have another deposit in your account by the time you return home. A new house? Fine, I will move you both . . . again, to the nicest home you will no doubt destroy and lower the property value of. However, a place within my organization? Let alone an heir? You are . . . how do the kids say now? Cray cray."

Paige said nothing. She walked across my office to the couch and sat down next to Randy. She put her arm around her son. I heard her sniff a few times.

"Julian . . . Jackson, we are the only family left. Mom and Dad are dead. We have no one else besides each other."

Damn. This speech again.

I rolled my eyes and snubbed out my cigarette and waited for Paige to finish her rehearsed speech. I'd heard it so many times before I could bob my head in time to the cadence while I pretended to listen.

Blah blah blah family. Senseless noise and rhetorical nonsense about looking out for one another. Poorly-constructed clause pertaining to the future. Some snot-drenched indecipherable babble. And, for the usual crescendo, the eventual question of what would become of them once I was gone.

Like anything was going to happen to me.

Once the speech was over, I took a sip from my drink and lit another cigarette while I pretended to consider her words.

"No. Go home."

Paige wiped away her crocodile tears and stood. "Fine, asshole. Give Randy a job and give me more money and I won't bother you ever again."

"I doubt that," I said as I considered the offer. "Fine. Here is my offer. I will take Randy with me to the realm of Caledon, to the Eastern Empire and Al' Garrad Baron Grimskull's capital, while I conduct my business. If he does not come across as complete idiot, I will consider a position in one of the far realms as a field operative and give him a chance to move upward. Will that suffice?"

"Oh Julie!" Paige cried out as she rushed towards me, wrapping me in a hug.

Again, my thoughts reached out to the Colt 1911.

"You won't regret it! I promise, Randy will pick up on your every word and surprise you!"

I doubted it. "Sure, sure." I nodded, trying to placate my sister to get her to release me. Based off her wild affection, I feared for her bedfellows.

"And of course, the money," Paige reminded me.

"Yes. And the money."

Me and my idiot nephew off to make an idiot warlock warlord a beloved ruler. What could possibly go wrong?

The Fourteenth Rule of Villainy

Trust leads to relationships.
Relationships lead to betrayal. Betrayal
is your own damn fault.
Ergo, trust is dumb.

Chapter Five

Where I Contemplate the Evil Nature of Horses, the State of the Poor, and Waste Teachable Moments on the Young

The sun was hidden behind a wall of gray clouds and the sky threatened rain. The entire Eastern Empire was in that perpetual haze between fall and winter. Most of the leaves had fallen and the ground seemed to be muddy and wet at all times. Everything smelled of musty, rotten wood and horse dung.

Essentially, everything was a moist bucket of cold shit.

Fantasy realm villains, sigh. Their concept of a kingdom was almost always the same. Cold, wet, and sad. They thought by using their magics and influence to keep the realm in a perpetual state of despair, the people would be ground into submission.

Idiots have zero agricultural sense. No sun and no seasons equals no food. Unless you count mushrooms.

Which I don't. Fungus is repugnant. It grows near death and excrement.

If you say "But it's good on pizza," then you will suffer my wrath. I will not destroy you. No. Instead, I will purchase the bank that holds the mortgage to your parents' home, sell the home out from under them and force them into the streets. Or worse, into your home.

And if your parents are already deceased . . . well, ha ha, you're an orphan.

But I digress.

I rode along on horseback with Courtney in the lead with and seven of my elite field operatives flanking the small caravan. All of them personally selected by Courtney.

Each of us had changed into appropriate garb for the location. I, dressed as a traveling merchant, wore my black leather trousers, matching thigh high boots, an emerald green silk shirt, a black doublet, a dark green hooded cloak, and forearm-length black riding gloves. Courtney wore a similar outfit, less expensive-looking of course, with bits of armor to pose as my man-at-arms. The remainder of my men wore their standard field tactical gear under their rough, homespun tunics and leggings. Each was armed with visible swords and daggers. Yet each also concealed a mixture of firearms and magical items in their packs.

And then there was Randy.

Randy was behind me trying to play a game on his phone while on horseback. He refused to wear traditional garb and settled on the fantasy realm equivalent of sweatpants and a hoodie. If questioned, I would refer to him as my servant. My simple, simple servant.

The trek from the dimensional gate to Grimskull's capital of Al' Garrad was not unpleasant. Except for the horse. I hate horses. They seem to exist to maintain as much air between my ass and the saddle at all times. Despite all my time working operations in the field in the fantasy realms, horsemanship was never a skill I mastered.

Laugh if you must. Horses are an instrument of the underworld. It's true. I've had dealings with the Never Realm. And I have it on good authority that horses were a creation of a darkest of lords. Don't believe me? Just talk to someone who is into horses. I mean, *really* into horses. Don't they act as if they are possessed? Don't they talk about their undying love for horses and how beautiful and majestic they are in the same wide-eyed, simple-minded way that cult members speak of their leader?

That is by design. Horses are trying to invade your soul at all times. They are sinister beings from the darkest realms of hell, moving from continent to continent enslaving the people they encounter. Why do you think it is called a night*mare?*

"Hey, dude, when are we gonna get there?" Randy asked.

"Tomorrow," I replied, for the third time in the last hour. "We will stop for the night in the town of Ashraven. In the morning, we will depart and make it to Baron Grimskull's fortress by the evening. In time for rest, baths, and dinner."

"So, why didn't we, like, y'know, just teleport into Grimm-dude's castle? Wouldn't that be faster?"

Because, you moron, the dimensional gates I establish across all the realms are set in locations that provide a strategic advantage for me. If I were to create a gate inside one of my client's lairs, they could potentially use their own magics and discover a way into my realm by analyzing the inter-dimensional residue left behind from the magical gate. Hence, I rotate my gates so they are never in the same place, and very few people know that schedule.

And, if you had listened the first time I explained this before we left, you would know. Since you do not care to listen, perhaps a training accident is what is needed, and I would once and for all be free of a barely vertebrate monkey child who happens to carry DNA similar to mine.

I sighed inwardly, wanting to scream and perhaps maim. Instead, I contained my frustration. "Randy, why are we here?" I asked, hoping to turn this into a teachable moment.

"To fix Grimm-dude's land or something like that."

"Yes. Correct."

"Then why are we stopping in this town?"

"Why do you think?" I asked. Perhaps the boy might at least have one natural instinct.

"Wench boobs?"

Well, so much for hope.

Hope is a stupid emotion anyway. Hope, like faith, only leads to disappointment. Those who say they hope for things are too frightened or weak-willed to make something happen for themselves. Those who say hope is the best of things clearly have never achieved a goal.

"No, dear, sweet, simple Randy. We are stopping in Ashraven because it is the last major township before we reach the borders of Baron Grimskull's capital."

"And?"

"And people who live close to, but not in, a capital have a strange sense of insulation against the regime that governs them. Much like the grandstanding morons who post political opinions on their social media accounts, these blowhards love to talk about the local politics but never truly do anything about it. Thus, what you get is an unfiltered, and often underinformed, opinion of the populace's disposition towards the powers that be."

"What was that, dude? I wasn't really listening."

"It means, dumb people talk too much and we can learn what they think of Grimskull."

"Oh, cool."

"Yes, it is rather cool." I smiled. Perhaps there was something I could kindle within the young man.

"Yeah. This phone you zapped for me still gets reception out here? So cool."

I opened my mouth, then closed it. It was not worth wasting my breath, nor my time. My dearest Randy was a brilliant example of this generation's ability to be distracted by colorful, shiny objects and pleasant noises. An indictment of the modern education system, free-range parenting, time-outs, and entitlement. Ah, youth . . . perpetual goldfish in a digital bowl.

"Courtney," I called out to my loyal man.

"Sir?"

"Please ride ahead to Ashraven and secure the rooms. I believe the Corolan Inn will suffice for the evening."

"Yes sir," Courtney acknowledged. He kicked his horse in the flanks and the beast took off in a gallop. Two of my field agents, wordlessly and without preemptive command, rode forward to take point along the forest trail as their commander departed.

I smiled.

Efficiency gave me a mental erection.

After another hour of two of riding, we reached the town of Ashraven. The town itself wasn't much to look at. It was little more than two dozen freestanding structures made of stone and wood and a wall surrounding the entire complex. Hardly a city, but big enough that a few strangers could get lost in the crowd.

Ashraven served as a trading station between the outlying farmlands and the capital. Even from outside the walls, I could hear the town still bustling with activity as night descended. The oil lamps were being lit among the streets and all the minor gates were being locked for the night.

My group came upon the main gate and several armed guards held out their hands for us to halt. Now was the time that I hated the most. The most odious of tasks that every field agent, myself included, must accept as a hazard of the job.

Common people.

It isn't that I hate people. No, that's a lie. I do hate people. But the common folk of these realms? Well, they are an acquired taste, like anal play and Morrissey. The grate and wail, stink and moan. They are generally disgusting and serve no purpose other than the delineation between the sane and damned. And yes, I am still referring to Morrissey.

"Put your hood up," I said to Randy as I placed my own hood over my head.

"Why?"

"Because I fucking said so," I hissed at the idiot. I had no time to explain the nuances of the realms. Like this one, for example. A group of armed men riding to a town's gate at night should be a red flag to any guard and denied entrance. But whenever said men have their hoods up and speak in unctuous tones, ninety percent of the time they are let into the city with only a few coppers for a bribe and a half-hearted warning that they will be watched.

"Whatever," Randy said, but the boy obeyed and placed his hood over his head.

"And stash the phone," I amended. "These people have never seen such a device and we are not trying to draw more attention than we already are."

"God," Randy said, rolling his eyes. But once again, he listened, and turned his phone off and stashed it into one of his pockets.

"May I help you, good sir?" I called to the lead guard. The overweight bruiser with the bulbous alcohol nose waddled over to me. I swear I could not tell where his chin began and his throat ended.

"Oy, what business do you have in Ashraven this time of evening? Respectable folks have already found their way inside the town's walls."

I smiled and pulled out a small wineskin from within my cloak. "Now, what fun is there in being respectable, my good man? Thirsty?" I asked as I shook the wineskin gently and discreetly.

The guard raised his eyes and took a step closer. "What fun indeed?" the guard replied.

I passed him the wineskin with a few coins. "My name isn't important. I am just a merchant with my guardsmen. By my honor, we are here for the night only and will be on our way at first light. And if you happen to be here in the morning when we leave, then perhaps another gift like this could find its way to your excellent town guard. My gift to the underappreciated guards of this fair town."

This was the moment of truth. I'd judged the guard's character as a bit of a lush and a bit on the apathetic side. However, I'd been fooled in the past. That was why I had my other hand under my cloak. I had the option of reaching for my silenced semi-automatic pistol or a Wand of Induced Memory if things went south. The wand had only a finite amount of charges and the item itself was very expensive. The pistol was more final.

Decisions, decisions.

"Welcome to Ashraven, Master Merchant. Enjoy your stay. If there is anything you require, then please, ask for Bircham."

"I will indeed, good Bircham. A pleasant evening to you." I nodded and then urged my horse forward.

"Damn, Uncle Jack," Randy said. "You totally Jedi mind-tricked that dude."

"Please, Randy." I waved my hand dismissively to him. "Getting past a town guard is Villainy 101. And besides . . . I prefer The Sith."

Chapter Six

Where I Discuss Shoes and Orchestrate a Bar Brawl

The Corolan Inn was pleasant, as poor, run-down crapholes go. The establishment was a simple rectangular building with a kitchen in the rear and a main bar lining the back wall. There was a fire pit in the center of the common area.

People had gathered in for the evening, with transients passing through like myself and my men. A few local farmers who couldn't make it back to their homesteads before nightfall had come in for the night. An obvious adventurer or two were mixed into the crowd. They were always easy to spot if you knew what to look for. Cleaner faces. Cleaner clothes. All their teeth. Weapons that radiated a legacy of magical energy. The lack of the human-shit smell.

There were other people in the crowd of the common folk definitely worth noticing. I caught the eye of Courtney, who was standing by the bar ordering a round of meals and drinks for us. I nodded towards several of the other odd people I noticed and Courtney nodded.

"What's up, dude?" Randy asked.

"What do you mean?" I asked the boy, curious that he caught the exchange.

"You totally just gave muscle-dude the eye about some of those dudes over there and there," Randy said. Before he pointed to them, I held out my hand to stop him.

"No, don't point, and for God's sake, don't whisper. Both draw attention. Speak normally. What do you mean? What do you see?"

"That's the same look I give my bros in the club when some douche is starting some shit. So, who are we going to have to fuck up?"

Hmm. It seems Randy the Useless Wonder has keen eyes when he wants to use them. And apparently, the mettle in him to get into a fight. Maybe he could make a field agent. With proper training, who knows.

"So, who are those dudes? Need me to put them down?"

"No." I shook my head. "Just tell me what you see."

"Hmm." Randy considered the command. I could tell he was interested because he put his phone away. "That dude is keeping to himself, but he's got his back to the wall so no one can sneak up on him." Randy inclined his chin towards a cloaked man standing just off the bar nursing a drink.

"Go on."

"And that dude over there," Randy said, nodding slightly at another hooded and cloaked man standing near a table smoking a pipe, "he hasn't moved in like fifteen minutes. And that chick over there, the one wearing dude clothes, is listening to the serving girl's conversations."

Well . . . go Randy. Granted, he missed the other three in the room, but points for noticing three of them. "So, what made you notice them?"

"Their boots, dude. Totally too fancy boots for this place."

"That is right. Why did you notice that?"

"Same way I can tell based on clothes which chicks in the bar want to get freaky instead of the ones who just want to be noticed. Or which dudes will start a bar fight. Fancy shoes on a dude might mean dude's a prima donna. But fancy shoes on a dude who doesn't smile means he's gonna throw down if you scuff his kicks. It pays to pay attention to feet."

Huh. A lesson learned from the dude-bro culture. Hell hath frozen over.

"Those men and women are secret police who work for Baron Grimskull. He uses them in the same purpose we are here for, getting information."

"Won't they like, not talk to us if the cops are around?"

"Of course not, so we need to get rid of the cops."

"How do we do that?"

"Easy," I smiled. "Courtney."

On cue, Courtney *accidentally* bumped into the first concealed secret police member that Randy had noted at the end of the bar. Courtney put on a drunken stumble and slur before he made his move. After the accident, he began apologizing profusely for spilling his drink on the covert cop's tunic.

"Buffoon!" the disguised agent said as he pushed Courtney away and reached for his sword. Courtney, appearing drunk, stumbled again into the guard, and in the confusion, struck him with a palm strike to the throat and knee to the groin. The guard gasped and hit the ground, but not until Courtney had a firm hand on the agent's cloak, tearing it off as the man fell.

The light of the lamps and the fire pit revealed, quite clearly (and by design), the heraldic sigil of a white laughing skull and a golden battleaxe on a field of purple. The banner symbol of Baron Grimskull.

"He works for Grimskull!" I stood and shouted, pointing at the man on the ground. "I bet he's not alone!"

The crowd immediately went insane, searching for the other spies. My men moved among the crowd and helped expose the remaining members of the secret police.

I returned to my seat and watched the ensuing battle unfold. Amazing what a few words could do. The members of the secret police pulled their weapons and tried to defend themselves, but they were really no match for a room of angry, disenfranchised country folk.

"Dude, aren't you going to get in there and fight?" Randy asked.

"Randy, sit down," I said as I helped myself to a drink from one of the nearby empty tables, the patrons having left it behind to jump into the scuffle. I passed another cup of beer to Randy.

"You see all that?" I gestured with my cup. "That is the power of words. The power of being in control. The power of being a villain. You take any situation and turn it to your advantage."

"Isn't the skull-dude like, your client?"

"Yes Randy, he is. And the entire reason for this trip is to create a new empire for him. Look at this. Look how the people hate his men. How they are willing to throw themselves at men with swords just because they wear his colors. That, dear nephew, is the mark of a weak villain. A shortsighted one. One who cannot see the bigger picture and would rather be feared than loved. And it is exactly why we are here. I am going to fix that. When I am done, the people of these lands will offer free drinks to any who wear Grimskull's colors."

"That's . . . cool."

"Yeah, it is," I said, agreeing with my nephew. "Now, go on, get in there. Kick a little ass and enjoy yourself."

"Fuck yeah!" Randy yelled. He hopped up and jumped into the chaos, putting his boots to the heads of the downed agents.

I didn't know what it was. Perhaps getting out from behind that desk and back into the field, into the job I once loved, allowed me to stop seeing and treating Randy as a worthless bag of crap. I mean, he still was, but he was at least listening a little more. I found myself taking him under my wing. And as revolting as that thought normally was, here in this rustic shithole, I couldn't help but smile.

So, let the idiot have a little fun. In a very short amount of time, the people were going to stomp the agents into submission. I wasn't sure if they would kill them. But they were definitely going to be in a world of hurt. And that was what I needed to see. What I needed to know. To what level the people would go to hurt Grimskull, even if it was only through his people.

By the look of things here, I had my work cut out for me.

Soon, the fight was over and what used to undercover agents were bloody heaps on the floor. The patrons picked up the bodies and moved them into the back kitchen. From the efficient way this happened, this was not the first time agents had gone missing in the town. And from Grimskull's attitude, I doubted he would accept failure on his agents' part.

Oh Baron, I am going to have to charge you double.

The inn returned to a surprisingly jovial state. The drinks flowed and the people talked. I did what I always did. I listened and stored the information to be used later. And I learned quite a bit that night.

One particular drunk in the bar was quite morose. After many, many rounds of drinks, he became chatty. And he told me a very interesting story, to which I paid keen attention.

When the drunk was done his tale, he got up and staggered out into the streets. I watched the young man leave and pondered the information he'd spouted.

Courtney came to sit next to me and also watched the man leave. "That him?" I asked.

"Yup."

"Curious," I said, considering the angles and the possibilities.

"Well, not much more we are going to learn tonight. Let us retire for the evening," I said, and Courtney rounded up the men.

Tomorrow would bring us to Grimskull's keep and a whole lot of work.

Chapter Seven

Where I Ponder My Time with He-Man and Encounter a Secret Servant

Let me just say this: Supervillains, regardless of their particular genre, have a need to create the most garish, gauche, and goddamn gaudy lairs possible. Hollowed-out volcanoes, for example. Underwater domes. Massive letter-shaped buildings in their initials. All of these serve as testaments to insecurity and expose deep underlying psychological weaknesses, or perhaps crotch-based shortcomings.

Baron Viktor Grimskull was clearly a devout subscriber to the belief that to rule over others, one's power must be expressed through outlandish architecture. Let me paint you a picture.

The Eastern Empire's capital city of Al' Garrad was nestled in the Grey Spire mountains along Caledon's eastern coast along the Nameless Sea. In the center of the city was the Bay of Barrak, which was fed by several rivers flowing from the mountain range. The bay itself then fed into the sea, which made the entire area perfect for imports and exports. The city was fairly impressive as fantasy realms went. Stone construction for the majority of the buildings within the city's interior, cheap wood and mud huts for the poor section along the docks.

Nearly everywhere in the city, there were statues of Grimskull, all of them in various poses, depicting battles he *claims* to have won. Some in white marble, others in black. Some in gray stone and others still in precious metals. And if that wasn't narcissistic enough, Grimskull's castle was high atop the easternmost peak. The castle's facade was carved to resemble his mask. The giant demonic skull face hung open as the main entrance to the castle, forcing those who entered the keep to be metaphorically consumed by the baron and reminded of his never-ending appetite for more.

Personally, I thought the entire thing moronic and self-serving. But I had to admit, seeing it in person did bring back pleasant memories of the He-Man Castle Greyskull action figure play set I had as a child. Oh, the battles I would create! The forces of darkness would mobilize and bring down the Eternians using their combined skill and raw ferocity.

Yes, even as a child, I knew the villains could and should win if they had proper leadership. The heroes' victories were not about their combined might and their righteous cause. They happened because Skeletor was a weak leader. His ego got in the way of using his people to the best of their abilities. So, episode after episode of that damned cartoon I watched as a child, and each time, I would spot the fatal flaw that would have turned the battle.

So when I called the shots, there was no moment of arrogance that ended the fight, forcing a retreat. No, I left ego out of it and meticulously brought down the champions to earn the victory and take the castle.

Now, as a man, I still think of those silly hunks of cheap plastic and the lessons they instilled. I control others as if they were my personal action figures. And it feels good.

My mother sold my Castle Greyskull in a yard sale and piece of my heart went with it. So when the time came, I made sure she was . . . taken care of.

No, you vicious asshole. I didn't kill her. Did I not explain earlier that I abhor psychopaths?

I made sure both she and Father had the best medical assistance money could buy. She was comfortable right until the very end following the accident. I loved my mother. And her selling my toys was a kindness bestowed upon me. She saw my mind. Even then as a child, she knew. She helped me put away my childish things so that I could evolve into what I am now.

****

By late afternoon, we'd arrived at the castle. My party was greeted at the city's main gate by one of the baron's chamberlains and an entourage of fifty armed soldiers. Hmm . . . only fifty? Should I be offended?

After pleasantries were exchanged and proof of our identity given, the chamberlain and the armed cohort escorted us inside the castle. The chamberlain prattled on about something or other. I really wasn't listening.

Not that I'm an aristocratic asshole or anything. Well, perhaps at times. No, I did not deem it necessary to listen to him because everything he was speaking was not meant for me; it was meant for the fifty soldiers. He had to give the appearance of his faithful employment.

Why do I know this? Because the chamberlain was actually a guy named Steve, and he worked for me. Surprised? Don't be. As I've said, I have operatives everywhere. And in this case, Steve was one of the first people I placed in this empire with two purposes: the infiltration of Grimskull's regime and the arranging of our initial meeting.

Spreading the legend of the Shadow Master across the realms was imperative for my business. And that required operatives in the field. During the time when I was doing this operation solo, I learned the ins and outs of manipulating my way through just about everything. I also learned it is a lot of hard work.

That guy on the HBO's *Game of Thrones*—the one who plays Littlefinger and looks like a cross between Gary Oldman and a rabbit—he makes it look easy. Trust me, it isn't. So as my power and legend grew, I began employing others. Like Steve.

Back in the real world, Steve was a former Marine who got out of the service to finish college. After graduating, the only job he could find was as a barista at a coffee shop.

Keep working on that liberal arts degree in anthro-poli-gender studies with a minor in theater, kids! Meanwhile, I'll have that venti caramel macchiato to go. Oh, and a lid protector, please. I'd hate to spill a drop inside my luxury car on my way to my job, for which I'm grossly overpaid, and after which I will return to my amazing home and have incredible sex with my supermodel maid.

Sure, one might say money doesn't buy happiness. But let's be honest. That's what poor people say. Being rich is awesome. I have everything I want. Every opportunity is afforded to me, and my job satisfaction is through the roof. Money might not buy happiness, but it damn sure lets me get there.

So I continued to ignore Steve, or rather the chamberlain, to continue the illusion. After we arrived inside, my men and I were shown to our accommodations in a private section of the castle.

"When the feast is ready, an escort will come and bring you and your men to the great hall," the chamberlain said.

"Thank you, Chamberlain," I said, escorting him back into the main hallway, outside the guest suite.

Both the chamberlain and I looked up and down the hallway, ensuring that we were alone. Once I was satisfied, I tapped the ring on my right hand's ring finger and spoke the word of activation. A magical spell settled between him and me, masking all outgoing sound. To anyone eavesdropping, we were simply communicating about the state of the ride there.

"Good to see you again, Mr. Blackwell," Steve said.

"Likewise, Steve," I returned. "Report."

"As you suspected, the baron sent agents of his secret police to all the inns along all the main roads leading to the capital."

"It is what I would have done."

"Six of the men have failed to return. They were dispatched to the Corolan Inn in Ashraven. I assume that was where you encountered them?"

Never admit anything is a rule I live by. One of many. Instead, I just smiled.

"I see," Steve commented, thinking. "Baron Grimskull suspects you, naturally."

"Naturally," I agreed. "But he cannot pin it on me. Not without any witnesses. And let me guess—his attempts to scry the information came back with nothing."

"Yes, sir, they did. How did you know?"

"Steven, I have been doing this a long time," I said with a slight chuckle. "When I am away from my dimension, I am no longer a god. But as long as I bring something with me that is imbued with the power of my realm, I am essentially a wizard in any realm I am in. All my items were fully charged by me prior to leaving. His meager attempts to learn anything about me will always come back clouded and hazy."

"Very good, sir," Steven said with a slight bow. "That is why you are the Shadow Master."

"Indeed. Now, has Grimskull given any legitimate thought to my plan to enhance his empire?"

"Yes sir, he has. Following the feast, the baron intends to invite you and your nephew back to his private chambers to discuss what he has already set into motion. I think you'll be pleasantly surprised with the amount of work he has put into this already."

"I look forward to it," I said, preparing to drop the spell.

"Perhaps he is not the idiot we pegged him for, sir?" Steven asked.

"Dear Steven, please, leave the thinking and planning to me. Grimskull, and all his ilk, are morons. They do not realize that they are bound to archetypal behavior. Like animals, they cannot think beyond themselves. That is why shepherds like us—well, me—guide their actions to a more beneficial outcome. Were it not for me, Grimskull would have been deposed by now. A casualty of his hubris and naïveté."

"Yes, sir."

"Good lad, Steven. Please, run along and let the baron know I am ready for the feast. We have much to discuss and an empire to seize."

"Yes sir," Steven said once more, then turned and departed.

I returned to the room, ready for a night of feasting and song, women and alcohol. Tomorrow—well, tomorrow would bring a new dawn for the Eastern Empire and a new toy for the Shadow Master to play with.

Chapter Eight

Where I Eat the Contents of the Monster Manual and Get Betrayed

Feasting is a waste of food. It is decadent and sinful.

I loved it.

Say what you will about Baron Grimskull. Moronic? Yes. Blind to the obvious? Oh, for sure. Unable to satisfy a woman? Well, according to his ex-wife Countess Skullgrim and testimony from several of his mistresses, then the good Baron's seven seconds of "lovemaking" set a new land-speed record while giving new meaning to the term "Two-Pump Chump."

All that aside, he laid out one hell of a spread when it came to a feast. Fruits and vegetables from all across the realm. Flavor combinations that played a melody in my mouth. There were little pastries with savory meat and exotic cheeses baked inside. For my carnivorous side, the baron's cooks presented nineteen different kinds of meats. Sure, you had your chicken, beef, pork, waterfowl, and mutton. But that was where the boring ended and culinary adventure began.

There was cockatrice and basilisk fillets. Roasted wyvern and brisket of minotaur. Sauteed chimera and barbeque dragon. spider legs, slow-cooked gorgon, haunch of hippogriff (mind the feathers), and bugbear stew. Hell, the cooks had managed to create their own version of a turducken by stuffing a phoenix inside an owlbear inside a roc!

And if that were not enough, the feast was topped off with baby unicorn chops.

Oh my gods above and below. The taste. Just perfect.

They say free-range unicorn is gamy, and you carry a blight upon your immortal soul for eating it. But the little ones, who are captured and forced to sit and eat so their meat is tender? Mmmwaaa! Perfect. You can truly taste the sadness. If you're lucky, you can fight with your friends at the table and break the horn like a wishbone. And unlike those good-for-nothing turkeys, when you break the unicorn horn and get the bigger piece, the wishes tend to come true.

It was a fantasy Fogo de Chao. As the meal progressed, I felt like I had eaten my way across the Monster Manual, and eventually, I had to decline another bite. I sat back in my chair in the great hall and just took it all in.

Baron Grimskull was sitting at the head of the twenty-foot-long stone table. He wore his typical armor and skull helmet. It was funny to watch him try to eat and drink. He refused to take it off, trying to maintain his powerful visage. But the real comedy was watching half the food and drink slop down his chin and onto his eating bib. I did notice that the good baron was now wearing the Amulet of the Ember Soul.

Good. Perhaps he was willing to start listening to me.

To the baron's right was his war general, a woman I had not met yet but had heard of. General Anders the Half-Giant. She was almost nine feet tall and beautiful (if half-giant women were your thing). She had flowing brown hair with flame-red tips to match her fiery red lips. Oh, she wasn't wearing lipstick, by the way. She was part fire giant. That was her natural heat radiating outward. To contain the inner heat from her mixed heritage, special armor made from magically-crafted petrified ice was created. She was a study in contrasts, ice and fire.

And I bet a blow job from her would melt your cock off.

To the baron's left was his archmage, Chaud. The bald man was my height and skeletal. He seemed to be perpetually shivering from the lack of body fat. He was wrapped in blue and black robes, yet he left his hood down for the feast. His piercing eyes and hawkish nose gave him the look of a bird of prey. While he radiated cold, dark power, he had a smirk to his mouth like he was recalling a joke. I liked him immediately.

My informant, Steve the acting chamberlain, stood behind the baron waiting for his command. I sat along the opposite head of the table, the seat for guests of honor. Behind me, Courtney stood a silent watch, keeping his eyes peeled for any danger. Just because Grimskull was a client didn't mean I trusted him. The rest of the table was filled with various retainers, local lords, the chief of police, and other such dignitaries.

And Randy.

Randy had all the dinner graces of a donkey in heat as he slurped his way through the meal, belching loudly and knocking over people's drinks while reaching over their plates for helping after helping of food.

All the kindness and goodwill I'd felt for my nephew in the Corolan Inn was swiftly melting away, leaving me with my original stance on him and my loathing for his breathing the same air as me.

The remainder of my men were downstairs, eating at the servants' tables, as was fitting their station. I would have preferred my men to be present in case Grimskull tried something stupid. Yet I was comforted, as always, in knowing Courtney was behind me, figuratively and literally watching my back.

As the meal died down, the musicians picked up their instruments in the great hall. The madrigal was soft and lively without being overbearing. Servants came forth with goblets of port, perfect for after dinner.

Grimskull took up his cup, and standing, presented it before the group.

"To the Shadow Master, Jackson Blackwell. With his guidance, I will transform my empire into the greatest realm in all the land. I am honored to have you in my home and look forward to a long and fruitful relationship."

Oh shit.

OK, for the uninitiated, when the villain raises a glass in a toast that flowery, wishing long relationships and blah blah blah, that usually means he is about to double cross you. Most times, you are about to be poisoned or drugged, then imprisoned, then killed.

So I held my glass out and refused to drink. Instead I locked eyes with Grimskull and waited. I sensed Courtney tensing behind me. My loyal badass was ready for a fight. With the amount of magical items and firearms on my person, I was ready to give these fantasy fucks a dinner they would never forget.

"Mr. Blackwell—Jackson, if I may—the wine is not poisoned," Baron Grimskull said in a obsequious tone. "Nor was a single bite of your meal. I would, after all, never think of trying to poison you. You are too wise and too cunning to fall for that. I assume you have no less than three different items on you that would detect poison."

I only had two, actually. Drinks were tricky since alcohol is technically a poison. The stone in the ring on my left thumb, the one I held my drink with, neutralized all poisons. I could drink any alcohol and only get the most pleasant buzz instead of full-blown drunk and a hangover.

"It is not your food nor drink which concerns me," I said as I tilted the goblet back and swallowed the port. "It is the manner in which you are addressing me. You mock my title and show contempt for me over a meal. Bad form, Baron."

"Jackson, you are no longer in your realm. As I told you in your awful dimension, you would be my guest. And my guest, you will remain forever, until your power is mine."

So that's why he wanted me here. I should have seen this coming. I was getting sloppy. Well, between Courtney and me, we could take them all. Steve, with luck, would neutralize the baron and the archmage.

Courtney could handle the big bitch and I would clean up the rest of the room. I just needed a signal to spring into motion.

That's when I saw Steve wink at me. I got ready . . . then realized.

He didn't wink at me.

He winked behind me.

At Courtney.

I turned just in time to catch Courtney's gauntleted fist on the bridge of my nose.

I dropped hard. My nose was broken and blood gushed everywhere. I couldn't see past the tears that were involuntarily welling up (I was NOT crying! It was a biological response!).

"Courtney, *et tu?*"

"You are such a fucking asshole," Courtney said just before his big boot connected with my temple and knocked me into unconsciousness.

Chapter Nine

Where I Recover from a Concussion and Plot the Demise of Seven Assholes

If you've never been knocked out, it is a hell of an experience. The sudden impact rocks your brain and your mind basically reboots like a computer. Everything goes black and you have a strange taste of metal in your mouth just before you pass out.

It is not good to be knocked out, as you have basically suffered a concussion. The longer you are out, the more damage has been done to your brain.

I was out for a good while.

The reality of coming to after being knocked out is piecemeal. Your senses return bit by bit while your mind and body perform a quick triage to assess the damage to the body and determine where you are.

I woke up cold, damp, and in pain. So that sucked.

My eyes were still closed, crusted over with blood. My head and nose throbbed in tremendous pain. That also sucked.

I felt cold, wet, abrasive stone underneath me and I was aware that I was only wearing my small clothes (that's fantasy realm talk for underwear). The situation was this: I hurt, I was on wet stone, and my head had been beaten in. If I had to guess, after being betrayed, I was stripped down and thrown into a dungeon.

Fucking great.

Blindly, I reached out and felt the stone ground and splashed my hands into puddles of water. Well, at least I hope it was water. I used the moisture to lubricate my eyes and wash off the blood. There was a gash on my forehead from where Courtney's boot must have connected after he kicked me in the temple.

What an asshole. That kick to the head knocked me out. The follow-up kick he must have delivered out of spite opened up my forehead. Oh, Courtney . . . now I will have to destroy you.

I sat up very slowly. When you have been knocked out, sudden movements afterward can be quite disorienting. Your head will swim and you'll vomit. I already had enough (hopefully) water on my face to wash off the blood; I didn't need to add partially-digested unicorn to the mix. I blinked and let my eyes adjust to the barely-illuminated cell.

I inched myself to a seated position, my back along a stone wall. Surveying the room, I was well and truly boned.

The cell I was in was nothing more than a hollowed-out alcove, carved into the mountain, deep below the castle. Before me were not steel bars, but a lattice of rock and stone. Since there was no gate and no lock, I had to assume that the cell was magical, and that either a mage was in charge down here, or the guards carried charms that controlled the stone, allowing them to manipulate the earth.

Crap.

If there had been a steel gate, like the ones in the stories and books, I could possibly pick the lock. But this? I would need a sledgehammer to get through it. Sadly, I had not thought ahead to hide one up my rectum in case of just such an emergency.

After a few minutes of slow breathing, my pounding headache subsided to mere annoyance. I slowly crawled over to the stone prison gate and peered outward. My cell seemed to be one of many, all carved into a long rectangular hallway with several fire pits positioned along it. The only source of light seemed to be those fires. Each end of the hallway had a door. My guess, one went up and the other went down. It would stand to reason that the upwards path went to the main castle while the other led to where all the garbage and sewage would go, the sea.

I returned to the back wall of my cell and waited. Calming my mind, I assessed the situation.

First, I was alive. So, someone wanted me that way—either to gloat, or to get something from me. Second, I was naked, or near enough. That meant someone knew what items I had on me, and more importantly, how to remove them safely.

I heard moaning and wailing from other prisoners, which was distracting. As was the stink of whatever shadow race creatures they had down here as well. Troll? Orc? The stench was so potent that combined with the sobs and wails of other prisoners, I missed that I had a visitor standing outside my cell.

Three of them, actually.

Randy, Courtney, and Steve.

"'Sup, dude," Randy said as he leaned against the stone gate and played with his phone.

"Mr. Blackwell," Courtney said. He stood there with his arms crossed and looked down on me, his expression showing nothing.

"Jackson. You look like shit, bro," Steve said.

Three of them. One of them was my Judas. My first instinct was Steve. Perhaps I'd left him here too long and he'd gone native. There was no way Randy could rub his three remaining brain cells together to do this.

But Courtney? He had to be mind controlled. There was no way he would betray me willingly.

"Mr. Blackwell, I want to explain why I betrayed you."

Fucking Courtney . . . I always knew I couldn't trust him! Bad news from the beginning.

"Mr. Blackwell . . . Jackson, you were the best employer I've ever had."

I crossed my arms and stared back at him. "Then why?"

"You would not understand."

"Not understand what? What in the world could possibly move you to betray me? I pay you very well. Your family is taken care of. You get to travel the multiverse and kick the crap out of people for fun. Hell, your niece is going to Harvard thanks to my donation!"

"Yale," Courtney said absently.

"Then again, why?"

"I told you he wouldn't get it," Steve said. Smug bastard just stared at me like I was an animal in the zoo. An exhibit to behold, then move on, forgotten moments after seeing it.

"Oh, I'll get to you soon. When I found you, you were nothing. I got you a job here and you started as a cook and moved up to chamberlain in six years. I had such high hopes for you."

"No, asshole," Steve said. "My last name is Cooke. You put me there as a joke and forgot about me. No communication, no orders, nothing! I've had to shit in outhouses and chamber pots for eight freaking years. You know what they have for dentistry here? Nothing! My teeth hurt. There are monsters. I never even saw the end of *Lost*!"

"You didn't miss much. Pretty much purgatory the whole time."

"Really? That sucks."

I turned my attention away from Steve and focused on Randy. "And what's your excuse?"

"Hmm? Oh, muscle dude's in love with my mom. He's cool. You're kind of a dick. No offense dude," Randy said without even looking up from his phone.

My sister. My freaking sister was behind this? And for love?

"You're in love with my sister?"

"Yes."

"And you," I asked Steve. "Greed?"

"You know it. I want back to the real world. Hot running water and air conditioning."

"Let me guess, you and your mom want my job?" I asked Randy.

"I guess," Randy shrugged.

"So, what's Grimskull's involvement?" I asked.

No one spoke. "OK, now we stop chatting?" I asked.

"Not stopping, waiting," a new voice said.

Grimskull's.

The bastard even started a slow clap. I guess that gesture wasn't contained to just the prime universe. The baron, General Anders, and Archmage Chaud came to stand before my cell while my trio of traitors moved aside. All of them smiled at me in captivity. Smirking. Gloating. Six people of power. Six controllers of my fate. Six people who brought my entire empire down around me, while my chubby, slutty sister was most likely redecorating my office. So, make that seven people.

Normally, I wouldn't count Randy, but when you are on this side of the prison bars, your perspective changes.

And with that thought, I smiled.

"And what could the mighty 'Shadow Master,'" Grimskull said with air quotes, "be smiling about?"

Chaud chuckled with an evil, creepy, thin-lipped smile. General Anders actually laughed out loud, tossing her mane of hair back. Her loud, bellowing laugh felt like it rocked the whole cell level.

Sycophants laughing in unison? Cliché bullshit was alive and well.

Well, so was the villain soliloquy.

Mine.

I was the villain here and these chumps were about to learn that.

"You stand there, in positions of power. And power is why I am laughing." I stood, as best I could, on shaky legs. If I was about to give a killer speech, it wouldn't be on my ass. "Laugh at me, if you must. Many have. And they are all memories. I am going to destroy you. All of you. Even my dear, bloated sister. Trust me, Courtney, I'm doing you a favor. You six see yourself as untouchable now that the infamous Shadow Master is trapped. But while you six stand there, I do not see six captors . . . no."

I inched closer, painfully, to the stone lattice cell. I rested my hands on the lattice, holding myself up as best I could.

Which is what I wanted them to see.

As fast as possible I snatched my hand through the opening and grabbed Randy by the collar and pulled hard, cracking his head to the stone. With my other hand I grabbed the smart phone before it hit the ground. Jumping back as Courtney and Steve reached for me, I smiled, baring my teeth.

"I only see six targets."

And with that, I vanished.

Chapter Ten...sort of

Where I Gloat

Don't act surprised. I'm the freaking Shadow Master.

Did you really think I was going to be stuck in prison?

Are you an idiot?

Probably.

Anyway, back to my tale.

Chapter Ten (The Real One)

Where I Exploit Fantasy Loopholes and Piss off a Sea Deity

"Boss . . . boss . . . BOSS!"

"Mmm?" I half grumbled, half gurgled as I sat up in the sand, coughing up what felt like a whole ocean from my lungs.

"Boss, can you hear me? Mr. Blackwell?"

Between my coughing fits, I faintly heard the voice of my receptionist, Sophia.

I shook my head and looked over my shoulder at the sea and smiled. "Heh, that always works."

"What? What works? Boss, are you OK?"

It was morning and I was on a sandy beach near a small fishing village. Some of the locals were walking toward me, and oddly, some of them seemed to be rejoicing. I saw Randy's phone lying on the beach next to me and picked it up. "Sophia, are you there?" I said into the phone.

"Oh thank fucking Christ," Sophia swore. "You're alive."

"Did you have your . . . doubts?" I wheezed as I tried to get more air into my lungs.

"Boss, I didn't know what to think. Shortly after you left, Paige came to your office, kicked out all your clients and then started using her goddess powers. She's making changes, Mr. Blackwell. Big ones."

I coughed a few more times, turning my head. Phone manners are important. "Changes? What kind of changes?"

"Praise be! A savior from the sea has been delivered!" the lead village fisherman said as he came up to me with his arms open as if he wanted to hug me. "The sea god has heard our prayers."

"Who the hell is that?" Sophia asked.

"Locals. Give me a second." I held my hand up, halting him. He looked perplexed, but obeyed. "Excuse me, terribly sorry, but I'm in the middle of something. You were saying, Sophia? Paige was making changes?"

"Everything, sir. The whole place has gone trailer trash, country kitchen, Pinterest kind of shit!"

Crap. Paige always did have the worst taste.

"Wait, how are you calling me?"

"I stole her phone when she wasn't looking. She's been in contact with Randy the whole time, texting, passing messages. Bad ones, sir."

Texting. I weep for the children of today. And the ridiculous parents who've adopted the juvenile practice. Is there a cluster of emojis that represents "Grow up, act your age, and suck my balls, you nation of vapid, non-verbal, entitled twats"?

"Boss, I've been reading through the logs, and it looks like Courtney—" Sophia began, but the fisherman, now with more people gathered around, interrupted us.

"Excuse me, but haven't you been sent by Nhal, god of the sea? We read the signs and we expected a blessing to be upon us today. Nhal was to give us a champion who would—"

"Yeah yeah, praise Nhal," I said. "Now, I am communing with the great sea spirit right now. Could you get me some clothes and something to eat and drink?"

"Uh . . . yes?"

"Great. Now, run on back to your village and I will be there soon. Go on, chop chop," I commanded.

"Yes . . . yes, very wise, sir," the fishermen said and left, confused, back to their village.

"He's . . . older than predicted," one of the fishermen said to the others.

"Never question the will of Nhal."

Once I was alone again on the beach, I returned to my phone call. "Yes, Sophia, I know all about Courtney and Paige. They are in love and he betrayed me. They all did."

"I know, boss. That was the last text received. Randy messaged her that you were in prison. Then when he stopped messaging, she went ballistic. How did you break free?"

"Simple," I said. "Courtney put his boots to me when I wasn't ready and knocked me out. They threw me in a dungeon, and true to form, Grimskull brought his whole crew of conspirators down to gloat."

"Then how did you escape?"

"It was that idiot Randy. The phone he was carrying was imbued with power from my realm. I sensed the power radiating from it. The power healed me and I put on an act. When they weren't suspecting, I cracked Randy's head, snatched the phone and used a little bit of the power to drop me off about a couple of miles away, down the coast and into the sea."

"The sea? Boss, you could have died."

"Sophia, you are forgetting the rules of the fantasy realms. People— well, main characters anyway—never die at sea. They always wash up on shore. It's kind of a trope. One I was very willing to exploit. Now, I have a couple of miles head start and an item with my power in it. So they will not be able to locate me."

"Until she realizes I stole her phone and she cuts off the power flowing from this dimension to that one."

Sophia was right. Once Paige realized what happened, she actually was smart enough to cut the flow of power. After that, the phone would only hold a charge for a limited amount of time. More than a regular phone, for sure. But the more power I used, the faster it would drain.

"Sophia, why didn't you try and contact me ahead of time?" I asked.

"She forbade any outside contact, sir. You know the rules of this realm and what my limitations are."

I did indeed. I wrote the rule. I also know Sophia's ability to circumvent the rules. "So, how did you manage to get around the command?"

I could practically hear Sophia grinning. "Oh sir, you know me so well. Too bad things could never work out between us."

"Sophia," I said, raising my voice.

"After Randy stopped messaging, she went a little crazy and started blowing up some of your possessions. Not the good ones, sir, those are still well hidden. So I calmly asked her if I could use the restroom. And she clearly stated 'I don't fucking care what you do'. So I took that to mean I was free and clear to behave as I wished."

"That's my girl," I said proudly. "Too bad Paige doesn't know you don't go to the bathroom."

"That's her fault for not paying attention," Sophia gloated. "OK boss, what's the plan? I can't open a gate to get you home. I require the permission of the dimension's sitting lord. At the moment, that is Paige. Perhaps if you could make your way back to the standing gate outside of Ashraven?"

I thought about it. I thought about how easy it would be for me to return to my realm. But I would have to battle my sister. Even though it was my realm, the battle between us could shatter the dimension and bleed over into others. I was already not well liked by my neighboring deities. A fact they made abundantly clear during the quarterly meetings.

"No, not this time. This needs to be done old school," I told Sophia. "A systematic destruction of my enemies. A lesson to them and a warning to others. You don't . . . fuck . . . with the Shadow Master."

"Oh sir . . . if I had a vagina—well, a real one . . ."

"I know Sophia, I know," I said. I saw something out of the corner of my eye that caught my attention.

The rising sun had caused a golden path of light from the horizon to the shore. Almost to the exact spot where I was standing. And on that watery path, a clam shell, easily six feet long, materialized and floated towards the shore. The clam opened and inside was a silver light that gave off a feeling of hope and power. As the clam floated up, I saw a child inside. She was blue, with white hair and strange red markings.

She was clearly the one promised by Nhal. A champion of justice and good. To be tended to and reared in the ways of humankind until the day came when the child would right a great wrong and bring peace to a war-torn people.

Well, I couldn't have that shit.

I put my foot on the shell and gave it a nice kick back out to sea.

"Sorry little one, but you're bad for business."

"Sir?" Sophia asked.

"Not you. I was just taking care of something. Let me go take care of these fisher folks and I'll call you back. In the meantime, I need to know the moment Paige cuts the power."

"You got it, boss."

I smiled as I watched the shell float back to sea, then turned to walk to the village.

****

After receiving clothes, food and a little rest, I thanked the people of the village and bid them farewell, promising them I would fight for their noble cause.

Whatever it was. I wasn't really listening.

I was more distracted by the garbage they called food and the rags they called clothes. Still, I soldiered on with a smile on my face.

Once I was out of sight of the village and moving to the nearby woods, I clenched my free hand into a fist and felt the power from the phone, my power, surging through me. I altered the driftwood and seaweed garments and fashioned myself new clothes. Nothing too fancy, mind you. But for what I had in mind, I had to look the part.

I stood, renewed, in my dark brown boots, black leather pants, a forest green shirt, a brown leather armor with silver plate inlay, and an adventurer's cloak. On my back were twin short swords and on my hips were two combat daggers. I created a small earpiece so I could keep comms open with Sophia. I also linked my vision to the phone. What I saw, Sophia could see on the smartphone on her end.

"Sophia, are you there?"

"Yes sir."

"Sophia, I am running out of allies. I need to know this is not another setup. Where do your loyalties lie?"

"Julian Jackson Blackwell, from the moment we met one another, we have been bonded. I have ever remained loyal to you. Of all who came before you, I only ensured their death. But you were different. I serve you because *I choose* to."

"Until the day you decide to kill me, that is."

"Well, of course, sir."

"That's all I needed to hear," I said. "Sophia, you know how I feel about trust."

"I feel the same way, sir. Now, what's your plan?"

"You are not going to like it," I told her.

"Try me, sir."

"I'm going to recruit some heroes."

The Ninth Rule of Villainy

A villain will use ANYTHING to win . . . even if it sucks.

Chapter Eleven

Where I Begin My Quest to Find Heroes and Expose Fantasy Realm Sexism

No doubt Grimskull and his forces were searching for me. His archmage, Chaud, would be able to tell where I teleported to. But from then on, I'd been covering my tracks magically. The phone still showed a full charge, so Paige had yet to realize she was inadvertently helping me.

I was weary from the last few days. The beating and subsequent imprisonment had taken its toll. The overland trek from the coast inland took several hard days of walking with little food or drink. However, it was blessedly free of conflict while also free of horses. It may have taken a considerable amount of precious time to get there, but if I never had to ride another one of those demonic hell-beasts, then I would walk without complaint.

Before me stood the Crossroads Inn and Tavern. I placed my hand on the door and took a deep breath, preparing myself.

"But sir, your reputation! Think about it!"

"There is nothing to discuss," I told Sophia. The comm link in my ear allowed me to hear her clearly, and I barely had to speak for her to hear me. Plus, having her as a second set of eyes with our inter-dimensional Skype had its benefits.

This was where the first step towards my vengeance would begin. I felt the wood of the door and admired the stained glass of the windows. The inn was aptly named, as it sat at a major intersection off the empire's capital road.

"But why this inn, sir?" Sophia asked. "Won't Grimskull be searching everywhere for you? Shouldn't you be hiding in less public places? Perhaps recruiting some goblins, or ogres?"

"Yes, possibly. No doubt that by now, Courtney will have informed the baron that, based on my threat, I would begin recruiting allies to take them all down. But, much like you, Courtney would not assume I would enlist the aid of noble champions. So Grimskull's people are more than likely searching the dark corners of his empire and inquiring among the Shadow Races. Also, Courtney knows where most of my secret caches of weapons, magical items, and gear are. With that in mind, both courses of action are off limits. I chose this inn because it is random and has no strategic value. But, according to the rules of the realms, an inn or tavern picked at random should actually prove to be my salvation."

"But sir," Sophia protested.

"Where do all the great quests begin, Sophia?"

"In a bar, tavern, or inn." Sophia sighed. "That's brilliant, sir."

"I know," I said. Sophia was clearly placating me. But she also knew I was correct, per usual. "How is my dear sister doing?"

"She created a pocket universe just to destroy it," Sophia informed me.

"That's Paige. She was always one to throw tantrums. Let me guess—she fears leaving the office and losing her power?"

"Yes sir."

"Good. Then she does not know how to store a portion of the power."

"Not yet, sir. That is why I have been avoiding her. I am sticking to her last command. But if she finds me, I will have to, at the very least, tell her anything she needs to know. To include our conversations."

"Sophia, do you still recognize me as the authority of that dimension?"

"Yes sir. Why?"

"Then that phone is now your phone," I said. "So, when she eventually asks you to help find her phone, you can say?"

"I have not seen nor have *her* phone," Sophia finished. "Sir?"

"Yes Sophia?"

"Are you stalling?"

" . . . I guess I am. To anyone watching, at best, I'm a drunk standing outside an inn with his hand on the door, talking to himself. At worst, I'm just a weirdo doing the same thing. I have not employed this tactic before. What if I were to fail?"

"Sir, permission to kick your ass for that line of thinking when you return?"

I laughed a little. "Granted. You are right. I did not push my empire to the heights that it is by not using every tool available to me. So . . ."

"So, time to be a—yuck—hero," Sophia finished. I nodded and pushed the door open and walked in.

The Crossroads Inn and Tavern was full that evening. People from all over were laughing and drinking, adventurers and locals alike. Music played and enjoyment was had by all. The drinks flowed and innocence was dying. Underneath the reverie were moments of creeping corruption. Pickpockets moved in the crowd, lining their pockets with ill-gotten gains via dexterous sleight of hand. Prostitutes solicited the unfaithful with whispers of promise. Gamblers attempted to cheat their way to small fortunes while honest folk let it happen.

In other words, it was a random bar on any given night, anywhere. Perfect.

You see, corruption is an aphrodisiac. Not just for the wicked like me, but for the just and the righteous as well. For the truly good cannot sit idly by in places of good. It's ironic. Places where the most good congregates often become corrupted by the existence of evil. Conversely, places of sin like this often bring in people seeking to help those who refuse the path of the straight and narrow.

So, all one had to do was peel back the layers and look. Under the filth was where I would find my champions. My heroes. My pawns to bring down my enemies.

"Sir, you do realize you are broadcasting your monologue again?"

Damn. I had not.

"Sorry, Sophia. It's a villain's curse."

"Not to worry, sir, it was isolated to the phone only. And I must say it is very good to hear you back in your element. You are a great businessman. But you were even better in the field."

She was right. I did derive a sick pleasure from being back in the field. Limited options, limited resources, hunted and alone. My mind reeled with the possibilities.

"OK, let's keep our eyes open."

"Who are we looking for?"

"Candidates."

I scanned the room and my mind did what it always did: assessed the potential in others and weighed my ability manipulate them for a net gain. The subtle trick was to keep any potential mark on the hook, unaware of my goals, and constantly take of their giving. Basically, an abusive relationship where they keep coming back.

"How about him?" Sophia said. "The redheaded kid who looks lost and probably shouldn't be in a tavern of any kind."

"No," I said, shaking my head. "What have I told you before about red-headed people in the fantasy realms?"

"That they are almost always a hero. Especially if they have strange eyes. Green, blue, or gray."

"Close," I said. "I said they were almost always a *chosen one*. A hero, yes, but their destiny usually has a much grander purpose. Saving the world from ultimate darkness and such predictable nonsense. I mean, look at him. Young and wide-eyed. I can practically smell the sheep dung on him. You have a pastoral kid looking like that, with just enough anger beneath the surface, I suspect he is looking for the answers to a familial tragedy, which will lead him on a winding saga and have him facing this realm's darkest forces. Oh, that's a grand story waiting to be told. So, for my purpose, it bores me. I've read that particular book over and over. And while I'm on the subject, do you how many red-headed people with odd eyes are littered about in science fiction and fantasy? The trope is disgustingly played out. Like recessive genes mean anything grander than they don't do well in direct sunlight."

"A simple 'no' could have sufficed, sir."

"You needed context."

"Fine. How about her?"

"The female in armor with short black hair and blue eyes?"

"Yes."

"Nope. She's a villain. Or soon will be."

"Are you sure, sir?"

"Yes, trust me. She has a very intelligent look and a desire about her. Being good won't fulfill her."

"Wouldn't she be perfect then? An ally?"

"Normally, yes. But for what I plan on, I don't need the eventual betrayal."

Sophia sighed. "Fine. And that one? The skinny girl in the corner with the rough homespun cloak."

"Runaway slave," I said. "While I do not condone slavery, her quest will take several books to tell. We don't have time for that."

"How about the tall, dark-haired, nondescript generic Caucasian over there? He seems to be a valiant warrior."

"Too noble. He is on a mission to right the wrongs of his past. No doubt everything he believed in is now a lie and he will stop at nothing to bring order to betrayers he once called allies. So, he will not be bendable to my will. Plus, they are always so enigmatic and boring."

"Fine, sir," Sophia said, sounding defeated.

She was clearly deflated by my critiques of her choices. It wasn't her fault. I just had a particular vibe I was searching for, and not a lot of time. I looked about the room and scrutinized my options.

A group of halflings? And me without a ring. No, no need to go down that path. I didn't want to get sued.

The fighter type in the back looked promising. Then I spotted the medallion he wore around his neck. The broken one. Nope. Half a medallion means he has a twin out there looking for him. No doubt an evil twin. Never get mixed up in family squabbles.

The magical lady in the dark corner levitating her silverware? That could be useful. Oh, wait. No, no thank you. I just saw her eat a small metal ingot to fuel her magic. No ferromancy, not in my company. A ridiculous magical system a good tale does not make. Ugh, just like all those hacks out there who have one hare-brained mechanic idea and build a thin plot around it.

I would never do something like that.

The dark elf and dwarf companion? No, too righteous and too cliché. Besides, I didn't need the dark elf to steal my spotlight. I wasn't a speciesist or anything, but few things entrance people, especially Caucasian women, like a beautiful, dark, exotic warrior. Hell, I was getting a little turned on looking at him. As they say, "Once you go Dark Elf . . . "

Here's a fun fact: All dark elves have overly white-haired nether regions. They practically glow in the dark. Off-putting, to say the least. Sorry if that ruined your image of them. But they are not all Brad Pitt à la *Fight Club*, hairless and lean muscle with impeccable manscaping. Nope, they are quite the burly unkempt beasts down there. Plus, the women have teeth in their vaginas. But what do you expect from people who worship spider deities?

"Any leads, sir?"

"The pickings seem to be slim," I said, "but I see a couple with potential. The overly built clergyman who's just short of being a walking mountain. The one nursing his drink and staring into the fire is obviously a former soldier with a tortured past who has turned to a warrior's religion. He has potential, but he's not a leader. And then there is the auburn-haired female warrior over there," I pointed out. She was the one thankfully *not* wearing fantasy armor bikini bullshit. Instead of steel, her armor was made of petrified wood. "She has potential."

"Which female, sir?"

"Over there," I said, staring at the woman.

"The skinny guy with the patchy beard?"

"No, that's a woman in disguise as a man. Pretty standard fare, I'm afraid."

"Really? I didn't see it."

"Hence the disguise," I smirked.

"Sir, didn't you just say that redheads were off limits? Chosen ones and all that?"

"My apologies, Sophia," I said. "Unfortunately, sexism is alive and well in the realms. And, not just the punk-rock, metal-underwear-armor kind of sexism, I'm afraid. In the realms, female redheads almost always turn out to be great warriors, no matter how they start off. Naïve princesses or bar maidens, sooner or later they all end up great warriors. The added bonus is they almost never die. They sure as hell get hurt a lot, but they usually pull through."

"Complete patriarchal bullshit."

"I know," I said. "If I had it my way, at least half of them would be clumsy, ugly, and dumb and die like everyone else."

If I had to guess, she was fresh out of some warrior sect, and once it was discovered she was female, they kicked her out of the boys' club. No doubt she was a natural combatant. The best the trainer ever saw. Hell, the trainer probably knew she was a she to begin with.

I sipped my drink and rubbed my eyes. This was going to be a long night.

When I opened them again, I spotted someone.

Check that. I spotted *The One*.

"Oh, this is providence."

"What, sir?"

"I just found our hero," I said. Cliché or contrived, I didn't care. I just loved abusing the fantasy rules.

Chapter Twelve

Where I Enlist My Team by Putting Innocents at Risk and Kick a Little Ass

"This is complete and utter horseshit, sir."

"What?"

"Are you telling me that this is the same man you saw in the Corolan Inn back in Ashraven?"

"Yes."

"The same man whom Courtney knocked out and stole the Amulet of the Ember Soul from?"

"It is indeed."

"So *he* is the bastard son of Baron Viktor Grimskull? Last descendant of the Eld and Prince of the Elder Men?"

"The one and only." I smiled.

"That's it, I quit!" Sophia yelled. "What kind of backwards, fucked-up, hackneyed, fan-fic bullshit is this?"

I put my hand over my mouth to stifle the belly laugh growing inside me, threatening to burst. "It is all very simple," I said. "If you understand the—"

"If you say 'The Fantasy Rules,' I am going to tear your foreskin off. Sir."

Gods above and below, Sophia had a flair about her. Well, at least when she was threatening me, she remembered to do it formally.

"Are you done with your tantrum?" I asked.

"For now, sir. But you have to admit, this is contrived."

"I never said it wasn't. But this is how things are."

"OK sir, so what's your next step? Are you going to go talk to him and enlist his aid in defeating Grimskull?"

"Oh, heavens no," I said.

"Then what?"

"Patience, Sophia," I told her.

In all honesty, if someone just walked up to you, made small talk, informed you that you had a common enemy, and enlisted your aid, what would you do? I'll answer it for you: Nothing. People don't work like that.

If you tell yourself any different, then you are a moron. Or an avid tabletop fantasy gamer, which is essentially the same thing.

People are dumb. People needed to be guided, to be led. And more importantly, people only truly come together for causes. They're just the pack animals they claim not to be. So to bring people together, to make them a pack, you have to give them a cause. I could sit around and wait for one to occur, but I was on a timetable.

I reached through my magic and released the warding spell that kept me hidden. Then, I slowly but surely enhanced my magical aura. I would be seen as a challenge to any wizards who were scrying for me.

OK Chaud. Tell your master where I am.

I went ahead and ordered another drink, then sat back down and waited.

"Sir, what did you do? I felt a shift in your power."

"I just made myself bait," I told her.

"You did what?!"

"Trust me, I know what I am doing."

Sophia stayed quiet, but I could sense her disapproval. Cards on the table. This was a very risky move. But in order to form a fellowship of idiots to do my bidding, I had to give them a common enemy.

Now to see if my instincts were correct.

A moment or two later, I had my answer. Outside the Crossroads Inn and Tavern, a brightness split the night. Reddish-tinged white light poured through the inn's windows and the sky rumbled with thunder. The music stopped all at once and patrons ran to the windows to see what the source of the light was.

"It's a legion of Grimskull's men!" I heard someone shout.

"What do they want?"

"Fuck that; *who* do they want?"

I scanned the room and looked for the people who were not reacting. And if I hadn't been in public, I would have patted myself on the back. The auburn-haired female warrior, the rough clergyman, and my wayward prince all remained in their seats and sighed.

Damn, I'm good.

"They're coming in!"

The patrons all moved back from the door. Some reached for their weapons, half drawing them, unsure of what to do. Other folk hid under tables or looked for a back door. Some poor bastards just got out their coin purses, hoping to bribe their way out.

Myself? I started rehearsing my lines. In between conquering worlds for fun, I take acting classes. I really like improv, but I've learned it's always good to have a well-scripted line or two ready when the situation calls for it. Best way to be an effective liar is to lace in just enough truth that whatever you say comes off as believable.

The door to the inn was kicked open and armed guards poured in. Each of the armored men was dressed in the livery colors of Baron Grimskull. I pushed my way past the people who were cowering, intentionally pushing hard against the young warrior who was still sitting at the bar so he would notice me moving towards the front of the crowd. Once I had enough of an opening, I used my best stage voice.

"Stop! They are here for me. If Grimskull wants me dead, then so be it. But no one else has to suffer!"

That was me placing the explosives. Now, I needed a spark to set off the fireworks.

"Are you Shadow Jack?" the lead guardsman asked.

"I am. Please, just take me and spare these people."

There are a few certainties in the world. Water is wet. Fire burns. And if you ask an evil henchmen to spare others for your act of nobility, they won't. So with my words still echoing in the ears of the inn's patrons, all the guardsmen immediately began drawing their weapons.

Heh heh heh. I even threw up my hands, protesting for dramatic effect. "No no no! Please, they're innocent!"

"Kill them all . . . ACK!" The guardsman was swiftly knocked flat on his back as the young warrior came to my rescue by leaping forward and planting a kick in his chest.

"No minion of Grimskull will harm anyone this night," the young man said as he drew his bastard sword.

Oh lord. A hand-and-a-half sword? Really? Besides their complete uselessness in an enclosed space, they were just too long and unwieldy in general. But when in Rome and whatnot. I drew my two short swords from my back and eased into an *en garde* position.

"Kill them!" the guardsman from the floor yelled the moment he had enough air back into his lungs.

As a visiting deity, I was not allowed to go around murdering my host realm's people. It is just bad form, not to mention illegal. But the workaround was simple. If a realm's citizen tried to inflict deadly harm on myself or a companion, I was allowed to respond in kind. The young man just came to my aid as we were about to be attacked, so this constituted a stand-your-ground rule. Even if I did pick the fight.

Hey, I didn't write the laws. I just abuse them.

The warrior and I fought well together. We fended off the first wave of the guardsmen's attacks with the clash of steel on steel, covering one another. The young warrior would turn in large, slashing arcs. If his target leaped back or ducked, then I followed up his attack with a one-two slash and lunge with my short swords, finishing them off.

"Not bad, old man," the warrior said as he came over my shoulder in an overhand chop, burying his sword in the neck and shoulder of the next of Grimskull's men who advanced. The guard's lifeblood sprayed everywhere, covering us and the inn's floor.

Old man? While I was firmly in my mid-forties, my body was barely thirty. I always kept myself in peak physical shape through rigorous Krav Maga and armed combat training. Plus, it helped that I cheated Father Time and refused to age myself while I was in my dimension. But leave it to youth to see anything past twenty-five as *old*.

"Better than you, boy," I said, thrusting my blade a scant inch from his head and into the open mouth of the attacking guardsman who'd gotten the jump on the kid's blind side.

"The name is Hawker. Kyle Hawker," the warrior said, deflecting an oncoming attack.

"I prefer 'Boy,'" I said to Hawker as I punched out with the pommel of my sword, catching a guard in the throat.

"Both of you talk too much," the large priest said as he joined our side. The big man picked up the nearest of the guardsmen and tossed him back into his comrades. "Damn you Vammar, damn you."

Vammar was the one of the gods of this realm. The god of duality. His iconography often depicted him as a burly male figure with a hammer in one hand and an olive branch in the other. People didn't actually worship him, so much as he conscripted people who amused him into his service.

Trust me, I know.

Not that I'm a follower or anything. Vammar comes to the celestial meetings sometimes. Kind of an asshole, really. Neither good nor bad. He just likes to expose the dual nature of man as both warrior and peacemaker.

The holy man had no weapons to speak of. Under his robes he wore heavy plate armor and on his fists were clam-shell gauntlets. All the armor was inscribed with the teachings of Vammar. The armor gave off both red and blue ethereal light.

With each thundering strike of his fists, a combined purple lightning flared, knocking the intended target back, then simultaneously healing them.

"Gods damn you, Vammar," the priest grumbled beneath his breath.

"Leave it to a warpriest of Vammar to be a blundering idiot," said the red-haired, bearded female pretending to be male. She was lean, yet strong and well-muscled, and wielded two wooden batons with steel caps on them. She whirled them and the air whistled with her movements. As if alone in her own world, she danced among Grimskull's men, snapping bones and knocking men on their asses.

I swear there was a moment when the four of us practically posed for an action shot.

"It looks like you found your team, sir," Sophia said in my ear.

I grinned wide and with delicious malice. "Was there ever a doubt?"

Chapter Thirteen

Where I Weave a Web of Lies into Half-Truths and Ensnare a Few Heroes

Before we get back to the story, I want to take a moment to recognize all the fallen henchmen across the realms.

Guards, militia, generic soldiers, and their ilk are basically fodder in moments like these. They never win or live unless they are named and have a backstory, or are part of an elite force— and if we're being honest, not even then. They are just there to show how awesome the heroes of the tale are.

Rest in peace, you dead bastards.

But do not weep too deeply for them. They are not really people. They are human window dressings who are dead inside and live to serve our amusements. Like strippers.

And authors.

OK, back to the show.

****

I sat down to the private table in the back of the inn with a tray of ale, cups, and food. "This small measure does not come close to how much I wish to thank you all for coming to my aid."

"You fight well," Hawker said. "All of you."

"The three of you are too slow," Cairn Hunter said. Cairn was playful and competitive, turning every opportunity into a chance to prove she (or he) was better than everyone.

She clearly suffered from a superiority complex. Someone's parents had told her she was the best at everything. Or she was just a middle child. A super-macho, arrogant act to fool people. At least I hoped it was. Otherwise, she was just an asshole.

Seriously, how had no one noticed he was a she? It looked like she had glued on patchy red pubes to her face. I imagined a ginger-haired dog with a bare ass out there somewhere.

"Our skills and speeds aside," I said, looking at Cairn with a sideways glance, "we will be hunted now. Grimskull's forces will come for us. By helping me, you have put yourselves in danger."

"Where Grimskull's concerned, we are all in danger," Hawker said with the resolute tone of someone barely old enough to shave every day. "His existence is a blight on this world. One that must be eliminated."

"Mmm," Wren grunted in agreement. "That, I understand." Up close the burly man was pleasantly ugly. He had a shaved head and a mustache that went down his jawline and terminated in his sideburns. His nose was permanently crooked from being broken on multiple occasions. His bright blue eyes were angry and piercing. Despite his monastic robes, and even without the armor, everything about the man screamed *fighter*.

"What about you, big man?" I asked. "What's your story?"

It is a time-honored tradition within these realms to share your backstory with your new traveling companions. It seems stupid, doesn't it? I mean, who does that? In the real world if you tell someone your tragic tale of woe after first meeting them, they are more than likely going to excuse themselves and not look back. Unless you were growing up in the 90s, and then it was a form of polite greeting. All of grunge rock was an excuse to complain about how rough you thought you had it.

"Me? Not much to say," Wren grumbled.

"Of course a follower of Vammar would be so dour," Cairn chided.

Wren cast him a sidelong glance and scowled. "Fine. Before I was an ammalar of Vammar, I was a simple mercenary in the Free Lands," Wren said, spinning his story.

The Free Lands was the middle kingdom between the Western and Eastern Empires. A place where they lived under the false delusion of democracy. A perfect place to eventually corrupt and exploit.

"I was serving with one of the militia groups, fighting back against the Grimskull's eastern purges. One night, we were camped close to the borders and were attacked by General Anders herself. Her forces came down on us out of nowhere. While the big bitch cut my men down with her giant mace, Coldfyr, the rest of her elite troops marched through us like we were rank amateurs. I was knocked out cold by Anders herself. The only thing that saved me was my armor and her lack of caring whether her victims were alive or dead. When I came to, her forces were gone. My training took over and I began tending to as many of my wounded men as possible. And that was when . . ."

"When what?" I asked, intrigued.

"When I found one of Grimskull's boneheads hurt badly, but alive. I should have let him die. Hell, I wish I had. But at that moment, I didn't see an enemy. Only someone who needed saving. Some scared kid. So I started patching him up. And that was when Vammar himself appeared," Wren said as he took a drink from his ale. "Damn god just appeared in a small thunderclap and a spray of earth and dirt. He points to me and says, 'You have proven yourself a man of true duality. A killer and a healer. You are now my disciple. My newest ammalar.' After that, I could no longer pick up an edged weapon. Only instruments that could hurt or heal. And when my emotions get the best of me, my attempts to help people end up hurting them. My attempts to hurt people heal them. A lesson I must learn one day about who I really am. Damn Vammar and the rest of his kin to the Never Realms."

"And you, what is your tale?" I asked Cairn. It was very important to know these things. You never know how you might use it against them at a later time.

"Unlike our ugly friend here, my tale is actually a tragedy," Cairn said, then looked at the rest of us at the table and said arrogantly, "What? He is. I am sorry, friend, you are far from comely. Rugged, yes, but fair you are not."

"Been called worse by better looking than you, ya ginger bastard," Wren said, taking another drink. By his tone, he was not grandstanding. Her insult had washed off him without the slightest care.

As it turned out, Cairn was from the Twilight Guard, a quasi-militant group from the Skyborn Forest north of the Free Lands who were bent on bringing order to chaos. The group comprised a mixed company who followed the beliefs of the elves while trying to serve justice above all. Unless you were a woman, apparently.

Oh, Cairn spun a tale about how he/she was too good for them and they sent him/her on a suicide run against Grimskull's men where he/she was wounded and left for dead. My guess was they discovered she was a female and left her behind. Since then, she's been on her own.

"Your turn. Who are you, stranger?" the big priest asked.

"And why do Grimskull's men want you?" asked Cairn.

"Why do you not speak?" asked Hawker.

Because I was preparing my dramatic moment. OK, remember, dramatic but honest. Give enough to hook them, but hold back enough to keep them coming back.

"I . . . gods, I'm not sure how to begin. My name, I guess, is the best place to start. I'm Jackson. Jackson Blackwell."

"One of the men called you 'Shadow Jack,'" Cairn said.

"Yes, that is one of my names. To be honest with you, I've not always been a . . . reputable person. I'm a merchant by trade, dealing in whatever people want or need. And oftentimes that brings me close to bad people. And in my adventures, I have come very, very close to that invisible line between right and wrong."

"That doesn't explain why were they after you," Cairn said.

Bless Cairn. She kept setting me up so I could knock them down. "Do you really want to know?"

"Yes," they all said, nodding.

"Very well. I escaped his dungeon. He didn't like that," I said while I smiled.

"You escaped his prison?" Hawker asked with a tone of skepticism. "How?"

I used a fraction of my power and made a small crackle of golden energy appear between my fingertips. "Magic is one of my many skills. I was captured by his forces when I was discovered as part of plot against him. I had spies inside his fortress feeding me information. My spies turned out to be traitors, and I was captured. But very few prisons can hold me."

"And why were you there in the first place?" Hawker asked.

"I was going to steal The Amulet of the Ember Soul and destroy it. His reign must come to an end. It's bad for my business."

No one at the table spoke as glances were shared across the table. "This is impossible. The amulet is lost," Hawker said.

"No, not lost. Stolen. Someone infiltrated the D'hoom Dungeon beneath the Peak of Inverness, defeated the Bray Beast and claimed the amulet. Shortly after, the amulet was stolen from whoever defeated the Bray Beast. Now, Grimskull has it. My spies were truthful on that. When Grimskull came to taunt me in my prison, I saw it on him. Damn it," I swore, slamming my fist on the table in mock dramatic flair. "I was so close. So close to ending it all."

The table was silent. My eloquent words and flawless delivery had left them speechless. Damn, I was good.

"And what about you, young Master Hawker?" Cairn asked. "What brings you to the Crossroads Inn and the Eastern Empire?"

Hawker stood and muttered something about getting another round of drinks for us, ignoring the question. I nodded, but put my palm over my mouth to hide a smile.

The art of manipulation was a favorite game of mine. A sickness, really. I liked making people do what I wanted. Here's a great tip: If you want people like you, or see you in a favorable light at least, learn one of their secrets. Then, present that secret in a way that aligns your interests with theirs. As long as you're sure not to reveal the fact that you knew the secret, then the person will look upon you as someone they can trust.

It works every time.

In Hawker's case, I just dropped a bomb that Grimskull had the amulet, the one I had Courtney take from him. But I also clearly painted myself as Grimskull's adversary. So to this young man, I was a wise, dangerous person who could guide him to what he wanted. All the while, he was doing my bidding.

Villainy is so, so rewarding.

I excused myself from Wren and Cairn to help get the drinks. I walked up to Hawker as he stood by the bar waiting for the pitcher of ale.

"Something is wrong," I said. "Men like you don't get rattled. And you are most definitely rattled."

"Your story," Hawker said, not looking at me.

"What of it? It's all true, I swear," I said.

"I believe you. But it is *you* that has me troubled."

"Me?" I feigned confusion. Maintaining an innocent look was difficult. *Come on, kid. Piece it together.*

That was the problem when dealing with weaker, slower minds. Sometimes you just had to let the rest of the world play catch up with you, no matter how infuriating it was.

"I remember you. You were in the Corolan Inn back in Ashraven, weren't you? I was drunk, but I'm sure I remember you helping start a bar fight that took out several of Grimskull's undercover agents."

"That was me," I confirmed. "I was on my way to his keep the following day. But I didn't need his agents reporting back that I was showing up early, or how many men I had with me. So the bar fight was the best way I could think of to get rid of them. As it turned out, my own men were betraying me."

"You are a dangerous man, Shadow Jack."

"Sometimes, yes. But that's not all that is troubling you, is it?"

"No. But I do not wish to speak of it for the now. For now, just know that our interests are the same. The removal of Baron Grimskull is my only desire. And I believe this meeting was fated. But come, let us celebrate our victory with more drink and stories."

I nodded and smiled as Hawker turned and took the drinks back to the table.

Kids are so damn dumb sometimes.

When we are children, we see the world as full of infinite possibilities as we try and make sense of our new existence. When we grow into our teens, we feel invulnerable. But, come our twenties, we begin to ascribe meaning to the smallest of events. We call it fate, or karma, or even worse, "meant to be."

And that is the mark of a still-developing mind.

"Meant to be" is the idiotic rhetoric that results when those who are ignorant of facts try to make sense of random encounters. They cannot understand that there is only random chance—or the machinations of greater minds. And if people still believe that things are fated and meant to be into their thirties? Well . . . they are the legion of corpulent morons who ensure reality TV, Netflix subscriptions, and professional sports remain at the forefront of entertainment.

Like my sister.

Hawker's naiveté was grounded in partial reality, though. The gods of the fantasy realms were arrogant bastards who enjoyed matching strangers up in order to play out their grander designs. They were assholes.

That was why I encouraged Hawker to believe our meeting was fated. He would follow that course, my course, to the end. He was, or soon would be, my weapon to use against those who betrayed me.

Alas, if I was to make this company of heroes my own, I had to join in their revelry. Under real world logic, we should have vacated the Crossroads Inn the moment the battle was over. If a military patrol or strike force went missing, reinforcements would surely follow. Yet in the realms, that rule almost always waited until the next morning. Luckily for us, this was not one of those grimdark realms, where hyperrealism and ultraviolence reigned. Beloved people like me often found themselves dead. Or worse, it could be a low-fantasy realm where everything is a rip-off of European history with TV-like melodrama and incest. The type of realm where you had to wait forever for a glimpse of something magical or a dragon.

So with the fortune of the rules on our side, we drank and talked into the night.

I thanked them. And that was sincere.

Because it was so much better having people who were willing to die for my cause by my side.

Chapter Fourteen

Where I Meet Two Gods and Wish for a Better Cell Phone Provider

The world—all the worlds—have cause and effect. And in all of them, when you drink too much, you have to eventually break the seal. In other words, I really needed to go to the Little Villain's Room.

In the realms, indoor plumbing is not normally present. Unless you are in a gnome community. Even then, there are cogs and sprockets, springs and contraptions that power the bathroom. A simple quick whiz can turn into a steampunk castration.

The lack of facilities has always baffled me. Hell, the Romans in our history could make ice in the desert and had open-flow toilets. In the realms though, it's privies. Which was fancy-speak for "outhouse." Such places were usually located outside, next to the stables. It stood to reason: Get all your foul-smelling business done in one place.

I excused myself and staggered out of the inn towards the privies out back. Once I was out of eyesight, I walked normally. While I enjoy a good drink of alcohol, getting bombed on cheap homemade ale is not my preferred method of intoxication. Without my poison-counteracting ring, I was forced to use a bit of my power to burn the booze out of my system.

I opened the door to the privy and braced myself for the smell of human waste. Immediately, someone bumped into me as they were walking out, knocking me down. It was the red-haired youthful farm boy from inside the inn.

"I'm so sorry, sir. Please excuse me!" the boy said as he offered me his hand. I took it and he helped me to my feet.

Along with his mop of red hair, he had grey-green eyes. On his hip he wore an antique sword. His grip was soft with no calluses, which meant he had no training with that, or any, weapon. As I stood up, I noted the boy was easily a full head taller than I was and his jawline was firm and strong.

"No problem, son, accidents happen," I said, affecting an easygoing tone. "What's your name?"

"Garreth La'Aghun sir," the boy said. "But everyone calls me 'Goose.'"

On Goose's forearm was a tattoo of a strange creature along with script of a language I was not familiar with. The boy caught me looking and pulled his sleeve down.

"You don't know where that came from, do you, Goose?"

"N—no sir," Goose said, looking away.

"And you are the only red-haired person in your village, aren't you?"

"Yes sir. How did you know?"

"And is that the sword you were found with when you were a baby? That and the strange tattoo?"

Goose went to speak, but I held up my hand, cutting him off. "Goose, I am going to do you a favor the world should have."

"Are you going to tell me where I'm from and what my destiny is?"

"Better," I smiled.

With a surge of my power, I briefly manifested myself as a monstrous demon with black skin and flame eyes. "GOOSE LAGOON, YOU ARE MARKED FOR NOW UNTIL THE LAST STAR BURNS FROM THE SKY! RETURN TO YOUR VILLAGE AND THROW AWAY THIS LIFE OF ADVENTURE OR ELSE I WILL FEAST UPON YOUR SOUL AND THE SOULS OF EVERYONE YOU HAVE EVER KNOWN! RUN, MORTAL . . . RUN!"

The color drained from the boy's face as he ran away screaming.

Well, that was fun. But I still had to use the facilities.

I returned to my human form and did my best not to breathe too deeply as I entered the privy. Looking around the lamp-lit room, I was again shaking my head in confused anger at the lack of evolution within the realms.

Lack of plumbing aside, at least the gold I took from them was still gold.

I fastened my belt buckles and unlaced my pants' drawstring to take care of my personal business at the trough. I was surprised when two figures stood next to me, one on either side. It was odd considering that only a moment before, they were not there and then had suddenly blinked into existence.

While I had my dick in my hands, no less.

Note I said figures, not people. One was a middle-aged man in white robes and crystalline armor with a slight elvish appearance. The other was a female in black robes, with light green skin, a horse's mane of black hair, and horns. Chitin-like scales covered most of her exposed flesh, accenting her female face and form. She had four eyes, a normal set and a smaller second set above the first. All of them were staring at me.

"I was wondering when something like this was going to happen," I said, putting away my manhood. "So, do we want to do this in here? I know I would prefer to have this talk outside in the fresh air."

"Jackson Blackwell, you do not belong here," the female said.

"No Khasil, you do not belong here. This is the men's privy," I countered as I moved away from them and used the wash bowl to freshen up.

"Impudence. I should cast you into my realm and let the thralls devour your entrails."

"But you won't," I said. "And technically, you can't. Besides, you know I am good for your business. In case you missed it, I just stopped a would-be chosen one from raining on your parade."

"Khasil, be silent," the male figure said. He was tall, with a grandfatherly appearance and a skin tone that did not indicate any particular race, although his almond eyes and pointed ears were clearly the mark of his favorite of races. His eyes glowed with a blue-white intensity.

"You stopped the promise of a great champion," the male figure said.

"Who? Goose Lagoon?"

"La'Aghun."

"Whatever," I said to the male figure.

He was Valliar, the High God of Justice. The leading "good guy" in this world's pantheon. His sister, Khasil, was the goddess of darkness and suffering. The leading bad bitch that sought to undermine her brother and bring chaos and misery into the world.

And if they were here together, it meant they had a unified mission. Me.

"Now why would justice and chaos wish to speak to me?"

"You are unbalancing the natural order," Valliar said, his eyes crackling with power.

I smirked. "Sorry, I'm not following."

"You know damn well what!" Khasil seethed. "You are abusing the laws of the realm."

"I thought you, of all deities, would appreciate that," I countered. "Using good people to help one's own cause is the true mark of a villain."

Khasil narrowed her multi-faceted eyes. "When I am doing it to defeat Valliar, then yes. You are a trespasser here."

"Sounds like you're jealous," I said.

"Enough," Valliar said with a chopping motion of his hand. "Jackson Blackwell, by altering the course of these mortals' lives, you are altering the karmic flow of this realm. All things operate within a balance of chaos and order. Cease now before you cause further harm."

"No," I said flatly.

"No?" Khasil and Valliar said in unison.

"No," I repeated. "I won't stop. Per the ancient accords, my status as a deity, even only technically a minor one, allows me clemency. You cannot directly attack me. As a born mortal, I have the right to interact with other born mortals as I see fit."

"Indirectly, we will crush you," Khasil threatened.

"I'd like to see you try," I said as calmly as possible. "Now, please go away. I have a lot to do and little time to get it done. Go on, be good little gods and leave the hard work to the experts."

Khasil and Valliar looked at one another, frowned, and blinked out of existence.

I dropped to my knees in the privy and let out a deep breath. "Holy shit that was close."

"Sir?" Sophia's voice came in sharp and clear.

"Yes, Sophia? I assume you were listening."

"Pardon my forwardness, sir, but what the fuck were you thinking? Those were high gods."

I got off my knees and stood, trying to present myself in a more dignified manner. "I am aware. I did it because I need to accelerate our timetable."

"Sorry sir, I'm not following."

"Stories, myths, legends," I said. "As you know, all of our world's pop culture sci-fi and fantasy is influenced by The Realms. It bleeds over through micro wormholes and influences certain minds. Those minds create our books, movies, and gaming."

"You're not making sense, sir. What does any of that have to do with your timetable?"

"Joseph Campbell's *Hero with a Thousand Faces*."

"Sir?"

"Long story short, mythologist Joe Campbell boiled down the monomyth, or the hero's journey. Whether that's Luke Skywalker, Frodo, King Arthur, or Achilles, they all follow the same path. Young pastoral hero joins wise mentor, is given a powerful token from the past, and goes on his adventure. They all cross certain thresholds, succumb to a madness, and come out on top."

"Well, that doesn't sound so bad," Sophia commented.

"Normally, no. But the shortest of those was Frodo and his trek across Middle Earth and even that took thirteen months. I don't have time to turn this into a trilogy. I need to get this done quick and dirty. I need to make an impact, a big one. One that shakes the underworld to its core and rings out a loud and clear message."

"Which is?"

"Fucking with the Shadow Master is a very bad idea."

"Yes, sir!" Sophia said. "So what's the next step?"

"Well, pissing off the high gods should have them sending every minion they have in my direction. A few battles with their minions will bond us as a team. Hopefully we can bypass a boring training montage and a magical weapon retrieval. Then we can take down General Anders and Chaud like bosses in a video game."

"Sir . . . I think we have another problem."

"What?"

"The high gods aren't sending minions. Oh shit . . . they are doing worse."

"What? What are they doing? Dragons? Giants? What?"

"Text messages."

"Excuse me?"

"I can hear your sister cackling. They just messaged your sister on her replacement phone. They told her that you had a relic of your power and she has cut off the flow of power, I can feel it."

I looked down at my phone and the battery read 99%.

Oh crap.

As I stared at the phone in disbelief, four men entered the privy. I was baffled that the high gods understood technology enough to send an interdimensional message. And that Paige understood how to cease the flow of power from the dimension so quickly. So baffled, in fact, that I really didn't notice that the men were armed with small hand crossbows.

I looked up just in time to see one of the men fire his crossbow into my thigh. Immediately, I felt the poison from the bolt course through my leg and unconsciousness took me.

While I always knew I would die one day, face down in a medieval shitter was never a consideration.

Chapter Fifteen

Where I Find Myself Poisoned, Robbed, and Planning on Going After a Pack of Bastards

"Jackson?" I heard a voice say. The voice sounded garbled, as if it were miles away. If I had to guess, it was Hawker.

"Jackson, are you alive?"

"I seriously hope so," I managed to say through half-numb lips, "because, from what I am tasting in my mouth, I am pretty sure that only happens when you die."

Strong hands lifted me up and put my back against the privy wall. A thick calloused thumb forced my eyelids open, and before my eyes rolled back into my head, I had a blurred vision of an ugly man with a hawk nose staring at me.

Ammalar Wren was giving me a combat medic once-over. Hopefully he didn't think I needed to be put down. My head was cloudy and I couldn't open my eyes. The world was spinning. I felt waves of nausea, and sweat was pouring from me.

"Poisoned," Wren stated.

"No shit," I commented as my head fell forward. Wren caught it and pushed me back up against the wall. Hard.

His big left hand gripped my forehead, enveloping it. Wren applied pressure to my temples with his thumb and pinkie finger. The pain brought me into a strange focus.

"Sorry," Wren said.

"For what?" I asked.

"This."

With my eyes cracked open, I saw Wren cock back his right fist. The red and blue energy mixed into a purple nimbus along his clam-shell gauntlets and the bastard punched me right in the face, breaking my nose and rocking my head back.

Stars exploded in my brain and blood gushed out from the impact.

"Mother fucker!" I screamed as I got to my feet and threw a knee strike into Wren's face.

The big man, as if expecting the attack, caught and held my leg in his strong grip. "Feel better?"

As rational thought returned to my mind, I realized that yes . . . I did feel better. I nodded and Wren released me.

"Vammar's will be done. The prick."

"What just happened?" Hawker asked.

I flexed my leg and then felt my nose. What was broken only seconds ago was now straight and whole.

"The duality of Vammar," I said.

The ammalar nodded. "In order to heal you, I first had to hurt you. If I had tried to tend to your wounds normally, you'd be dead," Wren said as he stood. "My conscripted god has a sick sense of humor."

"What happened?" Hawker asked. "What do you remember?"

"Four men," I said as I pulled my thoughts together and began patting myself down. "Four men came in here and one of them shot me in the thigh with a small hand crossbow. The next thing I knew, I felt my body seize up and I passed out."

I felt in my pockets, finding nothing. No swords, no daggers, and no smartphone.

Shit.

"And apparently, I was robbed."

"At least you're alive," Hawker said. "Their dart was only meant to incapacitate you."

"Nope," Wren countered. From a kneeling position, the combat medic was holding the crossbow bolt, sniffing it. "Manticore venom. This was meant to kill. Knocks you out, then over time your heart stops. Manticores prefer live, but placid, food."

Four no-name thieves almost killed the Shadow Master in a toilet with cheap poison? Oh, this would not do. And to top it off, I was only alive because of the kindness of strangers. If this were to get out, I would not be able to show my face at any of the villain meetings.

And yes, we have meetings.

"Any idea who they were or where they went?" Hawker asked.

Damn kid was nothing but questions. For a would-be hero, he couldn't shut up for ten freaking minutes and learn. But before I could scold him that I had no idea who the assassins were on account of being drugged and nearly dead, I realized that Cairn had also entered the privy and Hawker was speaking to him/her.

Oops.

"I don't know," he/she answered. The trail went cold about a mile out. But if I had to guess, they were part of the Forgotten Bastards."

"The who?" I asked, sounding like Hawker.

"Forgotten Bastards," Wren grumbled. "A clan of thieves and killers comprised of former soldiers who fled from the great armies, beggars, homeless, and all manner of societal cast-offs. All of whom have turned to a life of larceny and killing for hire. They raid and steal anything they can get their hands on."

"And," Cairn interjected, "fairly recently new-found followers of Khasil."

Well, that explained the manticore venom. "And the reason the town militias or police forces haven't done anything about them?" I asked.

Wren shrugged. "Because they attack Grimskull's men as well?"

"These crossbow bolts," Cairn said, holding them up, "are their preferred method of dealing with people. Rather than a straight-up fight, they would rather poison their targets from a distance, then rob them blind."

"That is Khasil's way," I said. I had to admit, I liked their method and ingenuity. "OK, where do we find them?"

"Why?" Hawker asked in return.

"Because they stole from me. I want my items back," I said.

"Items can be replaced," Wren stated.

Damn. I guess this was where I would have to—ugh—trust these people. A little at least.

If they thought I was confiding in them, then perhaps this would hasten the team bonding I would need if there were a life-or-death situation. Where the hero would lay down his or her life for a comrade.

Mine, specifically.

"What they stole from me was more than my weapons and some coin. They took my magical focus item," I admitted. "Without it, I cannot cast my magic."

My companions looked at one another silently, weighing my loss against their risk. If this had been me and my decision, I would have left me behind. Dead weight to the mission. Cut me loose and move on. Basically Robert DeNiro's entire shtick from the movie *Heat*.

I am, of course, not a nice person. But these people were heroes. Which made them idiots, idiots who would willingly help a relative stranger and co-champion of a greater cause.

This is how these adventures go: A party sets out on a grand adventure, planning on stopping the big bad villain. Naturally, conflict arises, which derails them along the way. Through such conflict, the bonds of friendship are forged even stronger than before.

And hey, sometimes, people even get laid. But looking at this group, I think I'd rather masturbate.

"We'll go," Hawker announced, while Wren and Cairn nodded.

"Do we have any idea where they went?" Wren asked.

"When I was in the Twilight Guard, we would occasionally venture this far south," Cairn said. "We came across the Bastards near the slopes of the southern range of the Greyspire Mountains and had a few encounters with them. They would only hit and run, fearful of a larger, well-armed force. The Guard was trying to put a stop to the zealots and their raids, but we never found their headquarters. There are a lot of hiding places there, in those mountain passes. And the tracks I found do point in that general direction."

"Makes sense," Wren confirmed. "A lot of battles were fought there a long, long time ago in the old wars. Plenty of stone fortresses were carved into those mountains. They were built to survive almost any attack. Legend says a small contingent of humans and elves staved off an orc onslaught for days there. A hardened place like that? Perfect location for thieves and killers. Easy access to multiple towns with fresh water from mountain streams. There was enough wild game to feed a relative force of people. Yes, it makes sense."

That was Wren. A military man through and through. He assessed the situation for its combat merit and logistical feasibility. If being a hero didn't work out, I could easily employ him.

"We should leave. Now," I announced. Without the phone and a source of my power, then my protection was off. Chaud would be able to scry my location easily. After Grimskull realized that his men were all dead, then what came after me next would be much, much bigger.

"He's right," Hawker said. "Grimskull won't be happy to hear his men are dead. He'll be coming for us all now. Best to put some distance from here."

"Agreed," Wren said, finding no tactical fault in the logic.

"Wimps," Cairn said, chastising us. But the look in his/her eyes said that she/he wasn't ready to take on Grimskull's full wrath just yet either. "But if you cowards must flee, let us at least procure some provisions from the innkeeper for the road. Possibly buy a few horses."

Damn.

Horses.

The Sixth Rule of Villainy

A villain will always pay attention.
You never know what you can learn and
turn to your advantage later.

Chapter Sixteen

Where I Fantasize About Equestricide and Forced to Listen to Back Stories While Sleepy

When we look at nature, something in our brains registers wonder and awe. We feel small and humble standing before the majesty of the Grand Canyon, the power of the Mississippi River, the sheer size of the Rocky Mountains. The Realms are no different. Landscapes untouched by moral hands spread over the vast horizon, displaying a jaw-dropping natural beauty.

But when you are being hunted, on horseback, traveling all night and into the morning without sleep, in the rain, your perspective on such natural phenomenon changes. Through my bleary eyes and with my saddle-sore posterior, the mountain plains were nothing more than undeveloped land. Nature could suck my cold, sweaty taint.

Without a proper bed and cover from the elements, all I wanted to do was bring a fleet of bulldozers there, level everything, and put up cheap condominiums to sell to poor assholes. Then, after ten years, gentrify the neighborhood, bring in rich yuppies, and sell it all back to them for three times the market price under the guise of urban charm.

"We're reaching the foothills of the Greyspire Mountains," Hawker announced. "We should rest up for a while." As adventuring-party logic would dictate, the idealistic young warrior had elected himself the group leader. No one had challenged him, myself included, because certain tropes must be followed.

I dismounted from my hell beast as best as I could. As I swung my right leg over, the beast twitched in such a way that caused my left leg to get caught in the stirrup. I fell flat on my back and the horse bobbed its head up and down in a horsey laugh.

I hated my horse.

And I was sure it was mutual. That was why I named him "Glue."

I looked at the young stallion from flat on my back and he stared back into my eyes, challenging me. I dislodged my foot and Glue took a snorting step towards me.

"Try it," I threatened the chestnut-brown equestrian demon. Glue shook his mane, considering my words, and stomped his hoof.

"Come on, big boy, make your move. No matter how this goes down, you'll learn what *gelding* means."

Glue turned away, walked two steps, and promptly shit. The arrogant horse had to the nerve to look back at me before walking off.

"You have a way with animals," Hawker said as he extended a hand to help me up. I took it and thanked him.

"Might I borrow your sword?" I asked.

"Is it to kill the horse?"

". . . Possibly."

"Then no," Hawker laughed. "Come on, let's get a fire going and get a couple hours of sleep before we move on."

Wren and Cairn had begun gathering some kindling and formed a stone circle under a small copse of trees. Despite the light yet constant rain, the two of them worked with smiles on their faces. I envied their blissful ignorance. The people of the realms had no awareness of our world. No knowledge of fine things like air conditioning, high-speed internet, pornography, and Taco Bell.

They were happy to have a little bit of rain on them. They were in the fresh air, on an adventure, with danger potentially lurking around every corner. This made them feel alive and that was what drove them onward. The human spirit at its finest. Confident in their hearts and their mission to vanquish evil.

Idiots.

That's why I so love manipulating people. These lovable clods were what every legend was predicated on. Happy-go-lucky do-gooders off on a grand quest, bumbling around with blind luck and divine interference. Every time one of them is in true peril, someone or something encountered earlier in the adventure comes along and pulls them from the fire—while thwarting the plans of the villains, the true masterminds.

Every damn time.

It disgusted me to the core.

So if these cretins could suffer through a little rain and some hard tack road bread, moldy cheese, and water that tasted like a leather skin, then so could I.

I pulled out my blanket roll from Glue, who was tied to the nearby trees with the other horses. Soon, Wren and Cairn had the fire crackling as the water inside the wood steamed and popped. I placed my bedroll beside the fire and lay there with an arm over my eyes.

"We know why Shadow Jack, Cairn, and I are here," I heard Wren said to Hawker, "but you dodged the question back at the Crossroads Inn."

I opened my eyes to watch Hawker set down his pile of damp wood. He set his bedroll down as well and got comfy.

"Yes, I did," Hawker said as he closed his eyes. "Jack and I will take first sleeping shift. Cairn and Wren, you keep lookout for any of Grimskull's men."

"Burn that," Wren said. "You haven't ever been a soldier before. Horses will alert us before anyone gets within a mile of this place. I need some sleep."

Wren and Hawker stared at one another in a male-dominance pissing match. I just grinned and waited for the outcome. Wren had years of experience on Hawker, but the boy was full of mystery and natural leadership.

"You all get some rest," Cairn said, breaking up the tension. "In the Twilight Guard, we were trained to go without sleep for days. I'll be fine."

I gave the woman masquerading as a man another appraisal. Nothing about his/her appearance and build said he/she had ever gone days without sleep. He/she had strong shoulders and a certain *denseness* to her lithe frame. But I also knew Wren was right about the horses. So I just rolled over and let them duke it out.

Sadly, both Hawker and Wren backed down and got comfy. So much for a good fight.

No one spoke for several minutes. I felt my mind drifting off to blissful, non-poisoned sleep. I felt the onset of a dream. A nice one where I was in my office, with a cigarette and a scotch, manipulating others.

"I came from a place called the Elder River Village," Hawker said, breaking the silence and waking me and everyone else up.

Seriously? A confessional backstory? Now? Damn it, I was almost asleep.

Well, tropes were tropes. No use in bitching and complaining. Steer into the skid and ride it out. I sat up like the others did and feigned interest. Being told a story you already knew was quite boring.

"Never heard of the place," Wren grunted.

"Wait," Cairn interrupted. "A little rustic place south of the Elder River's great lake?"

"Yes," Hawker said. "It was."

"The Twilight Guard moved through that area a year or so ago, following some of Grimskull's men. The whole area was burned to the ground. The land was still smoldering and the only thing we found was the remnants of a village. Burned down to its foundations."

"Yes, that was my home. Or it was," Hawker said. His voice had taken on the tone of someone reliving memories. Hawker's voice quavered slightly as it all came flooding back. "Men came one night. Like a flood. Led by a giant woman encased in ice. They . . . they began attacking us. They weren't there to steal. They weren't there to pillage or rape. They simply showed up and began killing my people."

"Kyle, I'm so sorry," Cairn said. Her maternal instincts were clearly kicking in. Her voice had raised half an octave. She/he caught himself/herself and lowered it back down. "Grimskull?"

Hawker nodded. "I didn't know at first. All I saw was the men killing and that damned giantess ripping the villagers apart with her bare hands, or smashing them to pulp with her giant mace. Then, when it seemed like her bloodlust could not be slaked, she cried out, 'For the glory of Baron Grimskull and the Eastern Empire!' Her crystal ice armor and breastplate retracted and I saw fire begin to glow in her bare chest."

Fire tits. Nice.

Hawker shook his head as a tear rolled down his face. "And then she . . . she began spewing fire from her mouth. Her mace lit up in fire and she used it to ignite everything I ever knew. The village was burning. Everywhere I saw my friends and my family dying, burning to death. I heard the children screaming. I smelled their skin crisp and sizzle."

"What did you do?" Wren asked. The stoic veteran was now sitting up and listening to Hawker's tale like a battle captain listening to a report from the field. "What did you do specifically?"

"At first, I was afraid. I was petrified."

"Thinking I could never live without you by my side?" I asked. Heh heh. What? I said I already knew this story.

"What?" Hawker asked.

"Never mind. You were saying?"

The young man gave me an odd look and continued. "I charged at the giant woman. I had my father's sword and I ran at her, screaming, intent on running through the fire and killing her."

"Did you?" Cairn asked.

"No," Hawker said, shaking his head. "I never got close. One of her guardsman jumped in my way. He struck me in the face with his pole-arm and it knocked me out cold. I did manage to stick him in the stomach, though, before I blacked out."

Hawker chuckled. "It's funny."

"What?" Wren asked.

"How clearly I remember the man's face who knocked me out. Big man with a hawk nose. He had mane of long, curly black hair and a scar under his nose and along his lip. I saw his bright blue eyes. All of that in a split second before he knocked me out."

"Then what happened?" Wren asked. His voice was barely above a whisper.

"I . . . I don't know. I woke up under a pile of burned bodies. I must have gotten lost in the chaos. Forgotten or overlooked. That was when I swore to kill Grimskull and all his people."

"There is something else, isn't there?" Cairn asked.

"You remember Jack's story? About the Amulet of the Ember Soul? About how it was recovered and then lost?"

"Yes," Cairn said.

"I was the one who stole the Amulet of the Ember Soul from the D'hoom Dungeon. I was going to use it to destroy Grimskull once and for all. But when I returned to my village after so much time, someone was waiting for me. Someone attacked me and took the amulet. And that was it. My quest was over. It had failed. Since then, I've been at the bottom of a bottle."

Hawker sat down on his bedroll and hung his head. "Does that answer your question as to why I'm here, Wren?"

The big ammalar rubbed at his stomach then got out of his bedroll. "Yeah, it does. Get some sleep. Cairn and I will keep first watch."

There was something there. Under the surface of the conversation. Something I couldn't quite put my finger on. I was sure of it. But as exhausted as I was, I let my hind-brain work on that problem while I got some sleep.

The melodrama of a hero's tale of woe was like a bedtime story for me. I was asleep in seconds.

Chapter Seventeen

Where I Prove Discretion in the Better Part of Valor and Enjoy a Final Show

My eyes snapped open.

Something wasn't right.

In the movies and television, when people wake up to something wrong, they sit bolt upright and pant. That is horseshit. When a person wakes up under distress, their primordial lizard brain kicks in. Immediately they freeze and listen, sensing and assessing the area for danger.

I did my best not to move and let my natural senses do their job.

It was getting dark. Long shadows played as the sun was starting to set. That was bad. We were not supposed to sleep the day away. We were only supposed to sleep a few hours and then get back on the trail of the Forgotten Bastards.

And it was quiet. I didn't hear anything.

Nothing.

Not snoring, not breathing, not the horses, not the ambient sounds of nature.

I repeat: Nothing. Not even my own breathing.

Something was blocking all sound. Which meant we were either under attack—or soon would be—by something magical.

Staying motionless, I darted my eyes around, taking in everything I could, which wasn't much. Hawker was appeared to be asleep, but I could not see the slow rise and fall of his chest. Was he dead? That would be bad for me. And I suppose it would be bad for him as well.

I dared to shift my head slightly, feigning natural sleeping readjustment. Wren and Cairn were sleeping. That was bad. Especially considering that they looked like they were sleeping in collapsed heaps as opposed to warm and snuggly in their bedrolls. Something had knocked them out.

Now, the question was, why was I awake?

"You are awake because we allow it to be," I head Valliar say, his voice breaking the stillness.

Valliar and Khasil popped into existence before me, sitting on logs by the extinguished campfire. The light rain had stopped and the two of them looked like they were enjoying a nice camping trip together.

"You've been warned a final time," Khasil said to me from her seated position.

I got out of my bedroll and looked around. Nothing was moving. The trees weren't swaying, and the reason the drizzly rain wasn't coming down was because it was frozen in the sky. Now that I had a clearer view, I saw some type of yellowish dust suspended in the air. The source seemed to be a couple of arrows sticking in the ground.

"You've paused time," I said. I did something similar in my own dimension so that I stopped aging while there. "Why?"

"Khasil is correct," Valliar said. "This will be your final warning." The god's voice boomed a rumbling basso. His mortal guise shimmered slightly for emphasis.

"So, those guys in the privy, yours?" I asked Khasil. The goddess only sneered and hissed her forked tongue. "I'll take that as a yes. Nice move using your people to try and kill me without doing it yourself."

And I meant that sincerely. Since the gods could not take open, direct action against one another, to include minor piss-ant gods like me, Khasil had her cultists from the Forgotten Bastards ready to go. They were prepared to rob me of my magic source and try and kill me. My guess was that Valliar only allowed it because I had Wren in my group, knowing the ammalar could heal me.

A godly warning indeed.

"Let me guess. Valliar's protection will be off once this moment is returned into time. Considering that Wren and Cairn are collapsed, it means we are under attack."

"Yes," Valliar confirmed.

"And what are my options?" I asked.

"Run," Khasil hissed. "That way. Run until your feet blister and your heart nearly explodes. Run in fear and hide the remainder of your days. Do that, and perhaps I will let you live in relative peace."

"So, my options are stay here and die with my companions, or run away? I assume I would forever remain in this realm as long as I didn't start any more trouble? And if I did begin my affairs, a swift end would come to the Shadow Master?"

"Yes," Valliar said, resolute. "But we all know these are not your companions. They are pawns to you."

"I don't know," I countered. "They are growing on me."

"They are not yours to use, interloper," Khasil said.

I arched an eyebrow. Hmm, I had touched a nerve there. By enacting the sacred rite of the summoning of the heroes, I had pulled these people onto a path that was breaking the gods' game plan. That meant the rules that governed this world would be askew.

And no villain worth a damn can resist the occasional bout of mayhem.

I know, I know, it contradicts my cold and calculating nature. But mayhem to the detriment of a rival is like catnip to us villains.

They were afraid of an imbalance. A shift in their power. My being here, in direct contact, was altering their grand plans.

But I had a theory. If I was right, then I knew what I had to do.

And it was delicious.

"Thanks, but no thanks. If running and living like a peasant or dealing with whatever you have planned are my options, then I'll take my chances."

"I strongly urge you to reconsider," Valliar said with absolutely no warmth or benevolence.

I took a seat on the log nearest my bedroll. I deliberately placed my hands under my chin with my elbows on my knees. I addressed Khasil and Valliar as if they were clients in my office.

"Do your worst."

"Fool!" Khasil screamed. She tried to rise, but Valliar placed a firm hand on her shoulder. The Queen of Darkness shrugged off her twin's hand and took a step towards me.

I did not move. Not out of bravery, but because I was petrified. I mean, she was the freaking embodiment of chaos and evil in this realm. But I had to hold on to my composure. You think showing fear to a dog is bad? Imagine doing it to a being of suffering and torment.

"Come at me," I said, using my elbows to brace my legs, keeping my knees from knocking. "Bring everything you have. Both of you. Bring your legion of undead, Khasil. You know I have allies in the Never Realm. Bring your elves and I will ruin them. Bring your holy masonic knights and I'll make sure a horde of whores descends upon your pious virgins with such temptations it will turn their gleaming white purity a nice shade of filth. You know, the butt-stuff kind."

"I will not miss you," Valliar said honestly.

"Mutual," I retorted.

"Goodbye, Shadow Master," Valliar said.

"Your suffering will never end," Khasil said. "Once you are dead, I will claim your soul as my own to play with until the stars burn out. You are nothing."

"Bitch, please. You've never seen a mortal like me. When I beat Grimskull and get back to my realm, know that I am coming for you both. Now get the fuck out of here."

As both gods blinked out of existence, I dove back for my bedroll as time restarted. I heard men coming, running towards the camp. The horses were whinnying and the rain was once again falling.

I did the bravest thing I could think of.

I pretended to asleep.

Don't knock it. You can learn a lot about people when they think you are asleep. Try it sometime. See if that conversation your boyfriend or girlfriend is having on the phone is in fact with "just a friend." I'll save you the time—it isn't. They're cheating on you or soon will be. If you have to ask, you already know the answer. Trust me, I'm usually the one on the other end of that phone call.

Now before you get all judgmental on me, I have to admit, while I am a decent fighter, I augment my skill and speed with my magic. Without it, I'd rather not take on however many people were coming.

Besides, Khasil had clued me in to what was going to happen next. Not on purpose, mind you. She said my soul would be hers. As a being from another plane of existence, she would have no claim on it—unless I was sacrificed in her name atop a place of power. Since the Forgotten Bastards were her cult, then I had a pretty good guess as to what was going to happen.

One of the Bastards confirmed it. "They're out cold. Get them on the litter," I heard one of the men say.

"Do it yourself," another responded.

There was a quick scuffle and the unmistakable sound of a foot kicking a crotch, and the second man hit the ground.

"Do it, or you'll be added to the sacrifice to Khasil, praise her dark name."

I only hoped that my plan worked. Otherwise, I surely would end up her toy for the rest of existence.

Rough hands picked me up and slung me over a shoulder. I dared to peek for a moment to see several men in leathers and furs looting our fire circle and moving my allies onto a makeshift litter.

I was dumped unceremoniously onto my sleeping friends, victims of the Bastards' knockout toxin. The Bastards took Wren's horse, the largest of them, and tied him to the litter, forcing him to drag us along to their lair.

The rest of the horses were slaughtered right there. Their blood was used to draw symbols into the ground as a warning to anyone who came too close to the area that this was the land of the Forgotten Bastards.

As we were carried away to be prepared for a ritual sacrifice, I watched as one of the cultists took a sword to Glue's neck. The horse tried to save himself, but he was tied to a tree branch and could not get away. The sword came down in a spray of hot blood. There was a singular moment when Glue saw me. He saw me watching him through my peeking eyes. I felt his sadness and fear. We were connected in that fleeting moment. I watched the life drain from his eyes.

So, all things considered, it wasn't that bad.

Chapter Seventeen-and-a-Half

Where I Don't Feel I Need to Explain Myself to You

Yeah, I enjoyed watching the horse die.
    Villain.
    Duh.

    ...That horse was an asshole.

Chapter Eighteen

Where I Point Out the Obvious and Plan an Escape

I slapped Ammalar Wren in the face so hard, I felt the bones in my hand rattle.

"What the damned bloody hell?!" Wren yelled as he sat up.

"You need to heal the rest of them," I said, shaking my hand and nodding towards Hawker and Cairn. The block of a man had one hell of a dense bone structure along his wide jaw. "They are not reacting well to the sleeping poison. I figured you were the best shot we had to wake them up."

"Why did you slap me in the face?"

I rubbed my nose.

"Oh, yeah. Right. Fair enough."

While Wren began inspecting his patients, I examined our cell. As cells went, I'd seen, and been in, worse. It was a simple room carved from the mountain stone. While Grimskull's cells were all black, jagged rock and perpetually wet, the cells the Bastards were using were smooth and tan with heavy wooden doors on hinges. Fresh straw was on the floor.

If I had to guess, these were once old military quarters. There was an oil lamp above us, suspended by a chain that led into the ceiling, giving off light. In the corner of the fifteen-by-fifteen room there was a singular small hole covered by a wire mesh grate. The hole led to a small underground stream. Back when this place was part of the mountain fortress, this was what people used for a toilet.

Great. In essence, I was once again in a privy. The gods hate me.

"Where are we?" Wren asked.

"The mountain fortress the Bastards use for a home base," I said, rubbing my hands against the wall and looking for cracks or any potential secret passages.

"How did we get here?"

"Maybe you should wake up the rest of our little group. I prefer not covering all of this multiple times," I said without looking at Wren. I continued my inspection of the room and turned up nothing. This was my second dungeon in so many days, and I was going to be very upset if I did not discover a secret passage.

The ammalar grumbled in his own way, not happy with my direction and curt way of speaking to him. Rather than doing as instructed, he watched me. Saddened by not finding a secret passage, I put my arms behind my back and took a deep breath. This was the price of dealing with people who officially did not work for you.

I turned my head just enough to see Wren out of the corner of my eye. "Do as I say. Or I will tell Hawker the truth about the night his village burned."

I made sure to hold eye contact with the reformed soldier until he turned away first.

"Fine," he conceded.

"Excellent."

Wren knelt beside both Hawker and Cairn and summoned his deity's power. The ammalar brought down the bear paws he calls hands in a mighty slap across the chests of his patients.

The energy provided to him by his conscripted faith woke them both instantly.

"Alianna!" Hawker cried out.

"I'm sorry!" Cairn yelled, his/her voice cracking.

Interesting.

I was fairly sure I'd finally figured out Cairn's real story as I had Wren's. A little more prying and I would have leverage over him/her as well.

"Good, you are all awake. Here is the situation," I said, preparing my address.

"Where are we?" Hawker asked.

"Where is my armor?" Cairn asked, and he/she did his/her best to loosen his/her clothing, hiding her true . . . assets.

"We were drugged by a sleeping mist back at the campsite and we have been captured by the Forgotten Bastards. We are in some sort of ancient mountain fortress, as Wren predicted. Our weapons and armor have been taken and they are preparing to sacrifice us to Khasil. Our souls will be removed from our bodies and given to the Queen of the Dark for all eternity. I counted over four hundred of the Bastards. Which means there should be at least the same number serving in some form of supporting role in the fortress. Probably the families and those who are not up for stealing, combat, and assassinations. Even still, this shouldn't be a problem."

I realized I was staring off and narrating. I turned to my group in case I had been doing it all in my head again. The three of them stared at me with their mouths open.

"How could you be so calm?" Cairn asked.

"Bugger that," Wren said. "How were you not affected by the sleeping mist?"

"Both of you be quiet," Hawker said with a stern glare. "It's obvious that he faked being asleep to gather intelligence."

Well, I'll be. A thinker in a world of idiots.

I nodded to Hawker. "Yes. From where the arrows hit, I was not affected by the mist," I lied. "But when the horses began making noise, I opened my eyes to see Wren and Cairn down. So I simply faked being drugged to learn what I could. Does anyone have an issue with this?" I asked.

Wren opened his mouth and I glared at him. He promptly shut it and shook his head. "Nope. Smart thinking."

"Well, Shadow Jack, we seem to be walking in a darker place. What's our next step?" Hawker asked.

"Simple. We have to stall for as long as possible. But not here."

"Why?" Cairn asked. "We need to get out of here as fast as possible before these cultists kill us."

I shook my head. "No. We need to stall."

"This room is a tactical advantage," Cairn countered. "Look," he/she gestured. "A singular entrance and no other way in or out. We could create a choke point by the door and when they come for us, we could take the first few. Steal their weapons and deal with those that follow."

Lord, was I the only one who paid attention?

I pointed up at the suspended oil lamp dangling by the chain that led out of the room.

Then I pointed down, at the dry straw that lined the cell. The highly flammable straw.

"Any other questions or dumb ideas?"

"What are we stalling for?" Hawker asked.

The young man continued to impress me. Perhaps this young hero could be turned to a darker path? An image of Emperor Palpatine came to my mind and it was all I could do to stop from wringing my hands together and saying "Good . . . good."

"We are waiting for our time to escape," I said. "Which will occur, most likely, right when they are about to ritually murder us. Until that time, we must do everything in our power to delay them. Make no mistake—if we resist, they will kill us. If we fight back, we will die. They have superior numbers and we are in their lair. So, the terrain is our enemy as well as the Bastards."

"How can you be sure a chance to escape will happen during the ritual?" Wren asked.

I could see his mind trying to form a coherent battle strategy. I didn't have the heart to tell him that his world, like so many, was prone to clichéd and contrived moments like rescues at the last second. So instead, I did something out of character for me.

I told the truth.

The Eight Rule of Villainy

A villain will plan for any contingency.
Should that plan fail, a true villain will
not only improvise, but they will also
claim any success as a well-constructed
backup plan.

Chapter Nineteen

Where I Discover Horrible Smells and Use the C-Word (If you find this offensive, imagine it said by a British comedian)

As cults went, The Forgotten Bastards were fairly blasé about their religious practice. Like snarky white people who say "I'm not really religious, but I'm spiritual." But the crossbows aimed at our backs as they escorted us into the mountain fortress's interior were deadly legitimate.

Throughout the mountain fortress, carvings and statues depicted Khasil in all her beautiful and terrible forms. The Seductress. The Queen of Torment. The Viper Beast (that last one was a complete rip-off of Tiamat, but thank goodness Babylonians weren't litigious). Each of the statues had small offering bowls with coagulated blood in them. There wasn't anything fresh in there, so Khasil hadn't received any real worship in some time from these folks.

The people who moved about the fortress were as I expected. Societal castoffs, runaway children, beggars and scoundrels.

In other words, poor people.

So naturally, they smelled.

Most of the realms were a knockoff of medieval or Renaissance Europe. Accents included. You know: those annoying fake British accents Americans ape when they go to the Renaissance Fair.

Since the Realms were stuck in that relative time period, so was their hygiene. But most of the people didn't smell as bad as they should have. I never figured it out. Seriously, think about it. Next time you watch *Game of Thrones* and things get *saucy*, consider the smell that should be stinking up the place. The ratio of bathing scenes to sex scenes ratio is woefully one-sided.

But this place reeked of unwashed asses, halitosis, and poverty. A cautious look back towards my companions told me that they smelled it as well.

As we descended into the keep's main hall, the air got warmer and more humid. Stolen goods lined every possible square inch of the stone interior. Tapestries, paintings, weapons, and carpets were strewn about, as in bad chain restaurants you peasants frequent. The ones with endless appetizers of deep-fried obesity and moderately-priced fruity drinks in type-2 diabetes commemorative mugs.

In the bowels of the fortresses was a grand hall, which held a raised dais carved with intricate unholy symbols and patterns. In the center of the dais lay a stone sacrificial altar. The reclined torture rack was recessed for a man-sized person to be held there. A cursory glance told me that the grooves in the stone were used for bloodletting. The contraption had buckles and harnesses to hold someone in place while the victim was drained of their blood. The offering for Khasil, no doubt.

Men and women lined the great hall and filled the overlooking balconies. Most wore threadbare clothing, while a few others wore leather armor and carried weapons. This must be their internal class system.

Braziers in corners of the room gave off flickering light and burned incense. But nothing they burned could mask that smell.

"Bastards!" a loud female voice said, distracting me from the poor-stink. "Your priestess comes!"

The speaker stood next to an arched doorway. She was a short and curvy with chin-length mouse-brown hair cut into a bob. Her clothing was made of soft leathers, which was finer than the rest of the people there. And she gave off a roguish, fun-loving, dangerous vibe. At first glance, she was cute, if a little too cherubic in her backside for my taste. But there was something distinctly *feminine* about her that I found oddly appealing.

The old crone that came through the arched doorway was definitely not my cup of tea. She was almost literally falling apart. Her skin was wrapped in bandages that seeped with infection. Her wispy hair clung to her misshapen head in intermittent sprouts and the remainder of her teeth were rotten and in various shades of yellow, brown, and black. She supported herself with a gnarled old walking staff made from the leg bone of some creature.

All of The Bastards remained silent as she shuffled into the room toward the dais. Her brittle bones and parchment-like skin threatened to split apart if she moved at anything faster than a geriatric pace.

Either that, or she was like my grandmother—the kind of old bitch that could haul ass when no one was looking but enjoyed the attention when the family had to wait for her painfully slow entrances and exits.

You know what I'm talking about. Every family has one of those attention-seeking elderly relatives. The ones who refuse to walk towards the goddamn light, and stay behind if for no other reason than to ensure other people are miserable.

Watching the priestess, I was not sure if I was supposed to be afraid of her or hug her and watch *The Price is Right* with her.

Then she spoke in a guttural, raspy voice.

"Slavish fools and mongrels of this accursed world, Khasil shows favor to us this day. The great queen, blessed be her unholy name, came to me in a vision and showed me a path to earn her dark grace. She showed me these four." The priestess pointed at me and my companions. "She showed me their faces and honored me. A glimpse of her divine plan. A plan to lure them here and kill them all, forever binding their souls to the will of Khasil. Blessed is She."

"Blessed is She!" the room repeated.

This old biddy was one hell of an orator. She had them all hanging on her every word and gesture. All around the room, the Bastards stared wide-eyed at her, awestruck. It was like going to a Baptist revival in the South. Religion really was an opiate for the masses. Everyone was enamored by yet fearful of the priestess.

Except the female speaker who announced the priestess. I caught her rolling her eyes when the priestess gave her speech. Interesting.

"Prisoners of the Dark Mother, embrace your fate and go willingly to your end. Her wrath is lessened by those who embrace her of their own free will."

"We shall never serve your foul goddess!" Hawker called out from behind me. "She will derive no pleasure from our servitude in life or death! Right?"

I turned to look at Hawker but turned back before I said anything biting. Sadly, the realms, for all their beauty, magic, and exploitable rules, suffered from both heroic bravado and bad dialogue.

"High Priestess of Khasil," I called out, "my name is Jackson. Some of you may know me as Shadow Jack."

A murmur ran through the crowd. Apparently my name still carried weight among those in the underworld profession.

"You have something of mine, and I want it returned. Do this, and you live. Do it not, and each one of you will die this night."

Now *that* is how you deliver dialogue.

"Dark manipulator, you have no power here," the priestess hissed. "Khasil herself has marked you as her own. We took your token of power, and as the Mother of Sin predicted, you have come for it. You are beaten."

"You angered a goddess?" Wren asked from behind me.

"Yes."

"Good for you." The ammalar nodded.

"How much longer do we need?" Cairn whispered.

"As long as it takes," I answered back, then turned my attention to the priestess. "Your goddess is nothing more than the spoiled kid sister to Valliar. She has twice shown herself to me in the last day alone, yet I walk away unscathed. She poisons your mind with the promise of power. But look at you all, hiding in the hills like goblins. Are you not men and women of the land? Or do you prefer scraping out a living? Are you the embodiment of this very place? Society's abandoned and forgotten, reeking of spoiled meat?"

This brought another murmur through the crowd. I saw several nodding heads. A few of the people even sniffed themselves, as if my saying they smelled was the first time they noticed.

"This priestess has turned the feared Forgotten Bastards into cowering sheep. Stealing and plucking like carrion birds. Mark my words, when she has killed us, she will turn on you all next. Her goddess will demand sacrifice. What do you think will happen to you, or your children, when she has no enemies before her to quench her thirst for blood?"

Several women burst into tears and husbands held their wives close. I had chosen my words carefully, knowing that all religious zealots sooner or later turn on their own people under the guise of sacrifice to maintain their power. And from the crowd's reaction, I was right.

Not that I cared about them or their loss, mind you. I just needed these idiots on my side. While I felt nothing for their pain, it does not mean I relished in it. I am a villain, not evil. There is a difference.

"Enough, manipulator. Khasil awaits you. Guards, secure him. He dies first," the priestess said. Instantly, I was gripped by two of the guards and hauled up to the dais. I was swiftly bound inside the altar and was unable to move.

The priestess started to walk slowly around the altar, chanting while she moved. The etchings and symbols on the stone dais started to glow with a sickly green light.

My allies struggled with their bonds, trying to reach me. Hawker and Wren were struck hard in the back of their legs by steel-capped cudgels, forcing them to their knees, while Cairn had tears streaming down his/her eyes.

I just smiled.

"I give you this one last chance," I said. "To all the Forgotten Bastards who hear my voice, heed my next words carefully: I am the Shadow Master. Bring me my token of power. Do this, and I will show you a new path. I will usher in a new era of wealth and prosperity for you all. Rise up and kill this old bitch. Do this not, and each one of you will die this very night. Choose."

No one moved.

I heard the whisk of steel on leather as the priestess freed her ceremonial athame. She used it to cut open my shirt. Then the priestess leaned in very close, letting the blade dance along my naked torso. I could smell her rotting teeth over the smell of the fortress. I felt the warmth of her breath only millimeters from my ear. The sharp blade drew blood over my chest with only the smallest amount of pressure.

"You lose, Shadow Master."

I leaned in toward her as best as I could, forcing the knife painfully into my chest. "Guess again, you old cunt."

The fortress rocked as explosions sounded in the night.

Chapter Twenty

Where I Make False Promises, Strike a Blow Against Sexism, and Get Kicked in the Balls

Another volley shook the fortress. Dust came down as the stone fortress was shaken to its foundation. The priestess's head snapped away from me towards the sound of the explosions. She hissed a curse in a language I did not recognize. Meanwhile, I laughed out loud.

"Bastards!" she bellowed, turning her head back to sneer at my mirth. Damn, the old woman had some lungs on her. "We are under attack. Respond as the Dark Mother would wish. Kill all the invaders. No mercy, no survivors, save two. One to torture and one to carry the message back to the world of the folly in attacking our home."

The room emptied in a flurry of movement. I'll have to say this: The Forgotten Bastards were indeed efficient when it came to mobilizing at a second's notice. I guess when you live on the fringe of society, you have to practice response drills in case someone comes knocking at your door.

The priestess watched her people react, and when the last of her people left the great inner chamber, the only ones left behind were my allies, a few guards, the priestess, and me.

I paused my infectious laughter to address the priestess. "You know, the offer stands for you as well. Release me and you will live this night," I offered her.

"I do not know what plot you have hatched, trickster, but it will fail. Khasil has foreseen it."

"Your goddess is blind to all actions that involve me. It is a lesson you should learn. One of two lessons, come to think of it."

The priestess cocked her head. "And what is the other lesson, scum?"

"The long version is that the very nature of villainy comes with the burden of knowledge. Knowledge of great power. Knowledge of your enemies. Knowledge that even at the height of your power, you must always beware the proverbial snake in the grass. The betrayer within our midst, as it were. Villains must always be prepared to be usurped by better minds. And sadly, sometimes by weaker ones. Nonetheless, that knowledge must always be on the forefront of your mind. There is a shorter version of this lesson that you failed to learn."

"Which is what?"

"You never learned to watch your back."

The woman who had acted as the priestess's speaker had walked up behind the priestess and waved off the guards. The priestess turned just in time to see the other woman, who smiled at the priestess and then proceeded to smack the old bitch over the head with one of the steel-capped cudgels. The priestess crumpled to the floor and bled like a stuck pig.

"Gods above and below, I always hated you," the woman said to herself. She then turned to the guards. "Either go outside and help repel the enemies at our gates or stay here and join her. Your choice."

The guards looked at one another, considering their options. The men were large and burly and none too smart-looking. But this short, thick woman might as well have been General Anders herself the ways their knees knocked together. They pounded a fist to their chests and left as if their collective asses were on fire, leaving my companions where they were and me still bound to the sacrificial altar.

"Now that feels so much better," the woman said before she bent over and began rummaging through the priestess's satchel. She stood, holding my phone.

"You came a long way and through a mess of trouble for this, Shadow Jack," the woman looking the phone over, not sure of what she was looking at.

"I did indeed, Ms. . . ?"

"Lydia," she said. "Lydia Barrowbride. And I only have one question for you. If I like the answer, you get this and you get to live."

"And if you don't like it?" I asked, amused. "You'll do what? Kill me?"

"I'll geld you," she said, flashing the dagger on her belt.

Oh, I like her.

"Ask your question."

"If you were released, would you live up to any of the promises you claimed? Would you see the Bastards returned to their full glory?"

"No," I said honestly. "I didn't mean a single word."

"That's what I thought," she said, pulling her dagger. She ran it up my leg and looked at my friends with a warning glare. "Move and I'll cut his artery. He'll be dead by the time you reach me."

"Seeing as I still have my balls," I said to Lydia, "I assume you wish something more from me?"

"I've heard of you. I've heard of what you do. I want the Bastards back. Back how they were before we took in this old bitch," Lydia cursed and spat on the priestess's unconscious body.

"I make this deal with you," I said, hoping my words conveyed their real meaning. "Release me, give me back my token of power, and I make my deal with you and you alone. I will show you how to form the Bastards into not just a thieves' guild, but a real power. An organization that will have the lands trembling when anyone hears your name. Do we have an accord?"

Lydia smirked. "We do indeed, Shadow Master."

Lydia used her dagger to cut the leather bonds that held me. Freed, I rubbed at my wrists and wiped the blood from my chest with my ragged shirt.

"You have something of mine," I told her.

Lydia held out her hand. "Shake on our accord."

I eyed her and smiled. I took her hand in mine, maintaining eye contact. I noticed she had a lovely pair of hazel eyes.

"My totem, if you please."

Lydia handed me the phone and instantly I felt my power rush back into me. It was euphoric. I felt like myself again. The wound on my chest stopped bleeding immediately and in seconds, the cut was gone altogether.

"Now that you are free and have your . . . whatever that is back, we need to help my people."

"No, we don't. And I do apologize for this," I said.

"For what?" Lydia asked.

"For this."

I punched Lydia right between the eyes. Her head snapped back and she was unconscious by the time she hit the floor. I stood there and smiled. Then I noticed my companions staring at me.

"What?"

"Why did you strike her?" Cairn demanded.

"Are you mad that I hit her after making our deal, or because I struck a woman?"

"Deal," Wren said.

"Woman," Hawker said.

"Both!" Cairn said the loudest.

Rolling my eyes, I took Lydia's dagger and belt sheath and strapped it onto my waist. Now that the item was mine by right of combat, I used a portion of my power to change the weapon into a shortsword.

"Look, her group is out there being slaughtered by Grimskull's forces. We can use that commotion to slip away," I explained.

"This was your plan?" Hawker asked.

Gods above and below . . . if I didn't need these people, I would very much enjoy putting them to work in particularly deep, goblin-infested mines.

"Yes. As I told you back in the cell. We would be attacked and we would use the confusion to slip out."

"You promised to help her after she freed you from the priestess. You gave your word," Wren chided me.

"You *want* me to assist in rebuilding a militant thieves' guild who accepts the occasional assassination contract?"

"No," Wren said, "not exactly. But . . . something to help these people."

"And you hit a woman. Have you no honor, sir?" Cairn said in mock righteousness.

"You, of all people, ask me that?"

"What . . . what do you mean?" Cairn asked, looking nervous.

"Never mind. Look, I hit a woman who threatened to cut my artery and let me bleed out. I hit a woman who, only moments ago, betrayed her superior. Thus, we learned she is not a nice person. So, I hit a woman who deserved to be hit. Are you telling me that women are not as capable or as deadly as a man?"

"Well, I . . . the thing is . . . " Cairn stammered.

"Exactly. Women are as lethal and cruel and dangerous as any man. And to treat them differently is to say they are inferior. And I won't stand for that kind of intolerance. I didn't just strike her; I struck a blow against sexism."

Yeah, that sounded good. At least it shut these idiots up.

"Hell of a speech, boss," Sophia said in my ear.

I smiled. The moment the priestess had come close to me, my link through the phone was re-established. I'd had Sophia feeding me intel ever since. What I didn't have was a handle on my companions. They all stared at me with shock, disgust, disbelief, and worst of all, broken trust.

"Fine!" I yelled, throwing my arms into the air. I stood over the fallen Lydia and tapped her on the forehead to wake her up.

"I've reconsidered our agreement. I promised to help you, not them. I will assist you in rebuilding the Bastards, but we have to go, now. Do you understand?"

Lydia kicked me square in the balls.

Yay. Equality.

Chapter Twenty-One

Where I Ladle Out Copious Amounts of Bullshit and My Companions Ask for a Second Helping

My allies and I reached the night air outside the fortress via an escape tunnel. Not the hidden passage I was hoping for, but I took what I could get. I let them go out first for several reasons. First, I was limping slightly while I sported a pair of aching testicles. Second, if there was a stray arrow or attack, let it hit them first. Human shields are very effective when used properly.

"What about the Bastards?" Lydia asked from behind me. "We can't leave them to be slaughtered."

"They won't be slaughtered," I reassured her. Sure, a few might get killed, others messed up pretty bad, while most of the others would be rounded up, captured, and forced into indentured servitude across the Eastern Empire for life. But I didn't want to tell her that.

"How can you be sure?"

Because the moment I stopped using my power to shield myself, I would be visible to the scrying magic of Chaud. Just like outside the Crossroads Inn, the forces of Grimskull would appear. Probably some sort of portal or gate magic. And since I had opened myself long enough ago, a few scouts no doubt had found this location and reported back. That would in turn bring a much larger force. One that could take a stronghold like this. The attack would create a distraction big enough that a small group could slip away. If I was smart, I could do it in such a way it would appear I was bravely leading my companions to freedom, thereby strengthening their trust in me.

I envisioned myself bravely leading my companions away. Instead, I waddled to freedom due to my busted nutsack. A busted nutsack that was directly my fault. All because I listened to those compassionate mouth breathers.

"How can you be sure?" Lydia repeated.

"Hmm? Oh, call it a hunch. But if you follow my instructions, you will be able rebuild stronger and better. Plus, if you look at it this way, you're better off."

"How the bloody hell am I better off?"

Because I am making this up as I go along? Oh hell . . . let's see. Her brotherhood was dead weight? No, she cares for them. Financially, it makes sense that—no, she doesn't care that much for money. Just look at how she's dressed. Damn, what's her angle to make me seem like a necessity instead of the guy who had her people turned into slaves?

Oh . . . that's it. Slaves.

"Lydia, look at me." I stopped and turned to face the woman in her eyes. She looked back at into mine and she regarded me in a way I couldn't describe with words. Only that I felt her disgust juxtaposed with her desire. I was dangerous and manipulating. An aphrodisiac for many women.

"Your men, your brotherhood, are gone. They were gone the moment that priestess showed up. Let me guess—you invited her in, she seemed like a nice old lady. And in time she corrupted the Bastards from within. Speaking out here and there, whispering. Before you knew it, your leadership had been usurped by her and the Forgotten Bastards were a cult of Khasil. How close am I?"

"Too close."

Thought so. "Lydia, listen to me when I say this: Khasil does not let people go. Ever. She is a spiteful bitch. If she has her hooks in your men, then she will never release them. Any fate, even that of death, is better than her twisted plans. If you escaped her grasp, then run free. You can rebuild the Bastards from the ground up. In fact, that is the only option before you."

"I . . . thank you. I needed to hear that. I know you're right. Damn it."

"I am. And I will help you. Now, we have to get moving. Let's catch up to the others," I said as I turned away and smiled.

That was an amazing amount of high-quality manure I just shoveled out.

"Jack, Lydia, get up here," Hawker called out. "You need to see this."

We crested a small hilltop and far below us in the valley was the fortress of the Forgotten Bastards. And it was burning. The night sky made it easy to see the flames. Even at this distance, we could hear the screams of the dying. The forces of General Anders, and thus Grimskull, were destroying everything,

I knew they were all looking at me, my allies. I had to ensure that my face did betray that I didn't care about what was happening below.

I did not enjoy the fact that people were dying. It just did not mean anything to me. People die every day, all over the known world and known realms. People claim to care. Mostly through social media. But they don't mean it. They don't do anything about it. It is just something they say to sound morally superior to their counterparts while they re-post other people's blogs and call it a day.

I, at least, am honest. I don't care. Kings sacrifice every other piece on the board to survive. And most of the people in the world are pawns to a king. Politicians, armies, and actual kings would waste the majority of their subjects if it meant they could live and stay in power even a moment longer.

"Jack, you are responsible for this," Hawker said.

"Yes," I said, not looking back.

"What kind of man are you?" Hawker asked. His voice wasn't as angry as I thought it should be. He was just honestly asking the question.

"I am the kind of man who considers the angles. I am the kind of man who plans ahead and improvises when needed. I am the kind of man who is willing to get his hands dirty. Just like each of you. But the difference is, I don't cry about it when it happens. You see that down there?" I pointed. "That is the result of planning and forethought. It should also be burned into your tiny minds that *that* is what happens to those who don't think ahead and who *don't* control their lives. Those people let their lives be controlled. So choose, right here and right now: Go down there and die like a servant, or follow me and learn how to live. Either way, I am going forward, and I am going to bring Grimskull down."

I turned and limped away.

"Boss, your speeches just get better and better," Sophia said in my ear.

"I know. It's what I do," I said. I looked down at the phone and the power read 68%. Damn it. "Sophia, why is the power so low?"

"Maintaining a connection is drawing a considerable amount of your power, sir."

"Understood. For now, let's just go into standby mode. No direct communication unless absolutely necessary. I need to conserve as much as possible."

"Understood, sir. I don't like it, but I understand."

"Sir?"

"Yes, Sophia?"

"Are they following you?"

"They will. There is just enough darkness in them that they will sense the truth in my words. Heroes are oftentimes just villains with a moral compass."

This is where a bad writer would make Person X look over their shoulder to lock eyes with his or her companions and exchange a "We're with you" look.

I just kept walking. I knew they were behind me. I'm the fucking Shadow Master.

Of course, being the Shadow Master and having the full knowledge of who is behind you does sometimes limit the field of view. I turned the next rocky corner and came face-to-face with a small contingent of General Anders's soldiers armed with crossbows, swords, and magic wands.

"Shadow Master, General Anders requests an audience with you," the lead soldier said.

"And if I say no?"

"I would not advise that, sir. We were warned of your powers. We are prepared."

At least he had manners. I liked that.

"What's the—?!" Hawker exclaimed from behind me. With no weapons, they had no chance. I held up my hand to them.

"Don't move," I commanded Hawker and the rest of my party as they turned the corner. "You." I addressed the soldier. "Take me but leave them behind."

"My apologies, Shadow Master. You know it doesn't work like that."

Of course I know that. But with as much damage I'd done with my credibility and trust with these people, I had to at least attempt to act altruistic while they were watching.

"We don't have a choice," I said as I hung my head in mock defeat. I could have teleported away or engulfed them all in fire. But that would not have mended their opinion or their trust in me. I didn't particularly want it. But I did need it.

They needed to see me vulnerable. At least, ever so slightly. The art of manipulation is subtle. Moments ago I gave them a speech about how not to be a pawn. Now, in their eyes, I was a weak hypocrite.

Until I turned in such a way so only they could see me. I used trivial amount of my power to make my eyes crackle, standing out in the night. I winked at them and smiled.

They got the message.

"Take us to the general."

Chapter Twenty-Two

Where I Go from One Prison to Another and Detail Why Elves are Assholes

"I'm so glad we listened to you. This is much better," Hawker said.

For the thirty-second time.

I did my best to ignore him. But being trapped in a tiny rolling prison cart with four other adult-sized people who were pissed off makes it hard to ignore. The cart was wood wrapped in banded steel. It was windowless, save for a tiny oval opening that served as an air vent and the only portal to the outside world.

"Another prison. Great," Wren grumbled. "I'm beginning to think all your plans are foolish."

"Tell me about it," Lydia agreed. "I thought you were the Shadow Master."

"Yes, what is this Shadow Master title people keep throwing around?" Cairn asked.

"One of reverence," Hawker whispered.

"You defending him?" Wren asked.

"No. Just stating a fact. When I was searching for a way, *any* way to defeat Grimskull, the name of the Shadow Master was mentioned several times. I was told he was a man of great power and means. One who moved in ways that made the underworld tremble. I considered very hard whether or not that was a person I even wanted to seek out."

"I'd heard the same," Lydia agreed. "That the Shadow Master made empires rise and fall on his whims. That he could make the impossible possible because it amused him. Imagine my surprise that he is this pathetic man who is nothing more than a weak manipulator."

She totally wanted me. I could tell.

"Why didn't you seek him out?" Cairn asked. "If he could help in stopping Grimskull, why wouldn't you do whatever it takes to win?"

Hawker looked at me. "Because I didn't want to become him."

"You didn't know him then," Lydia said.

Hawker shook his head. "No, but I knew enough about him. I knew that people like that were not good people. That they lied and manipulated

137

and cheated their way to the top. I knew that that kind of power came with a cost. Like your soul. I knew I would like it. And I would walk that path."

"You're a good person," Wren said. "You wouldn't fall to darkness."

"I don't know. There is something . . . in me. Something dark I can't explain."

Like your father is actually Baron Grimskull and your very soul is tainted by the dark power from the Never Realm whence Grimskull acquired his power?

"When I met my mentor, he sensed the darkness inside me. But he showed me a new path. One of perseverance and light. A harder road, for sure, but one that means more in the end."

Boring.

"Nothing to say, Jack?" Hawker asked.

I looked out the tiny air hole and watched the world bounce and roll slowly by, ignoring them as best as I could. But my temper was ready to boil over.

"Jackson, answer him," Wren demanded.

I was about to unload on these people when I heard a strange bird call out from somewhere in the night. Then another and another.

"What's the matter, Shadow Master? Nothing to say?" Cairn taunted. "So much for being all powerful."

That's it.

"I have many things I could say," I rasped through clenched teeth. "But I would not waste the breath on weaker minds. Sit there and mock me if you like, but when this is over, you would do well not to become my enemy."

"Shut up," Hawker commanded. "And get your heads down if you want to live."

"What? Why?" Lydia asked.

"Because," he said as he got as low as he could in the cart, "we're on the border of the Whispering Woods."

The broad head of an elvish arrow punched through the prison cart, accentuating the point. Followed by three more.

"Oh . . . damn it," Cairn said. "Oh damn it, no."

For a moment, it looked like Cairn was fidgeting in the corner, but in the darkness of the wagon, I couldn't quite see.

The cart came to a halt. From outside, we heard the muffled screams of General Anders's men dying. The elves of the Whispering Woods rained down death upon them.

When the sound of arrows stopped, everything was quiet. I heard the slight shuffle of feet outside. The elves were out there, finishing up their bloody business. They moved quietly. The stories of elves were true—they were basically ninjas. I would love to recruit them, but their moral compass is too closely aligned with their creator, Valliar.

There was the distinct sound of a sword being drawn from its sheath. The air whistled and the chain that held the prison cart was cut. The rear door opened and an elf in full green and gold battle armor greeted us.

"Welcome home, Hawker. You are safe."

****

I leaned against the balcony of my private room, which was high above the forest floor in a massive Suprenia tree taller and fuller than a Hyperian or Oak. The hidden kingdom of Lath'a'laria, or Grand Arbor, was deep inside the Whispering Woods. The kingdom was a lush, organic wonderland that made me think Ewoks would come singing *Yub-Nub* at any moment. Looking at all the beauty and majesty before me, I had only one thought: Elves are just . . . the worst.

Of all the creations of the gods, elves are without a doubt the dullest, most boring, and most arrogant of beings. Think about all the books and movies that have elves. And they are mostly right.

They are incredibly long-lived, incredible fighters, incredibly noble, and incredibly beautiful.

They are also incredibly boring. They do live in forests, high above in massive, ancient trees. Living each day in peace and tranquility. Learning wisdom by watching nature and singing to trees. Giving thanks for all the forest has given them.

Let me repeat myself: They sing to trees.

If you think that is somehow noble, poetic, or beautiful, then you are part of the problem.

Let me spin this another way. If I were to tell you that there was a group of people who had the power and the means to help the world, but chose not to, what would you think of them? Think of the pharmaceutical companies. The ones who get rich treating diseases instead of curing them. Or the politicians of the world who have the power to elevate mankind, but instead, they keep people fat, politically and racially divided, shopping at mega-centers and staying out of their corrupt business.

Think of the wealthiest one percent who do jack-shit for the rest of the world. What do you think of them? That they are beautiful? That you should want to emulate them? That they are the most noble creations and that you should get tattoos of their language permanently placed on your body?

Of course not. Because they are assholes.

Elves are the top one-percenters of the fantasy realms. They have remarkable resources and vast, incalculable wealth. They have advanced medicine, smithing technology, and architectural knowledge. They live so long that disease is a thing of the past for them. The elves of the realms could solve almost every problem across the lands.

But they choose not to.

Because they look down upon the other races as inferior. Not worthy of their help or salvation.

And you applaud them for it.

To be fair, I do as well. If they actually helped, it would put me out of business. The only thing that separates them from me is that they claim to be good and righteous, where I do not. Elves are, in fact, villains—just not seen that way because they are the creation of the higher beings.

Maybe I'm just grumpy because I have yet to turn an elf to my side. Their nobility will not allow it. But I always keep trying. Foolish, I know, but while the elves across all realms do not help others, they also do not go out of their way to stop the villains. They only march to war when war threatens them directly.

For now, though, I was their guest. The room they gave me, if you can call it that, was nothing more than a fancy tree house. Made from the living tree itself, the room was grown in such a way that the tree twisted and formed a living space.

The armed guards outside my room remained vigilant. When I tried to leave, I was informed that I must stay in my room while the Arboreal Court decided what to do with us.

I was once again a prisoner.

So I simply waited. I looked over at the plate of food they left for me on the small table in the room. I couldn't tell if it was food or potpourri.

I lay down on the bed and looked at my phone. Sixty-three percent. Damn. Even on standby, I was losing power. Things were moving along. I'd assembled my crew. I'd had a few bonding moments, a couple of captures, and a sense of betrayal. The story was unfolding as stories always did. I just didn't have time to wait much longer. I had to find a way to accelerate things without using any of my power.

The door to my room opened and a tall blond elf entered. He wore silken robes that looked like a cross between a Jedi robe and Ebenezer

Scrooge's sleeping shirt. I wasn't sure if I was supposed to be impressed or laugh.

"Jackson Blackwell, The Shadow Master, you have been summoned to appear before the Arboreal Court," the elf said in his best command voice.

"For what purpose?"

"To determine whether you live or die."

The Nineteenth Rule of Villainy

A villain knows the legal system of every location he is in and is prepared to use that system toward his advantage – preferably in a way that inspires shock and awe.

Chapter Twenty-Three

Where I Stand Trial and Drop Knowledge Bombs

I stood in the center of a massive tree stump beneath a canopy of trees. The stump was fifty plus feet across, and it was blackened on the edges, damaged from a fire long ago. The boughs of the nearby trees served as seating for those who bore witness to my trial. All around, luminescent pods from the trees provided soft colorful lights.

Being on trial to determine my life at least had a pleasant color motif. But the whole setup reeked of Valliar. I assumed Khasil had had her chance with a direct attack. Now, Valliar was using an alternative approach.

Before me, in the highest tree boughs, sat The Five of the Arboreal Court. The respective leaders of the five elvish tribes: K'annan of the Western Wilds, Allana'thas, Queen of the Northern Skyborn Forrest, Cellt'x Shaman of the Southern Wayfinders, Shallah, The She-Hammer of the Mountain Range, and lastly, Talisarian'de, Lord Protector of the Whispering Woods.

"Bring forth the witnesses," Talisarian'de commanded. In unison, the armed elvish guards who stood watch rapped their halberds on the ground three times in quick succession. Behind me, my companions entered the makeshift courtroom. Hawker, Cairn, Wren, and Lydia. All of them took a seat on the ground level next to a large human male.

Interesting.

Hawker hugged the man in a way that showed a connection. The man was burly and had the swagger of a ruffian. Nothing about him said he should be in the presence of elves. So who was he? My guess was Hawker's mentor. The one he mentioned who trained him and put him on a better path. But as I got a better look at him, his identity was undeniable.

How cliché.

"Jackson Blackwell," Talisarian'de, Lord Protector of the Whispering Woods, addressed me.

"Yes?" I said, the high elf's words bringing me back into the moment.

"You stand accused of being The Shadow Master, the mastermind of villains. How do you plead?"

I placed my hands behind my back and took note of all the androgynous elvish faces watching me. They were curious. Nigh immortal lives led to constant boredom. Despite their holier-than-thou shtick, they reveled in watching the suffering of others. It alleviated their boredom, if only for a little while. Hence this mockery of a courtroom.

Again, I could leave whenever I wanted. But that would only set me back. So I had to win these people over. And as they say, when lies will not work, let the truth set you free.

I looked at my allies once more and considered my words and my approach.

"Jackson Blackwell, I repeat, how do you—"

"I heard you, Lord Protector. I have just been ignoring you," I said, as bored as possible. "Lesser beings do not deserve my full attention."

Apparently my chosen approach was "asshole."

"What did you say, human?" Shallah, The She-Hammer of the Mountain Range boomed.

"You see us as . . . inferior to humans?" asked Allana'thas, Queen of the Northern Range.

"No," I responded. "I see you as inferior to me."

"How dare you?!" K'annan of the Western Wilds exclaimed while Cellt'x, Shaman of the Southern Wayfinders, began chanting a spell.

"Silence," Talisarian'de commanded. While in the Whispering Woods, the Arboreal Court obeyed the ruling leader. "Jackson Blackwell, your attempts to anger this court will not work. You have been charged with being The Shadow Master, the mastermind of villains. That charge stands open. How do you plead?"

I looked at Hawker and the rest of them. I watched watching me. They were waiting for a response. Waiting to see if I was the Bogey Man. Well, let's give them a show they'll never forget.

"Talisarian'de, I believe you have in your court a Truthseer? The maiden Alianna?"

"The charges stand open—"

"I know what the charges are, Lord Protector. And I will answer them. Everything and more."

"Why would you want an elvish Truthseer here? Considering the circumstances and your contempt for my people and our kind, a Truthseer would not improve your chances of living," the Lord Protector said.

"I wish a Truthseer to be present to ensure my testimony will stand uncontested. The one beauty of your people is your inability to speak falsehood. At least, not directly. A gift, or curse, from your maker Valliar. A Truthseer will know the truth from a lie and will be unable to speak a lie."

A young female elf stood from among the gathered crowd. "I am Alianna," she said. "And I will stand as the Truthseer."

Talisarian'de nodded in approval.

"Alianna, no," Hawker said.

But the female raised her hand. "Be still, my love. All deserve the law and the truth. Even scum like this."

Several of the elves nodded their heads in agreement while others gave her odd looks. I caught several whispering among themselves. I read their lips and made out the words "human whore."

Hawker grimaced, overhearing some of those elves, and sat back down. His mentor placed a hand on his shoulder in a reassuring way.

The elf woman made her way down the tree boughs with a slow elegance. She was beautiful, with elegant sculpted features, pale creamy skin, hair as black as night, and large blue eyes. She came to stand on the tree stump, just outside the outer ring of the old tree. I nodded my thanks to the elf.

"For the final time," the Lord Protector said, "you have been accused of—"

"Yes, I know, I know. And I will answer the charge. But first I wish, under the Right of the Accused, to speak on my behalf."

Talisarian'de narrowed his eyes. Obviously, he was not happy that I knew the judicial system of his people. A simple rule for all who walk outside the law: Know the laws and use them for your benefit.

"Elves of this court, I hold nothing but contempt for you all," I began.

"Truth," Alianna said.

Sigh . . . I looked back at her. "Could you hold the outcome for more dramatic moments? Otherwise, you are really going to break my flow."

"Apologies," she said.

"As I was saying, I do not care for your kind. Mostly because you are, in fact, villains yourselves. Although you do not claim the title."

"I will not sit here and listen to this lesser being befoul the nobility of our kind!" Sharrah said.

"Yes you will," I said, smirking at the muscular she-elf. "Under the Rights of the Accused, I am permitted to speak my entire case and mind uninterrupted. Under the law of the Arboreal Court, should any of the judges leave during that time, then it is the divine will of Valliar that the accused be exonerated, recompense be paid, and apologies be spoken at the four corners of the world. But feel free to leave."

Sharrah sat back down.

"A thousand years ago, when some of you here were still alive, the Eld were attacked in a war known as The Rift. Elves were the ones who led that attack, at least indirectly. They feared the technological growth of mankind. That it may win out over the immortal magic of the elves. So the elves rallied the lands against the Eld and watched as their pawns destroyed them. Do you deny it?"

"No," Tasliarian'de said through a grim mask.

"Truth," Alianna said with sadness in her voice.

"See, now that's how you do it," I congratulated the Truthseer.

"What is the point of this?" Wren called out from his seat.

"I'm getting there," I promised. "Kyle Hawker, you are, in fact, a descendant of the Eld. Your village, The Elder River Village, was built upon their ruin. You are a royal prince of the Eld, and these Elves orchestrated the deaths of your ancestors."

"Truth."

Hawker looked like he was struck below the belt. "But, Alianna . . . "

"Don't worry, she's not old enough. She had no part in their fall. But they did," I said, pointing at the Arboreal Council.

"Why are you trying to hurt him?" Wren asked.

"I'm not. I am here to speak the truth and speak the truth I shall, Ammalar. But since you keep choosing to interrupt, let us talk about you."

Well, I suppose it's about that time: the grand reveal.

"Kyle, do you recall your story, about how you stabbed one of the guards when you charged General Anders and got knocked out?"

"Yes."

"Did you know that Wren was the one who knocked you out? That he was one of General Anders' bannermen?" I said.

"What?" Hawker exclaimed, his head snapping to stare at the big man. "But I remember his face."

"You mean the big guy with a hawk nose, long hair, and a scarred face? And if that man shaved his head and grew ridiculous facial hair to hide the scar, he would look like . . . what?"

"Lie!" Wren said, jumping to his feet.

"The ammalar lies," Alianna said.

"Lift up your shirt, Wren," Hawker demanded.

Wren looked at me, then at Hawker with hate in his eyes. Then, something in him broke. He hung his head and then lifted his shirt, exposing the year-old sword wound in his gut.

"My guess is, during the battle he felt guilty and tried to save you," I said. "He was the one who hid you under the bodies of your dead kin, keeping you alive and keeping his conscience as clean as possible. No wonder Vammar chose him for one of his disciples."

"I . . . yes." Wren said as tears formed in his eyes. The big man sat down and sobbed.

"Truth."

"You bastard," Hawker said, staring at Wren.

"You're a monster," Cairn said to me. "Do you enjoy manipulating others for your amusement?"

"Sometimes, yes."

"Truth," Alianna confirmed.

I stared at the elf until she turned away from my gaze. "But what I am doing now is exposing the truth. The ones you all don't want to hear. Like you, Cairn."

"I have nothing to hide."

"Other than being a woman."

"I—I'm not a woman."

"Lie," Alianna said.

"I figured the Twilight Guard, for all their progressive ways, wouldn't balk at a woman in the guard. So your story seemed off. You're not the first female warrior posing as a man I've come across. But your patchy beard isn't makeup or cosmetic, is it? You're a half dwarf, half human, aren't you? And remember, the Truthseer will know."

"I . . . oh gods . . . yes," Cairn said, tears pouring from her eyes.

"Abomination!" Allana'thas, Queen of the Northern Range yelled in an exasperated voice.

"Xenophobia. Another of the elvenkind's least favorite traits of mine. You abhor the mixing of bloodlines. You see it as a dilution of your purity. An elf and a human, that you can almost forgive. But a human and a dwarf? No, those children are almost always terminated for fear of what they could be. The power and ingenuity of a dwarf coupled with the will of a human? Children like that would be strong and courageous. Free to pass over the earth as well as under it. And if they continued to breed, then elvish reign as the top life form in the realms would end."

"They . . . they discovered my secret and sentenced me to die. I only survived because—"

"Yes yes," I said, waving my hand in a "let's get on with this" motion.

I didn't have time for her to sob out a convoluted backstory, so I finished it for her. "Your dwarvish strength and facial hair, coupled with the height from your human blood, allowed you to pass for a young human male. So you adopted the name of Cairn and set out to make your way in the Twilight Guard. That is, until someone discovered your secret. But because the forces of Grimskull were on the move following the destruction of the Elder River Village, you were lost in the shuffle and ran away."

"Carina," Cairn said. "My name is Carina. How do you know all this?"

"So your secret identity was to change Carina to Cairn? Seriously, how did none of you idiots see this sooner?" I said. "And I know these things because I pay attention. I learn. I use knowledge, and people, to my advantage."

"What of me?" Lydia asked. "What dark secrets are hidden in my past?"

"You? Your surname Barrowbride means you were married to someone at some point. And since you eventually became the leader of the thieves' guild, it means you probably either killed him because he was abusive, or you started stealing to get out of poverty. Regardless, he's gone, and I would very much like to ask you out at a later time. When I am not on trial, that is. Plus, you have a thickness I normally don't find attractive, but for some reason, I am enamored of you."

"Truth."

"See?" I said pointing to Alianna.

"We can discuss my past over wine," Lydia smiled.

I smiled back. "But the important question you should be asking, Lydia, is this: If the Elves of the Whispering Woods, devoted followers of Valliar, have lived this close to the Forgotten Bastards, why did they never move against them when they became a cult of Khasil, Valliar's sworn enemy?"

"That is a good question," Lydia said as she looked at the Arboreal Council. "Why did you let Khasil's will spread like that? All the people she hurt and killed using the Bastards as her instrument. Why didn't you do anything to stop it?"

"You are a guest here. Do not presume you have the right to question us," Talisarian'de said.

"I'll translate that for you, Lydia," I said. "Because you're human. And the poor people who made up your ragged group were just that—poor. Your wealth may have grown some, but your political influence means nothing to them. Aiding you brought them no net gain. Plus, since Khasil is the sister of Valliar, he would not move directly against her unless his elves were in trouble."

"Truth."

"Blasphemy!" Multiple members of the Arboreal Court called out at once.

"Blow it out your narrow asses," I said. "It isn't a secret about the gods and their familial relationships."

"Also truth," Alianna said.

"Now you're getting it," I congratulated the Truthseer.

"What are you doing?" a voice cried out. It was the large man, Hawker's mentor. "Are you trying to destroy everyone and everything around you? Please, stop this. Let me set you on a better path."

I eyed him over and drew a few conclusions.

"Might I know who I am speaking to?" I asked.

"Zachariah Graywalker," the man named himself. "Battle-mage and ally of all the good races of this world."

"Uh-huh. And you are the one who set young Kyle on his path of redemption? The one who trained him?"

"Yes."

I nodded. "I see. And did you ever bother to tell him that you were his uncle?"

"No," Zachariah said, not even trying to act surprised.

"You're . . . my uncle? Are you one of the Eld?" Hawker asked.

"Sorry kid, wrong side of the family," I said. "You see, your mother—" I started.

"What about my mother?"

Hell, I didn't have time for this. "Look, sorry for the bluntness. But your real father is Baron Viktor Grimskull. This guy is his brother. Oh, don't look at me like that. Gods above and below, you're practically twins. Your dad is the big bad guy. He impregnated your mother when she was his concubine and then ordered the death of her entire village twenty-one years after she fled. The reason you have a big dark hole in your heart is because some of the dark magic that flows through Grimskull is also what flows through you. Now, act shocked later. I have a trial to conclude."

I turned to face the Arboreal Court and prepped for my closing arguments.

"When I leave here, I am going to continue my quest to bring down Baron Grimskull and end his tyranny, freeing the East from his influence. I am going to destroy his power base, removing General Anders and his

Archmage, Chaud. Yes, I am considered a villain by some. And I give counsel to the worst people. But I make the world a better place. I give the people a villain who provides medicine, money, food, and clean water. I control them so that others have a better life. You look at me in contempt, but I have done good for the people across this, and many, realms. I am in fact the greatest force for good this world has ever known. So make your judgment and be done with it. But if you cross me, I will end you all. You ask if I am The Shadow Master? You're goddamn right I am."

The entire outdoor court sat in stunned silence. All at once, eyes swept towards Alianna, who looked down and shuddered.

"Truth."

Chapter Twenty-Four

Where I Reacquaint Myself with an Old Ally and Perform Certain Necessary Acts

Walking through the Whispering Woods as a free man felt good. I even whistled "Walking on Sunshine" while I did it. Katrina and the Waves was lost on these people.

Granted, my freedom wasn't as enjoyed by the rest of the Woods. Almost every elf in the kingdom refused to meet my gaze and most actually avoided me at every turn. I guess outing them as the racist, classist assholes they were didn't win me any favor. You know, I never got that with people in general. When you show someone exactly what's wrong with them, they never say "thank you." Instead, they act all high and mighty and defend their faults.

Eh, life goes on.

I passed by a common room and saw my companions sitting by a fire and enjoying glasses of wine. Their conversation stopped when they saw me. Cairn—excuse me, Carina—was wearing a green dress that accented her red hair. She had even shaved her beard and was wearing cosmetics. Next to her Lydia wore a low-cut, night blue dress with black laces. Hawker sat next the fire with Wren, while Zachariah was in the corner of the room. I guess his being outed as the brother of the vilest man in the East wasn't exactly what he had planned that day.

As I walked by, all eyes were on me. I stopped to look at them.

"I don't care if you like me, or even trust me. But I am going to continue the quest. I'd . . . I'd like you all there," I said. "I know you have questions, and I will answer what I can. Do not let what I said in there cloud who you all are. Separately, you all are broken in your own way. Together, you are whole. The forces of the universe brought you all together for a reason. Your pasts all overlapping? That cannot be coincidence."

When no one spoke, I nodded my head and started to walk on. "Good evening to you all."

"Jackson," Hawker called out.

"Yes?" I said, pausing.

"Would you . . . care to join us for a drink?"

"I would like that," I said. "Soon. First, I must see to some business. Lady Alianna has requested my presence for an audience. Is there . . . anything you would like me to pass on to her?"

With their relationship out in the open now, the two had been separated. During Hawker's time in the Woods, their love had been forged in secret. Now, the lovers must stay apart. Sad, in a melancholy, star-crossed lovers way.

"Tell her that I love her. And we'll be together soon."

"I will tell her."

"Come back, Jack," Lydia said. Wren and Caitlin nodded their agreement. Zachariah eyed me warily, but said nothing.

"I shall."

I moved along the path of the treetop kingdom, across an open-air bridge to the section in the oldest part of the keep where the mystics lived.

I approached the standalone tree home that belonged to Lady Alianna. Two guards stood outside with crossed halberds.

"State your name and business here," they said in unison.

"I think it is bloody well obvious who I am now."

"Name and business."

I sighed. "Jackson Blackwell, Shadow Master, responding to a summons for audience from the Lady Alianna."

The guards uncrossed their halberds and I knocked at the door. A moment later I heard her call from within, "Come in, Mr. Blackwell."

I nodded politely to the guards and entered the tree home of the Truthseer.

The door shut behind me, plunging me into darkness. From the center of the receiving room, a small ball of blue light flittered in the air. The light illuminated the natural wood of the tree home, while giving off an eerie, supernatural feeling.

"Follow," came the disembodied voice of Lady Alianna. The ball of light flittered away, past the receiving room and up the stairs. I followed the light, passing shelves full of antiquated books and scrolls along framed, ancient paintings and etchings of majestic landscapes. The stairwell was lined with candles that burst to life with each upward step I took.

At the top of the stairs, the space opened to a large, loft-style room where the Lady Alianna waited. She sat on her knees in meditation. Her eyes were closed and the room was lit with candles that gave off a green flame.

Once I was at the top of the stairs in the Truthseer's presence, the ball of blue light winked out of existence.

"Shadow Master," Alianna addressed me.

I smiled. "Lady Alianna, Truthseer of the Whispering Woods."

Immediately we both began laughing.

"It's good to see you, Jackson."

"You as well, Bethany," I said. "Or do you prefer Alianna?"

Bethany Madison Jacobs was what you would call . . . a quirky girl, from our world. Along with her multi-colored hair, ear spacers, and facial star tattoos, she normally wore thrift-store clothing and items she made herself. She made her own outsider art and listened to bands you've never heard of (all of them shit, I might add). You know, a hipster.

Anyway, I met Bethany in a tattoo parlor (long story, don't ask) over ten years ago, before all of the things she was into were cool. What caught my eye was her ears. She had them surgically pointed to look like an elf.

I struck up a conversation with Bethany and as it turned out, she was a huge Everquest, Magic the Gathering, Tolkien, card-carrying super nerd. She went on and on about her fairy wing tattoos and how beautiful elves were and all that nonsense. The other thing that caught my attention was how after she got her third face star completed, she convinced the artist to give it to her for free. I watched as she manipulated this schlub into free work.

So I gave her my card and told her to call me if she ever wanted to really be an elf.

Normally, that line wouldn't work on anyone. People would assume I was crazy or slinging some new drug. But Bethany called me and we struck a deal. Fifteen years as my spy within the realms as an elf and I would return her, un-aged, to our world with fifteen million dollars in her account. Of course she didn't believe me. But one quick trip to my dimensional realm, and she was mine.

"As long as we are here, best stick with Alianna."

I nodded. "So, my dear Alianna, I must thank you for that performance in there."

"It's easy. I saw how your mind was working. Plus, with this," Alianna tapped the woven silver circlet on her head, "telling a truth from a lie is easy. Thanks for giving it to me."

"It's a loan only," I countered.

"That was amazing, Jack. I've never seen them so pissed and so speechless."

"It's a gift." I smiled.

When Bethany agreed to enter my service, I first sent her through several months of acting lessons followed by elocution lessons. My own Eliza Doolittle. When she was ready, I prepared her backstory.

Scouring the old legends, I came across a story. Twenty-five years ago, a pair of elven ambassadors went missing and never returned. They were presumed killed by orcs. Their infant daughter, the Lady Alianna, was also one of the casualties.

When the time was right, I used my power to transform Bethany into a real elf, then had her placed inside the realms in a previously abandoned castle, locked away by several orcs I have on payroll.

An anonymous tip to the Arboreal Council led the elven search party to the castle, where my orcs were killed and "the Lady Alianna" was rescued. Because she had grown up a slave to the orcs, the elves treated her as broken and never questioned her lack of grace. They did take note of her ability to see truth from deception, a very rare elven gift. So, seeing an opportunity, they took her *home*.

Thus, my spy within the elven people was born.

"So, what do you have to report?" I asked.

"I fucking hate it here," the Lady Alianna swore.

"Well, that's a succinct report."

"Dear God, Jackson, send me back home. If I have to eat another berry, listen to another poem about a leaf, or shag one of these wimps, I'm just going to die. These people . . . what was I thinking?"

"That living here was a perpetual renaissance fair come to life?"

"Exactly! I expected adventures and madrigals. Beautiful, sexy, buff men . . . and women, with impeccable grooming, ripe for the shagging. Action and dragons. You know, everything from the books."

"I take it you did not get those things?"

"Oh, I did. And at first it was great," Bethany conceded. "They fawned all over me and I saw so many amazing things. But then . . . boredom set in. Ever try to get laid in an elven forest? These people are near immortal so they play the long game in everything. They still court people, damn it! And get this . . . they actually watch grass grow. And they like it!"

"Sounds horrible," I said, trying to suppress a smile.

"Don't patronize me, Jack. I know my assignment. I just miss the real world. Oh hey, how did *Lost* turn out?"

"Horrible. Purgatory."

"Damn. What did Peter Jackson do next?"

"He made *The Hobbit*," I told her.

"Awesome! Was it good?"

"He turned it into a trilogy after bowing to the studio."

"A trilogy? It wasn't a big book to begin with. How were they?"

I raised an eyebrow and waggled my hand. "Bad to middling at best."

"That sucks. So what's your next step?"

"I am going to take the fight to Grimskull. I am going to wipe him off the face of existence. After that . . . a latte, I think."

"Oh god . . . coffee. And pizza. Free music downloads and all the internet porn a girl can have. Jackson?"

"Yes?"

"I know I said I would do this for fifteen years."

"No," I said, shaking my head. "You signed a contract to do this for fifteen years."

"I know, I know. But if you are going to kill Grimskull anyway, I assume you're done with this realm. I would like to request an early extraction. I've done two-thirds of my time and I will forgo half of my agreed-upon fee."

"Interesting. Why?"

"Jack, I'm tired," she said, with the persona of Alianna slipping away and Bethany coming through. "I miss the world. I miss my old life. I miss showers and air conditioning. Bad TV and technology."

"I see. What about Hawker?"

"What about him?"

"Nothing romantic?" I asked. "He is in love with you. He even asked me to pass his love along to you."

"I know. And yeah, he was fun. But he's . . . passionate. He's driven. He wants to save the world and then settle down and raise a family. I hate kids and I'm pretty sure my cat is dead."

"You'll break his heart," I said.

"And you care about that?" she asked.

"No, not really. But it gives me an idea," I said as I wandered around her living area. I picked up a small candleholder. It was simple yet elegant and carved of obsidian.

"What idea?"

"The guards outside. They're your guards, aren't they? Your personal guards."

"They've been with me since I was 'rescued' over ten years ago. They've sworn themselves to me for all their life. Why?"

"The transitive property."

"Meaning what?" Alianna asked.

"Well, in your contract, you swore yourself and all you have to me for the duration of our contract. In essence, you and all you have is mine."

"So?"

I used a fraction of my power and changed the candleholder into an obsidian dagger. An exact replica of the blades used by General Anders's elite assassins, the Night Fires. They used obsidian blades imbued by the general herself so that they burned with the power of the fire giants. The blades caused the body to burn from the inside out. I imbued the blade with the same kind of fire.

I crossed the space between us and slammed the blade into Alianna's heart, while I covered her mouth with my hand. Her eyes went wide with the shock. I wasn't sure if it was the betrayal or the knife in her chest. Either way, she began to smolder and burn from within. The fire inside melted her throat and lungs, and no sound escaped her mouth.

She was dead in moments, but the agony must have felt like hours. I lowered her body to the ground and watched as the fired consumed her from within, melting her organs. In seconds her skin turned black turning into a charred husk of ash and melted skin. In the center was the dagger.

Perfect.

"Bethany, your intel has been very valuable. And I will ensure your payment is sent to your next of kin. No one leaves my service until I am done with them. But don't worry. Your death serves a purpose. The young Hawker would have been traumatized by your leaving. But your death at the hands of the Night Fires will galvanize his resolve towards my purpose. Farewell."

I took a moment to open the window and turn over a few chairs to make it look like there was a slight scuffle. When the room looked complete, I went back downstairs and went through the front door and faced the guards.

Once again, I reached into my power reserves and touched the two elves on the shoulder.

"As you belong to Alianna, and she belonged to me, you are mine to command."

Both the elves' eyes went glassy and they nodded in understanding.

"In three hours, you will hear a noise and you will go upstairs to investigate. You will see two women dressed in black fleeing the scene through the window. You will see the obsidian dagger in the middle of the late Alianna's chest. You will then know without a doubt it was the Night Fires who assassinated her. After you report this to the Lord Protector, you will take you own lives for your failure. Do you understand?"

"Yes, Shadow Master," they said in unison.

"Excellent."

I walked away, picking back up my whistling of "Walking on Sunshine." A leisurely stroll and a hopping skip with a heel click later, I was heading back to the common room where my allies were. I joined my companions and had that drink with them. Hawker toasted me and we laughed and had a very pleasant evening.

It is so very good to be me.

Chapter Twenty-Five

Where I Negotiate Villainous Plots During a Funeral

The Lady Alianna's funeral was grand, yet tasteful.

When the Truthseer was found dead, her remains were gathered with respect and reverence. What was left of the wayward noble was placed on a small rowboat along the banks of the Lower Elder River. The boat was hand-carved from a fallen tree and adorned with fallen flowers gathered. Beside her, her sworn guards were placed. Silken scarves covered their throats to hide the self-inflicted slashes from their suicides after reporting their findings.

It was argued that the guards should not receive a place of honor. But it was Hawker who spoke up, demanding that they be with her. To guard her in the afterlife for all time. Forever making amends for their failing while alive.

All of the Arboreal Court and the Whispering Woods had gathered on the banks and in the trees that morning to say farewell to Alianna. The Treesingers' mournful song vibrated off each living tree and was repeated all across the woods.

I stood there with my comrades and watched as the Lord Protector spoke the eulogy in the high Elvish Tongue. He spoke of her beauty and grace. He spoke of her imprisonment at the hands of the orcs and how her life was one of torment. Yet, for ten years, she had found peace. He blessed her and thanked her for her life and love. Her smile and her joy.

God, I was bored. If I had a watch, I would have been looking at it.

Look, it isn't that I was unmoved by the situation, or the gravity. But I was on a timetable and an ever-dwindling supply of power. So forgive my impatience.

The problem was, elves rarely die. Natural deaths, anyway. The smug, fashion-model granola eaters were immune to almost every disease and healed from injuries at alarming speed. Coupled with their magical abilities and vast knowledge of herb-lore, they lived almost indefinitely.

When an elf died, it was almost always due to violence. War, assassination, murder. You know, the good stuff. The irony is, since they were always holding themselves on a higher level than other sentient beings, they did not grasp why anyone would want to hurt them. So, when said occasion happened, it turned into a rather large affair, sometimes lasting for days, weeks, or even months.

It was disgusting.

Have you ever seen a bunch of really depressed model-types, wearing black for months on end, acting all emo? It's like a high-end goth club, but with fewer people named Raven, Anastasia, Calliope, Caliban, Tempest, or Oberon. (Come on goths, get some new names. I literally googled "popular goth names" and it was the top link. Also, just because Shakespeare wrote it, doesn't mean you should change your name to it.)

When there was a lull in the thirteenth chorus of dead-elf mourning songs, I made my way toward Hawker. I knew the others would join me, but Hawker was their de facto leader. Getting him to come with me sooner would motivate them. Also, I didn't want to be the asshole who was trying to bail on a funeral early.

I was clearly that asshole and I didn't really care. But I needed the perception of me to be on the upswing. I did very recently get through a life-and-death trial using a planted witness, then murder said witness to further my personal gain.

Villainy. It's complex and very time consuming.

As I approached Hawker, Zachariah stepped in front of me.

"We need to talk."

I looked him up and down. "About?"

"Your plans with that boy," Zachariah said as he crossed his arms.

"If you're attempting to be menacing, then you are failing," I told Zachariah as I squared up on him.

"Ten minutes, please. In private."

I looked over at Hawker. The young man was staring at his beloved's corpse floating down river with tears in his eyes. Yeah . . . he was useless for now, anyway.

"All right. Ten minutes," I said.

Zachariah nodded and walked off to a small clearing. I followed, keeping an eye out. Strangers wishing to speak in private was often a setup for bad things to happen. I didn't see any traps, nor did I sense anything out of the ordinary. Still, I kept my guard up.

Zachariah spun toward me with his hands on his hips. "Excuse me for being blunt, but who the fuck do you think you are?"

"Excuse me?" I said, confused.

"Look, I get it. I know who you are. My brother told me all about you and your magical realm," Zachariah said, using air quotes, "but I have been working that kid's corruption for the better part of a year now. Now all of a sudden you swoop in and snatch him up for an easy win? No, that is not professional courtesy."

A bemused smile crossed my lips. I raised an eyebrow and looked at Zachariah. "Are you on the job?"

"What do you think? That Viktor's brother is a good guy? Oh, and thanks for outing me, by the way."

I had to keep from laughing at the situation. "The thought did cross my mind. You'd be surprised how many villains' siblings or relatives turned out to be heroes."

"Tell me about it. My own nephew, a hero. I blame his mother."

"Well, what was your plan then? You had a year to turn him—what were you waiting for?"

"I was taking my time, oh great 'Shadow Master.'"

"If you air quote one more time, I'll cut your fingers off," I said.

"Fine. But look, you should know how hard it is to turn someone. It takes time and subtle approaches. You have to build to a moment and then give them the right nudge to push them into the darkness. In the last year I trained him, I got him to go on an epic quest to recover the Amulet of the Ember Soul and defeat the Bray Beast. I was then going to use him as my instrument to kill my brother once and for all. Do you think you could have done better?"

"In a matter of days, I met him and fought alongside him, earning his trust. I have turned him to my way of thinking. I killed his girlfriend, implicating another. In doing so, I've severed his ties here and bent his mind toward murder. Now I have him rushing headlong into battle to kill his own father. And I did it such a way that I will most likely have the full power of the elvish nation behind me in an assault."

"Huh. OK, that's why you are the master," Zachariah said with a bow of his head.

"Thank you. But you still have not explained why you seek to bring down your brother."

"Viktor? You've met him, right?"

"Of course."

"Then you know he's an idiot."

"Naturally. While I abhor stupidity—and I confess my own idiotic sibling is destined for the grave when I am through with this quest—that is not necessarily reason enough for a death sentence."

"Because I'm the elder brother, damn it!" Zachariah barked.

I shushed him and looked around to make sure we hadn't drawn too much attention.

Zachariah lowered his voice. "I was groomed to rule the Eastern Empire. I excelled in combat training and magical studies. I learned about taxation and economy. But my late parents, may they rot in the pit, were also just as dumb as Viktor. They thought his tantrums and childish power displays reminded them of them. Instead of taking the time to learn, he used shortcuts. So my baby brother was anointed as the heir apparent and I was cast aside."

"So you wish to rule?"

"Yes."

"Intelligently?"

"Of course. A happy populace makes it easier to steal from them."

Interesting. "Then assist me, and I will place you on the throne. My deals with your brother will stand with you. Do you accept?"

Zachariah eyed me suspiciously. "What's your angle? What do you gain from this?"

"Many things. But do not worry about that for now. I will place you upon the throne to rule the Eastern Empire. You will have your birthright. I will act as an adviser for payments in gold. Do you accept?" I asked a second time.

"Yes. I accept. What do you need from me?"

"Three things. First, I need you to say farewell to Hawker. He is no longer your protégé. I need him focused and not looking for a mentor's approval."

"Why?"

Because juggling an extra character along the remainder of this adventure is too much.

"Because I said so," I stated. When Zachariah nodded his head, I continued, "Second, I need intelligence on his lieutenants, General Anders and Chaud."

"What do you need to know?"

"Everything."

"Fine. Anders is, as I suspect you already know, a half-giant from the Fire clan. She is equally beautiful and powerful. But she is arrogant and demanding. I think most of her troops would get out of the way and let the enemy attack her, given how she treats them. When she is not in Al' Garrad, she resides in her private island fortress Fyrheim, where she oversees all her battle engagements."

"How does she manage that?"

"Because of the real threat," Zachariah said. "The real power in Viktor's empire."

"Chaud," I said.

"Yes, Chaud," he confirmed. "The archmage is the only remnant of my parents' ruling council. And in truth, the only reason they stayed in power."

"Go on," I said.

"While my parents flaunted their power, imprisoned and tortured their enemies, built statues of themselves, and basically made the land a living hell for those who lived there, Chaud was the one who really ran the empire. He negotiated imports and exports with pirates. He secured funds from oversea banking institutions and kept crops growing through magical means. Chaud kept the empire's enemies at bay with displays of his magical abilities, and he ensured he had a place in my brother's regime."

"And how does this tie into General Anders?"

"Chaud was the one who facilitated it all. He installed seeing stones in her fortress, allowing her to see and give commands to her forces all across the land. Chaud installed teleportation portals for her to dispatch her forces. They also allow her to return to Al' Garrad when summoned. I assume the same is true for Chaud in his private sorcerer tower. But no one knows where that is."

"I see. So it sounds like the only way to sneak back into Al' Garrad is to go through one of these portals?"

"Yes."

"Excellent," I said, seeing a plan form in my mind. "I bet you know where Chaud's tower is."

He laughed. "I do."

"Then where is it?"

"What's in it for me?" Zachariah asked.

"Other than your brother's kingdom?"

"I will owe you a favor. A favor from the Shadow Master."

Zachariah told me the location and I committed it to memory.

"You said you had three demands of me. What is the third?"

"You are to travel to the west as my emissary to Countess Skullgrim. Extend to her my warmest regard and offer her a chance to destroy her ex-husband's lands."

"You mean *my* lands-to-be?"

"Do not worry," I assured Zachariah. "The Countess and I have a strange past. But she will not raze the lands. She would love nothing more than to strike at her ex-husband."

"Well, it would be good to see her again," Zachariah said.

"Oh?"

Zachariah smiled. "You didn't know? The reason they divorced in the first place was because Viktor found us in bed together. He may have gotten the empire, but I slept with his wife."

"You are quite the villain," I said approvingly.

"Thank you, Shadow Master."

"How long had you had the affair with her?"

"Oh, let's see . . . when did it start? Oh yes. Their wedding night."

Chapter Twenty-Six

Where I Try to Move This Along, but Certain People Refuse to Let Me

For the sake of brevity, let me give you the bullet points: After the funeral, we got a bunch of gifts from the elves and a cryptic warning from a deity and discovered an ingenious way to travel hundreds of miles to the live arctic volcano island that served as General Anders's lair.

But trust me, it's better to skip over everything to keep the pace going.

What?

Seriously?

You subscribe to that nonsense that it's better to show a reader than tell a reader information?

How did you get through high school or college? Was the lack of pop-up-book-based curriculum hard for you? You know, to stimulate the visual cortex of your moronic mind. Were the tests too hard?

Oh, never mind. Odds are, if you're reading this dreck, you never finished college anyway.

Fine.

Dumbass.

****

One week after the funeral, my companions and I stood on a remote beach on the banks of the Lower Elder River on the very edge of the Whispering Woods, as the Ceremony of Blessings was conducted. Talisarian'de, Lord Protector of the Whispering Woods, conducted the speech in high elvish while his keeper of the chronicles translated them into the common tongue. Which is English, in case you non-tabletop gaming nerds can't wrap your heads around that.

The last week to ourselves wasn't exactly beneficial to our fellowship. The time allowed them to consider me and what I was. They knew, now, that I was a villainous person. But they didn't see me as evil. And since each of them had a dark side, or a troubled past, my villainy was like a beacon. They circled me like moths to a flame. I simply kept my distance and remained silent. They would come to me.

They always did.

Yes, we would have a major discussion about who I was and what I do. But when that time came, I would ensure I spun it such a way that I came out as a dark hero in their eyes.

Hawker alone remained impervious to my allure. He was in a dark place following the death of his beloved and the revelation of his family lineage. But this was not my first time in this arena. Hawker would, in time, seek out a mentor—which was one of my main reasons for sending Zachariah away for the remainder of our journey.

I would be that mentor. And if he would not come to me, then I would bide my time and pick the right moment to engage him.

Corruption, when done right, is satisfying and delicious. But all things in their due time. We had a ceremony to complete and gifts to receive.

We stood in a formal line with the river bank behind us while flowers and leaves gently fell, thanks to the Treesingers lulling the trees into wishing us a safe journey. The Lord Protector honored our group as allies of the elves and decreed our names be written as friends to the forest, granting us free passage in the lands of the elves for all time.

If I knew I could get a lifetime free pass from the elves for killing one of them and framing another, I would have done it a long time ago. But I also knew elves. They would find a reason to rescind that gift in a moment's notice.

Talisarian'de approached each of us in turn. Behind him, his Keeper of the Chronicles stood maintaining records of the interactions. Behind the Keeper, several elves stood with new clothing and weapons in their arms.

The Lord Protector switched to the common tongue. "Wren, Ammalar of Vammar, leave these woods in peace, a friend of the elves," the Lord Protector declared as he made the sign of the leaf before the big warrior. "Your past transgressions are pardoned by the will of Valliar. No more are you a servant of the dark forces. You path now shines bright and forgiveness is your end."

The Keeper of the Chronicles passed Wren an elegant set of combat robes of dark blue and dark red, the colors of Vammar.

"Thank you," Wren bowed.

"Go in peace," Talisarian'de said, returning the bow.

Next, the Lord Protector moved to Carina and once again made the sign of the leaf. "Carina, lost child of the Twilight Guard. Leave these woods in peace, a friend of the elves. You cannot be held responsible for the union of your parents, no matter how bizarre or unnatural. Find your own path and the light of Valliar be upon you."

Wow. Even when he was being benevolent, the Lord Protector was kind of a backhanded dick.

The Keeper of the Chronicles passed Carina a new set of clothes that accentuated her feminine form, with divided skirts for combat and a tight top. The cloth was tan and brown elvish silk and meant to represent her human and dwarvish parentage.

Carina bowed as the Lord Protector moved to Lydia.

"Lydia Barrowbride, leader of the defunct Forgotten Bastards, leave these woods in peace."

That gave me pause. The Lord Protector omitted the sign of the leaf as well as the affirmation of "a friend of the elves." In his own aristocratic way, Talisarian'de just gave Lydia the finger and told her to get the hell out of his woods forever.

To Lydia's credit, she showed restraint. Rather than an attack with one of her hidden knives, she simply nodded in a small bow. She never took her eyes off the tall elf.

As the Lord Protector moved past her, the Keeper of the Chronicles handed Lydia clothes of modest make, which only the lowest-born elvish people wore. Last, The Keeper handed her a small bushel of nuts and berries.

"Our apologies for the cut of the clothing," the Keeper said. "But we seldom get females with your . . . posterior measurements. Forgive the tightness, but the food of the elves should assist you in the future for a better fit."

"Oh fuck you," I said before I realized the words had come out of my mouth.

"Excuse me?" the Keeper said, while the Lord Protector feigned disinterest.

"No, I will not. Lady Barrowbride is fine as she is. The only reason she hasn't punctured your precious skin in several vital areas is because she has shown more class and dignity as a thieves' guild leader than any of you. You disdain for humans aside, your body shaming of a woman with an ass is ludicrous. Most of you malnourished, scrawny snobs could use a little extra ass."

"Your opinion is noted, Shadow Master," Talisarian'de said.

After our standoff, the Lord Protector moved on to Hawker. The young warrior stood with his eyes down, not looking at anyone. Only his feet held his gaze, yet intensity radiated from him in palpable waves of seething anger.

"Kyle Hawker," the Lord Protector said in a booming, yet more cordial tone than any of the rest of received. "Friends of the elves this past year. We have come to accept you as one of our own. Accept these gifts as a friend to the elves."

The Keeper presented Hawker with a new elvish sword and magnificent green and gold elvish clothing and armor. As the Lord Protector went to make the sign of the leaf, Hawker whispered. "Don't."

"Kyle, what is wrong?"

"Did you truly let my ancestors die?" Hawker asked.

"That . . . is difficult to answer, young one. And it was centuries ago. We elves were different then."

"No, you're exactly the same now as you were then," I said, sticking my nose into their conversation.

"Hold your tongue," the Keeper of the Chronicles spat at me.

"Let him speak," Hawker demanded. Talisarian'de looked at Hawker and then me, but said nothing.

"Thank you, Kyle," I said, nodding. "Elves despise technology. In fact, they fear it. Elves are the only reason mankind, as well as the rest of the races, haven't advanced."

"What are you saying, Jack?" Carina asked.

"They ensure that you all stay in the exact same state for all time. A state from which they can control the world. Where I come from, there are no elves and the technological and industrial growth of man rivals that of the gods."

"Enough," the Lord Protector demanded.

Oh, good luck, pal. In case it isn't bloody obvious by now, speeches are kind of my thing.

"What do you mean by *advance*?" Wren asked.

"Silence!" the Lord Protector yelled.

Ignoring him, I continued. "A thousand years ago, what were all the races using to fight with?" I asked aloud.

"Swords, armor, and siege weapons, the same as now," Lydia said.

"Exactly," I said. "Why?"

"What else could there possibly be?"

"Oh, so much more, my dear Lydia."

Chapter Twenty-Seven

Where I Shine a Light on Fantasy Tropes and Go Swimming

Go back and read, or watch, ninety percent of books and movies. They always seem to have the same line: "A thousand-plus years ago . . ."

Whatever was going on back then was exactly the same in the current time. Wizards, armor, and swords. It was like their gods kept them from ever advancing past the corollary middle ages. And the few that did were then struck by a great cataclysm, which effectively hit the reset button.

Consider the master JRR. The elves talk about the Battle of the Ring three thousand years prior to the Fellowship. And since then, nothing had advanced. In real-world human history, we went from achieving flight with only the most rudimentary understanding of electricity to landing on the moon in less than seventy years.

The reason for this disparity is very simple. In fantasy realms, the gods and their children, the elves, refuse to allow advancement.

"In my lands," I said to the group, making sure I smiled while looking at the Lord Protector, "mankind has discovered how to harness lightning for power to run great and terrible machinery. We have carriages that fly through the sky. And, in only one hundred years of our time, those carriages reached the stars. We have machines that print books in the thousands, replacing scribes, and our vast libraries of knowledge are shared by all through wondrous devices called computers. In addition to sharing every scrap of knowledge ever written down, they allow us to communicate over vast distances instantly without the need of letters. I know you think I am only speaking in campfire tales, but it is true. And the people of the Eld knew this as well. Their advancement in science and medicine were a threat to the elves. So they were eliminated."

"Leave these woods," the Lord Protector growled through clenched teeth as he threw my gift of clothing and short swords to the ground.

"So, no formal sign of the leaf? No blessing for me either?"

"Valliar himself has marked you as a disruptor of the peace. Your existence is a blight on all sentient creatures. Your very mind, coupled with your actions, sickens, offends and corrupts. It is against the will of

Valliar to wish death upon any creature that is redeemable. But in your case, I see only a lowly human boy scared of his betters who surrounds himself in webs of corruption and lies. Therefore, I wish you nothing but misery until the end of your pathetic days."

I smiled. At least that was an honest moment.

But I was not the kind of person to *not* have the last word.

"Your allegiance to yourselves over every other race in the realms retards the growth of all. Were it in my power, I would see your entire race burned alive in your very woods."

"Sadly, little man, it is not in your power," Talisarian'de said. "Valliar protects us."

"For now," I said, smiling at the tall elf. "For now. But there will come a time when Valliar will not be there for you. I'll make sure of it. And I will make sure the entire world knows of your sins."

"Until that day, Shadow Master."

"Until that day, Lord Protector."

The Lord Protector turned and walked away. His coterie of nobles and sycophants followed, leaving us there on the banks of the Lower Eld.

"Talisarian'de!" Hawker called out.

The Lord Protector paused. He turned his head back slightly to regard the young man. "What?"

"I demand the Right of Recompense."

Oh . . . nice.

The Right of Recompense was an elvish tradition born from their sense of fair play. An accused party must pay recompense commensurate to the slight given to the aggrieved party.

"What do you seek?" the Lord Protector asked.

"When I call upon you, the elves must answer in force. For the slaughter of my people, yours must pay in blood and battle," Hawker said. And it was clear he wasn't asking.

I couldn't quite hear what the Lord Protector's advisers were saying, but from their wild gestures, they were clearly outraged. Talisarian'de silenced them with a wave of his hand. He turned back to Hawker and composed himself.

"When you have need of the elves, speak your request into any living tree rooted in the earth. We will come to save you weaker species," the Lord Protector said and finally departed.

Despite the win over the elves, Hawker looked defeated. Yeesh. You'd think he just found out his allies were responsible for the systematic murder of his ancestors and were single-handedly responsible for keeping everyone in the Middle Ages.

"We should go," Hawker said.

"Go?" Carina said. "Where are we supposed to go?"

"We have a quest to finish," Hawker said as he made ready a large rowboat tied to the river dock that the elves had left for us. They wished us to leave not over their sacred earth, but rather over the water. The traveling method of the commoner.

Wren nodded in agreement. "You're right. But first, I think a change is needed for us all." The big ammalar began shrugging off his old clothes, stripping down to his small clothes.

"You would accept the gifts given by . . . them?" Hawker asked.

"Yes," Wren said. The old soldier training in him refused to turn away fresh clothing and new armor. "And you would be foolish to spurn the gifts."

"Foolish?" Hawker asked with an edge to his voice. It was obvious the boy was ready to pick a fight. Self-righteous fury was dying to be set free.

Wren stood there in only his medieval underwear, a small mountain of fur and muscle. But he was ready to fight. Old white scars criss-crossed his body, peeking out through his black body hair. He resembled a patchwork man. And even nearly naked, he looked formidable.

"You wanna go, kid? Then let's do it. Might be time someone knocked some sense into you."

"Enough," Carina said.

Ever since her revelation as a woman, Carina had dropped the Cairn persona. With it went the brash, competitive person, and in his place, a wiser and naturally gifted mediator stood.

Also almost naked.

Carina had stripped down to her small clothes as well, revealing what the union of a human and a dwarf produced. While not quite as hairy as Wren, Carina had soft, ginger hair accenting her blocky broad shoulders, her medium bust, and her strong thighs and legs. And damned if it didn't look good on her.

"Wren is right. The gifts, it doesn't matter who they came from. Our old clothes, weapons, and armor were taken from us long ago. We now have better gear and provisions. So stop this grandstanding or I'll knock the shite out of both of you."

"Huh," Wren said.

"What?" Carina asked, eyeing him skeptically.

"You are prettier than me," Wren said while Carina blushed.

A loud splash and a womanly shriek caused us all to look at Lydia, who had also stripped down and jumped into the river.

"Holy gods above and below, that's cold!"

"What are you doing, woman?" Hawker called out.

"What you idiots should be doing. Going for a swim. It might be the last bit of fun we have until we all get killed."

Something in Hawker melted and a little smile crept up on his face. "Yes. Alianna liked swimming," he said softly. Hawker removed his clothes and ran towards the small pier. He leaped and dove headfirst into the water, a smooth practiced motion. It was clear this was something he had done with the late Alianna many times. And it was clear, that's where he was in head just then.

Carina and Wren both shrugged and followed, running like idiots, and jumped into the cold waters of the Lower Eld. I got a nice view of both of their hairy backs and jiggling buttocks as they ran.

Well, they were going to end up having sex. I could only hope I was not present to witness it.

"Jack, are you coming?" Lydia called out.

I began preparing my usual villainous response, laced with superiority and condescension. Then Lydia stood up and the primitive portion of my brain woke up. She stood there in her wet, curvy glory. And suddenly, swimming seemed like a good idea. What can I say? A set of wet boobs makes fools of us all from time to time.

I know, I know. It is sexist of me to see the wet skin of a woman and suddenly feel entranced. I blame her. Somehow.

But beyond the exterior, something about the woman intrigued me. Her confidence, her spark . . . the fact that she recently ran a villainous thieves' guild and that she could take a punch . . . all of that cast a charm over me.

So, like a damned idiot, I too stripped down to my underwear, mentally thanked myself for keeping away from the sweets and carbs while exercising regularly, and hoped the cold water didn't turn my outie into an innie permanently.

The five of us swam there in the Lower Eld for the rest of the afternoon like children. We splashed and carried on in the way companions did. A big discussion was coming, we all knew that. The one we'd been avoiding for the last week. The one where we hash out who betrayed who and when.

And of course, what our next move was going to be.

I had the answers ready for all of them. But for now, I took a little break from being the Shadow Master and just enjoyed being Jackson.

If Sophia had seen or heard any of this, she would have burned my soul to cinders while crushing my body to a bloody pulp.

She was like that.

Chapter Twenty-Eight

Where I Devise a Plan, Watch a Fight, and Listen to Barry White

"We are going to strike General Anders in her lair," I said, biting into the fresh cooked fish.

We ate the small meal beside the campfire on the riverbank as the sun set. Oddly, none of my companions seemed to be hungry. Was it something I said?

"Attack . . . General Anders. In her lair," Hawker repeated.

"Mmm, this is good," I said, finishing my food. "Yes. We are going to follow the Eld downstream to the Nameless Sea and then to Fyrheim. We'll infiltrate her lair and kill her. From there, we are going to use a teleportation gate in that lair to move on to Chaud. Once he is out of the way, we move onto Grimskull himself. So, let's say . . . five days?"

"What kind of plan do you call that?" Lydia asked.

"Setting up the third act?"

"What?"

"Nothing, never mind. Look," I said, addressing the group, "we have the rare opportunity of the element of surprise. No one in their right mind would dare attack her directly."

"That is us for sure," Carina said, biting into her fish. "Crazy."

"Isn't that the truth," Lydia agreed as she ate her meal.

"Well, Jack, what's the plan?" Hawker asked.

"Don't ask me, ask him," I said, nodding towards Wren. "He used to work for her, after all."

"Why would we ever listen to him?" Hawker said, looking at the ammalar with narrowed eyes. Clearly these two hadn't yet come to terms with their respective pasts. What were they doing in that week between the trial and now? Didn't we all just go swimming as a group? Team bonding and all that?

"Hawker, are you still mad about Wren's involvement with your village's slaughter?"

" . . . Uh, yes."

Huh.

It wasn't like anything could be done about it.

"Kyle, I'm sorry. Gods above, I am sorry. After knocking you out, and your stabbing me, I was in no shape to go on. I swear, I did nothing to harm your people," Wren said, practically begging. "I even saved you! After which I was left behind to die for my inaction."

"Do you want me to feel sorry for you?" Hawker asked. "So you didn't kill any of my people. Thank you. But how many other villages like mine had you destroyed while in service for that bitch?!"

"Too many," Wren whispered.

Carina put an arm around the crestfallen ammalar. "We've all made mistakes, Hawker," she said. "Don't act like you've always been innocent."

"I was," Hawker said righteously. "I lived a simple life before he came. Quiet. I never hurt anyone before that night. But now I see how the world really works. It is an evil place. One of violence, death, suffering, and pain. And the only ones who survive and thrive are villains like Grimskull. Villains like the elves. Like Lydia and the Forgotten Bastards." Hawker looked at me. "Or villains like Jack."

Kid had a point. Maybe he was learning?

"Are you a villain then, Wren? Like Jack? You got caught and are looking for absolution? If you hadn't had a conscience that night, how many people would you have slaughtered for General Anders?"

Carina held Wren tighter. "Shut up, Hawker."

"Defending your man, half-breed?"

Oooh. This was getting good.

The ammalar pushed Carina's arms off him and stood. He lumbered over to Hawker. Towering above the younger man, he stared down at him with a look most would find intimidating. Hawker, though, refused to budge.

"Say that again," Wren said.

Goddamn. If I had popcorn, I would be gobbling it up. Hmm. If I just used a little of my power? No. Best to conserve.

"Which part?" Hawker asked, staring up at Wren. "Where I called you a villain, or her a half-breed?"

Wren's left hand shot out and wrapped around Hawker's throat while his right fist cocked back, ready to knock the smaller and younger man's teeth out.

Hawker didn't flinch. He didn't react at all. In fact, he looked like he was begging for it.

Wren was happy to oblige. His meaty fist came crashing in, but was stopped at the last second. Not by Wren's sense of mercy, but by Carina.

The half-dwarf cut an impressive figure, standing legs askance, jawline set, and grim determination on her face as she held the big man's wrist in her iron grip.

"Don't," Carina grunted.

"Why?"

"Because Carina has the good sense you clearly lack," Lydia told Wren as she approached the scene. "For the sake of the gods above and below, Wren, Hawker's life has just been turned upside down. His woman's been killed, his mentor is his uncle, and his enemy is his father. Show some compassion."

"Save your sympathy, villain," Hawker rasped at Lydia. "Another vile person like you gets to live while the good people of this world die. The gods hate me."

"Yes, the Bastards were a ripe group of sodding thieves, but they were good lads. My lads before Khasil infected them. They only stole from the rich and kicked back to the poor. Don't speak of me, or them, as vile. Carina might have the good sense to stop Wren from knocking you on your arrogant ass, but I'll cut you and not think twice."

"Go ahead."

"You think you're the only one to ever feel pain? The only one who ever felt loss? Get over yourself, kid. You want to know why bad people survive in this world? Because we don't wait for fortune to find us. We make it happen. Now, tomorrow we are most likely going to die in some fool scheme to attack General Anders. So tonight, we just live like normal people. You get to make a choice—die tonight and every night thereafter by inches, wallowing in self-pity, or choose to live and maybe die tomorrow."

Hawker almost smiled. "Not much of a choice."

"I know. Sucks the milk right from the teat, doesn't it? But I have something to help."

"Which is?"

"Elvish wine," Lydia said, holding up bottles.

"Now where did you get those?" I asked.

Lydia flashed a smile. "I'm a thief, remember. And a bored thief is never a good thing to leave alone in your lands for a full week."

Wren lowered his fist and released his grip from Hawker's throat while the two men maintained eye contact.

"How could you work for her?" Hawker asked as he rubbed at his throat.

Something in Wren cracked. His cold interior demeanor fractured for a moment and he couldn't keep the young man's gaze. But I saw it in his eyes. Wren collected himself and looked back to Hawker.

"You're young. Too young to have had a family. One that loved you. One that relied on you. One that could be used as leverage against you. When you're poor, and your wife and child are sick and you don't have enough coin to pay for a healer, you'll do anything . . . *anything* to help them. Even joining a militia that serves a warlord like Anders.

"You won't care about anything as long as the money is good enough to help them. And when the medicine doesn't help them, and they die, and you're still in the militia, you find out that hurting others helps to soothe pain you feel. At least for a while. And one day, when you hate yourself and you hate the pain you have inflicted on others, something in you changes. Helping one young man doesn't wash the blood from your hands, but it is a small step to becoming the man you were before you'd ever taken life."

"Wren . . . I—" Carina started to say something, but Wren shook his head.

"Don't. It's all gone," he said to Carina before turning back to Hawker. "Kyle, I don't want your fucking forgiveness. I don't even really want your friendship. This whole endeavor is personal. A chance for me to try and wash a little of that blood away. I am sorry for what happened to your family, to your people. But you need to grow up and learn the world isn't about you and your pain. We all suffer. So, for now, I am going to drink too much of that wine. And, if Carina is willing, find a quiet place in the woods and try and feel like a man again."

Carina gently kissed Wren on the cheek and then took one of the bottles from Lydia. With Wren's hand in hers, she led them both away into the woods.

Told you they were going to bone.

Hawker in turn took another of the bottles from Lydia without a word and went in the opposite direction as Wren, into the woods alone.

That left Lydia and me alone. At night. By a fire. With wine.

In my head, Barry White was warming up.

"Shadow Master," Lydia said with a mischievous grin, holding two bottles of wine.

"Madam Barrowbride, leader of the Forgotten Bastards," I said, returning the grin. As I was still sitting by the fire with my back against a log, I patted the spot next to me. Lydia took her time and coquettishly walked over, swaying her hips as she did. As she sat next to me, I placed an arm over her shoulders and she snuggled in next to me. Lydia put the wine bottle to her mouth, pulled the cork out with her mouth and spit it into the fire.

Classy.

She took a deep swig of the wine then passed it to me. "So, if I lay with you tonight, will you see me differently tomorrow?"

I took a deep drink of the wine. A four-hundred-year-old red. Nice. The little thief had good taste.

"Honestly?"

"Yes, honestly."

I took another sip from the bottle and passed it back to her. "If we are being honest, I want to use you. Respectfully, of course. But I want to take you by the fire and let out all the stress I've had building up. Dark, twisted, erotic things that lurk in the dark corners of my mind."

"I see," Lydia said, pulling back slightly.

"Since meeting you," I said, "I've been enamored of your strength, your cunning, devious nature, your ability to use a knife, and of course, your curves. This will not be the start of anything beautiful. Does this bother you?"

Lydia set the bottle aside, then threw a leg over me and sat in my lap.

"Honesty is so refreshing," Lydia said.

She kissed me softly at first, then harder, then harder still. She tasted of wine and passion. Her kissing grew more intense as she ground her hips against mine.

"Will you still help me rebuild the Bastards?" Lydia whispered as she moved to playfully nibbling on my ear.

"That's business," I said. "This is pleasure."

Lydia sat back and removed her blouse and then her support shift, revealing her full breasts. The night air made her nipples stand erect. Which, coincidentally, I was as well.

"You know all those nasty things you said you would like to do to me?" Lydia asked as she guided my hands to her breasts, encouraging me to hold them while massaging her nipples.

"Yes," I said.

"Well, I have a devious mind as well."

With a quirky smile, Lydia pulled two knives from behind her back and slammed them down into the log I was using to prop my head up.

The edges of the knives were angled in such a way that if I were to move too much, I would cut myself open.

Interesting.

"I hope you enjoy this, but try not to kill yourself," Lydia warned.

Removing my hands from her breasts, Lydia slowly lowered herself down my chest as her hands found my belt. One hand reached into my pants and began to slowly stroke my erection while the other undid my belt.

She took me into her mouth and teased me at first with her tongue. Then she held me and began stroking me while she worked her mouth, wetly, up and down.

The ecstasy was intense. All the more so knowing that if I thrashed about, I'd cut my throat. And knowing that she was in control of the situation was an amazing aphrodisiac.

When I felt I couldn't hold on any longer, she stopped. "Oh no, not yet," she said, wiping her mouth.

Lydia stood, leaving me there pinned. She removed her boots and leggings first, taking her time to bend over and remove her small clothes. Naked and free, she stood before me with her hands on her shapely hips. The firelight crackled behind her, backlighting her naked form. Her silhouette reached up and she stretched like a cat waiting to pounce.

Lydia lowered herself on top of me, guiding me inside her. She was warm and wet and once again in full control.

"Don't you want me to take my clothes off?" I asked.

"Shut up, Jackson," she said in reply.

The rest of the night—well, let's just say things got a little more . . . graphic.

Chapter Twenty-Nine

Where I Nakedly Deal with a Deity and Have a Talk with My Sexual Partner

I stood naked by the banks of the Lower Eld river and smoked a cigarette. It was several hours before dawn and Lydia had finally fallen asleep. The woman had an incredible sexual appetite. My numb, wobbly legs were just now regaining feeling. And I desperately needed water for rehydration.

I smoked the cigarette, relishing a job well done. Normally I wouldn't waste the power, but I really wanted the cigarettes. I also needed the power boost during Lydia's and my sexual decathlon to keep up with her and to push her to the place her body begged to go.

Now, I consider myself a fair to good lover. But any man who thinks he can satisfy a woman every time is a fool. If they, or I for that matter, were as good as we thought we were, then the "personal massager" business would go bankrupt.

Besides, a little external help can be good for both parties if done right.

Sexual dalliances aside, I needed to use a portion of my power for the next leg of our adventure. As I cast the power into water, I looked at the phone. Forty-seven percent. Not good. But we didn't have an alternative. I may be able to teleport us all to General Anders's lair. But each person would have to swear themselves as belonging, mind and body, to me. While I relished the notion of more loyal servants, that would also break the rules of the realm. Heroes that belonged to me were not bound by the rules of the realms. Which was why I had to make sure that Bethany, or rather Lady Alianna, was kept safe within the forest.

"Nice night," a voice said from behind me.

Damn it.

"Valliar," I said, not dignifying the god by looking at him as he came to stand next to me. "You seem to enjoy appearing near me when my dick is out. Is this something we need to discuss?"

"No. I just enjoy mocking inferior gods," Valliar said. The god appeared in his full elvish form, a tall, white-haired, ancient elf dressed in forest-colored robes. "You were quite devious at the trial."

"Thank you."

"What are your plans for my chosen people?"

"Me? I have no plans for them," I said as I flicked the cigarette butt into the Lower Eld and lit another.

"Why don't I believe you?"

"You are just naturally untrusting?"

"Jackson Blackwell, do not toy with me."

"Why do you love the elves beyond all your other races?" I asked.

"They are most akin to myself," Valliar lied.

Yes, gods lie. They do it all the time.

"You have exposed certain facts that do not need to be dug up," Valliar said.

"You mean the ones where your chosen people have actively suppressed the expansion of technology and human growth?" I asked.

Valliar said nothing.

"I take your silence as confirmation. Then it is true. You gods are nothing without mortals to worship you. As you are bound to your realms, if the populace leaves you behind, you grow weak. You die."

"When you destroy Grimskull, will you leave this realm?" Valliar asked, ignoring my line of questioning.

"Yes," I said.

"Then I will not hinder you further. Provided, that is, you will do nothing to harm the elves."

"I swear it, Valliar. I will do nothing directly to harm your race of pointy-eared, xenophobic, arrogant acolytes."

"If you break that vow, then I will destroy everything and everyone you have ever held dear."

"Val, the best part of being me is that I do not hold things close to me. All things, all people, can be replaced."

"So you say, Shadow Master. But the Barrowbride bitch sleeping soundly over there would suffer in ways that only a god could perform."

That got my attention.

I finally turned to look at the god, who looked back at me. We stared at one another for a few moments, getting the measure of the other.

"Do not harm her," I said directly.

"Keep your oath and I will not."

Something about what Valliar said earlier bothered me. "What of Khasil?" I probed.

"I repeat, *I* will do nothing to hinder you," Valliar said.

I nodded. He could not offer aid directly, nor move against her directly. So, indirectly, he was warning me. That in itself held a deeper and more positive meaning for me, but I held on to that one little fact for the moment and tucked it into my metaphorical back pocket for later.

"Farewell, Valliar."

"Farewell, Jackson," the god said back.

Before Valliar vanished, he paused a moment and then tossed something to me. I caught it in midair.

It was a piece of obsidian carved into a candleholder.

Touché, you pompous prick.

Another noise caught my attention. Soft footsteps. Lydia, naked and sleepy-eyed, came walking up to me.

"Who were you talking to, Jack?" she asked as she sat down next to me. Lydia kept her distance, not sure how to behave.

Sex, while an amazing act, often led to emotional attachment. Real or perceived, it was there nonetheless. I could tell she was unsure if we were still basking in the glow, or if she were once again the leader of the Bastards and I the Shadow Master.

Truth be told, I wasn't sure myself. Before coming here, I would have thanked her, or whomever it was who shared my bed, for their time, and dismissed them. Once again, I was glad Sophia wasn't here. After berating me, she would have torn Lydia to literal shreds.

I sat down as well and put my arm around her. To comfort her, but also to stash the obsidian candleholder out of sight. I really didn't need her asking what it was or how I came to be holding it by the river, naked.

She was slightly chilly, and I shared my body warmth. "No one," I said, answering her question. "Why aren't you asleep?"

"I was alone. Plus, I had to relieve myself by the trees. I caught a glimpse of Wren and Carina."

"How bad was it?" I asked with a slight smile.

"Hairy and horrifying."

I laughed. An honest, from the belly, laugh.

"You shouldn't do that too much. People might think you are a nice person," Lydia said.

"Well, we can't have that, now can we."

"No. Jackson?"

"Yes?"

"What happens tomorrow?"

"We move on General Anders."

"No, what happens with us?"

"I don't know," I said honestly.

Lydia nodded. She clearly didn't like the answer, but she accepted it for the truth.

"Well, it isn't tomorrow yet," she said.

"No, it isn't," I said, not wanting to argue semantics.

"Maybe this time we won't need the knives," she said.

"Shut your dirty little mouth," I said. "We will always need the knives."

Chapter Thirty

Where I Lead Us on to the Next Leg of the Adventure, Have a Cold Awkwardness with Lydia, and Find a Job for My Dead Employee

I awoke to see Hawker standing over me. He looked pissed. But he was wearing the armor the elves had given him.

"Let's go," he said.

Lydia was still naked and asleep next to me. Hawker looked at her, then at me and sighed.

"Let's go . . . soon."

"Are you done with your existential crisis?" I asked, trying to unwind myself from Lydia's arms and legs. For a short thing, it was as if she had miles and miles of limbs.

"You mean learning everything about my life was a lie? That I'm questing to kill the man who had my mother and my village slaughtered? And it just so happens to be the same man who's my real father?"

"Yes, that one," I said as I pulled on my trousers and lit up another cigarette. Hawker eyed the smoke. I realized that cigarettes from my world really didn't have a place in the realms. "Pipe weed, but in a rolled form," I explained.

Hawker nodded, accepting the premise. "Where are Carina and Wren?"

"Here," Wren said as he and Lydia appeared from the woods wearing their new clothing.

And they were holding hands.

Cute.

I looked down at Lydia, who was now awake. She saw the two of them and noted their public affection. She looked at me for a moment and her face turned dark.

"We should get ready," Lydia said in a failed attempt to hide her disappointment in the potential notion of "us."

Rather than deal with a potential emotional time-bomb, I excused myself to go and empty my bladder by the river. As I stood there trying to urinate out a night's worth of sexual plumbing clog, I noted something odd.

There were weapons on the bank. Perfect, pristine weapons of unknown make. Each of them was presented in a way that suggested they were gifts. Beneath them were the ancient "V" script that represented the followers of Valliar.

Now, why would he give us gifts? Unless . . .

Hmm, it appeared my earlier hypothesis was turning out to be true. Good.

I counted four circles, each containing a gift. A hammer, shield, and armor decorated in red and blue exotic metals, which were obviously for Wren. A set of combat staves and new woodland armor for Carina. A complete set of battle blade and throwing knives with leather straps and holsters for someone with an ample bust and narrow waist. That would be for Lydia. And last was an exotic, oddly reversed S-curved war ax of elvish design, complete with a spiked hand guard. I assumed the weapon was meant for Hawker.

And yet, nothing for me. Wait, there it was. The weapons were perfectly in a line. And at the end of that line was the obsidian candleholder Valliar gave me last night that I'd had to quickly stash away from Lydia.

"Jack, look, about last night," Lydia said as she approached. "I know we said that—wait, what are those?"

"Gifts," I said.

"From whom?"

"The gods," I said.

The rest of my companions came walking to the riverbank and saw the gifts.

"It is the will of Valliar," Wren said. "I sense his power. These are his blessings. A sign that we are on a noble path."

"That was Alianna's!" Hawker said as he ran to the candleholder and fell to his knees. The young warrior clutched the piece of black volcanic rock to his chest and rocked slightly. "She would light this in her study when we made love."

Oh, lord.

In the prime universe, Hawker would be the guy who replayed the mix-tape he made for an ex-girlfriend over and over while he wrote bad poetry.

What's a mix tape? Hmm . . . it was like a mix CD, but on magnetic tape.

What's a CD? Sigh . . . think of it like an .mp3 or Spotify playlist you shared with someone you "watched Netflix and chilled" with. Does that make sense?

Goddamn millennial/Gen-Zeds.

I knelt next to Hawker. "I think this was meant to show you your path is illuminated and clear," I said, making it up on the spot. And, if I do say so, it was pretty good. Just the right amount of sincerity and nonsensical depth that young people eat up.

"Yes, yes," Hawker said, as he stood. I figured it was best he held on to it. In truth, the gift was mine, given to me by a god. Such things held power. But with him holding it, anything homing in on it would come for him instead of me. So, win-win.

"I believe the ax is meant for you as well," I said.

"Why do you think that?" Lydia asked. I felt like she was just trying to be part of any conversation I was in to still communicate, in some way, with me.

"Unlike the hammer, which is both a tool and a weapon, the perfect weapon of duality for Wren, the ax only has one purpose—to cut. And the shape of that wicked bastard has only one purpose."

"To cut wide a swath of blood in any of those who ally themselves with Grimskull," Hawker said as he picked up the ax, testing the perfect balance with a few swings.

"Indeed," I said.

"What of you, Jack?" Hawker asked. "I see nothing for you."

I shook my head. "You all may find it hard to believe, but the gods don't smile upon me. Not even the evil ones."

"That's for sure," Lydia said. "The priestess of Khasil said you were marked by her for unparalleled suffering."

"Yeah, that sounds about right."

"Take my sword," Hawker said, unbuckling the sword belt.

"The elves gave that to you," I said.

"And I am giving it to you. A gift."

"Thank you," I said, accepting the weapon.

"Are we going?" Wren asked as he shoved the boat into the river. He had already donned the god-wrought armor and weapons. Carina also had donned her gear and stashed her combat staves behind her back. She stood at the ship's aft with the guide pole.

"Yes, we are," Lydia said as she finished getting dressed and buckled on her new set of combat blades. Lydia waded into the water and then into the boat.

Hawker and I were the last to get aboard, the five of us fitting with little in the way of extra room. Beneath the bench-style seat, the elves had been nice enough to supply us with traveling rations. And, if I had to guess, several more bottles of stolen wine Lydia had stashed. I caught her eye, looked at the bottles and smiled.

Lydia just turned her head away.

Well, won't this be fun.

Carina pushed off the guide pole, and we were off on the next leg of the adventure.

Slowly.

Painfully slowly.

"Sit down, Carina," I said as I took her spot in the aft and gripped the guide pole.

"You think you have the strength and stamina over a half-dwarf?" Carina asked, bemused.

No, just the foresight to cheat the system. I closed my eyes and began to murmur an incantation. A fake one.

The water beneath the boat began to churn while the mud and clay from the riverbed kicked up, obscuring the clear water.

"What are you doing?" Hawker asked. "What sorcery are you conjuring, Jack?"

"We need to get to Fyrheim. A guide pole won't get us there, not with how far we have to go. So, a little magic is in order. Sit back and enjoy the ride."

Within a few moments, the boat was cruising at a fairly fast rate. Not at a speedboat level, but we were definitely moving.

"This is wondrous," Carina said while Wren grunted in agreement.

"You never cease to amaze," Hawker said.

"Or disappoint," Lydia whispered.

I let both comments go. For Lydia, I had not yet come to terms with what I may, or may not, be feeling. Her romantic longings would have to wait. As for Hawker, it was most assuredly best he did not know the means of the boat's propulsion.

I suppose it could be funny, for me at least, were he to know that it was the animated corpses of his beloved Alianna and her two guardsmen beneath us. The undead were clinging to the boat and propelling us with all the tireless power of zombies. It was fortuitous, for me, that my contract with her specified that she, and all she owned, belonged to me for fifteen years. The subordinate clause to that of course read: alive or dead.

So, my trusted elvish agent and her guards were, in essence, my medieval outboard motor.

The Tenth Rule of Villainy

Villains make mistakes. A successful one learns from them.

Chapter Thirty-One

Where Intelligence and Toilets are Key

"You want us to break into there and do what exactly?" Hawker asked, peering over the small rise.

"Eliminate General Anders," I said. "I don't see why I need to keep spelling it out for you."

For the bulk of our trip along the river Eld and into the Nameless Sea, I'd explained to my companions that in order to cause enough confusion, while simultaneously weakening Grimskull, we had to remove his top lieutenants. Their absence would degrade his power base and limit his reserves by creating a power vacuum. Those who served under Anders and Chaud would be chomping at the bit to claim that power for themselves.

Villainy 101: Whoever is under you wants you gone. Like the Rule of Two with the Sith.

My hubris aside, even I needed a reminder of the rules from time to time. Otherwise, I would have had a better countermeasure in place for Courtney's betrayal. There was going to be a reckoning between my former head of security and me.

Following our covert landing on Fyrheim, we'd secured our ship along the jagged, rocky shore of a small private beach. From there, we'd made our way to a small hill to hide and get a better lay of the land. The entire island was a contrast in nature.

In the middle of the island, a lone volcanic peak stood out with dark clouds circling. The active volcano rumbled constantly. Yet the island was perpetually covered in snow and black ash. The perfect place for General Anders herself. Unless I'd missed my guess, the abnormal weather was due to an ancient Frost Giant artifact. One that was a weapon to their Fire Giant cousins, but one that, in the hands of a half-giant like Anders, would cool her fiery side and allow her to operate without her magically enchanted ice armor.

"Gods above and below," Wren swore, "I'd hoped to never return to this dreadful hunk of rock."

"What can you tell us of the place?" Hawker asked.

"Wait for Lydia and Carina to return," I said. The two women were far better suited to scout the area. Lydia's thieving skills allowed her to be unseen; Carina's time in the Twilight Guard, coupled with her dwarven direction sense and terrain adaptability, made her more than suited to reconnoiter unfamiliar territory.

"Jack's right. Best to hear the report and understand the situation before making a plan of attack," Wren explained. Hawker nodded his head. For all his temper, the kid had an uncanny ability to listen to reason.

I turned and leaned my back against the hill. I took out my phone to see "39%" staring back at me. Damn it. Animating those corpses the entire voyage had eaten more of my power than I wanted. From here on out, I would be operating at critical-level conservation. No power unless absolutely necessary. I had no idea what it was going to take to destroy Anders, nor the more powerful Chaud, for that matter.

That's when I noticed I'd gotten a text message from Sophia.

Sir, we need to talk. Now!

Later, I texted back. In response, Sophia sent an emoji of a frowny face. What was my service provider going to charge me for trans-dimensional messaging? That frowny face better not cost me a small fortune.

A moment later, Lydia returned from her sweep of the area.

"What did you see?" Hawker asked.

"Is Carina back?" Lydia asked, and I shook my head no. I wasn't worried about being overheard, not with the crashing of the waves and other ambient beach noises. But it was best to not talk too much and remain vigilant.

"Then I'm going to hold off until she gets back. I don't want to create a false impression without collateral intelligence."

Wren failed to suppress his smug smile. Hawker just glared.

Almost thirty minutes later, Carina returned. She'd taken a longer route, hugging the coastline and staying low along the raised hill line.

"What did you see?" Lydia asked Carina.

Lydia held out her hand and Wren passed her a water skin. She nodded her thanks and gulped deeply. "I saw that that place is impregnable. Every entrance into the fortress I could find was guarded by armed men at all times."

"Agreed," Lydia said. "I noted that their shift rotation seemed random."

"I saw that too," Carina confirmed. "If I had to guess, the guards' positions were randomly assigned each day. So even following a particular weaker guard wouldn't lead you to the place you wanted to infiltrate."

"Agreed," Lydia said. "What do you all think?"

"There has to be a way in," Hawker said.

"It wasn't like this when I was stationed here," Wren commented.

I shrugged. "Looks like we passed the Bechdel Test." When I got the weird looks, I just shook my head. "Damn it," I cursed.

"What?" Hawker asked.

"All this—" I gestured at the fortress—"is wrong. It shouldn't be like that. There should be blind spots, paths to sneak in, unguarded water drains. That's how these things work. All of it points to someone rewriting the story."

"We saw what we saw, Jackson," Lydia said.

"Damn it," I swore again. Again I leaned against the hill. This time, I took out one of my cigarettes and lit up. I closed my eyes and thought about the problem.

Someone was changing the rules. It couldn't be the gods. They don't know how to operate outside their own rules. That meant it had to be an outsider like me. Courtney? He would have the military know-how to organize this.

But Grimskull distrusted outsiders. Even if Courtney had arranged a coup with my sister against me with Grimskull's help, there is no way he would start listening to them right away. He would keep them close, under observation. Still, an outsider would be the only one who could make this happen. So who did that leave?

"It must be that captain of the guard I saw," Lydia said. "He's running the guards in a way I've never seen before. He knows what he's doing."

A thought popped into my head.

"This captain of the guard," I said, thinking aloud. "What did he look like?"

"Handsome."

"Could you be a bit more specific?" I asked.

"Very handsome."

Could she be a little more scorned? "Did you see him?" I asked Carina.

"If it is the same person, then yes, briefly. He was about your height with a soldier's build."

"Narrow eyes and hawkish nose?" I asked. "Look of the eagles?"

"I believe so, yes," Carina confirmed.

"Cooke," I said under my breath.

"Who?" Hawker asked.

"One of Grimskull's men from his keep. A recent promotion," I said. "One of my own spies turned traitor."

Steve. The former Marine. That explained the tactics as well as someone Grimskull would trust. With his use of modern military knowledge, he'd have the place sealed down tight. His innate military need to command a situation, coupled with his experience, would make him an ideal captain for Anders.

I looked at the water of the sea and that raised another question.

"Wren, what does the fortress use for waste disposal?"

"Waste?"

"Garbage. Privies. Waste."

"The pipes lead to a cistern in the bottom of the keep, which then leads to a volcanic pit where it's all—oh. Oh no."

I smiled. "Yes."

"Please do not tell us that's your plan, Jackson," Hawker said, catching on.

Carina and Lydia just shook their heads.

"OK folks, time to get messy. We're going in through the toilet."

Chapter Thirty-Two

Where We Climb Through Human Shit and Wren Tries to Burn Us Alive

"This is repulsive and I hate you," Lydia said.

"Shut up and keep climbing," I said.

"I'm going to . . . vomit," Wren said, gurgling on his own bile.

"Please, not again." Hawker begged. "I'm under you."

"It isn't really all that bad," Carina said as she moved upward through the sewage drain. "When I was a girl back in the Mines of Gharlond, my father took me down a lot of different excavation tunnels. You'd be surprised what kinds of smells and nasty things you discover. One time, we broke through a vein of diamonds only to find a cavern full of methane and sulfur. The smell was . . . well, imagine a rotten egg that'd been eaten by a goblin, who then died, then shat out that egg after his corpse burst from four days of decomposition."

"Blaaargh!" Wren heaved and rained puke onto Hawker's head. "Sorry Kyle."

"I should have jabbed you harder in the guts with that sword and killed you."

"Right now . . . I wish you had."

"Just keep climbing," I reiterated.

Since it had become abundantly apparent I was never going to get my secret passage, I had to opt for the next best thing. A not-so-secret but underutilized passage in and out of any major keep or stronghold.

Waste disposal.

The simple fact is, you can't have that many people inside a structure and not have a place for the waste to go. Some may use bedpans and piss-buckets, but they all get dumped. And oddly, they have to make them large enough for a person to crawl through for when things eventually get backed up.

General Anders's keep's sewage exit actually fed into the volcano itself. Wren showed us an entrance just below the sea's water line. A small undersea cave that fed into the volcanic mountain. From there, we made our way into the bowels of the volcano. A massive lake of molten rock bubbled and churned. It didn't appear that it was going to blow anytime soon. I supposed Chaud's magic upon the island, keeping the entire region in perpetual winter, had slowed the volcano's natural cycle.

Once we were inside, it wasn't hard to find the chute we needed. It was the one with a carved stepladder going up towards it with a supply of scrubbers on poles nearby. It was also the one with a perpetual trickle of piss and shit. The ablutions fell into the lava and were incinerated into smoke and ash. In all honesty, the idea and execution were brilliant.

The lack of guards made sense as well. As I said before, the guards of this world often overlooked strategic weak points. And Steve, no matter how militarily brilliant and well-versed in the lore of the realms, didn't consider where his morning constitutionals went.

Carina had gone first up the narrow, curved chute. She tied a rope to herself and scurried upwards through the disposal shaft. Her dwarven heritage gave her the best skill set. As well, she was clearly the strongest of us all. Wren was a brute, but no human could match a dwarf, even a half dwarf, pound for pound in raw strength. With Carina being the strongest and most adept climber, she went first, followed by me and Lydia. Wren, with his size and bulk, was next to last, while Hawker brought up the rear. Hawker's strength and youth made him the best candidate to block Wren, should he fall. And had the big man been closer to the top, his collapse would assuredly have taken Lydia or me with him. This was our Mount Everest climb and Carina was our anchor.

If Mount Everest were a stinking slope of human shit.

The rest of us followed, each tied to the rope. The only way to move up the steeply angled chute was to place your back against one side with your feet and hands out in front. We had to brace ourselves and move inch by disgusting inch up the . . . well, *anus* of the keep.

"What can we expect when we get to the top?" I asked Wren, doing my very best to keep my lips as closed as possible, less a stray drip land in my mouth.

"More shit," Lydia guessed.

Wren gagged. "She's not wrong. This chute will lead to a cistern beneath the keep. A large circular room with a sloped floor. In the very center . . . gods, this is wretched."

"Focus, Wren," I told the ammalar. "We need to know what we're getting into."

Wren grunted as he moved his bulk slowly upward. The chute seemed to no longer be at an angle. Instead, we were moving straight up. From here on out, it was all our own strength fighting our body weight, gravity, and shit-slick slime-coated walls.

"We're going to come up right in the center of that sloped floor. All the garbage and waste flows into the cistern from other chutes and pipes throughout the keep. It won't be pleasant."

"Is there . . . any . . . nnng, good news?" Hawker asked.

"Yes," Wren said. "There is a door in to the cistern. One that leads into the keep itself. It is rarely guarded. And when it is, it is by the worst guards. The one they don't trust to look after anything other than everyone's waste."

"I can see the top," Carina said. "Give me a moment and I will begin pulling you all up."

With as much noise as we'd been making during our climb, I was amazed Anders herself wasn't there waiting on us. But Carina had assured us that the stone, and years of sewage buildup, would dampen any sound we would make.

Carina pulled me up and I in turn helped to pull Lydia though the chute's opening into the cistern. The three of us pulled Wren and Hawker up the rest of the way, while they grunted and cursed.

All of us took a moment to rest and recover. The climb had been a testament to our conviction. We had succeeded through sheer will and determination.

We reeked of decayed garbage and human excrement. Rest as we did, we were still in the bowels of the keep in an ankle-deep pool of piss and worse.

I spotted the door and nodded towards it. "That way?" I asked Wren.

"Do you see another door?"

"No," I said, narrowing my eyes. "I do not. But please enlighten us on where we go from here."

"Depends."

"On what?" I asked.

"What you want to do."

"Are your being obtuse on purpose?" I asked.

"Dunno what that means. If you're asking if I am tired, angry, and mad about being back in the one place in creation I don't want to be so I am acting out in terse responses, then yes, I am being 'obtuse.'"

"Let's all move up to a higher point in the room, by the door perhaps," Lydia suggested. "Maybe we can have a rational discussion when we're not standing in the epicenter of the keep's asshole?"

"Works for me," Hawker said, while Carina nodded.

The five of us slogged through the waste and made our way across the massive cistern to the exit. Carina held her ear against the door and listened.

"All clear. No one is on the other side."

"Small miracles," Hawker said.

"How do we get clean?" Lydia asked.

"Afraid of a little dirt?" Wren said.

"No, I am not afraid of a little dirt. But what we are is coated in shit."

"And vomit," Hawker added as he tried, in vain, to wipe his armor clean.

"And vomit," said Lydia. "Anyone past this door will smell us long before they see us. There has to be something we can do."

"She's right," I said, trying to think of something. I could clean myself. The power it would take was a mere fraction and it was a necessity.

"I have an idea," Wren said. "Link hands."

We all did as instructed. I reached for Lydia's hand and she recoiled at first, giving me a venomous look. Reluctantly, she took it as the rest of us joined hands and stood in a circle.

Wren seemed to concentrate and warm, purplish fire flared up around his hands and enveloped his body. The fire spread, catching Hawker and Carina, then spreading to Lydia and me.

The fire was warm. Pleasant even. It was like a hot shower. The flame burst and crackled as everything that was filth upon us hissed and evaporated. The smell was awful, but considering where we were, it wasn't anything new.

In moments, all of us were clean and revitalized. I didn't know about the others, but I felt healthy and strong. All the aches and soreness my muscles had endured from the climb were now a memory, replaced with hope and newfound strength.

"What did you do?" Carina asked.

"I tried to burn us all alive," Wren sighed. "Praise Vammar."

"Where to next?" Hawker asked.

"We find General Anders," I said. "And we kill her."

Chapter Thirty-Three

Where I Skulk, Learn About Giant Sex, and Contemplate Romance

The keep was blissfully devoid of soldiers and guards. Being a wanted fugitive had its benefits from time to time. In this case, it meant that most of the general's guards were out scouring the empire looking for you, leaving their home base running on a skeleton crew.

"Where would Anders be?" Lydia asked as she put on the oversized tabard and belted it around her waist.

"How do we know she's even here?" Hawker asked, doing the same thing over his armor.

Wren had opened a storage container near the cistern, where fresh, laundered livery was kept. He distributed tabards in the colors of Grimskull and General Anders to each of us. The disguises were not fully convincing. But they would pass a cursory glance. Wren explained that new recruits flooded in all the time. So new faces were the norm here.

"She better be," Carina said. "I didn't crawl through all that for nothing."

"She's here," Wren said.

"How do you know?" I asked.

"It's what she does," Wren said. "When she is not on assignment, this is where she resides. Thanks to Chaud's magical enchantment on this isle, this is the one place she can walk freely without her ice armor."

"So, where would she go without her armor?" Hawker asked.

Lydia smiled. "Well, if you spent all your time in the field wearing cold, hard armor, once you were free of it, where would you want to go? Or better yet, what would you want *to do* when you were free of it?"

"Oh, well that makes sense," Carina giggled.

"What?" Hawker asked, clearly not getting it.

"Kyle, dear, what do adults like to do when they are not wearing anything . . . restrictive?" Lydia asked.

"I don't know . . . oh." Hawker blushed. "Well, yes, *that* I suppose."

Wren nodded in agreement. "Yes, the general was quite fond of her extra-curricular activities. She frequently would visit the barracks for . . .

inspection. Otherwise she would spend all her time either in her private quarters or in the great hall. It was from there she could view the empire via Chaud's scrying device and order her troops, or assassins, wherever she wished."

"The general never enjoyed her dalliances in her own chambers?" I asked.

"No." Wren shook his head. "Her chambers were for her alone. She deemed no one worthy of stepping foot in her living area. She always said we were all too unclean."

"We? So you know from experience?" Carina asked, raising an eyebrow.

"Um, I prefer not to discuss that."

"Oh, you are cute when you're embarrassed." Carina smiled. "I know there were women before me."

"OK, enough of this. We need to split up," Hawker announced. "We have three areas of the keep to search. Carina and Hawker, you take the great hall. I'll check the barracks. Lydia and Jack, you check her private quarters."

"Um, about the pairings," Lydia said. "Can we rethink the teams?"

"Just do it," Hawker said. "Wren and Carina work well together."

"Yeah we do!" Carina said as she swatted the ammalar on his backside. Wren just grumbled.

"And you two need to get over whatever your issues are. So a fighter and scout in pairs. I work better alone. Meet back here by the cistern in one hour and report what we've found. Agreed?"

"Agreed," Lydia mumbled. I simply nodded my approval as Hawker turned and left. Wren and Carina practically pranced off together.

"So, what was it like, you know, being with her?" I heard Carina ask as they made their way down the long hallway.

"Awkward."

"How so?"

"Bitch is almost ten feet tall," Wren said, shaking his head at Carina. "Had to use a step ladder to do any of the fun positions."

I watched them leave and then turned to Lydia. "Alone at last?"

"Let's just go," Lydia said, turning to leave.

After following the general path Wren had described, we moved down the hall towards where I believed General Anders's quarters to be. As we searched, the keep's features transitioned from a functional design to one of luxury. I assumed this meant we were entering the living quarters of General Anders and her top military retainers.

I turned a corner and stopped. I backed up and allowed myself another cautious peek. There were two guards standing beside one another in full armored livery with pole arms crossed. They were blocking a door that was easily ten feet tall.

Unless there was another half-giant here, I'd wager we found her room.

Lydia had her head down and she walked past me. Her mind was obviously on other things, like being pissed at me.

"Lydia, stop," I hissed as I reached my hand out and snatched her back before she turned the corner.

"What?!" Lydia half barked.

"Pull your head out of your ass," I whispered, holding my finger to my lips and then pointing towards the guards. "Act like a professional."

"Go to the Never Realm," Lydia said. "Who are you to tell me what to do?"

I shook my head. "Are you still angry about . . . us?"

"Do you want to have this conversation? Here? Now?"

"No, I'd rather not have it all," I whispered harshly. "But clearly, we need to have this talk. I recall when you asked me by the fire what I wanted, I told you bluntly it was carnal, and you said, if I recall correctly, that the honesty was refreshing."

"I know," Lydia said, sulking.

"And," I continued, "when you asked me by the river what happens with us the next day, I said that I didn't know."

"I know, damn it!" Lydia screamed.

"Then why are you so mad at me?!"

"Because!" she yelled.

"Because why?!" I yelled back.

"Halt!" yelled the pair of Anders's guards as they rounded the corner on us. "Who are you?"

"Fuck off!" Lydia and I yelled at the guards in unison.

"I thought you were someone special," she said, her voice deadly serious. "Someone like me. I thought you were more than just . . . a tryst."

"And where in the hell did you get that notion?!" I yelled back at her. My sense of control and villainous conditioning had gone out the window dealing with this incredibly infuriating woman.

"I don't know, perhaps when you were inside me? When you held me with passion and emotion? When you didn't treat me like an object? At least, not until you were done with me."

"Emotion? You had a knife to my throat the whole time!"

"Um . . . excuse us, but who are you?" one of the guards asked again. "Are you one of the new hires?"

"Shut up," I said, holding my hand up to the guard. I then turned my attention back to Lydia. "Because I treated you with respect and dignity while we were having sex, that makes me a monster?" I asked, ignoring the guards who were now very curious who we were and why we were fighting. "Because if that's the case, then the problem is with *you* and with the type of men you choose to take to your bed. Not me."

"Oh, so this is all my fault?"

"How could it be mine? I'm not the one who inflated good sex into something more than it was," I said.

"You arrogant bastard," Lydia said, her face contorting with seething rage. "Was I the one who kept commenting about your body all the time? Was I the one who mentioned you during the trial, or defended you to the elves? No. That was you flirting with me. Was this all a game for you, Shadow Master? To make me feel special, seduce me, and then slip away?"

"No—I—" I stammered.

Damn it. She had a point. I had said nice things about her. I had defended her.

I had also punched her in the face. And between that option and dealing with a real emotional connection with someone, I preferred the punch.

"OK, enough of this," the guard said. "Both of you, drop your weapons. You're coming with us until this gets sorted out."

"Sod . . . off!" Lydia said, swinging her arm wide and releasing a pair of throwing knives. The blades buried themselves into the guard's chests, missing vital organs. Both of the guards dropped their weapons and fell to the ground, unconscious.

Poison on the blades? Nice touch.

"Sir?" Sophia's voice said in my ear. "I know you said to contact you only in emergencies, but I think this counts. I've been listening to everything and, right about now, you should probably just kiss her."

"You've been listening? The whole time? Is that why my power is drained so low?"

"Sir, I have to monitor. But please, do not change the subject. I will forgive your moments of lighthearted frivolity if you just kiss her."

"Who are you talking to?" Lydia asked, confused and angry.

"My assistant," I said, holding my finger up. "Frivolity? What are you talking about?"

"Your little camping trip? Carousing and playing by the river like a normal person? Like a . . . hero? For shame," Sophia admonished me. "Sir, our arrangement is mutually beneficial. And I enjoy it. Normally, I would make every effort to undermine your power from this day until the end of the time for your weakening, caring for these heroes."

"Then why don't you?" I asked, challenging her.

"Because I'm a sucker for romance!" she exclaimed. "You're the Shadow Master; she's the leader of a thieves' guild! It is the sweetest, most ruthless, and downright sexiest thing I've seen, or rather heard, in a long time. Big points for the sex, sir. You two work well together. But Jackson, please, trust me. Just kiss her. Sometimes, even the villain gets the girl."

I looked back at Lydia, who had another pair of throwing knives ready. She looked at me and I could feel the anger coming off her.

To be honest, it kind of turned me on.

Oh, fuck it. This was not going to end well.

I crossed the distance between us and wrapped my arms around her and kissed her as hard as I could.

She, in turn, stabbed me in the kidney.

Sigh...Fuck romance.

Chapter Thirty-Four

Where I Get Healed, Get Robbed, Entertain an Offer, and Get Rescued

"Move back!" I heard Wren command. I felt his hammer hit me square in the chest, crushing my ribs and breaking my sternum. I felt bone piece my heart.

Then a wave of energy hit me, and just like that, I felt better.

"Praise Vammar," Wren sighed.

"Sir? Sir?! Are you OK?" Sophia's voice said in my ear.

"You're . . . fired," I groaned.

"You couldn't fire me if you wanted to, sir," Sophia said. "Sorry for the bad advice. I really thought she'd go for it. You humans seem to eat that stuff up. I will have to reconsider all those romantic comedies I've watched. Damn that Channing Tatum, but Magic Mike is so pretty."

I propped myself up on my elbow and wiped my face. Wren and Lydia were kneeling beside me. "This adventure has gone to hell. I quit."

"What was that?" Lydia asked. "Why did you kiss me?"

Not much of an apology.

"A bad attempt at romance?" I said as I tried to stand. Wren's god's magic had stitched me back together, but everything inside me felt like it was still finding the right place to be in.

"Did you honestly think a pathetic attempt like that was going to . . . do what? Win me over? Make forgive the way you treated me?"

"And I'm supposed to assume the knife in my side was a completely rational reaction?"

"Will you two please shut up?" Wren rumbled. "We checked the barracks and Anders wasn't there. I assume from this little scene that you didn't make it inside her bedchambers?"

"We were distracted," I said, getting to my feet. Once I was up, my knees buckled. Wren reached out to steady me.

Damn.

"What's wrong with him?" Wren asked. Lydia simply crossed her arms and looked away.

"I'm poisoned," I said.

"Is it lethal?"

"Ask her," I said.

"He'll live," Lydia confirmed.

Carina appeared a moment later. "Guards are stashed," she said.

"Bedroom?" Wren asked.

"Clear."

"Hmm," Wren grunted. "Then she has to be in the main hall. Think you can walk?"

"In a moment," I said. "Go on ahead. I'll catch up."

"You sure?" Carina asked, looking at me and Lydia. "It's not wise to split us up again."

"Go," I said. "Hawker may need you."

"He'll be fine," Wren said. "Vammar's power will clear him out soon. Let's go. Jackson is right. Hawker may need us."

Wren released me, and I leaned against the hallway wall. He and Carina nodded to one another and took off down the hall.

"You want me to stay?" Lydia asked with a bored sigh.

"No."

"Oh. Well . . . fine."

Lydia stared at me a moment, considering my curt reply. She walked over to me and placed one hand gently on my cheek.

Then she hauled backed and smacked me so hard my teeth rattled.

I snapped my head back and stared daggers at her. But she simply left without another word, leaving me behind. I watched her leave, and when she was no longer within earshot, I collapsed.

The poison was affecting me a lot more than I wanted them to see. Getting belted in the face by a scorned lover didn't help.

I'd rather let the poison run its course than use any more power. So I had to just rest. Deep inside, I felt a lingering trace of the ammalar's god working to counteract the poison.

So. There I was, the Shadow Master, collapsed in a heap of idiocy, poison, and bad romantic decisions. Speaking of using too much power, I needed to admonish my assistant.

"Nice going with the kiss," I said to Sophia. "If I paid you, I'd cut it in half."

No response.

"Sophia? Sophia?" I said as I placed my hand to the earpiece.

It was gone.

I looked on the floor and saw nothing. Where did it go? I just had it a moment ago when Sophia was waxing on about her romantic comedies.

"The slap," I said out loud. I replayed the altercation in my head and it had to have been then. When Lydia went all Ike Turner upside my face, she must have palmed my earpiece. She'd seen me touch it when I'd talked to Sophia earlier.

Which means she could be speaking to Sophia now. How in the world could that be a bad thing? My ancient, powerful, villainous assistant having a tea-time chit-chat with my scorned lover.

I felt my genitalia shrivel at the prospect.

"You've looked better," Khasil said from behind me.

I rolled over to get a better look at the goddess as she stood with her hands on her hips, looking down at me.

Khasil appeared in an almost human form, dressed in her black robes and battle armor. Her greenish skin, hair, horns, and creepy bug eyes were the same. But she was now sporting a scorpion tail and a second set of pincer-like arms.

"Khasil, to what do I owe the honor of this visit? Last time we spoke, you seemed like you wanted to murder me."

"I still do," Khasil said. Her tail bobbed above her head, accenting the point. "But, I am here to make you an offer."

An offer from the Queen of Chaos? This should be petrifying.

"Go on," I said.

I tried to sound brave, but it wasn't like I was going anywhere. My body was still sluggish from Lydia's poison and I was flat on my ass. Even if gods cannot attack other gods directly, nothing stopped her from summoning monstrous creatures from the underworld to feed on my defenseless form.

Or she could just sound an alarm. So I just lay there and waited to hear whatever horrid plan came out of her mouth.

"Give me the girl," Khasil said.

That piqued my interest. "What girl?"

"The Barrowbride. Give her to me."

"Why?"

"My reasons are my own. But, if you give her to me, I will help you raze Grimskull's empire to the ground. His allies will perish. His associates will perish. All who knew of his once vast lands will know his end came at your hands."

"And if I refuse?"

"I will kill you."

"You can try," I said, smiling.

Hopefully she didn't opt to follow through with her threat. One principle of villainy is to always appear to be more powerful and deadly than you are. While my reach and skill were formidable, I was just a man who happened to lease a dimension and was only technically a god. To the real gods, though, I was an anomaly—a mortal who achieved god status. Therefore, I was something they were very wary of. And because my success continued, I was deemed dangerous.

Khasil considered me. "Fine. I will kill her and your new allies," the goddess threatened. "Not just kill them—I will torture their souls for millennia. Their anguish will resonate so loudly, you will hear their suffering in your own tiny dimension."

Something about this was wrong. She was offering too much and threatening too violently. The gods of the realms weren't true universe-creating deities. They were higher beings, but beings nonetheless, complete with hubris and fallibility. This whole deal was *off*.

Khasil saw my face and read my expression. She altered her stance and knelt down beside me in a very human way.

"Jackson, do you love her? Is that why you are hesitating? I watched your lovemaking. There was something special there. A passion. A connection."

What is with these gods? Why is it they seems to have a sick perversion of watching me and my penis every chance they get?

"What if I do?" I said. "My feelings are . . . conflicted in this matter. Who I am and what I do is not conducive to maintaining relationships. So what exists between the Barrowbride and myself is private."

"She stabbed you."

"Hell of a woman," I smiled.

"If her safety is what concerns you, I promise, she will not be harmed."

I'd heard enough.

"No. You cannot have her."

"You have doomed them all, mortal," Khasil sneered.

"No, you are wrong. They are heroes. And we know how that works out for people like us." I smiled at the goddess. I felt my legs gaining strength and the poison all but gone. If I had to move, I should be able to at least run, if not fight.

"Damn the High Accords!" Khasil screamed. "Die!"

Her scorpion tail drew back, the stinger quivering with anticipation. I scrambled to get my feet under me, but Khasil swept her leg out, knocking me back to the ground while her clawed hand clamped onto my wrist, holding me in position.

"Hey, bitch!" Lydia called out. "Get away from my man!"

Khasil looked up just in time as a pair of Lydia's poison-coated throwing knives pierced the goddess's eyes. The blades slid into her primary and secondary left eyes.

Khasil roared and the fortress shook.

I was free from Khasil's grip and I ran, narrowly dodging her scorpion tail blindly stabbing the ground where I had been only seconds before.

I ran to Lydia, who held her hand out. I took it and the two of us ran down the hall. A quick look over my shoulder and I saw Khasil rage again, lashing out. Then the violence stopped and the goddess blinked out of existence.

"You love me." Lydia smirked as we ran down the hall.

Damn.

I was never going to live this down.

Maybe it wasn't too late to sell her to Khasil after all?

Chapter Thirty-Five

Where I Spy From Above, Give Sage Villain Advice, and Am Betrayed

From my perch high in the vaulted rafters, I could see the great hall below. General Anders towered over an expansive circular wooden table. The structure was intricately designed to hold a massive cauldron in the center. The water within the cauldron rested flush with the table. Anders swept a hand over the water and a map of the entire Eastern Empire was displayed. As Anders gestured, the water shifted, showing her forces throughout the empire.

The table was magical—a gift from Chaud, no doubt—allowing her the ability to view wherever she wished and deploy her forces through the portals in the training field. She gripped the railing and studied the map. So what was she doing now?

Well, that was simple: She was searching. No doubt for me. I looked at my phone and it read 34%. Keeping me cloaked from outward scrying was slowly draining my power. And, it appeared, the closer I was to the magical source looking for me, the more quickly it drained.

The rest of the hall was empty besides two of her captains and several attendants. One of the captains was a female in black lightweight scout armor designed to make little to no sound. She was most likely Gale Korva, the leader of the Night Fires, Anders's assassins. She was dark-skinned with a shaved head. Her eyes scanned everywhere.

The other person was Steve. The former chamberlain-turned-captain was dressed in shiny new armor complete with single off-shoulder cape denoting his rank.

Across from me, in the rafters on the other side of the hall, Wren and Carina were perched. They nodded at me. Lydia was on my right, and all of us were looking for the same thing.

Where was Hawker?

"What made you come back?" I whispered.

Instead of answering, Lydia just gave me a dopey smile then passed me back my earpiece. I glared at her, already seeing the story play out in my head. I placed it in my ear and immediately Sophia began a torrent of romantic babble.

"Oh sir, she is perfect. Once I explained who you were, what we do and how we approach our work, she completely understood. Do you know how devious she is? Did you know she planned on poisoning you and not giving you the antidote until you apologized and bowed before her?"

"Sophia, the point. Get there."

"Sorry, sir. I am such a hopeless romantic."

"I once watched you destroy an entire city."

"Well, did you see the color schemes they were using? But that's beside the point. Sir, she is good for you and good for us. I think you know why."

I looked at Lydia, who was still smiling like a goon. A self-satisfied, smug goon. "Yes. My assumption as well."

"Well, then stop jabbering with me, sir, and get this done."

"Agreed. Go to standby," I said, and I heard the line go dead.

"Where is Hawker?" I said, looking around. I nodded toward Wren and Carina and signaled them with a hand over my eyes in a searching gesture, then pantomimed a muscled simpleton, giving them my best Hawker impression. Wren shook his head while Carina held her hands up, not knowing.

Damn it.

"How should I rebuild the Bastards?" Lydia asked.

Her question was odd for several reasons. First, because it was not germane to the situation. Second, because it completely ignored what had transpired between us. Lydia inched closer to me, into the intimate zone people have.

"Supply and demand," I said absently. Something about how Gale Korva was looking around, or rather *not looking*, was bothering me. For an assassin clan leader, she should have been more wary.

"I don't understand," Lydia said.

"Hmm? Oh, recruit smarter members."

"I did that."

"Form a brotherhood. A sense of family."

"I did that."

"Poorly," I said while I watched.

"Hey," Lydia hissed. She snatched her hand out to grab ahold of my tabard. "Pay attention to me."

I looked at her hand, then into her eyes. "This new found *relationship* aside, you ever grab me like that again and I will be involved with a one-handed woman."

"You go on ahead and try," Lydia said. But she released me.

With that bit of business aside, I returned to watching Anders and her captains. "Your Bastards failed the way all small business do. You tried to grow too fast. You assumed that becoming bigger meant success. You allowed the impoverished in, along with their families, to create your illusion of family. After that, you let in refugees, which was ultimately your downfall. By doing so, you did not know your people, inside and out."

"Aren't you in this situation because you didn't know your people well enough?"

"... Yes," I agreed reluctantly. "A lesson we villains must learn over and over, it seems. But we are talking about your mistakes, not mine. Besides, in my realm, I am a god."

"You don't look too godly hiding in the rafters."

"Be silent, woman," I said while Lydia smiled. "As I was saying, you need to create a supply and a demand. You need to create two groups. The Forgotten Bastards, mercenary group, and a sub-contract company that attacks caravans, robs, and all such petty larceny. The Bastards then will stop said company of thieves, again your own men. Perhaps the ones you don't trust and don't mind having killed off. Regardless, once word spreads that the Bastards are performing a public service, they will be hired for other jobs. Jobs that involve stopping your own men. Thus, you control the crime and the protection in your region. But that is just an idea off the top of my head."

"That's ... brilliant," Lydia said, sounding surprised. "How many people can know about it?"

"In application? No more than three. You, as the leader of the Bastards, whomever you appoint as the leader of your thieves' guild, and me. But in principle, only one person. Since that is impossible, I suggest you keep the number low. Ben Franklin once said, 'Three men can keep a secret, provided two of them are dead.'"

"Who was he?"

"A wise, treacherous old villain from my world. He helped to found a country by advising the leaders but never serving in a position of actual leadership."

"He sounds formidable."

"He was. The lech even managed to manipulate a position as an ambassador to a country where the women were notorious for their sexual liberty. I am fairly sure he died of disease from his liaisons. What a way to go."

"Indeed. Well, do you have other great advice for an up-and-coming villain?"

"Yes. Learn to play dead," I said, scanning the room.

"Are you serious?"

"Yes. Playing dead, or at least unconscious, allows you gain intelligence you might not otherwise be privy to. Try it now. I could use the silence."

"You so love me," Lydia smirked.

"I am beginning to regret it. Now be quiet. Where the hell is Hawker?" I asked, my temper getting the better of me.

"Do you want to know?" General Anders's voice boomed though the great hall, answering my question.

Crap. We'd been made.

"See what you did? You should have been quieter. Perhaps play dead?" Lydia said with a self-satisfied smile.

My paramour was a bitch.

"Come down, little rats, and I'll show you the fate of your companion," she announced.

Steve placed his fingers in his mouth and made a sharp whistling sound. I'd always hated people who could do that. For all my power and reach, that was a skill I could never master.

The main hall was quickly flooded with armed guards in heavy plate armor. Their tromping and clanking echoed through the hall and bounced around in the rafters where my companions and I were. Each of the thirty or so guards were armed not just with swords, but also with crossbows. Each of the men aimed their weapons towards the rafters.

"I will not ask again," Anders said. She moved her hand over the table and a small oval portal opened behind her. Through the portal I could see two of her guards standing at the edge of lava pit. They had Hawker bound, his toes inches over the edge.

"Upon my orders, my men will cast your friend into the lava. Then, my guards will open fire and kill you all. Your move, Shadow Master."

They knew we were up here, but due to the poorly lit hall, they weren't sure exactly where. Perhaps we could use this to our advantage?

"How did they know we were here?" Lydia whispered in my ear.

"Because I told them," Carina said.

The half-dwarf dropped from the rafters all the way to the stone floor. She fell into an easy stance as if a twenty-five foot drop was nothing. She stood and smiled.

"Well done, my new servant."

"Your will be done, General," Carina said, bowing.

That hairy bitch just pulled a Lando Calrissian.

Chapter Thirty-Six

Where I Am Forced To Listen to Two Traitors and Plan a Counterattack While Not Moving

"He's weak," Carina said the moment my feet touched the ground after the climb down from the rafters. "He is low on his power. His thick-thief uses poison-coated knives. The ammalar is . . . surprisingly flexible for his age."

"You did the right thing, leaving that message for us at the beach," Steve said.

"You missed the note she carved in the prison wagon, directing us to the elven lands," Korva said.

"I missed nothing," Steve said.

"Enough," Anders said, silencing the captains. "At least she provided what my captains could not—results." The general looked both Steve and Gale Korva over as one looks at dogs who shit on the floor while you were away.

"I told you he would come here," Steve said. The former Marine would not back down to the giant woman's glare.

"You only knew that because the one called Courtney suggested it first upon his visit here," Korva corrected.

Steve glared at her, but the assassin paid him no mind. No doubt several members of the Night Fires were hidden in this very room, ready to move on her orders.

"Silence, both of you. I am in command here. Learn to follow or learn how to swim in a lake of molten rock," General Anders bellowed. "Carina of the Twilight Guard, you have earned a place of honor in my retinue. Name your reward and you shall have it, among countless riches."

"I seek no riches, General. I only wish the complete and utter decimation of The Twilight Guard. For their treachery upon me, I wish for their order to be wiped out to the last members and all records of them blotted out of history for all time to come."

God damn. That woman was vicious. Selling us out to get what she wanted? I'd be angry if I wasn't so impressed. She was this devious the whole time? Right under my nose? Was I slipping? Perhaps I had gotten too complacent. If I hadn't realized my moron of a sister was sleeping with my head of security and they were plotting against me, hence my current situation, then perhaps my judge of character was also now suspect.

"You bitch!" Hawker yelled from the other side of the portal.

"Oh please," Carina said to Hawker. "You bore me with your little sad stories. Oh no, my parents are dead, but my real father is the ruler of an entire empire. Just accept him and imagine what kind of power you could have."

"I can't believe I defended you," Wren said, sounding defeated.

"Be calm, lover, or else you may end up joining young master Hawker out there."

"Well said," Anders said, as she moved away from her desk to stand over Carina. "But I will have to dispense with Wren regardless. He betrayed me. And I cannot allow a traitor in my midst. Even a plaything."

Carina turned and bowed to General Anders. "Yes, General, I understand."

"Stand, Carina. You have proven yourself capable and ruthless."

"How do we know this isn't a trick?" Korva asked. "What if she is simply playing us?"

"Look at Jackson's eyes; he never saw this coming. No way this is a trick," Steve said.

"Silence, Captain Cooke. The women are talking," Anders said. "Carina, I would be remiss if I didn't ask why. Korva is correct. This could all be an elaborate deception."

"Because I figured you of all women knew what it was like to be considered a freak simply because you possessed strength. At first, I joined this group out of sense of adventure. I beg your pardon, General, but if I could be part of the movement to dethrone Baron Grimskull, then the power and fame that would come after would be immeasurable. But as we continued our adventure and after many captures, it was clear we were but children playing at a game for more powerful people. So I decided I wished to be on the winning side. And now that I stand proud as a half-breed woman, I refuse to hide who I am. Nor shall I hide my desire to dominate those weaker."

Oh, she's good.

"You are a rare gem in this disgusting world. But *never* refer to yourself as a half-breed again in my presence. You are a whole person. Strong and beautiful." The general nodded her head to her side. "Take your place."

Carina quickly moved to stand next to her and then the giant turned her attention to me.

"Well, Shadow Master, you gave us quite a little chase. The baron wants you back alive, but I am starting to think that is not possible. For all our best efforts, you managed to elude us. I applaud you for that."

"Thank you. Now I must warn you that you should very much consider letting us go."

"Why would I do that?" the general asked. "Look around. You are reduced to yourself, a broken-down old warrior who's protected by a fickle god, and a thief who appears to not miss many meals. You are surrounded by heavily armored guards with crossbows and Korva's Night Fires. What exactly is your brilliant escape plan?"

"I never said escape," I said. "I said you should let us go. You are far too beautiful a woman to die today. Hmm . . . unless you come back in a sequel?" I said, pondering the idea. Eventually I shrugged. "Regardless, this is not going to end well for you if you press the issue."

"Boss, what are you doing?" Sophia said in my ear.

"I am going to do nothing," I said, responding to both women. "I will do absolutely nothing. And in so, I am removing myself from the equation."

"What are you talking about?" both Sophia and General Anders said.

"No . . . NO!" Captain Cooke yelled. I turned my head towards him and smiled. He'd figured it out. Too bad Anders and the rest of them had not.

"Wren, would you be so kind as to wish these guardsmen health and prosperity?" I asked.

The ammalar of Vammar picked up on what I was alluding to.

Quickly, Wren raised his war hammer in the air, a nimbus of purple energy glowing like a beacon, and slammed the weapon to the stone floor, screaming "Blessings upon mine enemies!"

The hammer struck the stone and the room itself rocked as the energy from the will of Vammar was released through the room in a blinding flash. But only the forces of Anders were affected.

That's the nature of Vammar. Wren specifically blessed his enemies, so only his enemies received Vammar's curse. In that flash of brilliant light, crossbow strings snapped, armor shattered, and General Anders, along with all her allies, was blinded.

Except Carina. The crafty, hairy bitch just smiled as she quickly moved to Anders's magical table.

"Duck!" Carina shouted as she began swiping her hands over the instruments. Wren, Lydia, and I obeyed, throwing ourselves to the ground.

A dwarf's mind instinctively knows how machinery works, even magical machinery. The table appeared to be no different. In moments, small black discs of energy—Anders's transportation portals—appeared in midair among the blinded guards. Instead of appearing vertically, they were horizontal, parallel to the ground.

Carina swiped an instrument and all the portals widened and then closed in a flash, slicing the guards in half. What once was thirty armed guards was now sixty pieces of dying people. Blood pooled along the floor as soldiers died. The great hall was flooded with the screams of men and women who were quickly bleeding to death.

Carina had killed everyone in one quick action.

Almost everyone.

Captain Cooke had not been blinded. Traitor or not, he still belonged to me. And as my property, he was unaffected by the Curse of Vammar. The resourceful Marine had tackled General Anders to the floor, sparing her life.

Korva, on the other hand, was not so lucky, as she too was cut in half by one of the offensive portals. I watched her bleed out. The great assassin's eyes were in a state of shock and disbelief as she died. But at least that was a loose end tied up. If she lived, Hawker might question her about the murder of Alianna/Bethany.

The captain was to his feet in seconds while Anders remained blinded on the floor. Vaulting over a table, Cooke threw a vicious kick that connected to Carina's head. His armored leg carried with it additional weight that knocked the woman to the floor.

"I'll kill you!" Wren roared, swinging his war hammer with all his might at Cooke's chest. Had he connected, Wren would have crushed Steve's chest and killed him, barring any trickery by Vammar.

But Wren did not connect, because his target was a former Marine who was well trained in close combat tactics. Cooke turned with the blow and pulled the war hammer from the bigger man's grip. Continuing the motion, Cooke spun and slammed the hammer into Wren's kidneys, dropping the ammalar to his knees.

"Stupid fucking medieval combat bullshit. You've never fought one of the toughest warriors Uncle Sam ever created," Cooke taunted. He lined up his next shot, aiming the blow at Wren's unprotected head. If he connected, Wren's head would explode in broken skull, blood, and brains.

Cooke looked at me. "Call them off or he dies."

"I'll tell you what I told Anders, Steve. I won't do anything. But if you stop, you will live. Otherwise, you will die today."

"Wrong answer, motherfucker."

Cooke shifted his body into a batting stance. Pulling his arms back, Cooke began to swing the hammer, but as he did his foot stepped into the ever-growing pool of blood. He slipped slightly, losing his balance for just a moment.

And a moment was all it took was for Lydia to launch a poison-coated throwing dart across the space between them. Lydia's aim was true and the knife hit Cooke in his only unprotected spot, the head.

"OW!" Cooke screamed as he fell to the ground. It appeared that Lydia's throw, while accurate, wasn't strong enough to penetrate his thick skull. So only one half-inch of the small throwing dart was embedded into the bone along the top of Cooke's forehead.

"Ow ow ow! Goddamn it! Why the head?! Jesus Christ!" The former Marine screamed and writhed on the bloody floor.

"Nice shot," I said to Lydia, who came to stand next to me, watching Cooke try and pull the dart free.

"Thank you."

"You didn't kill him," I commented.

"Oh god, why the head?! It's in the bone! It's in the bone!" Cooke wailed.

"Oh shut up," Lydia told Cooke, then turned to me. "And I lost my heavy throwing knives saving you from Khasil."

"Ha!" Cooke yelled as he wrenched the dart free. He stood and pulled the sword on his hip.

"Hey Steve?" I said.

"What?!"

"That dart was poisoned."

"Oh shiiiiiii . . . " Cooke tried to say as his knees buckled. The armored man with a hole in his head collapsed and was asleep in seconds. His immediate snoring blew bubbles in the congealing blood on the floor. It was almost cute.

"Enough!" Anders roared as she drew herself up to her full height. With her eyesight returning, the giantess was once again on her feet and a power of her own. With a flick of her wrist, black clouds jetted from her bracelet. The clouds condensed and hardened, forming her giant mace, Coldfyr.

Anders brought the mace down onto her magical map table, splintering it. The broken wood simultaneously caught fire while freezing.

Damn. There went my plan to sneak into Chaud's tower. It was amazing (or contrived) that the portal to where Hawker was stayed open. The general began swinging the weapon around her head and was moving directly toward me.

An inconvenient thing, considering I had to stand perfectly still.

Chapter Thirty-Seven

Where I Witness the Fury of a Half-Dwarf and Ponder Vaginal Relativity

"You die!" General Anders boomed as she stomped towards me, knocking over tables and kicking corpses away.

Lydia threw two more of her throwing darts at the oncoming giantess, embedding the blades in her chest and the shoulder of her weapon arm. Anders simply ignored the attack. Her internal temperatures were growing and her skin began to glow, as her fire giant side was coming through.

The throwing darts melted away. With each step she took, the puddles of blood hissed as they evaporated from the heat she was generating.

Wren lunged in with his hammer, but the god-given weapon was turned away by Coldfyr. The dark magic contained within the weapon crackled and sparked when it came into contact with the hammer.

Anders reached out with her free hand and grabbed the ammalar by his armored shoulder pauldron and squeezed.

The armor squealed as her grip crushed it and the metal began to glow red. Wren screamed while Anders laughed. She tossed the smaller man aside like a child and continued her deliberate march toward me.

As she approached, Anders considered me. "You're not going to even try and run?"

"No," I said.

"Very brave and very stupid little man."

"Smarter than you," I said, trying to look as bored as I could.

"Somehow I doubt that. Goodbye, Shadow Master," Anders said as she reached back with Coldfyr, aiming to bring the weapon down directly on the top of my skull.

Hawker leaped from an overturned table, his hands still bound in chains, and brought his battleaxe down right between Anders's shoulder and bicep, severing her arm.

Anders and Hawker screamed, both from surprise and pain. Anders from losing her arm, Hawker from the gout of flame and burning blood that erupted from her stump of an arm.

During the confusion when Carina had opened the portals and killed the guards within the great hall, I had seen Hawker take advantage of the chaos and dispatch his guards, knocking them into the lava. The hero that he was, Hawker had retrieved his weapon and stalked the most dangerous target, waiting for the right moment to strike.

Hawker dropped the battleaxe and brought his hands to his face, where the fire-giant's blood had burned his face like acid.

Anders stood in shock, looking down at her arm on the floor while still holding her weapon. Her mouth hung open, and for once, she had nothing to say. Carina used the opportunity to teach Anders a lesson in physics.

Anders was of giant descent, which meant she was incredibly large and strong. But Carina was of dwarven stock. And while dwarves are strong, they are not giant strong, even half-giant. But dwarves are far more *dense*. All that power packed into a smaller package means they are like tungsten. Heavy and nearly unbreakable. When that much power and density decided to focus a shit-load of anger into a small fist and throw a punch into a heavier, yet less dense target . . . well, let's just say physics is a bitch.

General Anders's eyes widened in another wave of shock and pain. Each of Carina's punches was like a sledgehammer to the gut.

"You! Ruined! Everything!" Carina shouted each word with a haymaker punch into Anders's sternum, breaking the bone of the giant. The temperature that Anders was emitting didn't seem to register to the half-dwarf's fist. Her skin seemed blackened along the knuckles, but the ginger pugilist showed no sign of pain.

"I had a good life until you came along! When you attacked the Elder River Village, the Guard had to move out fast. My elvish captain woke me, and saw me in my bed. Not only did he see a female, but seeing me in my tent in my small clothes, he realized I was a dwarf. He commanded me to be gone, because gods saw me as an abomination. I lost everything!"

Carina punched Anders so hard, the giantess stumbled backwards into Hawker, who was still reeling from the burns to his face. The two of them fell through the portal that remained open, the one from which Hawker had been held captive by the two guards by the open lava pit.

"Carina, stop!" Lydia called out. The thief went so far as to jump onto Carina's back, but the stronger female simply shrugged the nuisance away.

"Everything I was was taken by you. And now, you threaten the only friends I've had since then. The only people who accept me for me!" Carina screamed, following Anders through the portal.

Carina, in a blind rage, did not see that Hawker too had tumbled through, and was once again back along the edge of the lava pit. She brought her burnt and bloody fist back once more, intending to finish the general once and for all.

Wren ran through the portal and grabbed Carina's wrist, stopping her. The half mad half-dwarf spun and kicked Wren in the groin, launching him several feet. He hit the ground with a painful *thump* and teetered dangerously close to the edge of the molten rock.

Carina turned her attention back to Anders, but the brief pause in her attack was all the time the general needed. With her good arm, Anders delivered a powerful, well-placed, open-handed blow that struck Carina in the temple and bowled her over. Anders winced and shook her hand.

"You're . . . good," the giantess puffed. "You would have gone far in my regime. But you have chosen the wrong side." Anders picked up her massive foot and aimed for the back of Carina's neck.

Wren dove and shielded Carina with his own body. The general's kick cracked several of his ribs along his back with a sickening pop. Wren screamed, but he refused to move.

"Stupid Wren. You could have fought by my side during the day and warmed my bed at night. Instead, you chose this . . . creature."

"At . . . at least . . . she has . . . a proportional vagina," Wren wheezed. I heard the bubbling sound in his voice. His lungs were filling up with blood.

"My vagina is perfect!" Anders screamed, bringing her foot up, ready to deliver her final blow to kill Wren and defend her apparently abnormal vagina.

Wren rolled over and whispered something I could not hear from where I stood, but it sounded like a prayer.

Anders's foot came down and was met by a domed shield of intense magical energy. The shield shone a brilliant pure blue.

The ammalar had made his choice.

And his god approved.

Wren held his defensive magic, protecting himself and Carina from his foe. Anders ground her boot down, trying to crush them both. But with each strike, a wave of blue-white light flashed under Wren's protective dome. And unless I missed my guess, the waves of energy were healing both Wren and Carina.

That clearly went unnoticed by the general, as her only mission was to try and grind them both into oblivion. But young Hawker had other ideas.

Hawker jumped up and looped the chains of his manacle around Anders's throat and pulled her back hard. The giantess struggled and fought back, reaching back with her one good arm, trying to find the smaller man.

Hawker held her tight, refusing to let go, but Anders refused to succumb to being choked out. The general was a force of nature. Despite Lydia's sleeping poison, broken bones, and missing an arm, she would not yield.

And Hawker knew it.

"General, I'm afraid I haven't properly . . . introduced myself," Hawker said through gritted teeth. "I am Kyle Hawker. The only survivor of the Elder River Village massacre. And while I wanted to destroy Grimskull for his actions, your death will bring my people the peace they need to move on in the afterlife."

Summoning all his remaining strength, Hawker pulled as hard as he could.

And that was when both Kyle Hawker and General Anders fell into a lake of molten lava and disappeared below the fiery surface.

True to my word, I never moved from my spot.

Chapter Thirty-Eight

Where I Sacrifice a Life to Save a Life

"Boss, that was incredible!" Sophia said in my ear.

"I know."

"How did you do all that?"

"I didn't. I just abused the rules."

"Sir?" Sophia asked.

"I've had a little time to reflect. And what I came to realize was that most of the adventures this little band was having followed the normal hero pattern with captures and escapes and all the normal tropes."

"Naturally, sir."

"But there are the pivotal moments in the stories, moments where the heroes have to save the day. And my presence here disrupts the flow. It was what Khasil and Valliar were trying to say without saying it directly. I am not of this world, so I disrupt that flow, causing events to unfold in ways that are not the norm. Hawker was meant to stop Grimskull and I altered that part of the pattern. Wren and Carina were more than likely meant to be heroes, and Lydia was supposed to fall under the will of Khasil or else die. But by bringing them all together, I've created a new pattern. So if I wanted to win, I had to do absolutely nothing directly. I had to let the heroes do what they do best."

"A big gamble, sir," Sophia commented.

I shook my head. "Gambling is for idiots who do not have the foresight to rig the game, Sophia."

"What of Hawker?"

"What of him?" I said. "He did his job."

"Sir, if I may," Sophia said, choosing her words, "he didn't. If Hawker was meant to stop Grimskull, and you removed him from the pattern, it interrupted everything. When you put him back on that path, the pattern corrected itself. Now, he's dead. Doesn't his absence mean that the pattern will now . . . I don't know . . . collapse?"

Hmm. She had a point. Sophia was a creature who had seen her share of heroes fail over the millennia. Mostly by her own actions. She really loved to screw over would-be heroes and thieves.

Regardless, that didn't make her incorrect. The gods wove their pattern in with fluid strokes. If a problem arose, the pattern would flow around it like a river around a rock. But if a piece was missing, then the flow would cease, causing unexpected, and potentially horrid, consequences in random places.

I know, because it is what I do to them all the time. But now that I was riding that flow, involved in the pattern, the matter became personal. The very pattern could now turn on me. Well, continue to turn on me. Hmm . . . that could be bad.

But what could I do?

Oh.

Of course.

Valliar, you tricky bastard.

The god did not like me; that was clear. But he still wanted his plans seen through. He wanted tyranny, and thus villainy, to fall. While that grieved me, I too wanted it to happen. But on my terms.

So it appeared that in this, Valliar and I were allies.

Hence, his gift.

I crossed the bloody floor of the great hall, pausing only to pick up Coldfyr. The mace reduced in size to match my body type. With a mental command, the weapon reverted back to smoke, only to reform as a cold black bracelet around my wrist.

Nodding at the fit, I walked through the portal into the open lava pit. The cavern was similar to the one where we first entered the keep. Lydia, Wren, and Carina knelt by the lava pit. They openly wept at the loss of their companion.

It was annoying.

"Move," I demanded.

"Jackson, what are you doing?" Carina asked.

"What I must. Go, fetch me the sleeping captain."

"Why?" Lydia asked.

"If you wish Hawker to live, do not ask questions. Move."

"You can . . . bring him back?" Lydia asked.

"Impossible. Even Vammar cannot bring back the dead," Wren said.

I looked at the ammalar and let a small strand of my power touch his mind. Not to alter it, or bend it to my will, but to allow him an awareness of my capabilities.

"Do what he says," Wren said, getting to his feet and moving back slightly, his body reacting with fear towards me.

Good.

Holding out my hand, I opened myself to my limited store of power, trying to use it as efficiently as possible. Reaching out with my senses, I searched the lava for a particular item. A homing beacon of sorts. One that could not be destroyed by the lava, nor any item under creation.

The gift from a god.

There.

I sensed the little black obsidian candleholder given to me by Valliar. The lava began to bubble and then ripple. Swirling red and black, the lake of fire bent to my will as I used my power to bring the candleholder, and its bearer, up from the liquid hell.

"Gods above and below," Wren gasped.

The charred body of Kyle Hawker floated there in midair, turning slowly as the remains of the lava dripped from him. Considering his time in the lava pit, his body was surprisingly well preserved. The gift of Valliar had kept most of his body intact.

But it was not enough to save his life.

Not directly, anyway.

Through my power, I could sense what was the soul of Hawker now stored within the very volcanic rock-shaped candleholder in his pouch, protecting it. It was fitting that the little holder of light was deemed a gift by the god to hold the light of life.

But his soul could not return to its body. Not in that condition. So I had to give a life to save a life. And since I owned none of my companions, I instead turned to the one life I did own.

Captain Steve Cooke's.

Carina returned with the drugged captain slung over her shoulders. With my other hand, I reached out and sent a wave of my power into Cooke. His body jerked and then rose into the air. Carina jumped back, afraid.

Then I made the conscious decision to end Steve's life.

His body began to burn and wither while Hawker's body began to regenerate in waves of golden energy. The charred skin was now turning back to light brown. His armor was again filling back out. In moments, my servant-turned-traitor was a burnt husk of blackened meat.

Kyle Hawker of the Elder River Village took a sweet, deep breath of life.

I released Hawker while dropping the corpse of the late Captain Cooke into the lava. His remains sizzled and disappeared.

"What . . . what happened?" Hawker said. "Am I . . . alive?"

In response, Wren, Lydia and Hawker hugged their friend and ally. Their reunion was joyous. They had accomplished a great feat together. And I did not want to ruin their happiness. I'm a villain, not an asshole.

Besides, it was best not to tell them the only reason I brought Hawker back was because I didn't want the rules of the realm to turn on me before I could finish my mission and get back to my own realm.

I looked at my phone. Down to 22% power. The large power drain was necessary. Power used to keep me alive and safe was always worth it.

I walked back through the portal into the great hall, surveying the damage. The stone floor was one large puddle of blood. The walls and what was left of the furniture was practically coated in it.

I turned to look at the magical table. It was beyond amazing that when Anders smashed it, the one portal we needed to kill her stayed open. In fact, it was downright improbable bordering on impossible. The whole thing stank of lazy and contrived writing. And I am not just referring to fantasy novels and most JJ Abrams movies. This was . . . divine intervention.

For just a brief moment, out of the corner of my eye, I swore I saw Valliar there. The phantom image of the god smirked, mimed tipping a cap, and then was gone.

"I think I'm starting to like you," I said aloud.

"Jackson, who are you talking to?"

"Apparently myself," I said to Hawker. I turned to look at the young man. "Welcome back."

"I . . . I don't know what to say."

"Say nothing. Don't ruin the perfectly awkward moment with words."

Hawker reached out and hugged me.

Gross.

But I hugged the young warrior back.

I'd most likely have to kill him later anyway. Best to let him still consider me a friend.

Chapter Thirty-Nine

Where I Check on the Recently Deceased and Deal with Steve

I released the hug and regarded him with as earnest a smile as I could muster. Then, Hawker looked at me with an odd curiosity.

"Who's Steve?"

"Excuse me?"

"Steve? I keep hearing a voice. He says his name is Steve and he wants to talk to you?"

"Oh, that. May I?" I reached into Hawker's pouch and held the small obsidian candleholder.

"Alianna's candleholder?"

"It was what held your life while I healed your body. But there were some . . . side effects. Please, go sit and rest. I will take care of it."

"But the holder," Hawker said. "It's all I have left of her."

"No," I said shaking my head. "You have all you need of her inside you."

I turned and walked through the portal, back into the volcanic chamber. As I passed the rest of my allies, I paused.

"Look after him; he is hearing things."

"Thank you," Carina said, while Lydia and Wren nodded in agreement.

"You are welcome," I said. "I will be there in a moment. There is something I have to do. In the meantime, Carina, please look over the table and see if you can make it work again. There is a portal I need to be opened."

"You got it."

I walked to the edge of the lava pit. Once I was alone, I held the candleholder in my hands.

"How's it going in there, Steve?"

"God, I hate you," I felt Steve say from within the obsidian.

"It's mutual," I said. "But this is fitting. For your betrayal, you deserve a prison."

"You left me here to rot."

"No, I gave you a job and you betrayed me. Now be quiet. I am waiting."

"Waiting for what?"

"Shh."

I set Steve the Candleholder down in the ground and stared into the lava. I waited for the inevitable cliché.

The blackened and burned yet living General Anders burst forth from the lava.

Dumping a fire-giant, even a half-breed, into hot lava? My companions were idiots.

General Anders swiped a large hand towards me. I stepped aside easily. Her bloody and burned clawed hand gripped the edge of the pit and she began to pull herself free. The molten rock dripped from her as she hauled herself, inch by inch, out of the lava.

"Sorry. I've watched far too many movies to think the enemy was dead without checking."

I commanded the black metal bracelet to form Coldfyr in my hand. I wound up and swung for the fences. The mace connected with Anders's head, breaking her skull. I followed the swing with another and another until the only thing that was left of her once-beautiful face was bloody brains and burned pulp.

With that done, I commanded the mace away and kicked her corpse back into the lava. I then picked Steve the Candleholder back up from the ground.

"What are you going to do?"

"What I have to."

"I will serve you! Please don't," Steve pleaded.

I looked at Steve the Candleholder once more and considered him. Perhaps it would be nice, keeping him around? A sarcastic voice to talk to from time to time, if nothing more than comedy relief?

Nah.

There were enough ridiculous literary heroes and anti-heroes in the fantasy realms who abused the spirit-in-an-object motif. It was becoming the norm and boring.

I absently tossed Steve into the lava.

I heard him scream one last time. It made me smile.

Especially since that little candleholder was a gift from Valliar and would last for all time, impervious to lava.

A suitable prison for the ex-Marine who forgot to be forever faithful to his master.

Semper fi, motherfucker.

The Fifteenth Rule of Villainy

A villain will always assess everything
and everyone for a net gain.

Chapter Forty

Where We Question Carina, I Dodge a Bullet, and We Move on to Chaud

"Can you make it work?" I asked Carina.

"It's amazing that even that one portal stayed open," Carina said as she inspected what was left of the magical table. "I might be able to make it work, but I don't think a new portal will stay open for long."

"I don't need it to. We just need the one location."

"Chaud's?" Wren asked.

"Yes. Chaud's," I confirmed. Now that the action was over, I got a look at the ammalar. His armor was now completely blue, all the red washed away. He and his armor had been reforged as Vammar willed it. Neither the armor nor the man was marked by Anders's touch.

Wren, conflicted, ever walked the path of warrior and defender. The former father and family man who turned to a life of violence had found his calling as a protector. No longer would he be an ammalar, an undecided disciple of the fickle god. Wren was now a Templar of Vammar. One of his chosen who defends the weak.

I was hoping he would return to being bloodthirsty. Besides red being a better color for him, I had no real use for a heroic champion. When this was done, so would be my need of him.

While I was on that train of thought . . .

"That was quite devious of you, Carina," I said with actual respect.

The half-dwarf smiled while she worked on the table. "I thought you would like that."

"For a moment, I thought you were actually betraying us," I said. "You were very convincing."

"I was living a lie while in the Twilight Guard. Acting as someone and something I was not is essentially lying. And I've had years of practice."

That was a very good job of dodging the issue. Perhaps there was something to cultivate within her.

"Your plan went back as far as when we were captured by Anders's forces and locked in that rolling prison cart?" Wren asked.

"That's some foresight you have there," Lydia said.

"We were all mocking Jackson after we learned that he was the Shadow Master. Hawker had expressed a darkness within himself and how he never wanted to be like that. I even said something to ridicule him. But when Hawker mentioned the elves, I was afraid. The Twilight Guard was, after all, a group led by elves and based on elvish principles. Since they had discovered me and abandoned me, I saw it all happening all over again."

Carina stood and checked the desk again, trying to set pieces of wood back into place. "I'd found a loose nail in the cart, and was holding on to it as my only weapon. Guard training never really leaves you. But with the elves coming, I took the time to scratch a note in the wood. 'Anders, we've been taken to the whispering woods. A half-breed ally.'"

"So you planned to betray us?" Lydia asked.

Carina nodded. "For a moment, yes. But during the trial, when I was exposed and none of you judged me for what or who I am, then no. I decided I'd never betray you. So when we got to the island, I used that time to leave another note behind detailing that we were here. I kept it a secret and used it as a last chance should we be captured. You couldn't know in case we were captured and you had to act shocked."

Inside, I was fucking applauding.

"I don't have an issue with this, but I am a confessed villain. So do any of you trust her less?"

"I'm the leader of a thieves' guild," Lydia said. "Or I was."

"I use what I need to finish my quest," Hawker said.

"Trust less? Perhaps. Love less? No," Wren rumbled.

Chaotic Neutral, True Neutral, and Chaotic Good. I felt the dice practically rattling in my head.

"OK, I think it will work now," Carina said, finishing her work on the portal table.

"Excellent," I said.

I looked over the table and moved my hand over the remaining water. The map moved. Slowly and with great distortion within the water, but it moved. The device was like a computer tablet back in the real world. I scrolled to the location that Zachariah gave. A small island off the east coast miles away from Grimskull's capital. A desolate and small place.

The open portal behind me swirled as I moved the map. Place after place spun by as a magical hole in space-time tore through the scrolling map locations. I settled on the targeted island. The portal showed what looked like the inside of a tower, a circular stone room complete with rows upon rows of bookshelves. The cold stone floors were covered in exotic animal furs and expensive tapestries hung on the walls.

It looked like the place. But there was only one way to find out.

I looked up at my companions. "Are you all ready?"

Lydia had replenished her knives from the bodies of the dead guards and was now carrying a small sword across her back along with a crossbow. As she strapped on several quivers full of crossbow bolts, she gave me a nod.

Carina smiled as she twirled her battle staves, while the newly christened Templar Wren stood ready with his hammer and shield.

"All right," I said, addressing them all. "It wasn't that long ago we were strangers. And since we've allied ourselves together, we have been through a lifetime of adventure. We've fought together. Been captured and escaped multiple times. Relationships have been formed and secrets have been revealed. For that and so much more, I thank you. We accomplished an incredible feat today, bringing down the military arm of Baron Grimskull. The majority of his troops are either trapped on this island or wandering aimlessly around the empire without centralized leadership. We have defeated his brawn. Now, we move on to the brains. Chaud is a powerful mage. When we get in there, we must be quick and show no quarter. Do not give him a chance to cast his magic. From there, we move on to Grimskull himself. Are you all ready?"

"Aye," my companions said in unison.

"Then let's go. Gods above and below be with us, or else get the fuck out of the way."

We moved quietly through the portal and walked into Chaud's tower.

And right into a trap.

The moment we entered, lightning crashed all around us. The floor literally glowed with burning arcane symbols, and gale force winds and rain ripped through tower. All of us were gripped by unseen waves of magic and slammed hard against the walls.

Books and loose parchment flew around in the miniature indoor hurricane. The whole scene was a cross between *The Exorcist* and *The Wizard of Oz*. Which was fitting. As Chaud entered the room, he looked like the wicked witch in his black robes and demon-possessed by the look in his eyes. The really disturbing part was that none of the wind or the storm seemed to affect him at all. His robes hung loosely as he casually walked.

The thin, bald man came to stand before us. His disinterested eyes looked us over, and with a slight smile on his thin lips, he addressed me first.

"Shadow Master, if I could have a moment of your time, please. We need to talk."

Chapter Forty-One

Where I Have Polite Villain-to-Villain Discourse and Enjoy a Glass of Wine

Chaud, Archmage of Baron Martin Viktor Grimskull, sat calmly as a small table he conjured from thin air and enjoyed a tumbler of port.

"This was your juvenile plan? Break into my tower and do what? Kill me?"

When you say it out loud, it does lose some of its luster. "Yes!" I yelled.

"What?" Chaud asked, turning his ear towards me.

"Turn off the storm so we can talk?! Just a suggestion!" I yelled over the howling winds while random wet bits of paper kept smacking me in the face.

"Oh, yes. My apologies."

The winds and rain stopped. The burning arcane symbols winked out. But my companions, and more importantly I, remained pinned against the curved stone wall of the tower.

"There, that is better. Now, where were we? Oh yes, your premeditated murder of me. So, now that you are here, and conditions being what they are, what is your plan?"

"We both know I can free myself. And that I can destroy you," I said.

"I do. But I also know it would greatly deplete your ever-dwindling supply of power."

Damn it.

"Don't look surprised," Chaud said. "I've learned so much about you ever since your sister moved into Grimskull's castle."

"Paige . . . has moved in?"

"Yes. Your sister has been taken as Viktor's latest . . . consort."

I imagined the worse. Her sense of design alone was criminal. Let alone her incessant chatter in her shrill voice. I could just see her now, asking everyone why they had never heard of the Kardashians.

"Is it as bad as I imagine?"

"Worse," Chaud said as he sipped his port. "But between her braying and mewling, I learned quite a bit about you, your power, and the world you come from. I see now why you are here and why you do what you do."

"Jackson, are we seriously having a polite discussion about this?" Hawker asked.

I rolled my eyes. "Apparently so. Please be quiet now. Apologies, Chaud. My young comrade is ill versed in the ways of civilized discourse."

"Understood. Considering his parentage, I am surprised he has remained silent for this long."

"You knew Grimskull was his sire?" Wren asked from his position along the wall.

"Disciple of Vammar, there is next to nothing I do not know about what transpires in the Eastern Empire. The only reason the empire remains whole and functional, such as it is, is due to my considerable efforts."

"What is it you want from us then?" Lydia asked. "Since we are still alive, it only stands to reason that you need something that you think we can deliver."

Chaud looked at Lydia, then at me. "Your training?"

"I'd like to take credit, but Madam Barrowbride has an incredible mind. She is adept in the ways of thinking as we do. And she has a point."

"Indeed," Chaud agreed. "While I am not pleased with the death of General Anders, her battlefield blood lust and bullish blustering will not be missed. With her no longer in the way, I will have a better control over the empire's forces. Which is why you are still alive. I want to know, right here and right now, what your plan for Grimskull is. And, if you lie, I will know."

"Jackson?" Carina said with hesitance in her voice.

"Be at ease, Carina," I said.

This was moment where, once again, honesty was required. If Chaud was angling the way I think he was, then telling the truth very well might set us free.

Or have us incinerated. Life is its most thrilling when death is a gambling variant.

"My intent, in all honesty, is to remove Baron Viktor Grimskull from the throne of the Eastern Empire, by any means necessary, for no other reason than he dared to double cross me. After which I will turn my sights on my misguided family and remove their presence from the realms, and quite possibly, from this mortal coil. When those actions are complete, I will place Zachariah, the elder brother, on the throne. He will serve until Kyle Hawker, the heir apparent, is ready to assume his birthright. I imagine both leaders require a magical adviser who served the empire and seeks to further its glory in expansion, rather than hold together the plaything of a tyrannical child."

"Excellent," Chaud said.

Instantly, all of us were released from his magical grip and we fell to the tower's floor. I stood and dusted myself off, looking over my companions who likewise checked themselves over. I saw no apparent injuries. Only wounded pride, my own included.

I walked towards Chaud, who remained seated. He looked up at me and held up a second glass.

"Port?"

I almost laughed. "Please."

As Chaud poured the dark wine, a second chair manifested itself and I took a seat.

"What of my companions?" I asked. "Surely they deserve refreshments."

"Are you sure you're the Shadow Master I've heard so much about? That particular person isn't overly concerned with such niceties."

"That person is a myth. The real Shadow Master considers all who work for, and with, him as valuable. That includes future associates, Archmage Chaud."

Chaud nodded and his thin lips curled back in a smile. A table manifested for Wren, Carina, and Lydia, complete with food and wine.

"Thank you," I said.

Chaud held out his glass, and I raised mine. Together we clinked the tumblers.

"To your success," Chaud said and then drank.

"This is . . . it?" Wren asked. "A polite meal and wine?"

"You expected more?" Chaud asked.

"Well, yes?" Carina said. "Considering everything we went through with Anders, this is rather . . . "

"Anti-climatic?" Chaud offered.

"Exactly!"

"You complain too much," Lydia said. "Never turn away free food or wine."

"Do you ever think beyond your base desires?" Carina asked.

"Clearly, you have never been poor," Lydia said as she tore into Chaud's provided bounty.

"If you prefer, we could resume where we left off," Chaud offered. "With you pinned on the wall like insects while I unleashed the power of a miniature storm upon you."

"No, that is OK," Carina said.

"I thought so. You have to understand, I have served the empire for a long, long time. Before the Grimskull familial line was in power, I was here, guiding the land to greatness. I saw both great and weak rulers come and go. The only thing that endured is Chaud."

That last line gave me pause. Chaud was clearly more than an average human with magic. Mages could expand their lives a great deal, but the way Chaud spoke, it was reminiscent of something older—and far more sinister.

I believed he was, at least partly, from the Never Realm. But as much as I wanted to talk shop, we had to finish what we started.

"Archmage, I request that you house us for the remainder of the evening. Come tomorrow, we will infiltrate Grimskull's castle and put an end to his reign, once and for all."

"Agreed. You may use my tower as you see fit. Please, do not rush. Devise your stratagem well. Take a few days. But be warned." Chaud paused. "He may seem like a buffoon, but Viktor is not an idiot. His martial prowess and his power gained from the Never Realm make him formidable. He has recruited from the shadow races to reinforce his guards at the behest of the one you call Courtney. Goblins, Orcs, Dark Elves, and all manner of filth now patrol his home and the streets of Al' Garrad."

"Can't you just create a portal inside his castle?" Hawker asked. "Surely that is how you travel from here to there."

"It is," Chaud said.

"You will not help us?" Lydia asked.

"No, Madam Barrowbride, I will not. In fact, I will most likely be forced to hinder you when the time comes. Please understand, it is business. Should you fail, I do not wish to have committed occupational suicide. A device very similar to the one used by Anders is on the level above this one in my study. That should allow you access to the city. From there, you are on you own."

Chaud stood and finished his wine. Setting down the tumbler, he spoke to us all. "Now, would you be so kind as to threaten me with horrific physical violence and perhaps a display of power?"

"Why?" Hawker asked.

"Because in order to explain, truthfully, to Grimskull, Chaud must say that we infiltrated his tower, fought him, and from the power displayed by us, he felt he needed to retreat to Grimskull's castle. At least, phrased in a way it would pass a lie detection incantation," I said.

"I do not know what you mean," Chaud said with a smile.

It was so nice to work with a professional villain again. It seriously warmed my heart to know that civilized discourse was still a viable option. Of course, what Chaud was hinting at indirectly was that once he left here, he would flee to his "master" and tell him that he was attacked. Chaud would then detail us and our abilities and naturally inflate them a touch. Grimskull would not believe he was overpowered otherwise. So Grimskull would then increase his defenses. After that, anything he did would be unpredictable.

For now, formalities must be seen to. "Chaud, I will destroy you. I will use my great and terrible power to rip you apart and send a portion of your soul back to the Never Realm from whence it came. Flee now, and you may survive another day," I said in pro forma.

I used a fraction of my power to make golden energy dance between my fingers. Chaud saw it and nodded. He cleared his throat and recited the required words. "No. Please. Do not destroy me. Oh, I must flee. Oh, thou art the great and terrible Shadow Master."

Chaud stood and raised his arms. A portal appeared behind him and he stepped through. Before the portal closed, he paused.

"Please, leave my home in the manner in which you found it."

I managed a look of mock offense. "I'm a villain, not a savage."

Chapter Forty-Two

Where I Have a Heart-to-Heart with Hawker and Consider My Grandmother's Cryptic Adage

After we finished our meal, my companions and I laughed and drank, enjoying a brief reprieve from our normal activities. Strategies were discussed, but none seemed plausible. I needed to consider our options and our resources.

So, after our merriment, we retired to the guest rooms Chaud had prepared within the tower. For a narrow wizard's tower on a tiny, desolate island in the middle of the sea, the rooms were very spacious and luxurious. Obscenely so. Chaud must have been experimenting with pocket dimensions to give his tower added space.

My own guest room was nothing short of monolithic. Of course, Lydia insisted we share.

"What to do, what to do?" Lydia said as she circled the ornate canopy guest bed, running her hands along the dark engraved wood. "All this time on our hands before we go into battle and possible death. If only there was something we could occupy our time with."

Lydia flashed me a playful smile as she crawled onto the bed. She moved like a coquettish predator. She made sure that as she crawled on all fours, the cut of her shirt was low enough to give me a view of her ample cleavage.

"Life-threatening and incredibly dehydrating sexual liaisons aside, I still must formulate a plan to infiltrate Al' Garrad, defeat my former head of security who knows far too many of my tactics, and destroy Grimskull himself while wrestling power away from my idiot sister and reestablishing my dominance as the Shadow Master."

"Wanna do it in the butt?"

"I've got twenty minutes."

****

Several hours later, I stood on an outside terrace overlooking the cold Nameless Sea. I smoked a cigarette and let my mind wander.

I thought of what was before us.

What was behind us.

The challenges we had yet to face.

The throbbing pain in my ass.

Lydia's devious trap for sexual gratification was set so perfectly, I hadn't realized I was to be on the *receiving* end as well as she. But as my senile grandmother used to say, "Anything up to the second knuckle is just playful curiosity." Sadly, Grandmother's adage about bodily exploration neglected to dictate how many digits at once.

As always, a small tryst turned into something more. Rubbing at my wrists, I was thankful that this time, the bondage contained fewer knives. Not to say that none were involved, just fewer of them.

The sound of someone's shoes on the stone brought me back to the present.

"Jackson," Hawker said as he approached.

"Hawker. How are you this evening?"

"I am well. I'm surprised you're even standing. Madam Barrowbride can be . . . vocal."

I smiled. "That she can."

"And vulgar."

"Yes," I agreed.

"Obscenely descriptive and commanding."

"I get it," I said, growing intolerant of Hawker's jibes. "You heard us."

"I'm pretty certain the entire tower heard you two. As did all the local marine life and most likely the god of the sea, Nhal himself."

"I am growing to dislike you, Hawker."

"Are we going to live?" Hawker asked, his voice growing sober.

"I believe so, yes."

"How can you be sure?"

"I know the rules."

"You say that a lot," Hawker said. "What does it mean?"

"Just that I have an understanding of the universe. If I move correctly, we will all survive."

"You sound like Zachariah. He too spoke in riddles."

"You miss him?" I asked as I flicked my cigarette over the balcony and into the ocean.

Hawker stared over the water, watching the cigarette fall. "Sometimes, yes. He found me. He trained me. He gave me a purpose. I went on that quest thinking I was on the side of righteousness. Now, thanks to you and everything we've done, I learned that Zachariah was not only my uncle, but the brother to my real father, Grimskull. I guess I was being groomed to remove my father to make room for my uncle the whole time. I was a pawn."

"Do you want to be?" I asked, lighting another cigarette. I offered one to Hawker, who took it and eyed it warily. "Relax, it won't kill you. Well, eventually, but that's beside the point. Consider it a gift."

I lit the smoke for Hawker, who held it all wrong as he tried to inhale.

"Give me that. You're not an adolescent European food critic," I said, taking it from him and placing it correctly in his hands. "There, that's better. Small puffs until you get the hang of it."

"No, I don't want to be a pawn. And that means yours also, Jackson."

I smiled. "You're referring to what I said to Chaud."

"Yes."

"Hawker . . . Kyle, I meant what I said. The Eastern Empire can be yours to do with as you see fit. You may rule as a kind and benevolent leader. Or as a tyrant. Both are within your blood. But that is the duality of all men. The good and the bad."

"So says the master villain."

"Yes. But I am a villain because I choose to be one. I like subverting the rules. I like making others dance to my plans. But you don't have to choose that path if you don't want to. Yes, your father is a villain. But more than that, he is evil. He enjoys the suffering of others, whereas I do not. Your mother, however, is a descendant of The Eld, the most technologically advanced and benevolent people this realm has ever seen. You could be the one who ushers in a new golden age of human advancement. If you choose."

"I need time to think it over."

"Of course. I need time to plan our next move," I said.

"That device of Chaud's," Hawker said. "The one that generates portals."

"What about it?"

"Can it make one to go back to my village?"

"Back to the Elder River Village? I suppose. But why?" I asked.

"I think that is where I need to think. Give me a few days there and then come for me. Regardless of my decision, I will help you bring down my . . . father."

"Go then. We will come for you in a few days. Here. Take a few of these. You seem to like them," I said as I passed Hawker a few of my cigarettes.

"Thank you, Jackson. For being honest."

"You are welcome. See you in a few days."

Hawker left and I smiled. This level of self-doubt and vulnerability was like catnip to a villain. I had to consider my words carefully. If I pressed too hard, he would think I was working an angle, which I was. If he decided to take the throne he would learn, like all rulers do, that power corrupts.

And every ruler needs an adviser.

Of course, I did promise Zachariah the throne. But I never said for how long.

"Jackson," I heard Lydia call out. "If I have to come out there to get you, I'm just going to throw you over the rail. Now get back in here."

Well, I could think of worse things to be than the plaything of a homicidal sex fiend. I waddled back to the bedroom with as much grace and dignity as my violated anus allowed me.

Chapter Forty-Three

Where I Put My Plan into Action and Receive a Threat

Several days later, we all sat in Chaud's study, by his portal table. "Is everyone clear on the plan?" I asked.

"Nope."

"No, sorry."

"No."

"Which part? I really wasn't listening," Lydia said.

I wiped my face and imagined murdering each of them in turn. If this was the level of competence I was expecting for this final assault, I may as well resign myself to being Randy's "bro-migo" for the rest of my life.

I envisioned myself as a club-going middle-aged man in hipster clothing. I could just see myself with multiple scarves, purple-tinted horn-rimmed glasses, a patchy beard, an ironic t-shirt, and a fedora.

Oh lord, I was Johnny Depp.

I shuddered at my possible future.

Seriously, what man needs that many scarves, bracelets, and rings to go out?

Lydia led the rest of my allies in a chorus of laughter. "Oh Jackson, you should see your face. Of course we understand the plan. We just thought it would be amusing to mess with you."

"I hate you all," I said as I sat at Chaud's portal table in his private study and lit a cigarette. "So, there are no questions? Once this starts, everyone must play their part perfectly."

"I have a question," Carina said.

"Yes?"

"What happens when this is over?"

"What do you mean?" I asked.

"What happens to you? To us? Will we ever see you again?"

"I don't know. Perhaps the fans will demand a sequel."

Once again my comrades looked at me like I just spoke Greek. I had a choice. Tell them the painful truth or lie. The truth was simple. It was the reality where I go back to my world and continue living like an obscenely rich god-king, bending every law to my will. Or I could just lie, and make them feel better.

"The universe is a giant place. And very easy to get lost in," I said, taking the time to look each of them in the eye. "But with how we all came together? How we all accomplished so much in such a short amount of time? Most assuredly we will all meet again, my friends."

Carina smiled. "I believe you."

Yeah, the lie was the better option.

Oh, don't look at me like that. People lie to each other all the time. Your parents lied to you just like you'll lie to your kids.

Your puppy or kitty is dead and not living upstate at a farm.

Santa Claus is a fabrication.

And yes, she faked her orgasm. Hopefully, your parents didn't tell you that one.

See? All the classics.

Lies make people feel better. People always, *always*, deep down know the truth in virtually every situation. But the lie is what makes them feel accepted, normal, and functional.

"Well, when I do see you all again, we will either be victorious or dead. My vote is victory," I said.

"Until then, Jackson," Hawker said as he stepped through the portal. He was the first part of the plan.

"This is going to be insane," Lydia said. "I love it. See you soon, lover."

Lydia stepped through her portal, but not before she slapped me on my behind. As much as I wanted to be angry, I just smiled. That vivacious brigand was becoming almost too close. But if I got rid of her, Sophia would butcher me.

"My turn," Carina said. "I don't like this. But I'll do it."

"I know, Carina. But you stand proud and strong. Never forget who you are. You are the dwarf who punched out a giant."

That made Carina smile. She walked through her portal and vanished. Which left me alone with Wren.

The Templar stood in front of his portal but did not move.

"Jackson, there is something we need to discuss first."

Oh lord. Did these people not know we were on a very tight schedule? But in making sure my plan was completed, I had to ensure my moving pieces were in place. Mentally and physically.

"And what do you feel we need to discuss?" I asked.

"A while back, you threatened to tell Hawker my secret. You knew that I was there the night his village burned."

"Yes, I did threaten that. And I did know you were involved. Are you going to ask me how?"

"No." Wren shook his head. "It's obvious you just know things. But there is something I know."

"Which is?"

"You were behind Hawker failing his mission. You stole the Amulet of the Ember Soul. You gave it to Grimskull."

"I don't know what you are talking about," I lied.

"In the Crossroads Inn you said you had spies in Grimskull's castle. And that you saw the amulet."

"I did."

"That amulet was a legend the guards used to talk about. I know, since I was one. No one had ever heard of it, let alone knew where it was. But you knew about it. You knew where it was located. You knew it was retrieved. You knew it was stolen. And you could properly identify the amulet. How? Unless you were behind it. If Grimskull was one of your Shadow Master clients, then you organized it all. And that was when you were betrayed. That was when you began this quest."

"Do you have a point?" I said. For my cold outward appearance, I was simultaneously excited that someone had a mind and pieced it all together, while also trying to quell the growing dread that I'd been sloppy.

The feeling was exhilarating. Every thief will tell you that the fear of getting caught is an incredible rush. They are addicted to that as much as to stealing itself.

"Only this: Do not hurt that boy. Fate has deemed him a hero. Me? I'm just an old bastard who's found a better way. But I sure as damnation can spot another scoundrel. I only tell you this as a warning. If you harm him, I won't just expose you—I'll kill you."

"Templar Wren, there is nothing I can say to you that will sway you one way or the other. I just ask you look back on my deeds and see every time I saved us. Every time I held the group together."

"Those were the same things I told myself to justify my own actions when I was in General Anders's service. Amazing what a man can justify when it means his soul is damned. But I will offer you a bit of advice. It is never too late to walk away from it all. And when you do, your heart feels the freedom of all the pain it has suffered under. All the pain you didn't realize you were carrying is washed away."

"Just do your fucking job."

Wren held my gaze for a moment longer than necessary, then stepped through the portal.

Pompous born-again hero.

But I found myself smiling.

Not only did I find a surprising adversary in the old warrior, but I also learned a nifty little speech I could add to my repertoire. Surely I could turn those words into something I could abuse. Perhaps convince someone to do bad things in my name?

The next part of the plan was the most difficult for my allies, but the easiest for me.

I had to wait in Chaud's tower for three days. Being the brains of the operation is so hard sometimes.

I kept myself occupied by reading through several books in the Archmage's library and running through any potential obstacles to the plan. But in the end, there was boredom. I assumed it was the waiting. But in truth, it was my missing the simpletons who I called my allies. Over the last few weeks, bonds had been forged between us.

And I was having difficulty, as a villain mastermind, separating my personal attachment from my professional one. If I had to end them, could I do it?

Of course I could. But I may actually feel regret.

For an hour or two, at least.

But perhaps, just perhaps, I could turn things so they could continue being useful to me and my operations. I had clearly laid enough groundwork that they could see where my way of doing things was superior.

Or would the hero in them force them to become my enemy?

Only time would tell.

On the morning of the fourth day, it was my turn to go through the portal. My allies' hard work was both behind and ahead of them.

And I? My job was the most disgusting of all.

I had to visit my sister.

The Twenty-First Rule of Villainy

The enemies you make speak louder about you than your allies.

Chapter Forty-Four

Where Families Reunite and I Learn that Snitches Get Stitches

I was once again inside Grimskull's castle. This time I was not a guest, nor a prisoner. I was a fugitive. I could be caught. And that held a certain electricity. An invigorating sense of danger. Yet complete subterfuge was not my plan. In fact, being seen was what I was counting on.

A quick glance at my phone showed I had seventeen percent power left. Not as much as I'd hoped for. I still had to maintain my anti-tracking shields. At least for a few more minutes. While Chaud was no longer actively looking for me, that didn't mean Paige wasn't. So she was the first stop. Hopefully, she had enough of my items on her to give me a recharge.

Besides, when I was done with her, she wouldn't need them.

The portal I came through brought me just outside the guest wing of Grimskull's castle. I knew Paige was there by simple reasoning. When I was here last, there was no guest wing. Only ready-rooms within the main keep. It appeared that Paige was already flaunting her new position. The entire wing itself, aside from being newly built, no doubt by magic, was in a state of mismatched decoration. Statues of Grimskull were in the alcoves, while knick-knacks and cheaply made tapestries hung on the walls.

Looked like Paige and Grimskull were at odds on how to decorate.

I moved within the wing, keeping myself almost invisible. Hugging the shadows of the keep kept me unnoticed while scullery servants moved everywhere with their heads down, quickly flitting from place to place. Given Chaud's reports of shadow race creatures operating within the city and the keep, a semi-transparent man moving about would not seem out of the ordinary.

From the look of the faces of the servants, they were tired and overworked. They looked like they were frustrated and nearing exhaustion. I knew that look. I had the same expression at every family gathering I'd ever attended. From the distance I heard Paige bellowing

orders and moments later issuing commands that directly opposed her
original orders.

While Paige was an idiot, this was not her normal low-functioning
mind. No, this was her version of a power trip. All my life she liked to do
this. If the family ever went to a nice restaurant or hotel, Paige would take
sadistic delight in commanding the help to do inane tasks, then berate
them, claiming she never asked for said tasks.

Long story short: Paige was a bitch.

I stopped outside the wing's reception hall. Listening by the main
entrance, and looking through the massive door's crack, I saw her and
heard her shrill voice continuing to command servants.

"No, imbeciles! Why would we decorate in cold colors when this land
is perpetually cold and bleak?"

"Mistress, you commanded us to honor Baron Grimskull by
decorating the wing. Purple is the primary color on the lord's standard,"
one of the braver maids answered.

"As is his golden battle ax!" Paige shrieked. "Nice warm, golden tones
would brighten this room and make the entire wing come alive. Never
mind. It is clear from your narrow jaw and oversized brow you come from
poor breeding and are therefore stupid."

Raising her hand, Paige launched the maid across the room. "Dispose
of this trash. And if this room isn't glowing in brilliant golden tones by
nightfall, well, let's just say you'll feel as if this dumb bitch got off lucky."

"Yes, mistress!" the rest of the maids said, running off. No doubt
looking for golden things to make my sister happy.

I continued watching through the crack of the doors to the hall when
I felt a presence.

"'Sup, dude."

I turned and Randy was sitting on one of the hall benches. The greasy-
haired idiot was playing with another smartphone, no doubt a gift from
his mother. He had sneaked up on me and could see me while I was
nearly invisible.

"Randy?"

"'Sup. Mom's like, really pissed off. She hasn't been able to find you.
And she couldn't find that Sophie chick to make her do what she wanted.
So she came here to be, like, I dunno, that Grim dude's new woman. Or
whatever."

"Well, that's good for me, then."

Randy shrugged, not looking up from his phone. "I guess. You gonna
take her down and then like, get your revenge?"

"Yes."

"Cool." Randy nodded. He looked up at me from under the mop of hair and actually looked me in the eyes. "Sorry about before, Uncle Jack. Mom set you up and threatened to like, kill me. Plus, she said I was like, a godling, or demi-god, and I could use her power. It's how I can see you. It's kinda bitchin'."

"Yes, it is . . . bitchin'."

"When you get your revenge, are you going to go back to the prime universe?"

"Yes, I am."

"Cool." He nodded again. "Can I come with?"

"Are you going to stop me when I am forced to deal with your mother?"

"Nah. Bitches and snitches get stitches."

"There might be hope for you yet, Randy."

"Cool," Randy said. And just like that, he went back into his own little world, then teleported away.

Interesting.

Turning my attention back towards Paige, I decided it was best to approach this like ripping off a Band-Aid. It would be fast and painful. But first, I needed to make a call.

"Sophia."

"Yes sir?"

"Send the signal," I said.

"Are you ready, sir?"

"I better be. Send the signal."

"Yes, sir. Good luck, Jackson."

"Sophia, you know better."

"Yes sir. Luck is for idiots and people who do not plan."

Sophia broke contact and sent out the signal to my allies. Regardless of how well they had accomplished their mission, it was time.

Dropping my invisibility, I expelled just a little bit more of my power and blew the hall's ten-foot doors off their hinges. The massive, ornately-carved doors blew inward, smashing into the gaudily-decorated tables and destroying cheaply-made plates and serving ware.

If I'd given the doors a little extra effort, perhaps the door would have shredded the giant oil painting over the hall's fireplace of a much slimmer Paige atop a throne. I assumed the painter had taken liberal license with the subject matter rather than risk getting his neck snapped.

"Hello Paige."

"Julie?" Paige asked as the blood drained from her face.

Clearly she wasn't expecting me. Which only proved she did not belong in my position. Rather than see an adversary as capable and as willing to commit as much as she was, Paige only thought of herself. She saw all others as inferior to her, despite never proving her own worth and value by the sweat of her brow or the machinations of her mind. A trend prevalent in today's youth culture. Those we call "entitled."

That thought struck me as odd.

How could one as dense as Paige have orchestrated a coup against me? Even with the assistance of Grimskull, the execution against me was near flawless. At the risk of countering my own sentiments of underestimating an adversary, I felt the plan against me was something those two could not manage on their best day against my worst.

Sadly, I could not consider the thought any further, as Paige decided to take advantage of my deep reflection and hurl a giant chunk of the remaining doors back at me.

Quickly, I rolled to the floor, dodging the makeshift projectile. The door crashed behind me, destroying even more of the gaudy, cheap furniture. Paige reached out with her power and grabbed another large piece of the broken door and hurled it at me.

From the ground, I threw my hand up and used my power to stop the incoming debris. As much as I needed to conserve power for my inevitable fight with Grimskull, I had to show her she was a child in the villain equivalent of the kiddie pool, while I was Michael fucking Phelps.

But, you know, without the enormous eyebrows. And I didn't look like an anorexic Andre the Giant.

Whatever, the metaphor stands.

I hurled the door back at Paige with more force and more velocity than she was ready for. To my surprise, she didn't try to catch it. She was adept enough to pull all the nearby tables towards her, creating a makeshift shield around herself. I was a little proud.

So I ignited the wood of the tables.

"Goddamn it, Julie!" Paige yelled as she exploded the tables away from her. "Why aren't you dead already?!"

"Is that what you want, Paige? For me to be dead like our parents so you can have it all?" I asked as I walked towards her.

"Yes!" Paige yelled. I saw immediately in her frazzled eyes that the answer had inadvertently slipped out.

She had never meant to say it. But she had said it nonetheless.

It was one of those perfect moments of honesty. The ones that only come with a scattered mind or alcohol.

I pulled the sword given to me by Hawker and threw it at her. Not to kill her, but rather so it landed at her feet.

"Pick it up," I commanded. Dropping to my knees, I pulled open my shirt, exposing my chest. "If you want me dead, then just do it."

"Julie, I—"

"Pick up the fucking sword!" I yelled so loudly the words rang off the walls and hung in air.

Paige obeyed, for once, and picked up the sword. It looked awkward in her hand as she pointed the tip at my chest. She looked at me with a mixture of sadness and contempt.

"It's OK, Paige. One quick thrust, right here, and it will all be yours."

Paige took in a deep breath and I saw the muscles in her shoulders tense, ready to strike.

"Goodbye, Paige."

"Goodbye, Julie."

Then my sister jammed my sword deep into my chest.

Chapter Forty-Five

Where I Explain Some Rules, Deal with Paige, and Suffer from a Gunshot Wound

If you've been paying attention, you've noted a few facts along the way. The first being how magic works. As a god from another realm, I cannot directly alter the structural matter of an object I do not own while visiting another realm.

For example, the poor clothes I was given when I first escaped Grimskull's lair would remain threadbare, foul-smelling rags that only thrift-store hipsters would enjoy. Until they were *given* to me. Once they were mine, they were mine to do with as I pleased. Same with people. I couldn't act directly upon, or kill, a person unless they posed a direct threat to me. As for things like the doors, if I unleashed kinetic force, physics took over. As long as I did not alter the molecular construction of the matter, I violated no laws.

It happens all the time, believe it or not. Gods visiting planes of reality, changing things, stealing items. Worse, being gifted items allows said divine power to play with the gifts as a child with a new toy.

Still unconvinced? Where do you think your left socks keep going? If you knew the true purpose of what millions upon millions of missing hosiery were meant for, you wouldn't sleep again.

Ever.

So, in cases like this, where I am on my knees with a sword in my chest, the story would normally be over. Except, the sword was *my* sword, gifted to me by Hawker. With that little fact in mind, how could *my* sword hurt me?

Answer: It can't, and it didn't. It was just meant to scare the ever-living shit out of Paige when her dead brother sat up.

"I hate you, Julie. You always thought you were better than me."

I snapped my eyes open and smiled at my sister. "Because I am."

Paige screamed in shock and fear. The sword obeyed my commands as the handle and hilt melted like liquid metal and flowed upwards, covering Paige's hands and wrists. The sword's blade practically came alive as it elongated and narrowed into a flat, edged snake and wrapped itself around Paige's throat. The blade constricted, drawing blood. As Paige tried to scream, the remainder of the blade moved upwards and wrapped around her open mouth.

"This coup is at an end," I decreed as I stood. I walked over to Paige and allowed my senses to open up, detecting every item in the room that held any power from my realm. Holding my arms wide, I commanded the power to flood into my phone, refilling me and depriving Paige.

"Stop moving and you will bleed less," I told my sister. "You have me in a unique position, Paige—unsure." I circled my captive sibling, looking down at her and wondering what to do with her. With almost no power in her, she was mostly a mortal. Only her hereditary connection to me allowed her to have base-level goddess status.

"Sis, I spent a lot of time, effort, and energy getting to this moment. And now that I'm here, I am not quite sure what to do with you. Kill you? Banish you? What sends the best message to my enemies, allies, or potential business partners?" I asked my unresponsive sister.

I could barely make out anything intelligible between her bleating whimpers of pain and frustration. Not that it mattered anyway. This whole line of questioning was largely rhetorical. It was nothing more than psychological catharsis.

If you cannot afford therapy, I highly recommend binding your siblings in painful mechanisms that contort their bodies while you get off your chest all your built-up stress.

Then again, if that's your particular kink, perhaps you do belong in therapy. Hmm . . . what does that say about me?

"Paige, what would you do with me if the roles were reversed? Oh, that's right. You wanted to kill me," I said as I knelt down next to her so we were eye to eye. "And you even tried to do it. The only reason I'm alive is because you were too stupid to ever bother learning the rules I tried to teach you a long time ago. And the only reason you are alive is because I am currently cursed with a lingering sense of family. Maybe that is all I need to be free of to truly spread my wings and accomplish even more? What do you say, Paige? Do you think you deserve to live?"

I set my phone down for a second to take Paige's head in my hands. I held her there, with my forehead resting on hers. With my mind made up, I kissed her forehead.

"Goodbye, Paige."

"Step away from her, Jackson," I heard Courtney say from behind me.

Damn it.

I turned to look over my shoulder and Courtney stood there in his full tactical response gear instead of realm-appropriate garb. To top it off, he was aiming a .45 pistol and a magical wand of unknown power at my head.

I looked at my phone on the ground. It was right there, less than two feet away. But I was not fast enough to beat the muzzle velocity of the weapon, let alone whatever the wand did.

So I did what I normally did in situations like these. I talked.

"You know she doesn't love you, right?" I said to my former head of security. "She is with Grimskull now. I don't know if this land-whale even knows what love is."

"Jackson, this is your last warning. Step away from her."

I complied. Raising my hands, I moved away from Paige and stood, facing my former employee.

"So what's your plan? Do her bidding while you watch her with another man? Hmm? Are you going to be her little slice on the side? Do you think she's going to realize she was supposed be with you the whole time?"

Courtney didn't answer me with words. Instead, the prick shot me in the leg. The large-caliber bullet ripped a huge chunk of flesh out of my left leg, just below my hip. The impact spun me around as if I were a rag doll, and I hit the floor hard. Both my hands went to my gaping wound as I tried to apply as much direct pressure to it as possible.

My hands trembled in shock as blood poured from the wound. I immediately felt faint. Courtney didn't shoot me in the artery, but the .50 caliber weapon had done so much superficial damage that he may as well have.

"I never said that she loved me," Courtney said. He walked in a slow arc around me, keeping the weapons out.

"What?" I asked through gritted teeth.

"You said she never loved me. I know that. I never said she did. I only said that I loved her."

The comment made me stop thinking about the hole in my leg and look at my former employee as a person. As a man. A man who suffered from the age-old pain of loving someone who didn't love you back. I looked at him with new eyes and a new perspective on the man. On Courtney.

And I laughed in his face.

"Ha ha ha! Oh, fuck that hurts. Oh my God, that is too funny! Seriously? That's what the mighty Courtney has been reduced to? The sympathetic loser in a romantic comedy? Oh Jesus, just put a bullet in my head now and end this."

"Stop laughing, Jackson. I'm serious."

"So am I," I said. "Do you think that makes you noble? You're Duckie from *Pretty in Pink*. Paige only loves powerful, evil men and what they can do for her. This whole thing only makes you weak and stupid. Two traits I abhor. I am glad our partnership has been terminated."

"Free her," Courtney demanded.

"I need my phone to do it."

"I know. But the moment I sense anything other than you freeing her, I put another bullet in you."

"Can I heal myself?" I asked, but Courtney didn't answer. "Fine. But I must reiterate my pleasure that our contract is no longer valid. Especially since you never took any of my lessons to heart."

"Such as?" Courtney asked.

"Like the rule where you don't announce yourself when you plan on shooting someone. You just shoot them. Otherwise, it gives your opponent time to plan a way out of the situation. Like now, for example. You are going to die. Goodbye, Courtney. When you're dead, I am going to have your niece expelled from Harvard for cheating and running a drug ring."

"You're not getting out of this one," Courtney said. "And she's at Yale."

"I always forget that," I said. Then I chuckled.

"What's so funny, Jackson?"

"I never said I was the one who was going to kill you."

"What?"

A bullet ripped through the back of Courtney's head, exiting between his eyes.

"'Sup dude," Randy said, lowering his own pistol.

Chapter Forty-Six

Where I Ponder Paige's Fate, Compare Myself to Tolkien, and Consider Public Nudity

"Randy, you beautiful idiot, thank you," I said as I grabbed my phone and immediately healed my leg. Power washed over me and I felt whole.

"It's cool, Uncle Jack. Sucks I had to smoke muscle-dude. But he was a punk. Yammering about love and bitches."

"Yes," I agreed. "Love and bitches are just the worst."

"That skull-dude is in his throne room. He's pretty pissed off. I guess the city is, like, under attack? A bunch of people showed up."

"That would be part of my plan, Randy. I need Grimskull distracted."

"Is killing Mom a part of your plan?" Randy asked.

I looked at my sister, still bound on the ground and covered in Courtney's blood and brain matter. "Yes."

"Dude, don't." Randy said. "I know she's a bitch sometimes, but she is still my mom."

"What happened to bitches and snitches get stitches?" I asked.

"That's just an expression. 'Sides, stitches ain't murder."

"You just killed Courtney."

"That's different."

"She betrayed me," I said rather than argue the point of Courtney's death. "She orchestrated this insurrection against me. She is responsible for my capture and imprisonment, and the attempt to remove me from the very empire I built. Any leniency I show is an invitation to enemies to attack me. Especially if it is known I was bested by this idiot. I am sorry, but this is business."

"Come on, Uncle Jack, you're a smart dude. Why not, like, imprison her in some mine somewhere? Or, like, I dunno, make her an immortal statue. She'd make a cool coat rack."

My nephew had a point. An endless living punishment served an example just as well as death.

"I will consider it. For now I must attend to Grimskull. What did you see out in the city?"

"I'll show you," Randy said. "Follow me."

I cast several spells on my still-immobilized sister, rendering her completely silent and asleep. I basked in the joy of not hearing her for a moment before following Randy.

Randy led me up a long narrow staircase that opened up onto an overlook tower. From the open cylindrical design, I could see in every direction. Far below, war was being waged throughout the entire city of Al' Garrad and within the castle's grounds. My allies had come through exceedingly well.

In the distance, I could see the green and gold of marching forces. Hawker had called in his favor and rallied the elves of the Whispering Woods. The elves had marshaled their forces and marched on Grimskull's capital.

Within the city, I saw combat forces fighting against Grimskull's army of men and shadow races. This combat force wore a white hammer on a field of blue and red as their herald. If I was correct, then Wren had convinced the remaining soldiers of General Anders on Fyrheim to convert to the ways of Vammar. This new group would most definitely take glee in attacking their former emperor, who had never paid them.

To the north, I saw a line of warriors riding, dressed in gray. The Twilight Guard moved on Al' Garrad with speed and ferocity. I was sure that Carina would gain their support once it was known that she carried with her the blessing of Lord Protector Talisarian'de.

The main force of soldiers, the ones that surrounded the city and occupied the majority of the battlefield, was courtesy of Zachariah and Countess Skullgrim. I knew the Countess would like nothing more than to return to these lands if for no other reason than to cause her ex-husband misery.

Last, there was Lydia. Her role in this was slightly less extravagant, but equally important. Her job was to free any remaining loyal members of the Bastards from prison, along with whomever else she deemed worthy, and get the majority of the civilian staff and populace to safety.

Civilian casualties were inevitable. But it would go a very long way for whomever I put on the throne to have the backing of the people. Once word got out that the usurper of my choice ensured the smallfolk were safe, they would have the people's blessing. It made it so much easier to rob them blind in the chaos. Which I was sure Lydia was doing regardless.

Looting and war profiteering go hand in hand. And that woman had an appetite to take whatever she wanted when she wanted.

The thought made my asshole shudder.

Lydia's deviance aside, I watched the battle play out before me with satisfaction and more than a touch of pride. This was a testament to my mind. With little prep and using the natural talents and connections of people, I was able to bring together a battle of seven armies.

Seven! Two more than Tolkien! I am the champion!

Sure, I was counting Grimskull's forces twice. But in my numerical defense, Grimskull's standing internal army was completely separate from the shadow race auxiliaries, or orcs, goblins, and the like. Those monsters would no doubt turn on Grimskull the moment it suited them, so they definitely counted as an independent army.

And yes, Lydia's force of escaped prisoners and slaves weren't exactly an army. But the civilians who chose to fight instead of hide would join up with her. So I counted them.

Yes sir, seven armies. Suck it, Ronny-Rule.

The battle unfolded, a grand overture to my own personal symphony of destruction. The thrums of bowstrings and siege engines were the driving beat, reverberating deeply and powerfully. Steel clanging against steel provided an atonal melody. The war cries and screams floating above the clash of battle served as lead vocals, accentuating the overall composition.

I almost felt like dancing. I wanted nothing more than to hold my arms above my head and gently sway to the beautiful noise of battle and blood. This was my song, my opus of carnage. Not too bad for a man with only a cell phone and his wits.

If Randy hadn't been there with me, I would have dropped my pants and conducted this overture with my erection. As it were, I kept my pants on and simply soaked in the product of my own beautiful mind.

"Are you OK, dude?" Randy asked as I stood there with my eyes closed.

"Yes, Randy. I am absolutely perfect."

"Aren't you gonna go and throw down with Grimskull?"

"Patience, Randy," I said, not letting his questions ruin my mood.

"What are you waiting for?"

I sighed. "A coward like Grimskull is currently sitting in his throne room directing his orders via his magic, rather than stepping foot on the field of battle. With war on all sides, he is at his limits—mentally, physically, and magically. This is more than a battle for him. This is an affront to his will and the whole of the Eastern Empire, especially since his ex-wife herself is leading one of the prongs of the attack. Grimskull is taking this very personally, and anyone who turns a fight into a personal matter gets sloppy. There is no reason to confront him while he has even an iota of strength. No, young Randy, time is my ally. So I will wait until he has pushed past his limits. Then I will move. And then I will destroy him."

"You're a cold motherfucker, Uncle Jack."

"Yes, yes I am," I agreed. "Now please, do me a favor and find me a glass of wine. I would very much enjoy a nice drink while I watch my favorite show."

Chapter Forty-Seven

Where I Question Whether or Not I Possess Guilt

The Battle of Grimskull's Fall, as it came to be known, lasted for a full day.

Through the night and into the following morning, the war continued. When night descended, the burning city provided enough flickering light for the combatants to continue the slaughter. Destruction and death were found in the shadows that night.

Both the beautiful and the ugly died together, their life's blood mingling in the gutters with all the grace and dignity of an emptied chamber pot.

Yes, all seven armies bled rivers of blood that day.

All for me, whether they knew it or not.

Perhaps the death toll was too high? In the pursuit of salvaging my wounded pride, I'd knowingly put these warriors into harm's way. This was not the first massive battle I'd orchestrated. But those were all business-related. This was the first war I'd put together for personal reasons. Did that make me . . . evil? I'd always prided myself of being a villain who didn't take delight in the slaughter of others.

Hmm, perhaps a quick recap.

The elves of the Whispering Woods? Like all elves, they were xenophobic, aristocratic assholes who allowed the deaths of anyone who they considered lower than themselves or who held no political advantage. So, no guilt from me for their demise.

The Twilight Guard? They followed the same principles as the elves. Plus, their treatment of Carina could not be forgiven. So, let them burn.

The remainder of Grimskull's men whom Wren organized? They were just recently trying to kill me and my allies. Fair is fair.

Countess Skullgrim and the army of the Western Empire? That one was tricky. She was a former client. Her presence here meant she agreed to battle her ex-husband of her own accord. And her warriors chose to follow her, so they knew the risks. The bonus for me was this: As a former client who terminated our business relationship, she would most likely need assistance in rebuilding her forces when this was over. So this was in fact a guilt-free positive for me.

The remnants of the Forgotten Bastards and the city's civilian population? Well, the Bastards did try and kill me. And the civilians who die will die as martyrs. So, win-win there.

Grimskull's army? Well, again, they were actively trying to kill me. Some of them even smiled at me before I was captured. They must have known the betrayal was coming.

The shadow race auxiliary of goblins and orcs? Come on now. Not to sound like an asshole, but I am almost completely sure that Khasil and other dark gods breed them just to die in battles like these. They are fantasy-realm filler. The equivalent of the generic blue-suited Cobra trooper from *GI Joe* or the no-named *Star Trek* redshirt. I am certain they are happiest when they are fighting and dying.

Based on that reasoning, the answer was simple: no guilt for me.

I kicked my feet up on the banister of the overlook tower and continued enjoying the show all through the night.

Come morning, when the sun crept over the horizon, what was left of Grimskull's forces had rallied to the gates of the castle in a desperate attempt to protect their lord and home.

Smoke from the long-dead fires wafted upwards while the morning breeze brought the stink of death, fires, and human waste to my nose. Battles were truly a disgusting medley of olfactory sensations.

As I watched the last-ditch attempt of Grimskull's forces try to hold out, I knew that their master must be pushed to his breaking point. Without General Anders leading the defense, Grimskull ineptly tried to serve as the leader. I was sure Chaud had a hand in some of the battle. But the crafty mage knew a sinking ship. So, most likely, Chaud only did the bare minimum to obey his lord's commands.

That meant it was time to pay Viktor a visit.

"Come, Randy," I said, nudging the sleeping young man in the ribs with my foot.

"What?"

"It's time."

"To do what?" Randy asked.

"To confront Baron Grimskull."

"Good luck, Uncle Jack," Randy said, rolling over. "His throne room is downstairs."

I considered kicking my nephew in the ribs. Hard. But I stopped myself. My sister's slacker son would most likely find a way to screw up my triumph. An amazing feat for sure, considering his primary mode of existence was apathy. So I left the young man sleeping on the stone. He would no doubt find his way into events. It seemed to be his superpower. The gods must have blessed the idiot in utero. He was not gifted with a sharp mind, drive, or desire, yet he was always able to be in the right place at the right time despite having no idea how he got there. Randy was a millennial Forrest Gump or Candide.

I cast one last look over my shoulder on the ruin of Al' Garrad and smiled. Where some may have seen a field of horror, death, and loss, I saw more. I saw promise and a hopeful future.

For me, that is. Not for those poor dead schlubs.

When this was all over, perhaps I'd keep Grimskull's helmet as a trophy as well as a reminder. To never let my guard down again when dealing with anyone I saw as weaker.

Well, it was time.

Time to put down my wayward sheep and skin him alive while he bleats.

Chapter Forty-Eight

Where I Witness Grimskull's Tantrum and I Learn a Bit More About My Conspirators

"We will never surrender!" Grimskull screamed from his throne.

"My lord," Chaud pleaded. "Viktor. If you stay, you will die. The empire has fallen."

"No!" Grimskull roared as he leaped from his throne. "Tell the men to fight harder! I will infuse more of them with my powers and push back these invaders!"

"There are almost no warriors left."

"Because they refuse to fight to their full potential!" Grimskull yelled. "I will not be defeated due to the ineptness of others! The empire—*my* empire—will endure. We—I—will not be beaten by a coalition of elves, mercenaries, and traitors."

"You've neglected to mention the vastly superior and better-trained forces of your ex-wife," Chaud said before he sarcastically added "My lord."

Grimskull stood and grabbed the archmage by the front of his robes. He pulled Chaud close so they were face to face. "You are walking a very thin line, mage."

Chaud rolled his eyes. Clearly, he had had enough of Grimskull's excuses and grandstanding. The archmage brought his hands up and concentric circles of orange light erupted from his palms. In a flash of power, Chaud launched the unsuspecting Grimskull backwards, down his dais and onto the marble floor.

I peered out from my vantage point, just outside the archway leading into the great hall, to get a better look. Grimskull scrambled to get to his knees after taking the fall.

"Guards! Apprehend him!" Grimskull commanded his personal guard. The twenty men and women in the ornate armor and visored helms represented the last remnants of Grimskull's personal forces.

"You forget yourself, Viktor," Chaud said. With an arcane gesture, lightning burst forth from Chaud's hands. The electricity crackled and snapped as it arced from guard to guard. In seconds, all twenty guards had fallen to the floor, dead. The air smelled of ozone and cooked meat.

Chaud then sat on Grimskull's throne with a defiant look. "I was there when you were born, boy. I watched you come screaming into the world, take your first breath, and piss on your mother. And I think it best you know that half the castle enjoyed pissing on her as well. Your mother had strange . . . appetites."

Grimskull snarled like an animal.

Chaud ignored Grimskull as he continued. "I watched you grow from a spoiled, barbaric child into a spoiled, barbaric adult. You have only ever succeeded because I allowed it. Now, at the end, you still refuse to accept that it was your own folly that brought your empire down."

"Get off my throne."

Chaud rubbed the bridge of his nose with his slender fingers. "Oh, blow it out your ass, Marty."

"What did you call me?!" Grimskull said, his body practically shaking with rage.

"Your birth name. Martin Viktor Grimskull. Martin apparently means 'powerful warrior.' But in this case, you are simply Marty, the giant child."

"Get off my throne," Grimskull repeated.

Chaud slapped his hands on the throne's armrests and stood. "Your throne? That's a laugh. Your parents were also idiots. The pair of them. The only reason they, or you, ever kept the throne is because of me behind the scenes, running the empire. Do you even know how trade, taxes, and tariffs work?"

"Lower your voice when speaking to me."

"You are not threatening, Marty," Chaud taunted the warlord. "This chair, this uncomfortable monstrosity, should belong to me for all the work I've done for the empire. But here you and your moronic family have sat, while loyal Chaud shuts his mouth and does the real work. No wonder Jackson Blackwell wants to place your brother or your son on the throne. Either one of them could do an infinitely better job than—"

Chaud's speech was cut off, on account of his no longer existing.

Where the archmage once stood was now a smoldering empty space with the residue of spectral green energy. The same energy glowed from Grimskull's outstretched right hand. His left was clasping the Amulet of the Ember Soul.

Grimskull had used the most powerful and most forbidden magic in all the Never Realm: The Curse of Unmaking. The Curse of Unmaking was exactly as it sounded, a spell that caused its victim to cease to be, erasing him completely. Even the gods of their respective realms feared using the curse. The ripples it sent into the great flow of existence caused unknown and terrifying events to happen. Everything Chaud could potentially do, in any possible timeline, was gone.

The curse messed with potential futures, and the universe did not care for that.

I stepped out into the open from my hiding spot and walked down the great hall towards the throne.

"Hello, Viktor. You have looked better."

"You! You did all this!" Grimskull yelled.

"Yes, yes I did," I yelled back.

"I have lost everything!"

I stopped and looked at him for a moment before continuing. "Can you wait a moment, please? The banter isn't nearly as good while we are this far away! Yelling to your opponent isn't all that menacing! Plus, the acoustics in here are not very good!"

"I know! Yes, please, just hurry up!" Grimskull shouted back while making a hurry-up motion with his hand.

I closed the distance until Grimskull and I were in normal speaking range. "Better. Now, where were we?"

Grimskull sighed and repeated himself. "I've lost everything . . . "

Ah yes.

I laughed. "Yes. And do you know why?" I asked, slipping back into my villainous tones.

"Because—"

"Shut up," I said. "The question was rhetorical."

"Oh."

"You lost it all because you chose to try and take me on."

"I had you beaten!"

I shook my head. "No, you had me disadvantaged. And I will give you credit for that. Very few ever have. Between you and my sister, I am humbly surprised. How long had that been going on, may I ask?"

"From the first time I entered your realm, coming to you for your advice. I was in that horrible waiting room of yours, being bored to death sitting next to your nephew Randy. You sister was there, leaving a meeting she had with you. She was upset and I offered her my handkerchief. She was so incredibly charming and beautiful. The attraction was immediate between us. We struck up a very interesting conversation. It was like fate had brought us together. She was the one who first suggested that we rise up against you. And to be honest, I said no. All the legends of you were daunting. But after meeting you and being in your arrogant presence for only seconds, I knew I wanted to see you removed and your sister placed in power."

"Then why go through with our meetings and consultations?" I asked.

"Because they worked," Grimskull replied. "You are an insufferable man. But your methods and outcomes work. Thanks to you, I expanded my empire into the Middle Lands and the through several of the island chains. You are a horse's ass, but you get results."

I nodded. "Then why betray me?"

"Because I learned all I needed from you."

"Oh?"

"Yes," Grimskull said. Behind his skull helmet, I saw his eyes narrow. "I learned you would always keep me coming back, taking more of my gold for yourself. I learned that I would never be rid of you. I learned that your appetite for power and status is equal to your ego. And I learned that if I made your sister my wife, then all your power could belong to me."

At that moment, I was honestly not mad at him. I was impressed.

But he still had to go.

Reputation and all that.

"I thank you, Baron, for your honesty. But it is time. Surrender to me now, swear your life to me, and you may live."

"No," Grimskull said, shaking his head. "Now is not the end of Grimskull."

Oy . . . third person.

"Goodbye, Shadow Master."

Grimskull snatched his left hand to the Amulet of the Ember Soul and raised his right hand towards me. At this range, there was nothing I could do but watch as the sickly iridescent green energy of the Curse of Unmaking washed over me.

Chapter Forty-Nine

Where I Confront a God and I'm Forced to Do the Unspeakable

Oh ye of little faith.

The Curse of Unmaking, as I said before, erases a person from the flow of life. The river of time that makes up the entirety of a realm's existence.

I was not from that realm.

I was a god.

Sort of.

Visiting gods were not beholden to that realm's flow. They were unique in that they could bend the flow's will around them. So to me, The Curse of Unmaking was nothing more than a warm shower in green energy goo. It smelled of hand-sanitizer and pine.

"Impossible," Grimskull whispered when he saw me standing there, not erased from existence.

I would have taken the time to explain that it was not impossible at all, that it was in fact logical if one knew the rules. But explaining everything would have greatly diminished how imposing I looked standing there, amid the swath of destruction the curse gouged out.

"If you are done, then it is time for you to surrender," I said, brushing off nonexistent dust and debris from my clothing.

"Fool!" A female voice echoed through great hall. The massive doors to the hall slammed shut. The vaulted windows were darkened as shadowy clouds from nowhere rolled in. "You were instructed to not use the curse upon him."

The voice was a throaty hiss and unmistakable. It resonated from nowhere and everywhere within the darkness of the hall. The air had dropped several degrees, and I was able to see my breath.

"Khasil, how are you?" I asked. "Here to witness my moment of triumph?"

Khasil manifested within the great hall's balcony seating. She stood there in a deeply v-cut formal gown of black and green. Her ringlets of black hair were tied up in an intricate weave, accentuating her horns. The entire piece was held together by a net of emeralds and black diamonds. She now wore a two black eye patches with dark green leather cords to cover the wounds done to her two left eyes from Lydia's deadly accuracy.

"Great mistress." Grimskull lowered his head and dropped to one knee. "You grace me with your presence."

"Stand up, worm," Khasil hissed. "You were commanded to destroy him. Complete your task."

"Great mistress, I tried. I used the most powerful spell I know. It was not enough."

"Again, I name you fool. Powerful and dark from the Never Realm the Curse of Unmaking is, but useless against a god."

"Of course," Grimskull said, shaking his head. "Paige Blackwell tried to warn me of that. I could not believe that either one of them were gods."

"Only technically," Khasil said, glaring at me.

"I am standing right here, you know," I addressed them both.

"Do not address the dark goddess," Grimskull warned.

"Shut up, Marty," Khasil and I said together.

"I will give you one last chance," Khasil said to me. "Give me the Barrowbride and I will let you live."

"How are your remaining eyes doing?" I asked in response. "Lydia's knives sure are sharp, aren't they?"

Khasil bent her knees and held out her arms like a feral animal and roared. Her scorpion tail stood erect and quivered.

"Rise, my avatar! You shall be my vessel. Destroy the Shadow Master. I bestow upon you the power of a god to kill a god!"

Baron Martin Viktor Grimskull began to swell and grow, nearly doubling in size. Small, insect-like legs sprouted from his body and along his trunk. Each stalk grew into thick armored legs and a second set of pincer claw-arms. His flesh turned a pale shade of green, and black chitinous scales began to form, overlapping one another down his arms.

The baron's helmet did not grow with the rest of him; instead, it stretched and cracked, cutting into him. The mangled helm embedded itself into his bleeding skull, and what was left was a human-arachnid hybrid with the power of a god and only one mission—to kill me.

Grimskull tested his new body, scuttling from side to side before his new eyes set upon me. Instead of a mindless beast, there was an intelligent creature. He smiled.

Grimskull shocked me even more when he spoke. "Arise!" he commanded. He raised his front legs and then slammed them down, releasing a ripple of power. The remnants of his dead personal guard rose up, controlled by the necromantic power that flowed through him.

Well, shit.

The first of the guards came at me, wildly slashing its sword. I leaped backwards and raised my hand, releasing a gout of flame so intense that it would melt steel like an acetylene torch.

Nothing happened.

I narrowed my eyes in contemplation, then looked up at Khasil, who smiled back at me.

Of course. My power would be useless against them while her power possessed Grimskull and by proxy, the guards. The only way to defeat them would be through martial skill, as the Old Accords demanded.

With enhanced speed and strength from my power, I turned aside from the guard's attack and mentally activated the bracelet on my wrist. Nightfyr sprang into my hand. Catching the weapon in mid-turn, I shifted and brought the mace's weight to bear against the guard's helmeted skull, crushing it. One down and too many to go.

As fast and as strong as I could enhance myself, Grimskull and his minions could match it. I was talented, but I was not good enough to take on nineteen heavily armored zombies and a Scorpion King knock-off.

"Sir," Sophia's voice came into my ear.

"Busy," I responded as I swung Nightfyr again, only to have it *clang* against the broad shield of the nearest undead guardsman. They were trying to surround me and wear me down. Grimskull reared up and down on his insect legs in anticipation.

"Sir! I'm afraid you have to do . . . the unspeakable."

Ignoring Sophia for a moment, I released a blast of pressurized air from my fist just to push the attacking armored zombies back. I grabbed the shield from the first guard I downed just to have some kind of off-hand protection.

"I can't!" I yelled. "You know I can't!"

"Sir, would you rather be the live Shadow Master who abused the rules, or the dead one?"

Damn it. She was right. I had to swallow my pride and do the one and only thing I could do in this moment.

"Help," I whispered.

Next to Khasil, Valliar appeared in the balcony. He was adorned in his usual white robes and crystalline armor. But this time he had a new adornment.

His smug smile.

Valliar held his hand to his ear. "What was that, Shadow Master? I could not quite hear that. Would you be so kind as to repeat it?"

"Please . . . help," I grunted as I fought to fend off more and more of the guards.

"Now, was that so hard to say?"

"Yes."

Beams of light burst through the windows, penetrating the gloom of Khasil's presence, and the doors of the great hall burst open.

My allies, my salvation, rushed into the hall and ran headlong into combat. I was saved. All because I asked for . . . help.

Gods above and below, I'll never live this down.

Chapter Fifty

Where I Receive Help, Say Goodbye to Bad Business Partners, and Pray

Hawker led the initial charge. His enchanted battleaxe cleaved through the nearest zombie guard's shield and armor like a hot knife through butter. His weapon, like all their weapons, were gifts from Valliar. A gift from a god. So their power met Khasil's on equal footing.

Following Hawker came Templar Wren and Carina. The duo fought in tandem, with his shield blocking incoming attacks, while Carina's battle staves knocked the guards to the ground. One swing of Wren's hammer and the undead guards were no more.

Lydia and her Bastards stuck to the corners of the hall, providing assistance where needed by way of a well-timed throwing blade or a stab in the back. Last, the Lord Protector Talisarian'de and Zachariah entered the battle. Talisarian'de maneuvered his dual-bladed battle-staff with spinning, deadly precision, and Zachariah unleashed a combination of magical attacks and incredible swordsmanship.

In moments, the last of Grimskull's raised guards were nothing more than pieces of dead flesh and broken armor.

Which left Grimskull himself. The monster opened and closed his clawed hands while a sliver of drool escaped his elongated jaws. Grimskull was smiling.

"Good," Grimskull's barely human voice formed. His new lower mandibles interfered with his speaking, causing a chattering, lisping sound. "I want the pleasure of tearing you apart myself."

The monster lunged at us, snapping his pincers in wide arcs, forcing us to scatter. The only thing on our side was there were too many targets to focus on.

"Go for his legs!" Hawker shouted, swinging his battleaxe. Grimskull in turn scuttled aside and swiped a clawed arm, connecting with Hawker's breastplate. The impact launched the young warrior across the great hall. Lydia was there immediately to assist him in her own special way.

"I think he can understand us, idiot."

"Yeah, I figured that out," Hawker groaned as Lydia helped him up.

"Move!" Lydia yelled.

Grimskull leaped through the air and crashed down to where the two of them had been only seconds before. The deadly stinger missed Lydia by a fraction of an inch as she shoved Hawker away, then rolled the opposite way herself.

Zachariah threw conjured balls of fire at his brother. "Hey little brother! I didn't think it was possible for you to get any uglier. But this look suits you!"

"Graaah!" Grimskull roared as turned his attention on his older brother. Grimskull turned, then began to scuttle at full speed toward his brother, shrugging off the fireballs as mere annoyances. At the last moment before Grimskull struck, Wren blindsided the beast. With a war cry, Wren rammed his shield into the monster's side with all his godly strength, knocking Grimskull to his side.

Talisarian'de took the opening, springing into the air, twirling his twin-bladed combat staff, and bringing the weapon down into Grimskull's vulnerable underbelly. The weapon struck home, driving into the scaled flesh. Blackish blood sprayed like a geyser as the elf cheered his strike.

But wounded was far from dead.

Grimskull shifted, knocking the Lord Protector to the ground and into one of Grimskull's outstretched claws. The monster gripped the elf's throat so tightly that Talisarian'de's eyes bulged and his face instantly turned red. Grimskull's grip tightened and Talisarian'de released his battle staff and punched vainly against the heavily armored claw.

Carina, Wren, and Zachariah ran in and tried to help, but Grimskull flailed with his other appendages, keeping them at bay.

With no help able to make it in time, it was only a matter of moments later that the noble elf's head rolled free, severed from its body.

The room fell silent as a creature who was over a thousand years old ceased existing. Blood pooled on the stone floor as we witnessed his last breath, perhaps his soul, escaping his rapidly cooling lips.

Talisarian'de, Lord Protector of the Whispering Woods, was dead.

So, hey, things weren't all bad.

Before anyone could properly react, Grimskull scrambled onto his many legs. My allies moved back defensively, watching to see what the monster's next move would be. Even I was amazed when he simply picked up the dead elf's head and tossed it into the air a couple of times like a baseball.

"Who's next?"

"Me," a new voice echoed over the sounds of battle.

Through the great hall strode a very confident and very powerful woman. She took her time walking in, ensuring all eyes were on her. After all, the last time she'd set foot in this castle, she was fleeing for her life. Now she returned as The Power of the West.

Countess Elsbeth Skullgrim had returned to Al' Garrad, and she was reveling in it. The countess stood tall, proud and regal in her fur-trimmed black and silver armor. She wore a flowing cape made of a virgin griffon's skin and feathers. Atop her head, the countess wore a skull headpiece similar to her ex-husband's. Hers was more delicate and ornate, and her flowing blonde hair cascaded from under it.

"Oh Viktor, Viktor, Viktor," Countess Skullgrim said, relishing the moment. "You look terrible. I love it."

"You insufferable bitch! How dare you assault my home?!"

Countess Skullgrim's smile was wide and proud. "Because I can . . . Marty."

"Whore!" Grimskull hurled the severed head of Talisarian'de at his ex-wife with enough velocity to put a hole through the stone.

With a bored expression, Countess Skullgrim held out her right hand and stopped the dead elf's head in mid-air. "Whore? I did not have relations with your brother for money. I did it because it was fun and he is so much more of a man than you. But I am bored with this. Your time has come to a close. And I am ever so grateful to be here as it does."

"Elsbeth, I am glad you were able to make it," I said, greeting the countess.

"Jackson," Countess Skullgrim greeted me, ignoring the giant monster in the room. "I just had to come. I could not believe it when Zachariah told me that you were here. You really let *that* trick you?" Countess Skullgrim thumbed her well-manicured finger at the monstrous form of Grimskull.

"It is a long story," I said, dodging an armored chunk of twice-dead guardsman. Grimskull was now picking up anything in reach and hurling it at us. The dead guard's severed torso sprayed all manner of blood and entrails along the wall of the great hall.

"Oh, that will never come out. Once blood is in the stone, it stays there. My slaves are still scrubbing blood from my last public beheading."

"So business is good then?" I asked. Talking shop was always important when dealing with clients, past and future. You have to do it, really. It's the mark of good business.

"Really? Now?!" Hawker yelled as he dodged another inbound corpse missile. "I don't mean to be rude, but we are in the middle of something!"

"Right, of course," I said. "Countess, how is your power from the Never Realm these days?"

"I am doing rather well. Thank you again for brokering the deal."

"You are welcome. And your amulet?"

"Not in a secret dungeon, if that is what you are asking, Jackson. Only a fool would do such a thing."

"It was a brilliant plan!" Grimskull roared as he moved towards us.

I grabbed Countess Skullgrim's wrist and pulled her away before her ex-husband could impale us with his stinger.

"Thank you," the countess said. "Why do you ask?"

"Because dear Viktor here is brimming with the power of Khasil."

"That scaled bitch?" the countess asked.

I almost winced. Poor Countess Skullgrim, like the rest of the *mortals* here, was unaware that Khasil and Valliar were present. She no doubt heard the comment and would remember that.

"Viktor was dumb enough to throw in with her?"

"Apparently," I confirmed. "My power can match him, but not beat him. Not in this realm. It's a god thing. Therefore, we need to cheat. The Never Realm touches all planes of reality and its power should be enough to repel Khasil's influence and return him to normal."

"Well, won't that be grand. But . . . " The countess paused, considering the ramifications. "That level of power will have a fairly large toll. The cost to me will be great. What's in it for me?"

I actually stopped dodging to regard the arrogant witch. "What's in it for you? I made you. You owe me."

"And now, I no longer need you. Yet you need me. So what are you offering, Shadow Master?"

In my line of work, the only way to succeed is to have an enormous threshold for stupidity. But there are several things I cannot abide. For one, people who wear fashion scarves. Unless you are a foreign correspondent for a major news network, then you just look like a douchebag.

And for another, professional discourtesy.

And Elsbeth was being very discourteous. So when Grimskull lunged for us, I grabbed the back of Elsbeth's cape and pulled hard. I yanked her backwards while propelling myself forwards. As the old adage says, when being chased by a bear, you only have to be faster than the person ahead of you. I rolled away from Grimskull's attack, while poor Countess Skullgrim was left behind in shock as her ex-husband got his claws into her.

Within seconds, the countess was nothing more than a puddle of wet goo in a very expensive cloak.

In gratitude, Grimskull turned his attention to me. The monster smiled and lunged.

Lydia tackled me from behind, knocking me out of Grimskull's destructive path. The monster slammed against the wall, missing us both by only a hair.

Lydia rolled with the momentum, came to her feet, and grabbed me by the scruff of my shirt.

"Move!"

Instead of responding, I just listened and ran as Zachariah once again tried attacking Grimskull with bolts of magic.

"You killed her!" Lydia yelled as we ran across the hall.

"No," I countered. "Grimskull killed her."

"You pulled her back!"

"I had my reasons."

"Which were?" Lydia asked.

"She tried to extort me."

"Oh, well, that's fine then," Lydia conceded. As a thieves' guild leader, she understood the bad business practice of extortion. "Bitch had it coming."

"Indeed," I agreed. "Besides, her usefulness had run its course."

"That's funny," Lydia laughed. But her voice didn't carry any humor.

"What's funny?"

"It looks like I've reached the end of my usefulness also."

"What are you talking about?" I asked.

Lydia stopped running as we took cover behind the throne. Panting, she pulled back her leather vest to reveal a puncture wound oozing with a thick, sickly yellow fluid.

Venom.

Grimskull hadn't missed her when she saved Hawker. She had been hit and poisoned minutes ago.

She was already dead.

Her body just didn't know it yet.

"Lydia, I . . ."

"No, it's better this way," Lydia said as she began coughing. "Better to die young and pretty than old and ugly."

Lydia's body was convulsing. Spasms were contorting her face and body. The sprint after saving me must have hurried the poison through her body.

"Boss, is there anything you can do?" Sophia's voice said in my ear.

"No," I said, as I held her hand while she died. "She doesn't belong to me."

Lydia closed her eyes. Tears rolled down her face. She was in incredible pain, but she refused to scream out. I peeked out from behind the throne to assess the situation.

Grimskull was locked in combat with Hawker, Carina, Wren, and Zachariah. Above, in the balcony, I saw the two gods watching. Khasil caught my eye and the evil goddess winked at me. Well, considering her eye patch, it was more of a blink.

I turned my attention back to Lydia. I knelt next to her, in awe of her strength and grit. She would not let anyone hear her scream. It was pointless and meant nothing, as death was going to happen. But to Lydia, pride meant something. She would die, there was no stopping that. But she would determine how she would go out. And there, with her at the end, I knew when my time came, I wouldn't have even half the strength.

Because I knew how to cheat.

"Forgive me," I whispered.

"Boss?"

"My apologies, Sophia. But I have to do this."

"Sir?"

"There is nothing *I* can do."

I closed my eyes and I prayed.

"I know you want her. I know what she carries and the power that it can afford you. Save her life and I will give her to you," I said aloud.

I paused, took a breath, and added, "Valliar."

The Seventh Rule of Villainy

A villain will never claim victory. Victory only comes when all enemies have either perished or submit to you and they claim you victor.

Otherwise, you are bound to be beaten just when you think you have won.

Chapter Fifty-One

Where I Sell Lydia and Take Cover While the Avatars Battle

A burst of white lighting crackled down through the great hall and struck Lydia in the chest. The blast knocked me back and Lydia sat up immediately, gasping for air.

Lydia looked at me and instead of her normal brown eyes, orbs of pure white stared back at me. She looked at me as if for the first time. Her unnatural gaze regarded me with a look of disgust, as one would if they were forced to stare at a steaming pile of dog feces.

Valliar, the god of order and light, had empowered her as his avatar. She now carried a portion of his power and his temperament. No doubt as she looked on me, all she saw were my various sins. No doubt she would view me with disgust.

"Well, hello, dirty boy. I knew you were bad, but never *that* bad."

"Um, what?"

Lydia didn't really stand up as much as she simply *ascended* to her feet. "Smart move, giving me to Valliar over Khasil."

"I thought so as well."

"But the question is, *how* did you give me to Valliar? You don't own me."

"That is true. I don't. Which was why I could not save you. I do co-own what grows inside you. And thus, by the rules of this realm, patriarchal as they are, you fall under me. So I could sell you."

Lydia's white eyes regarded me, once again, as dog feces. "You knocked me up?"

"Apparently so. It is the only reason the gods would want you. No offense. The offspring of a god and a mortal is often powerful, and apt to unbalance the universal flows. It's what demi-gods do."

Lydia placed her hand on her stomach. Then slapped me in the face. Hard.

"When this is over, we are going to have a long talk."

I rubbed my stinging face. "Of that I have no doubt. Now, would you be so kind as to go and remove Khasil's influence over Grimskull so we can finish this?"

"How?" Lydia asked.

"Just do what comes naturally. You will want to . . . cleanse him of her taint."

Lydia nodded and walked around the throne, then paused and looked back at me. "Heh. You said 'her taint.'"

"Just go."

"Boss, what does this mean?" Sophia asked.

"She will have to make a choice. Valliar has imbued her with his power. So, she will feel a pull to do good. But she is still control of her choices. Unless she knows they are morally wrong."

"I know that, sir. I meant . . . for the child."

"That I do not know. This is a first for me."

I never had a child before, at least none I knew of. But this child would no doubt be special. Now, it was nothing more than a rapidly growing cluster of cells, but the bastard blastula growing inside my baby-momma had been exposed to the power of several gods. There was no way Junior wasn't going to be something special. This child was going to exact a terrible price upon the world.

Not to mention how much it was going to cost me in interdimensional child support.

Lydia, now aglow in white light, glided inches off the floor towards the monstrous Grimskull. The scene was surreal as the two godly avatars squared off against one another in the great hall.

Grimskull seemed unsure at first, but an upward glance at his godly benefactor renewed his commitment to her cause. The monster swiped a massive claw at Lydia's head, but the newly deputized agent of—yuck—*good* simply raised her arms. The resulting impact sent shock waves of power rippling through the great hall. Masonry broke free at the explosion of power.

From behind the throne I saw my allies hunkered down behind a makeshift barricade of overturned tables. With the amount of power these two divinely inspired beings were slinging, the tables might well have been made of tissue paper.

I reached out and wrapped Carina, Wren, Hawker, and Zachariah in ripples of telekinetic power and pulled them across the room to me. The quartet landed in a heap behind the throne. Once they were safe, I threw up a dome to shield us from the backlash of power.

"Jackson, how is Lydia doing that?" Hawker asked.

"Nnng . . . long story, kid," I said as I fought to hold the shield.

Lydia blocked each of Grimskull's blows with perfect precision. The ensuing blast of power destroyed more and more of the castle. Silvery-white and greenish-black lightning snaked in all directions as the battle raged.

As Grimskull began to tire, Lydia chose to go on the offensive. The former thief used her martial prowess to dance and dodge around Grimskull's massive form. Lydia began to rain blow after blow against Grimskull's armored carapace. With each strike, Valliar's power rocketed through the baron's body, knocking pieces of his chitinous armor off and cleansing more of Khasil's taint.

Heh heh . . . Khasil's taint. OK, it *was* funny.

With each display of raw power, more lightning crackled across the room. Grimskull's hulking form began to diminish, as did the remainder of the great hall. The effort to maintain the shield was growing more and more taxing as the shield deflected both stray strikes of energy and debris of the crumbling castle.

"Jackson, what can we do?" Wren asked.

"Nothing. Just be ready."

"Ready for what?"

"For an opening," I said. Holding the shield against the flying rock and stone wasn't so bad, but the power of the gods' avatars was incredible to defend against. I had a horrible feeling that all the power I had siphoned from Paige was quickly being depleted.

"What kind of opening?" Hawker asked.

"If this goes right, Grimskull will revert back to his mortal form. But he will still be empowered by his own magics, enhanced by the Never Realm."

"The Amulet of the Ember Soul," Hawker said.

"Exactly. It is around his neck. If you see an opening, you take it. Destroy it, and you destroy him."

"I'll be ready."

In one final attack, both Grimskull and Lydia circled each other, like two animals looking for the weak spot in the other's neck. Then at once, both avatars swung wild for one another, placing all their godly power into their attack.

Both connected.

The ensuing blast was like a bomb going off. The wall nearest to the blast simply evaporated as the destructive force blew it completely away, exposing the castle's main courtyard far below. Stonework and debris rained down upon the allied forces gathered there.

The explosive power of the attack scattered everything that was not bolted down to the far corners of the hall. The massive doors leading into the hall were reduced to splintered driftwood and barely hung on their steel hinges.

My semi-spherical shield held at first. But by the tail end of the concussive force, the reserves of my power had been reached. My shield popped like a soap bubble in the wind, and the residual detonation flung us like ragdolls across the room.

All I remembered after that was hitting my head. Oh, and realizing I was completely powerless. A mere mortal playing war games with gods. That was when unconsciousness claimed me.

Chapter Fifty-Two

Where Hawker Gets His Revenge and Grimskull Gets a Visit

A hard smack across the mouth let me know I was still alive, even if my eyes refused to open. The second smack let me know I detested being struck in the face. I sensed the third strike coming and I threw my hand up clumsily, blocking the hit while I fought to open my eyes.

"Jackson!" I heard a voice scream. "Are you alive?"

"Of course I am, you fucking idiot," I tried to say, but the only thing my mouth said was unintelligible babble. I tasted coppery blood, and my eyes were sealed shut. I ran a barely functioning hand over my head and felt a deep head laceration along my hairline. The wound was bleeding at an alarming rate, as head wounds tend to do. The blood was congealing in my eyes, making it hard to open them.

"Jackson!" the voice screamed again. I realized it was Hawker's.

"Hawker. Where's Wren? I need healing. Fairly sure I have a concussion and I think my shoulder is dislocated," I said.

I heard Hawker spit on his hands, and then I felt his thumbs wipe the blood from my eyelids, allowing me to pry them open.

I was on my side and all around was complete devastation. The air was thick with masonry dust clinging to the blood. But as my eyes focused, I saw what kept Wren from attending to my wounds. Zachariah was knelt down beside Carina, holding her hand.

Her hand was the only part of her not covered in blood or sprouting steel.

When my shield gave out, we were thrown across the room, but not until the majority of the blast was over. So, when we went flying, we flew into the room's contents. Wren and Hawker had been protected by their armor, and I had hit my head and shoulder against one of them.

Carina had been the first to fly. She was the first to land on a pile of discarded weapons. Her body served as a human shield, protecting the rest of us from her fate.

Broken swords and broken pieces of wood impaled her body. The last wound was particularly ironic; the jagged shard of wood that pierced her throat was from her own broken battle staff. Her lips were already turning blue as her body was cooling. There was no dignity in this death. Yet her sacrifice, inadvertent as it was, saved the rest of us. Of all of us, she was the most innocent.

Wren, who had been standing there watching the body of his newly beloved, collapsed and wept. As a Templar of Vammar, he had great power to heal. But healing could not mend the dead.

Grunting, I stood and found that my right ankle was swollen and in pain. I couldn't tell if it was broken or sprained. It didn't matter. I limped over to Carina's body and laid a hand on her head.

"May you find the peace in death you never found in life," I said. And here I thought that the redheaded females always survived the story. If I had put money on it, I would have bet that Wren would have been the one to die. Her death, while of no consequential loss or gain for me, still had a strange impact.

I felt . . . grief?

I was glad, if only for this one reason, that my power was burned out. If Sophia heard, or sensed, my feeling remorse, then she would no doubt plot my ruination.

"Jackson," Hawker said, getting my attention back to the moment. "Look."

Hawker's outstretched finger pointed to the epicenter of the destruction. In the middle of the blast crater were two bodies. Lydia was unconscious and barely breathing. Her clothing was shredded to the point of rags. She no longer glowed with Valliar's light. But she and my unborn child were alive.

The other body was that of Baron Viktor Grimskull, back in his mortal form—all the power of Khasil wiped away. The baron too was reduced to shredded clothing and destroyed armor. Around his neck dangled the Amulet of the Ember Soul. The baron stood on unsteady legs and began to laugh.

"I have won! Khasil's power has overcome Valliar's!" the baron rejoiced, shaking his fists above his head.

"You have won nothing," Wren said, standing. The Templar cast one last glance at Carina, then began marching towards Grimskull. Zachariah and Hawker flanked him as they marched towards the baron.

"Fools. Even now you dare defy me?"

"Brother, you are the fool. Look outside." Zachariah pointed out the gaping hole to the courtyard below. "Your army is destroyed. Your lieutenants are dead. The castle is surrounded."

"Let the peons watch as I snatch victory from them and life from you, brother," Grimskull said as his hands began glowing. While the power of Khasil had fled, the power from the Never Realm afforded Grimskull by the Amulet of the Ember Soul remained.

"Stop now and I will let you live," Zachariah offered.

"The hell we will," Hawker said. "He dies."

"Spoken as a true son of mine," Grimskull said.

"I'm not your son. My father was Bjorn. He was a simple man, from a simple village. He raised me to fight monsters like you."

"And how well did that work out for him?" Grimskull taunted.

Before Hawker could reply, Grimskull hurled a bolt of fire at Hawker. The miniature comet struck Hawker in his left side, melting away armor and burning flesh. But before Hawker fell, Wren laid his hands on Hawker, washing him in the blue healing energies of Vammar. Hawker's side healed instantly and the young man barely missed a step.

"If you live, you live. If you die, you die. All we may do is play our parts and let fate decide," Wren said as he continued his slow march with Hawker towards Grimskull.

"Pretty words. Empty and pointless, but pretty," Grimskull said as he released a barrage of green lightning upon the trio.

Zachariah quickly muttered his own words of magic and released his own burst of red lighting. The spells slammed into one another in a cascade of multi-colored sparks as each bolt canceled the other out.

A blast hit Hawker in his side, but Wren was there immediately to heal him. They continued to march. Another spell breached Zachariah's defense and singed the older brother, who began to fall. Once again, Wren caught him, healed him, and set him on his feet.

Spell after spell Grimskull threw at the approaching men, and each time one struck, Wren healed them instantly, or Zachariah countered.

Grimskull could only stare wide-eyed in disbelief.

I, on the other hand, wished for a bowl of popcorn while I sat next to Carina's corpse, watching the show. In my wounded and powerless state, it was best for me to do what I did best: letting others fight for me. For good or bad, this was the end of my journey. These were the final moves, my pieces and pawns playing out the roles I designed.

Zachariah and Hawker had closed to within melee range and the former student and teacher were locked in two-on-one mortal combat with Grimskull. Wren had skirted the outside of the battle and was attending to Lydia. The Templar pulled my lady friend free of the wreckage and placed her still-unconscious form safely behind a chunk of mostly whole stonework.

As much as I highlight Grimskull's mental deficiencies, his martial prowess was something to behold. Summoning a sword of magic, Grimskull matched all his attackers blow for blow. As Zachariah attempted to blend magic into the battle, Grimskull was ready with a counter to each of his brother's spells.

Hawker deftly wielded his battleaxe, but Grimskull moved and weaved with grace and precision. His own sword snaked in and out of Hawker's defenses, drawing blood with each strike.

I was honestly shocked that Hawker was doing as well as he was. Just over a year ago, he was a simple village boy before his fate found him. But I guess that was the way of the realms. A simple kid can turn from a bumbling hayseed into a heron-marked blademaster with a few quests and an obligatory training montage as long as the fates decree it. Never mind the fact that every opponent said kid goes up against is a student of combat day in and day out. Sickening, I know. But tropes are tropes.

Grimskull sensed his impending loss. His blocks were coming a half second too slow. His steps and evades were slightly off. Zachariah pressed the advantage, stepped in close, and swept his sword in a straight line, meaning to cleave Grimskull's head from his body.

At the last second, Grimskull snapped his sword upwards into a textbook-perfect block. The surprised Zachariah only had a moment to recognize the trap he'd stepped into before Grimskull released a burst of howling wind, sending his brother flying.

Hawker screamed his war cry and hacked downwards with his battleaxe. Grimskull simply moved backwards, allowing the chop to miss him completely while at the same time exposing Hawker. Grimskull repeated the same wind spell and launched his son across the room to land in a heap next to his uncle. Grimskull brought an empowered foot down on Hawker's battleaxe, snapping the exquisite weapon's shaft.

Oh . . oh, that was nice. I damn near applauded. Grimskull had lulled Hawker and Zachariah into his own version of the Muhammad Ali rope-a-dope. If this weren't bad for me, I would have been laughing.

I mean, let's face it—that was some excellent villainy right there.

"You have tried. You have failed. In the end, Grimskull stands supreme," Grimskull said, his left hand grasping his amulet while his right hand prepared the Curse of Unmaking. He pointed at his brother and son. "Goodbye, fools."

Damn! We'd come too far to lose to this buffoon! I scanned the room, looking for something, anything to turn the tide.

"Do you have any ideas?" I asked Carina's corpse.

And damned if she didn't.

Her broken battle staff was still in her throat, covered in her blood.

The blood of an innocent.

"Wren, stop him!" I commanded as I pulled the staff from Carina's throat.

"Vammar's will be done!" Wren screamed as he hurled his battle hammer in a side-arm motion. The weighted projectile spun horizontally, scant inches above the ground. The weapon glowed in a blue-red nimbus as it struck Grimskull's shins, breaking them and dropping the tyrant flat on his face as the Curse of Unmaking went wide, missing Hawker and Zachariah.

"Now!" I screamed.

What happened next seemed to happen in glorious movie magic, slow motion.

I threw the weapon as well as I could with my wounded arm. The broken staff tumbled end-over-end. Hawker ran and leaped for the weapon while Zachariah's magic gave the young warrior a boost into the air. Snatching the weapon in midair, Hawker brought it over his head, pointing the blood-covered tip downward.

Grimskull sat up to his knees just as Hawker came slamming down on top of him, driving the weapon directly into the Amulet of the Ember Soul. The amulet shattered into thousands of shards.

The air of the room immediately turned dark. Purple and black smoke erupted from every shadow. Demonic script glowed violet along the floors and what was left of the walls. A large nine-pointed star in a circle flared into being beneath the baron while spectral flames shone with a terrible blaze. Grimskull screamed as the fires burned him and him alone. Skeletal claws burst forth from the nine-pointed star, gripping the baron's legs, holding him in place to continue his agonizing immolation.

A screeching sound echoed through the hall, overpowering the screams of Grimskull. The sound was the heralds of the Never Realm, announcing the coming of one of the Infernal Exalted.

Monstrous red and black muscular arms burst forth from the burning star. The arms heaved and pulled the rest of their master forward as Y'ollgorath, Exalted One from the seventh plane of the Never Realm, peered into this realm with his five yellow eyes.

Those eyes scanned the room until they saw me. The demon smiled.

"Hey there Jackson! Long time!"
"Hey there, Y'olly."

Chapter Fifty-Three

Where I Reconnect with an Old Ally and Discover a New Enemy

Y'ollgorath and I went way back. He was something of a friend. Well, as much of a friend as one could be with a demon. Let's call him a longtime business associate of mine. He was my primary liaison between my realm and the Never Realm. Each time I met a would-be villain who was seeking power and cared little for the price, I always used Y'allgorath.

He was an incredibly devious—and dangerous—ally.

He also had something of beer gut. So when he tried pulling himself the rest of the way out of the nine-pointed star portal, he got stuck.

"A little help here? Jackson, could you give me a hand?"

I started applauding.

"Oh ha ha. Fine," Y'ollgorath said as he heaved and pulled his corpulent form the rest of the way free.

The naked Y'ollgorath stood an impressive fifteen feet tall on his reverse-jointed legs. His barbed, serpentine tail swished back and forth while his black wings stretched the reddish, translucent membranes to their full width. Y'ollgorath's horns were black and smooth, curling like a ram's. His head was bald and his mouth opened to reveal razor-sharp teeth and a forked snake's tongue.

As he stretched, his massive belly shook and rumbled like that of a demonic Santa Claus. Well, a Santa who liked flashing his red, barbed penis at everyone.

"Y'olly, I thought you were going to go on a diet?"

"I tried the low-carb thing. But come on. I'm a demon from the Never Realm. The whole place is sugar and carbs. Well, for us at least. But not for you, is it, little Viktor?" Y'ollgorath said as he smiled down on the still-screaming Grimskull.

"Slick move breaking the amulet," the demon said to Hawker.

Hawker looked at me. His face read "What the fuck?!" I nodded to him and gestured to Y'ollgorath. "Go on. You may speak to him. It would be rude not to. He cannot do anything to you without your permission. Just be careful what you say."

"Thank you?" Hawker said to the demon, who in turn nodded.

"You are very welcome. OK, I am going to drag this sack of flesh back home and do unspeakable things to, in, and on him. Unless anyone would like to trade his soul for theirs? It is part of the rules. Any takers?"

Whether it was a demon's presence, his candor, his cordiality, or that he was giant and naked, the room was shocked into silence.

"No, nobody?" Y'ollgorath asked. "How about trading your immortal soul for near limitless power? We have new rules and terms I think most of you would find amenable."

"Y'olly, come on. No shop talk. You claimed your soul," I said.

"Come on, like you don't use every opportunity to do a little shop talk. It's called networking," the demon said, crossing his arms.

"Fair enough. But not right now. We just had our final confrontation. So, a little peace, please."

The demon looked me up and down. "I'll say you all did. You're looking in a bad way, Jackson," Y'ollgorath noted. "Want a little healing? Nearly free of charge."

"I'll live."

Y'ollgorath shrugged. "Suit yourself. I'll be seeing you all. Very soon." The demon smiled.

"I have a request," Hawker said before the demon returned through the portal with Grimskull, his claimed prize, in tow.

"Oh really?" Y'ollgorath paused. "Do tell. What can this humble servant do for you, young master Kyle?"

The demon knew Hawker's name? That was never good. Since the Never Realm was one of the very few planes of existence that tangentially touched all others, it meant the demons there could view any and all things. Y'ollgorath had taken notice of Hawker. Because of his familial lineage, or another reason?

"I want you to make him suffer," Hawker said.

"Trust me, mortal, he will," Y'ollgorath confirmed.

"No." Hawker shook his head. "I want him to suffer more than any mortal ever has."

Hawker's turn towards a darker path was not unexpected. But I was sure he'd justified his request in his mind. With the deaths of his family and village, he most likely thought he was seeking righteous vengeance.

All corruptible heroes do.

I threw Y'ollgorath a nod and the demon winked back.

"You know what, kid? For you, I'll make sure of it personally. Free of charge. No strings attached."

"Thank you," Hawker said, bowing his head.

"Unless there are any other offers or deals I can make, I'll be on my way," Y'ollgorath said.

As he began his descent into the nine-star portal, Y'ollgorath waved goodbye, then grabbed Grimskull by his leg. "Tell me baron, have you ever had you urethra violently probed by a barbed demon penis? I believe it's called 'docking,' but with a few infernal twists. You're going to love it. Well, you won't, but I will!"

As the demon and his heralds departed, the inky smoke dissipated and the room returned to normal.

"You know the most interesting people," Zachariah said, and I nodded in agreement.

"So, that's it? It's over?" Hawker asked.

"Something of a letdown, isn't it?" I said as I limped over to Wren and the still-unconscious Lydia.

That was the thing with quests. Once they were over, so was a person's sense of purpose. Like a soldier after war, or prisoner released back into freedom.

"What are we going to do now?" Hawker asked.

"Whatever you want," I said. "I promised Zachariah the throne of the Eastern Empire. It was his by birthright. And he promised to rule the empire with a benevolent guiding hand. I'm sure he will need help."

"Will you truly rule with peace and kindness . . . uncle?" Hawker asked Zachariah.

The old mentor looked his young apprentice and nephew in his eyes and lied through his teeth.

"I am not, my brother. I wish you had learned of our relationship a different way, Kyle. But I will make this land, and that of the late Countess Skullgrim's Western Empire, into a unified kingdom that will bring peace and prosperity to all who dwell within. If you want to be part of that, then there is a place by my side."

Damn. That was an excellent line of bullshit. The best lies always were.

"I will," Hawker said.

Deep down, I think the kid knew his uncle was a villain. And deep down, Hawker knew one day he would be as well. But like I said, those without purpose feel lost. That's why some retired soldiers become mercenaries and soldiers of fortune. And why this young man would stand by his uncle's side to enslave the land under the guise of unification.

"What about you, Wren?" Hawker said. "Would you join us?"

"No," the big man said. He finished attending to Lydia, making her sleeping form as comfortable as possible.

"Why?"

"This place is not for me. Too many bad memories. I will walk the land and go where Vammar directs me. There are people out there who need help. And I will find them, and help them."

"But we're going to unify the kingdoms. We are going to need help."

Wren shook his head. "So you say. But right now there is a power vacuum. Too many warlords and tyrants died today. When that happens, the little people suffer as new would-be conquerors rise. I will be there for them. Not you."

"What are you saying?" Hawker asked Wren, his tone taking a serious edge.

Wren held his hammer a moment and considered the head of the weapon. He tapped it several times in the palm of his hand. "Only that power corrupts. Even those who set out to do good oftentimes hurt the weak they claim they are helping."

Wren took a breath, then looked up at Hawker. "If that day comes, should that day come, then you and I will be on opposite sides."

Hawker narrowed his eyes. "I'll take it under advisement."

"I wish you luck," Wren said, extending his hand. Hawker took it in his own. The two men shared a moment.

Ah, bromance.

"Well, isn't this nice. Hail the conquering heroes," a voice rang out. Magnified and ominous. Enhanced by godly power.

Randy's?

I looked up and to the balcony railing where a section of wall had slid away, revealing a secret passage. Randy stepped forth, his eyes glowing a blazing orange and white. A vulpine grin was etched into his face.

Finally, a secret passage. And Randy got to use it.

Fate hates me.

Randy dove off the balcony in a perfect swan dive, rolled in midair, and landed on his feet. A ripple of orange power blasted outwards as he did, knocking us all to the ground. With my existing injuries, I crumpled like paper. The others did not fare much better.

I saw Khasil and Valliar watching the scenario play out from their seats in the opposite balcony.

Randy followed my eye line and smirked. Raising his hands, Randy released another blast of energy at the two gods. The beams hit them both, binding them in bands of power.

Randy then turned his attention to me. He smiled as he knelt down beside me.

"Hello, Uncle. It's time to die."

Chapter Fifty-Four

Where I Am Dumbstruck

Randy.

A secret villain genius.

I am going to need a moment to process this.

In the meantime, do me a favor. Look back on this tale and see if I missed something I should have seen.

Seriously, go ahead. I'll wait.

Fucking Randy.

That was supposed to be my secret passage.

Fuck.

Chapter Fifty-Five

Where I Witness Evil and Receive a Lecture

"You should see yourself, Uncle Jackson. The look on your face is priceless. Confused is an exceptional expression for you. It highlights your hubris and your foolish belief that you control all villainy."

What . . . the . . . fuck?

"Still not grasping everything, I see. Fine. I will use smaller words."

"Jackson!" Hawker screamed. The warrior ran headfirst towards Randy, still gripping Carina's broken battle staff. Randy gazed upon Hawker as if he were bored. With a slight gesture, Randy unleashed a wave of power that slammed Hawker against the nearby wall. Stone and debris the size of small boulders fell on the collapsed Hawker.

Randy spotted Wren trying to move in behind him. Randy's wicked smile grew even wider. He gestured at the back of the room and released another wave of power.

Carina's body began to rise. The corpse stood awkwardly on newly empowered legs. Her body moved jerkily towards Wren, still bearing the broken blades that had killed her.

"Vammar, help me," Wren whispered.

The walking dead shrieked and charged the Templar. Wren raised his shield as Carina's corpse slammed into him. With her magically augmented strength, Carina gripped Wren and picked him up. She ran, carrying them both towards the open wall. At the last moment, Wren threw his legs down, digging in and slowing them both.

It was a battle of wills. A battle of strength. A battle of gods. Randy's power pitted against Vammar's.

Wren's legs buckled.

Carina and Wren fell out the opening to courtyard below.

Randy next set his gaze on Zachariah, who threw his hands in the air. "I'm not a threat! All hail the new lord."

"Smart," Randy said.

"Thank you."

"Smart people concern me. They rarely accept the fact they are being mastered," Randy said.

Randy held out both his hands and the orange-white energy coalesced around his hands once more. Randy contorted his hands as if he were crushing a beer can.

Zachariah's body bent and broke inward. His bones snapped with audible pops. His skin ripped open as splintered bone and blood spewed forth.

Zachariah screamed. He screamed until there was no air left in his body.

Zachariah would not scream again, as his twisted body collapsed, crushing his lungs. In a final gesture, Randy suddenly pulled his hands apart and Zachariah's body was simply torn in half. Each hunk of flesh was tossed to either side of the hall. Randy was like a child torturing animals out of boredom. Each act was nothing more than a display of cruelty.

"Now, where is that chubby mistress of yours?" Randy asked.

Lydia was lying closer to the great hall's main doors. The blast from Randy's entrance must have blown her further away. She remained unmoving.

"Hmm," Randy said, considering whether or not to waste the power.

"How?" I asked.

"Hmm?" Randy said bringing his attention back to me. "Oh, how am I able to do things you cannot? How I am able to touch those from another realm who are not directly threatening me? How I can modify what is not mine? How I can bind two gods?"

"Yes."

"Come on, Uncle Jackson. Use that brain you are so proud of."

This new Randy was vile and wicked. He wasn't just a villain; he was evil. And watching his astonishingly evil acts had blinded me to the answer I already knew.

"You're a demigod," I sighed, shaking my head. "That's why you wanted your mother alive. So your power would remain intact."

"Bravo, Uncle," Randy said. "Demigods don't play by the same rules as the rest of you deity types. For those who are daring enough to seize power, then there really isn't anything that can stop us. If we're smart."

Randy sat down next to me, as if we were longtime drinking buddies. The little bastard had the audacity to put his arm around me. Randy surveyed the destruction of the great hall and had a satisfied look on his face. He even reached into my belt pouch and took out one of my cigarettes and lit it.

"See, the trick was playing the long game. Once I learned about the family secret from Mom, I knew I wanted in. She always talked so poorly about you. Yet the moronic cow kept going back to you for more money whenever she ran out. Do you want to know a little secret, Uncle Jack?"

"Must you talk?"

"Good one, Uncle," Randy said, shaking me with a good-natured hug hard enough to break bones. "I'm the reason we were always out of money. Sure, she spent a lot drinking, buying useless things. All the things uneducated trash do with their money instead of saving, investing, and spending wisely. But whenever she went out, I was stealing it. Hiding large sums here and there in various bank accounts I set up. She, of course, assumed she spent it. Woman never was good with money. But the reason I stole it was so that she would go back to you, hat in hand, asking for more. And it was on those trips I got to come to your little dimension. I learned more and more about you and the rules of realms."

I didn't know what to say. I looked at him, smoking my cigarette and speaking eloquently. Here, in this realm, among destruction and blood, *I* was being lectured on villainy.

By Randy.

The gods above and below were laughing at me. Come to think of it, there were two of them here. Even bound, I could tell they were taking joy in this.

"When I was eight years old," Randy said, speaking aloud if not to me, "I came to the conclusion that I was smarter than my mother. Something I must have inherited from whomever my father was. At least he was smart enough to get away from that woman. You were the smart one of the family. And it was you I wanted to get to know and become close with. But let us be honest, that is not something you ever wanted. You made that abundantly clear."

"Randy—" I tried to speak, but Randy grabbed me by my hair and slammed me against the ground with his enhanced strength.

Coupled with the concussion I already had, I was like a child in his grasp. Randy set me back up as quickly as he'd slammed me down. My head was spinning and pain lanced through my now clearly dislocated shoulder.

"Do shut up, Uncle," Randy said.

Thus far I'd say my fall to my own arrogance was going fairly well. Beatings aside, Randy fell into a villain trope: the monologue.

And while doing that, he missed a couple of key actions that happened right under his nose. Now all I had to do was keep my usurping nephew occupied and focusing all his attention on me.

If this worked, I might actually survive.

The Second Rule of Villainy

A villain will know every rule through and through. And when in doubt, a villain will always refer to rule #1.

Chapter Fifty-Six

Where I Am Forced to Listen to Randy and I Test a Theory

"Now, where was I?" Randy asked. "Oh yes. Please do not take this the wrong way, Uncle, or do, I honestly do not care, but people like you look down on those you feel are intellectually inferior. And most of the time, people like you consider nearly everyone to be your inferior. Thus, it is amazingly easy to hide in plain sight as long as one puts on the proper imbecile affectations while speaking in contractions and shortened words. It helps to wear the moronic clothing my slacker generation seems to gravitate towards. From there, all I ever had to do was sit on the couch, pretend to play with my phone and listen. And listen I did. Over the years I learned all your rules, as you are prone to wax on. My god, you like the sound of your own voice."

"So, over the years I stole items from your realm. I know you knew I stole them. I wanted you to see me steal them, Uncle. That way, you considered me inept and not a threat. But what I was doing was testing my powers. As my mother was technically a goddess, then I as a demigod had to practice my power. But my real skill was in mental manipulation. It was not hard to convince mother that she needed to usurp you. It was easier still to convince Courtney that he had feelings for my mother. Your receptionist, though—she was impossible to crack. What is her story, anyway? How do you have someone that loyal to you?"

"Go ask her and find out," I said as my head cleared a little.

"I think I might. So once I had the players set, all I had to do was put the plans into motion. Grimskull was easy enough to seduce. I placed both mother and him under a charm, where they felt they were in love and their only goal was bringing you down. With Courtney similarly bewitched into loving mom and doing anything for her, the mission to come to this land was the perfect trap. You were doomed the moment we came through the portal here."

"You planned all this?" I asked.

Randy smiled. "I did. And I can see your mind moving, Uncle. Why bring you here? Well, I needed a place with vengeful gods who hated you.

Once here, and the trap was sprung, I needed you to do what you do so well. The infamous Shadow Master would not allow himself to be bested by anyone, let alone a buffoon like Grimskull. You had to be convinced you were set up. Which you were. Your hubris refused you to consider me a threat. All I needed was for you to escape Grimskull's and set everything into motion."

"Of course," I said, thinking it all through. "You were leaning against the prison bars with the phone in your hand."

Randy laughed. "I was this close to just throwing the damn thing at you and screaming 'Run, Uncle Jack, run!' But I was pleased you eventually figured it out. From there all you had to do was raise an army, get the gods involved, eliminate your competition, and return. You bent the rules to your benefit, as I knew you would. And every time anyone got close to you, I made sure you escaped."

"You protected me?"

"What? Did you think that you did it all by yourself?" Randy asked. "Well, fine . . . for the sake of honesty, you did most of the work. I just made sure they were always a step or two behind you. Is your ego properly stroked now?"

"Sufficiently. But how could you track me when no one else could?"

"Uncle . . . seriously?"

I shook my head at my own stupidity. "Of course, it was your phone I empowered. They couldn't track me, but you knew where your phone—and thereby I—was at any time."

"Duh."

"I deserved that," I said. "But, may I ask you a question or two, Nephew?"

"Why not."

"What are you using as a totem? I don't see a phone and you clearly are imbued with my realm's power."

"Simple, really. Phones, totems, items and the like are very cumbersome and very old-fashioned thinking. If you had used your mind a little, you would realize that internalizing your power would be far more useful."

"Internalizing? You mean you swallowed something? Doesn't that just get messy when you need to . . . retrieve it on the back end?"

Randy rolled his eyes. "Twelve-hour time release capsules, Uncle. Imbue the power into a long-lasting pill and you have all the power you need."

"Smart," I said honestly. "When I get out of this I will keep the tip in mind."

Randy laughed.

A lot.

"Oh, Uncle Jackson. You are beaten. You have been bested. And now *I* am the villain. And now, here you sit. Wounded and all your power burned out because you didn't have the conviction to kill my mother."

"He's kind of a big softy like that!" Lydia called out from on top of the balcony. She had my sister in a chokehold with hand and one of her knives held to Paige's throat. "But I'm not."

"It's nice to know you took my advice," I called to her. While Randy was bloviating, I saw Lydia look up and smile at me. She had kept up the unconscious charade in order to learn information. And learning that Paige was the key to Randy's demigod status was indeed key intelligence.

I'd pat myself on the back if I could for instructing her. The reward I received instead was a vicious backhand from Randy.

"Silence, Uncle," Randy said. "You! Release my mother!"

Lydia laughed. "Now why would I do that?"

"She is a god, you cow! Your weapons can't hurt her. And even if you could, I would then destroy you."

"First, watch your mouth, little boy. You couldn't handle this body. Your uncle can barely keep up."

Despite the pain, I laughed. She wasn't wrong.

"Second, I was very recently chosen to be the avatar of Valliar. I am literally coursing with godly power designed to smite the wicked. And this knife was a gift from Valliar himself. A godly weapon with the power to kill other gods. So, what exactly do you think your odds are?"

"I am a god!" Randy screamed. His voice echoed with power as everything that wasn't nailed down rattled and shook. Amid his little tantrum, Randy missed another key piece of the puzzle.

Templar Wren had stealthily sneaked back up and through the section of missing wall where he was dragged by Carina's corpse. For a big man, Wren could move scarily quietly. Perhaps an enchantment of Vammar's? With Randy's attention still on Lydia and his captive mother, Wren was able to move into position. Wren looked at me for permission and I nodded.

"Listen to me, you low-born whore, I do not care what deity has chosen you for his meat suit. If you harm her, I will kill you. This is my moment, not yours. I am the new Shadow Master!"

"You're barely practice," Wren said from behind Randy. "Ready for round two?"

Randy snapped his head around in shock and disbelief. "But . . . you died!"

"Dead ain't dead unless you see the body, kid," Wren said, swinging his massive hammer.

Randy went flying as couple hundred pounds of pissed-off Templar put all his godly enhanced strength behind his swing. The sound of a snapping spine was audible as Randy was launched into the air. My nephew landed in a heap of broken stone and rubble.

"Gods above and below, he is related to you," Wren said.

"Please, do not remind me," I said. "Do you have enough power to spare for a little healing?"

Wren smiled and slammed his hammer down on my head. The impact broke my skull. And as always, Vammar's power healed me immediately.

I grabbed my head in phantom pain. "I thought you didn't have to do that anymore?!"

"I don't."

"Asshole," I said, holding out my hand. Wren grabbed it and pulled me up.

Wren nodded, then looked around. "Where's Hawker?"

"Here," the young warrior said, pushing his way up from the rubble where Randy had left him for dead. "Somehow the rubble landed in a way where it braced itself instead of crushing me."

"Yeah yeah, praise the gods, for your dumb luck," Lydia said. "Now, do you want me to kill this bitch or not?"

All eyes turned to me.

In a moment that felt like an eternity, I had to decide whether or not my sister died. On one hand, her death would remove Randy's power instantly. On the other hand, I was not a murderer. Well, I was, but those killings had purpose.

But didn't this one as well?

Did my sister's life have . . . value? Did she have meaning to me?

I was right back to where I was only the night before. Paige defeated, and my having to decide her fate. In that moment I had let her live because Randy convinced me to, in order to retain his power. But the choice, and the impact of that choice, was just as true then as it was now.

A thought popped into my head. I looked up to Valliar, who only smiled back at me.

No. Could it be that simple?

I thought about everything that had happened since coming here and a ridiculous theory formed in my mind.

Valliar, you crafty bastard.

"No," I said. "Do not kill her."

Chapter Fifty-Seven

Where the Heroes Unite and Randy Tells a Very Unfunny Joke

"Why?" Lydia asked, sounding both confused and disappointed.

"You couldn't if you wanted to," I said.

"Watch me!" Lydia said. She tried to jab her blade into Paige's throat, but her muscles refused to move.

"What's wrong with me?"

"Nothing. You are Valliar's mortal avatar."

"Meaning?"

"Meaning you can't do anything morally wrong," I said.

"No killing? No theft? No . . . dirty stuff?!"

"Sorry," I said, shaking my head. "I don't know the ins and outs of Valliar's credo. I'm sure there are loopholes. But I don't see one where cold-blooded murder is allowed."

"And you gave me to him because why?"

"Because he is weak. And stupid," Randy said angrily, trying to rise to his feet. It was clear he was trying to use his power to heal himself and was having a difficult time.

"Godly imbued weapons, what a bitch," I said, taunting Randy. "Now please be a dear and just stay put; adults are talking. Lydia, I did it because you and our child were going to die."

"I guess you have a point. My life is worth a lot, even if it means I can't stab this bitch. Ow!" Lydia screamed as she struggled with Paige, who was now completely awake and running away. "She bit me!"

"You more than likely have rabies now," I said. "Possibly several sexually transmitted diseases."

"So do you."

"What?"

"Nothing," Lydia said. "Do I go after her?"

"No, leave her. She is powerless now," I said. It looked like Paige also knew the faking-unconscious-to-learn-secrets trick. Once she knew that Lydia couldn't hurt her, she hauled ass.

"Uncle! This is not over," Randy yelled.

"It was over the moment you considered crossing me, boy."

In response, broken rubble began to rise and float in an intricate pattern around Randy. Faster and faster the stones spun. While it was clear his body was partially paralyzed, Randy's power was not.

Throwing his arms forward, Randy hurled a hail of deadly rock at me. Wren leaped to my side and raised his shield. Blue light beamed from it as the protection of Vammar intercepted the attack. Rock and stone bounced off Wren's shielding magic.

"Remind me again why I save you so often?"

"Because I'm endearing," I said with a smile.

Hawker came to stand next to Wren and me. He nodded silently to us and simply took up his battle position. There the three of us stood, squared off against my nephew. Three—ugh—heroes, ready to go down fighting a common enemy.

It was so poetically beautiful, it made me want to throw up a little.

"You have a plan?" Hawker asked, keeping his eyes on Randy and staying ready.

"Yes. We kick his ass," I said, looking at Hawker's hand where he was still clutching Carina's broken battle staff for a weapon. "Not much of a weapon."

"Not much of a plan."

"Trust me, I have a bigger backup plan," I said.

"Last plan you had got us here. Then all this happened. Perhaps you're not as smart as you think you are," Wren said.

"Seconded!" Lydia yelled from the balcony.

"Not funny," I said.

"Exactly. It's hilarious."

"Just get your ass down here. We have other matters to contend with."

Lydia jumped from the balcony over the spot where Grimskull was dragged into the Never Realm. Just before she crashed, soft light and warm winds buffeted her descent. She landed as softly as if she had rolled out of bed. It appeared that Valliar was still inside her.

Metaphorically.

Well, literally.

Damn it—not like that!

Perverts.

Lydia picked up Hawker's broken battleaxe from where she landed. Snatching the weapon, she ran over to stand the line with us. Lydia set the weapon's head onto the broken battle staff in Hawker's hand. The weapons united as if meant for one another. Hawker now held a very deadly, if much shorter, godly weapon.

Hawker nodded his approval and we all turned our attention to Randy.

"Fucking heroes. Look at you four," Randy spat. "What are heroes without the villain? Nothing! It is the villain that sets the stage. It is the villain that causes the drama. Without us, the villains, the hero is nothing. Has nothing. No motive. No ambition. Nothing!"

I swear I'd heard something very similar not too long ago. No doubt orated by a much smarter, better-looking, more worldly individual with clearer execution.

Amateurs.

"You will not take this moment from me," Randy yelled while he vainly hurled more and more massive chunks of stone at us, only to be deflected by Wren's shield.

It was clear Randy's power was running out. His attempts to heal his body were exacting a massive toll on his power reserves. Throwing rocks was all he had left in him. "I have worked too long and too hard to get here."

"If you cease now, Randy, I will let you live," I said, ignoring the "long and hard" comment.

"N-never!" Randy seethed, his eyes glowing with hatred and power. Corpses from all over the room began to animate, standing up and preparing for battle, while thunder and lightning manifested within the great hall.

An impotent gesture from a beaten man.

"Zombies?" I asked.

"On it," Hawker said, diving into the undead. The warrior swung his new weapon with reckless abandon, cutting the zombies down before they had a chance to attack *en masse*.

"Weather?"

"I've got this one. I still have a little bit of Valliar in me," Lydia said.

"Uhh," I sighed. "Phrasing?"

Lydia laughed as her eyes turned white. She raised her arms to her sides and white nimbus energy accumulated around her hands. Her feet slowly rose until she was once again hovering above the floor. Lydia's light grew brighter and brighter, encapsulating her body. The power that raised the storm was pushed further and further back to its source, and in moments the storm ceased entirely. Lydia returned to the floor and her light dimmed. It was almost sad.

"Look, I am very tired now and I want this all over. Do you have any other tricks, Nephew, or can we just please end this story?" I asked, mocking Randy. To my surprise, the kid had one left.

Randy pushed himself to his knees and looked at me. His face was bruised and broken from his landing. I could read the pain on his face from where Wren's hammer had hit him. Yet he was smiling.

"This . . . isn't over."

"Unless you have one last joke to tell, boy, this farce is over," I said.

Randy pulled out a gun. A gun I forgot he had. The gun he killed Courtney with.

My nephew shot me in the chest.

"How's that for a punch line, motherfucker?"

Chapter Fifty-Eight

Where I Have a Near-Death Experience

From my perspective, that was *not* funny.

"Jackson!" I heard someone scream, but for the life of me I didn't know who it was. It could have been some or all of my allies. Getting shot has an odd way of distorting one's perception of the world. Perhaps it was the shock?

My knees bent of their own volition and I felt myself fall flat on my back. My head bounced against the stone floor. To be honest, I barely felt it.

Yeah, I must have been in shock.

From flat on my back I saw Valliar and Khasil looking down at me from the balcony. While they were still bound, they were looking intently at me. Something in how they stared at me hinted that I was missing a bigger picture.

I heard Randy screaming at my allies. He was saying something about not moving or not helping me, or else the next one went in my head. I guess he meant another bullet. Wren could most likely heal this, but dead was dead. If Randy shot my skull, then Wren would only be trying to heal a sack of meat.

Why the hell was my mind wandering and thinking about that crap? Oh. Yes.

Randy shot me in the chest and I was bleeding out.

Julian Jackson Blackwell, a deep male voice said in my head.

Yes?

Snap out of it! a second female voice said.

Khasil? Valliar?

Obviously, Khasil said.

Damn it. I can't even die in peace.

Then figure a way out of it, Valliar said.

A way out of dying? If you have a tip, I'm listening.

I told you he would not grasp it, Khasil said.

What I grasp is that you two are stuck and you need me to save you.

Yes, this is mutually beneficial, Valliar said.

And you need me, because my allies can't do it by themselves? I said.

Your friends *you mean,* Valliar said.

Friends? Why did he say that? In all my time here, I'd only considered them my allies. They had their uses. Lydia in particular was something more. But to see them as friends . . . That was not who I was. I was a villain. And my rules, while sometimes lengthy, were ultimately simple. At the top of that list: One does not have friends. Friends are a liability. Friends lead to caring. And caring is the path to being—

Oh. Oh, damn it.

Damn it, damn it damn it damn it damn it.

Realization hit me harder than Randy's bullet. My theory was all but confirmed. I thought I'd done enough already. I guess I still had more to give.

Is there anything you all could do to help me? I asked. *I am in a lot of pain here.*

Which was becoming more and more pronounced as the shock wore off, and my nerve endings were realizing there was a hole through my body.

We already did, Valliar said. *Your bleeding has stopped. We can sustain you slightly. But that is all we can directly do for you.*

How?

The mortal weapon missed your heart. As small a target as it was, Khasil said.

I'm not The Grinch, bitch.

I do not understand the reference, Khasil said, confused.

Then understand this, I said as I started to push past the pain and bring my mind back to the present world.

I am the one who does not lose. Not to you two, and damn sure not to some punk kid demigod who is only in existence because my slutty sister can't be bothered to use a condom or use her ass for another purpose. I'm the rule breaker. The villain of villains. I am the motherfucking Shadow Master. And if this is what it takes to win, then so be it.

I opened my eyes and sat up to a world of pain and agony.

But I was alive. And as long as I was alive, I would win.

Chapter Fifty-Nine

Where I Take a Painful Walk and Accept My Fate

"Impossible," Randy said as I began to rise.

"No, not impossible," I grunted. "Just—oh goddamn that hurts—just improbable."

"Jackson?!" Hawker exclaimed as he came to my side, helping me stand. "What did he do to you? What was that?"

"A weapon from my world."

"How are you standing?" Hawker asked, his hands red with my blood.

"Grit, Hawker. Grit."

Wren put himself between Randy and me. He held his shield up and stood in defiance. I placed my hand on Wren's shoulder. The big man looked back at me.

"No. Don't. That will puncture your armor and your shield."

"Vammar's power will—"

"Will do nothing," I said. "Not this time. This is bigger than Vammar. I have to do this alone."

"Do what?" Lydia said as she came to support me on the other side.

"I have to face him. Alone. This . . . this is between Randy and me."

"Are you an idiot?" Lydia asked.

"Most likely, yes," I said. "But it still has to be done."

"Uncle? What are you getting at?"

"You and me. Just you and me. We finish this story together. All I ask is that no matter what, my friends live."

"Now why would I do that?" Randy asked.

"Because they mean nothing to you. If you beat me, then you win. You beat the Shadow Master. After which you take all that I have. This place. Them," I gestured back to my friends. "They mean nothing."

"What is your angle, Uncle?"

"This time? No angle. You and I, and only one of us walks away. Well, maybe not 'walk' exactly. Because unless you get up, you're going to die on your knees."

Slowly, Randy stood on shaky legs. It was a testament to a will almost as strong as my own. Almost.

"As turned on as I am with this, don't do it," Lydia said. "We can take him together."

"Lydia's right, we can beat him together," Hawker said.

I put a hand on Hawker's armor and looked him in the eyes, "No. You did your part." I took a moment and looked at each of them in turn. "You all did your part. We would never have gotten as far as we have without you. I thank you, my friends. But this is my time, and mine alone. No matter what happens, you'll be OK. I will never forget any of you. My friends."

Lydia grabbed the front of my bloody shirt and pulled me towards her. She kissed me with passion and fever. If I hadn't lost so much blood, I would have had an incredible erection.

"Kick his ass," Lydia said as she broke the kiss. "Then come back to me."

"That's my plan," I said.

I walked away from my friends and took a few steps towards Randy. My nephew still had his gun trained on me. His newfound strength was inspiring, but his legs trembled with effort to stand. His power output must have been reaching its max.

Which was why I taunted him into standing.

My hand came to rest on the pommel of the sword at my side. It was the sword Hawker had given me on the banks of the Lower Eld. Randy saw my hand and pointed his gun at my head.

"It looks like you brought a sword to a gunfight, Uncle."

I unbuckled the weapon. The belt, sword, and scabbard hit the floor of the great hall.

"Jackson?! What are you doing?" Wren yelled.

I ignored my friends. Holding my arms out wide, I took a deep breath and started walking towards my nephew and his gun.

Randy fired the gun.

The bullet zipped past my left temple, grazing the flesh and tearing it open. I felt searing hot pain as the skin ripped open, but nothing more.

I kept walking.

Randy fired again.

The bullet tore past my right pectoral and through my lateral dorsi. Another bullet wound. Yet I kept walking towards Randy and his gun.

Randy fired again and again. Each bullet missed me, or tore through painful but non-life-threatening parts of my flesh. I stopped when I was within arm's reach of Randy.

"You're shaking, Nephew. Nerves, or the strain on your power reserves?"

Randy ignored the question and aimed the gun directly at my head. "At this range, I can't miss."

I took one last step and placed my forehead against the barrel.

"I don't want you to miss," I said, looking down the weapon's barrel directly into my nephew's eyes. Odd as it was, I noticed, perhaps for the first time, that we had the same eyes.

"Jackson! Stop!" my friends yelled from behind me. I ignored them and continued looking into the younger reflection of myself.

Perhaps in another life, another place, Randy and I could have been allies. Perhaps if I had been nicer to him? Or if he had been more forthcoming with me? Who knows what we could have accomplished together.

Now, it was just Randy and I on opposite ends of a loaded gun.

"You want to be the villain?" I asked.

"Yes, Uncle, I do."

"Will you let my friends live?" I asked.

"No."

"I didn't think so. I had to ask."

"Any last words, Uncle?"

"Yeah."

"It isn't one of your speeches, is it?"

I smiled a little, considering the circumstances. "No. No speeches. Just this: If you are the villain, then I guess that makes me the hero."

"Yeah, I guess it does. How the mighty have fallen."

Behind me were pawns I had used. Pawns who became allies. Allies who became friends. And I was between them and Randy. A trail of my own blood led inexorably to this moment. Something about the finality of it all made me smile, just a little.

"Just pull the trigger, Randy. You only get one shot. Make it count, kid."

"I will. Goodbye, hero."

Randy pulled the trigger.

Chapter Sixty

Where I Reveal the First Rule of Villainy

The gun's hammer fell. The impact struck the firing pin. The firing pin hit the bullet's cartridge primer. Once the primer ignited, the charge would ignite the gunpowder, pushing the bullet down the length of the barrel, spiraling like a football, directly through my skull and my brain and out the back of my head.

Except the primer didn't ignite.

It happens sometimes, like when an automatic pistol jams. In the world of gun enthusiasts, this is called a misfire. Right then and there, it was a miracle. And I took full advantage of that miracle.

I swung my right hand down, springing Nightfyr free from its magical bracelet, and slammed the heavy mace over Randy's head. His eyes showed complete shock up until the moment when the mace collided with his skull. After that, his eyes glazed over as he hit the ground, knocked the fuck out.

I rummaged thought Randy's pockets and found a pill bottle. I popped it open and took a couple of the twelve-hour release capsules. Immediately I felt power, my power, surge through me.

"Jackson!" Lydia said as she came to grab me from behind. "That was amazing!"

"I know."

"Ass."

"Also true."

"How did you know that was going to happen?" Wren said as he came to stand next to me.

"Honestly? I didn't," I said as I looked over my shoulder at Valliar. "I just had faith."

"That's quite a leap of faith indeed," Hawker said. He placed his battleaxe next to Randy's throat. "Should we finish this?"

"No!!" Paige screamed, running into the room and throwing herself on her unconscious son. "Julie, don't kill him. Please!"

"Move, Paige," I said.

"Julie?" Lydia, Hawker and Wren asked together.

I closed my eyes and exhaled slowly. "My first name is Julian. Paige likes to call me Julie because it makes me angry. Do you wish to taunt me now that I have my power back?"

"No," Hawker said, smiling.

"I am going to mock the shit out of you," Lydia said. I guess she gets a pass. We had seen one another naked, and she was my baby-momma.

"You?" I asked Wren.

"My first name is Gaylord. I don't have room to mock you."

"Gaylord? Really? Did your parents not like you?"

"You see why I just go by Wren now?"

"Good choice."

"You'll let him live, Julie?" Paige asked.

"Paige, he was going to kill me. The only reason you are alive is because Randy forced you to rebel against me. You are a complete and utter worthless human being. But you are innocent of that sin. He is not."

"If you kill him, then you have to kill me," Paige said, laying her body against her only child's.

There it was. Primal, animalistic nature. A mother protecting her son.

"Get . . . off me . . . Mother," Randy said as his eyes flickered open.

"He's trying to kill you," Paige said.

"He would have done it already," Randy said as his eyes came into focus, looking at me. His hands went to his pockets, searching.

I held up the pill bottle and shook them at him. "I've got your stash, kid."

"How?"

"I took them from you while you were knocked out."

Randy shook his head, then immediately regretted it. He turned away and then threw up. Concussions were like that. I'd had my share of them recently.

"How . . ." Randy spat out drips of vomit and bile, wiping it with the back of his sleeve. "How did you beat me?"

I smiled.

"How, goddamn it?! I followed all your rules!"

"Oh Randy," I said, smiling. He really had been listening. I felt (slightly) sad about defeating him. There was an apt pupil in there. Perhaps too apt. Maybe that was why the Sith kept the Rule of Two. Train your replacement to take you out one day and become the master. If they succeed, then they deserve the position. If they fail, then they were never strong enough to be the master.

I knelt down next to Randy and lit a cigarette. I handed it to him and then I lit one for myself.

"Randy, I am truly impressed. I honestly am. You took to my lessons like no one ever had before. And you were this close to defeating me." I held out my fingers a fraction of an inch apart. "But that was not close enough. Because there is one Villain's Rule you never learned. The first rule. The most important, absolute rule. The one rule upon which all other rules are predicated."

"Are you going to bore me to death, or are you going to spit it out?"

"Come on, Randy. You're a smart young man—much to my surprise. Figure it out."

Randy said nothing at first. His mind was replaying the events of our final showdown. I could see him searching for the missing piece of the puzzle. Over and over the look came across his face, the look that read, *What did I miss?*

Then it hit him.

Randy's eyes went wide.

"No," he said, looking at me in partial disgust and partial awe.

"Exactly. And the best part was, you made it come true. You said it yourself. In that last moment, you were the villain and I was the hero. So, Nephew, what is the First Villain's Rule?"

Randy looked away and muttered something under his breath.

I flicked my cigarette away as I reached for my nephew. Grabbing the boy by the shirt, I shook the ever-living shit out of him.

"Say it!"

"The hero always wins!"

Epilogue

"Welcome back, sir!" Sophia said as I sat down at my desk.

"Thank you, Sophia."

"And welcome, Ms. Barrowbride."

"Um, thanks? And please, call me Lydia."

"I most certainly will. May I?" Sophia asked, touching Lydia's stomach before permission was given. "Oh, this one will be quite special."

"Sophia, please see to our newest employee. She is most excited about starting right away. I'm sure you would take great joy in overseeing her orientation as her direct supervisor."

"Oh indeed, sir," Sophia said, heading to the door. "Oh, there are some new contracts on your desk for you to look over. A few realms' overseeing gods have lifted their sanctions. Word has spread of your success and they would like you to come and shake things up for them."

"Thank you. I will look them over soon."

"Very good, sir."

"Oh, two more things before you go."

"Sir?"

"First, thank you for re-re-decorating," I said.

"You are welcome, sir. And the second thing?"

"Are you mad?"

"Mad, sir?"

"With how I succeeded?"

"Sir?"

"Becoming the hero. If only for the moment."

Sophia paused at the door and then turned her attention to me. "May I speak freely?"

"Sophia, like you need permission."

"Jackson," Sophia said, choosing her words carefully, "you used every means available to you win. And win you did. You were dangerously close to becoming an anti-hero. But in the end, you got exactly what you wanted by manipulating the rules to your benefit. I couldn't be more proud."

"So you're not going to kill me?"

"For this? No. Oh, please do not take this clemency for absolution. When you cease entertaining me, I will be the one who kills you. I will rip your soul from your body and burn the remains to ashes. I will feast off your life force until there is not one single atom of your existence remaining," Sophia said. Her eyes now resembled a cat's, and her mouth was filled with needle-like teeth.

"So, our deal stands?"

Her monstrous face snapped back to that of her normal human self. "Of course, silly! Now be a lamb and look over those contracts. I think you may like the top one. It is for the comic book realms."

"Oh, that is interesting."

"I thought you would like it. Take care, Lydia."

"Bye?"

Sophia squinted her eyes when she smiled goodbye and left through my office door.

"Gods above and below, what is she?"

"Hmm?" I asked as I perused the comic book realm contract.

"Your . . . receptionist?"

"Sophia? Oh, she's a Djinn."

"I've heard of those, but I've never seen one before."

"Every realm has them," I said. "In each and every known realm, including the Prime Universe, legends speak of mystical creatures who have unfathomable power. In some legends they grant wishes. In others, they are bloodthirsty monsters. And as far as I can tell, they are descendants of the True Beings that created all known reality. Hence their power and ability to move across the dimensions with ease."

"How did you capture one?"

"I didn't," I said. "My parents did. An archaeological expedition many years ago before Paige or I was born. They found the lamp that housed her. And through her, they amassed an incredible fortune. I was let into the family secret when my parents deemed me worthy. Sophia orchestrated the accident that claimed my father and maimed my mother. So when my mother passed on, Sophia's lamp, and thus the right of ownership, passed to me. When I confronted Sophia for the first time, I did the one thing no one ever had."

"What?"

"I released her."

"Why?"

"To see what would happen."

"And what did happen?" Lydia asked.

"She was going to kill me as well, but curiosity stopped her. She asked why I did what I did. I told her she was not mine to own. It was then that she asked me what I wanted in life. And I told her I wanted to be the greatest villain in this or any known world. She agreed to help me. I let her choose her own name and she in turn showed me the known realms. Our partnership began and has been mutually beneficial ever since."

"So, she is evil?"

"Oh, most definitely. Well," I paused, thinking about it. "Not evil-evil. She is . . . chaos. Yes, that's a better description. She's an elemental force for change and disruption. Sophia is neither evil nor good. A primal force of the universe."

"And she is going to kill you?"

"One day," I said. "Nothing I can do about it. My family trapped her and used her. So for several generations, the Blackwells carry her curse for vengeance. Part of our agreement is as long as I continue to be the greatest villain, while entertaining her, I have a stay of execution. Although now that I think about it, I am convinced she made Randy as smart as he was while Paige was pregnant. Perhaps that was Sophia's way of testing me to see if I was still on my game. Djinn are very patient creatures."

Lydia's hands went to her stomach. "What of our child?"

"Also cursed, I'm afraid. But he or she will also be a demigod. They have a way of bending the rules."

"So," Lydia said, "what do we do now?"

"Whatever we want. Especially since you are no longer Valliar's avatar, we can be as nefarious as we wish to be."

Lydia smiled. "That was tricky of you."

"Thank you."

"How did you know Valliar would transfer his power from me to Randy?"

"I wasn't offering him much of a choice. Stay imprisoned or make the switch. But Valliar saw the benefit in using an evil person for good purposes. Now Randy will have to wander your world, forced to do good deeds."

"Won't he try and destroy you somehow?"

"I hope he does."

"But won't he be the hero then?"

"Oh, no," I laughed. "He is forced into doing good. That will never make him a hero."

"Besides, there are already two other new heroes running around."

"Exactly," I said. "Although if Wren does his wandering the countryside righting wrongs bit, he will eventually come to blows with Hawker."

"I thought he was going to try to unify the empires."

"That's my point. If Hawker tries, he *will* become corrupt. It's too big. When he tries, he will start down a dark path. It's in his blood. Even the Eld tried to bend people to their way of thinking."

"I don't think you give him enough credit. He seems to do things no one else can."

"Backwoods farm boys only become emperor if they have magic and red hair. Strange dragon tattoos or birthmarks help. Oh, poor Lydia. Don't worry, I'll teach you. "

Lydia rolled her eyes. "Do you think your sister will accept her new job?"

"Let's see," I said. I reached out and touched the intercom. "Sophia?"

"Yes sir?"

"Ms. Barrowbride and I would like some scotch."

"Yes sir. I'll bring you a bottle."

"No need, Sophia. Send the new girl."

I could feel Sophia's smile. "Very good sir."

A moment later Paige opened my office door. She was dressed in a servant's uniform and her face was most displeased. In her hands was a silver tray with a bottle of scotch and two glasses. "Here Jul—Mr. Blackwell."

"Thank you for the scotch, Paige."

"Yes . . . sir."

"Please set the drinks down here, Paige. Thank you. Afterwards, please clean the toilets."

Paige gritted her teeth. "Yes . . . sir."

The door shut a little too forcefully. But I let it go for now. Paige would settle into her new role as my employee. It was the only way I would spare Randy. She had to swear herself to me mind, body, and soul. In turn, I pay her a fair wage and she works fair hours.

But in *my* realm, I can make an eight-hour shift last as long as I want.

"So, with Valliar gone, I miss having a little god inside me," Lydia mused while she bent over my desk, showcasing her cleavage. "Do you have a little god for me?"

"Only a little?" I asked.

Lydia crawled over my desk, knocking paperwork and items askew. She pulled my face towards hers and began kissing me.

"Did you bring the knives?" I gasped, trying to catch my breath.

Lydia pulled a blade and held it to my throat. "Always."

About the Author

M. K. Gibson is a husband, father, a retired USAF MSgt and a lifetime geek. Ever since he saw the Rankin-Bass *The Hobbit* movie in 1980, all he ever wanted to do was create and tell fantastical stories.

M. K. Gibson lives in Mt. Airy, MD with his wife, and first-line editor, Valerie, their son Jack, their schnauzer Murphy, newfoundland Sully and their cat Mini.

Follow M. K. Gibson on Twitter at @GibsonMK1, Facebook author page and read updates and insane blogs at MKGibson.com.

Made in the USA
Monee, IL
22 February 2022

91640763R00203